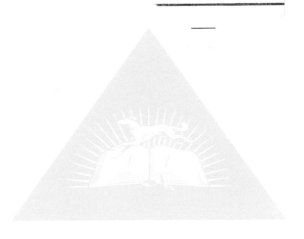

EVERYMAN'S LIBRARY

EVERYMAN,
I WILL GO WITH THEE,
AND BE THY GUIDE,
IN THY MOST NEED
TO GO BY THY SIDE

MURIEL SPARK

The Prime of Miss Jean Brodie
The Girls of Slender Means
The Driver's Seat
The Only Problem

with an Introduction by
Frank Kermode

EVERYMAN'S LIBRARY

Alfred A. Knopf New York London Toronto

274

THIS IS A BORZOI BOOK

PUBLISHED BY ALFRED A. KNOPF

First included in Everyman's Library, 2004

The Prime of Miss Jean Brodie
First published in the USA by *The New Yorker*, 1961
Copyright © 1961 by Muriel Spark
Reprinted in the USA by permission of HarperCollins Publishers.
First published in Great Britain by Macmillan, 1961
© 1961 Muriel Spark

The Girls of Slender Means
First published in Great Britain by Macmillan, 1963
© 1963 Muriel Spark

The Driver's Seat
First published in Great Britain by Macmillan, 1970
© 1970 Copyright Administration Limited

The Only Problem
First published in Great Britain by The Bodley Head, 1984
© 1984 Copyright Administration Limited

The moral rights of the author have been asserted.

Introduction Copyright © 2004 by Frank Kermode
Bibliography and Chronology Copyright © 2004 by Everyman's Library
Typography by Peter B. Willberg

The verses from 'Moonlit Apples', *The Collected Poems of
John Drinkwater*, are quoted in *The Girls of Slender Means* by permission of
Sidgwick and Jackson.

All rights reserved under International and Pan-American Copyright
Conventions. Published in the United States by Alfred A. Knopf, a division
of Random House, Inc., New York, and simultaneously in Canada by
Random House of Canada Limited, Toronto. Distributed by Random
House, Inc., New York. Published in the United Kingdom by Everyman's
Library, Northburgh House, 10 Northburgh Street, London EC1V 0AT, and
distributed by Random House (UK) Ltd.

US website: www.randomhouse/everymans

ISBN: 1-4000-4206-2 (US)
1-85715-274-3 (UK)

A CIP catalogue reference for this book is available from the British Library

Book design by Barbara de Wilde and Carol Devine Carson
Printed and bound in Germany by GGP Media, Pössneck

MURIEL SPARK

CONTENTS

INTRODUCTION

When Muriel Spark's first novel, *The Comforters*, came out in
1957 there was an unusual stir of interest. She had as yet
published no novel but was not unknown in literary circles,
having previously published books on Mary Shelley and John
Masefield, as well as editions of the letters of the Brontës,
Newman and others. There was also an admirable volume of
poems and a short story, 'The Seraph and the Zambesi', which,
in 1951, won first prize in a well-publicized *Observer* competition. More stories followed, and these successes led to her
first venture into full-length fiction. *The Comforters* was at once
recognized as a novel of unusual originality and skill; it was
warmly praised by Graham Greene and Evelyn Waugh, and
not merely out of sympathy for a newly converted Roman
Catholic writer but from an understanding that here was an
artist, writing fiction that has the quality, scope and variety of
ambitious poetry, and which could be at the same time comic
and deeply serious.

The Comforters is a novel that looks into the question as to
what kind of truth can be told in a novel; in fact nearly all of
Spark's fictions have this reflexive quality, though never in
an ostentatiously theoretical fashion. *The Comforters* is always
conscious of the fact that to make up fictive narratives is, in a
way, a presumptuous activity, because the characters of a novelist, unlike those created by God, are not endowed with free
will; she enjoys power at the expense of her characters.
Caroline, the heroine of the book, resists the will of her creator,
who nevertheless goes on creating coincidences, arbitrarily,
sometimes impatiently, dealing with her characters as she
pleases. A fascinated interest in the relation between life and
plot persists in the later fiction, notably in the novella *Not to
Disturb* (1971).

Spark's writings were now assured of attention, and she
proceeded to publish novels with quite remarkable frequency.
In *Robinson* (1958), *Memento Mori* (1959), *The Ballad of Peckham*

Rye (1960) and *The Bachelors* (1960) it is possible to trace some permanent or recurring interests, but they are nevertheless all quite astonishingly original and ingenious, imbued not only with the author's preoccupation with the supernatural and with the shadier aspect of religious belief and various other kinds of crookedness, but also with her intelligent and unfailing contempt for stupidity and weakness. Sometimes it appears that for Dame Muriel one of the prime duties of the artist is to clear away as much as possible of the monstrous accumulation of stupidity in our world. Hence a certain ruthlessness of tone, a steady refusal to countenance failures of common sense. The dull or in other ways unworthy may be represented as negligible, even as unreal. Forgiveness, even of one's own creations, is not, in this case, a necessity of art. Muriel Spark's novels are rarely short of wit and high spirits, but they are sternly deficient in sentimentality. As Rebecca West remarked, this writer 'observes reality more exactly' than others, and 'lacks the cowardice which makes us refuse to admit its lack of correspondence with our expectations and desires'.

Few writers have so natural a command of the techniques available to the modern novelist. One has the impression that for Spark there somehow exists, in advance of composition, a novel, or more usually a novella, which can be scanned as it were in a satellite's view of it, from above – a map, rather than a temporal sequence. It can be surveyed in all its parts and details, and it ignores the conventional notion that to write it down requires one to treat its events in their temporal order. From the outset the end may be just as visible as the beginning, and on the same page may be found conversations and revelations that took place, in the 'real' time of the narrative, years apart. In these manoeuvres there may sometimes be a certain playfulness, serving as an indication of the writer's absolute control (though one device may be to confront that control with evidence of its fallibility).

Nothing is absolutely new in the novel; what we think of as the mainstream English novel had barely got under way before Sterne wrote *Tristram Shandy*. And two generations before Muriel Spark began her experiments Conrad and Ford Madox Ford were doing extraordinary things to persuade us that the proper order of a fiction may not be, perhaps rarely is, a mimicry of the notion that the momentum of a story depends on its sticking to what passes for the commonsense process of 'Then ... and then ... and then'. Yet Muriel Spark never sounds like these august predecessors, self-consciously exploratory; and she has a surer sense of the right order of things than Ford, who worked so hard at such matters as 'progression of effects' and the interrelation of disparate narrative sections. It is true that she loves complicated plots and expounds them with the confidence of an expert thriller writer, giving, as she once said, 'disjointed happenings a shape'; but to do that is only one of the techniques, and probably not the most interesting of them, at her disposal.

Nowhere are these powers more evident than in *The Prime of Miss Jean Brodie* (1961) and *The Girls of Slender Means* (1963). They are short books and they are often funny, but they have very serious themes. Exquisitely formed, they give pleasure by their very existence, by the way they illuminate with their own plots the plot of the world, the writer matching her own presumption of providential powers with a truth beyond them. The puzzle is that fictions, if we are not to think of them as lies, must offer a kind of truth; yet they must be seen as shadowed by a truth more absolute than any they can aspire to. Or, as she once put it, 'I don't claim that my novels are truth. I claim that they are fiction, out of which a kind of truth emerges.'

It is of course important that the truth is that of the Roman Catholic religion, an absolute truth, but treated quite unsentimentally in these books. God, as Barbara Vaughan discovers in *The Mandelbaum Gate*, Spark's longest novel, does not play by the human rules. Barbara is half-Christian, half-Jewish, and experiences the mysterious union of these religions in Jerusalem. She reflects that Jacob tricked Isaac into blessing him instead of Esau, and, having stolen his brother's inheritance, became the father of Israel. God doesn't necessarily play fair; it is one of the facts of life we have to live with. It is a recurrent theme, and is perhaps most explicit in *The Only Problem* (1984).

In *The Prime of Miss Jean Brodie* the order of telling may appear almost random. Attention moves from 1931, when this very odd teacher first gathers together her girls with the intention of shaping their lives, establishing them as the *crème de la crème*, to the post-war period, alighting at many separate points between the beginning and the end of the tale. Here are the girls in their first year, and here they are at the end of their schooling, six years later; and so to their final meetings with Sandy, or Sister Helena of the Transfiguration. But these disparate moments are denied strictly consecutive treatment. The tone of the narrative is one of amused and mannered irony, as in the recurrent use of the same tags to characterize the girls, especially Sandy, who is rarely mentioned without some allusion to her piggy eyes. For these she was merely 'notorious' – her early fame depended on her beautiful (English, not Scottish) vowels. The effect of the repetitive mentions of Sandy's piggy eyes is almost Homeric. It could be hard to find anything like it in other modern novelists. The reader is left to relate Sandy's tiny eyes ('which it was astonishing that anyone could trust') to her subsequent conduct as the betrayer of Miss Brodie – though we know her to be precociously capable of treachery, for example at the expense of the unhappy scapegoat Mary Macgregor, who is famous only 'for being stupid and always to blame'. The other girls are famous for this or that: for sex, acrobatics, and so on. Brodie seeks to transfigure them, and they play their parts in her attempt to achieve this secular 'Transfiguration of the Commonplace', later the title of Sandy's famous book.

Despite its boldness of method the novel has some old-fashioned virtues of plot. We may wonder why a strange girl, wearing the wrong uniform, is introduced near the beginning and then apparently disappears from the story; but she returns and turns out to be important to the plot. Mary Macgregor, as a young girl, is panic-stricken by the flaming Bunsen burners in the science laboratory, and at twenty-four she is burnt to death in a hotel fire. These events, years apart, are virtually simultaneous in the telling; in a single page we are taken back from the fire to the moment when, at ten years old, she is, no doubt wrongly, accused of spilling ink on the floor (at the beginning of Chapter 2). Spark has no compunction about repeating herself, even word for word (the last words in the book are an instance) if her overview of the fictional proceedings seems to demand it. There is what might be called a recursive quality about her narrative manner; but none of these apparently wanton departures from the normal procedures of duller novelists can be attributed to clumsiness; they are part of the story, and also part of the joke.

The unrivalled deftness of the narrative would be a source of pleasure in itself, but to praise that quality is to risk missing the more important point that the entire book is a testimony to the sheer, if somehow rather guilty, delight of the novelist in the possession of such powers. *Brodie* is charmingly and always relevantly funny. In the course of the story the girls grow from childhood to early maturity, questioning one another about sex as they are on their way to experiencing it. The characters of the two masters, art and music, are masterly sketches of obsession and abjection. That one of them lost an arm in World War I is a neat moment of historical placement, and, like Brodie's romance about her lost lover, is linked to the plight of all the spinsters of the period, their possible husbands killed in France. The children's walk through the Old Town of Edinburgh gives them a fleeting view of the poverty of the Thirties, the decade during which these girls are growing up: 'Walk past quietly,' says Miss Brodie. As middle-class girls they have no more direct knowledge of the unemployed – 'the idle', as they were called in Scotland – than they have of sex.

The two themes come together in a Sparkian joke, as the girls study Tennyson's poem 'The Lady of Shalott', which is sometimes regarded as an allegory of the menarche – a word that makes Miss Brodie's girls giggle.

> 'Down she came and found a boat
> Beneath a willow left afloat,
> And round about the prow she wrote
> *The Lady of Shalott.*'

'By what means did your Ladyship write these words?' Sandy inquired in her mind with her lips shut tight.

'There was a pot of white paint and a brush which happened to be standing upon the grassy verge,' replied the Lady of Shalott graciously. 'It was left there no doubt by some heedless member of the Unemployed.'

Meanwhile Miss Brodie follows her disastrous course. It is her ignorant affection for Italian Fascism and for Hitler that precipitates her fall, but her extraordinary teaching methods adumbrated it. Yet the expression of her dangerously free-thinking opinions cannot conceal her Edinburgh-Calvinist background, evident in her correct Sunday observance as in her fussing about manners and propriety.

In plotting the careers of her élite girls she imitates the predestinarian God and goes wrong in the process: 'I do not think ever to be betrayed,' she boasts, and is as confident of her victory over her superiors as she is of the accuracy of her forecast for Sandy: 'I fear you will never belong to life's élite.' God, as we know by hindsight (a power freely conferred on us by Spark) has other plans, and a different idea of election. It might be said that Brodie's interests are on the whole aesthetic, whereas God's are spiritual. Thus Sandy's conversion is facilitated by her loss of interest in the artist Teddy Lloyd as a lover and her accidental absorption of his Catholic religion – another of God's plots, and not one that could have occurred to Miss Brodie. We learn of the early end of her prime, and of her life, in various places, first in Chapter 3, later in grim conversations with Sister Helena in the nunnery. Her end is everywhere implicit in her prime, as the end of the story is implicit in the conduct of the whole.

Something of the manner of this remarkable book persists in Spark's next novel, *The Girls of Slender Means*. Here, too, the tale is of a conversion miraculously wrought. The story occupies the period between the end of the war with Germany and the end of the war with Japan, roughly May to August, 1945. We notice the familiar attention to detail in the rendering of that period of relief and rationing, a time of which it could be said, however inaccurately, that everybody in Britain had slender means. The girls at the May of Teck Club are mostly, though not without exception, of slender bodies, and on suitable occasions can wear the Schiaparelli dress, informally held in common. When the wartime bomb explodes in the garden and the building catches fire it is to recover this dress that Selina returns from the safety of the roof, through the aperture from which only thin girls can make their way.

Her action is noted by Nicholas, her lover; they had slept together through the summer on this roof, she arriving by the strait opening, he from the roof of the building next door. But now, seeing her emerge with the dress, Nicholas crosses himself. He is on his way to the martyrdom of which we have already, by means of Sparkian time-shifts, been made aware. Selina's action grants him a vision of evil that eventually changes his life, as Sandy's was changed by what remained of her feeling for a discarded lover. Another divine trick, another meditation on God's way of choosing his élite.

That was a pedestrian account, reducing the story to the kind of thing an ordinary writer might produce. Of course Spark is more than equal to the demands of realistic narrative, witness, for example, the force and accuracy with which she describes the effects of the bomb, with much detail of fire-fighting, rescue and disaster. But to speak of the novel thus is to falsify it. Once again one has the sense of its having been conceived as a whole, so that the details of life in such a community, and in the strange post-war atmosphere of 1945, are already related to the whole, already cohere. Spark achieves the ambition of her butler-novelist in *Not to Disturb* – she makes everything pertain.

She likes to find occasions to quote poetry in her fiction, and in this book the elocutionist Joanna provides a sort of obbligato of anthology pieces. Her recitations assume great seriousness at the time of disaster, when she chooses Hopkins's 'The Wreck of the Deutschland' and the Anglican liturgy for the appropriate day. The victims in Hopkins's poem were nuns, and the Anglican verses for the twenty-seventh day suit the scene of a collapsing house: 'Except the Lord build the house: their labour is but lost that build it./ Except the Lord keep the city: the watchman waketh but in vain'. 'Any day's liturgy would have been equally mesmeric. But the words for the right day was Joanna's habit.' She perishes with the house, and Nicholas, after the event but long before his martyrdom, has to deal with her father. He shows him the house; but there is little to see, and the old man makes nothing of it, and despite his priesthood cannot find any but the feeblest explanation of how such a fate should have overtaken his daughter.

The inhabitants of the club are all sharply sketched and knowable: the girl who pretended to have dates with the musical star Jack Buchanan, the older ladies, permanent residents and not under thirty, as they ought to have been by the rules of the institution. Jane Wright is important though not slender; her dealings with shady publishers bring Nicholas to the club. When we hear from her at the very beginning of the story the war is long over, and she is on the telephone telling another May of Teck survivor about Nicholas's martyrdom. We are not to expect events in sequence, but we are to understand their place in the whole. We start in the battered London of 1945: 'Long ago in 1945 all the nice people in England were poor, allowing for exceptions ... at least, that was a general axiom, the best of the rich being poor in spirit.' And we end in the park, at the rowdy and dangerous celebrations of VJ day. Nicholas protects Jane from the mob, and as she stands, bedraggled, fixing her hair, Nicholas marvels at her stamina, and will recall her 'years later in the country of his death', as 'an image of all the May of Teck establishment in its meek, unselfconscious attitudes of poverty, long ago in 1945.' The life of Nicholas has not yet gone forward to its conclusion, but the novel has, in the middle of a sentence.

The Girls of Slender Means was followed by a very different book, *The Mandelbaum Gate* (1965), and then by *The Public Image* (1968), a dark tale of a film actress who sheds her fraudulent public image. Two years later came *The Driver's Seat*, the most chilling and desperate of all the novels. Written almost entirely in the present tense, it cannot avoid reminding the reader of the French *nouveau roman*, especially the novels of Alain Robbe-Grillet, which had appeared some years earlier and were attracting much attention at the time. It is said that Spark owed something in the conception of her narrative to Christine Brooke-Rose, the most successful English exponent of what has come to be called post-modern experimental narrative, though Spark had certainly made her own experiments and cannot really have needed this model.

Indeed the atmosphere of this book is, as one realizes on reflection, quite different from Robbe-Grillet's habitual mysteries and puzzles. Sudden time-shifts and unapologetic repetitions were, as we've seen, a feature of her earlier writing; and she was already a mistress of the macabre, especially in her short stories. Here she extends an idea that might once have made such a tale into a longer narrative enacting a pathological obsession, represented with accuracy in the intensity and strangeness of the prose.

It seems that Spark remembered a newspaper story about a German woman, garishly dressed, who went to Rome and on her first evening walked into a park, was assaulted, tied up, raped and stabbed to death. She is reported as describing the book as 'conceived at white heat ... it is supposed to give the reader nightmares'. It does not contain many jokes of the kind that enlivened some of the earlier fiction; there is, however, a satirical feminist speech by the slightly dotty Mrs Fiedke about the impudence of men in claiming equal rights with women: 'the male sex is getting out of hand'. Mostly such laughter as there is arises from Lise's sinisterly absurd clothes.

That a woman should wind up her life and choose, with the greatest care, her own murderer, is the material of dreams. That she should not only seek out and compel her assailant to kill her but lay down conditions – no rape permitted, only murder – is to go beyond human powers of foresight and planning. Much happens during her day that is merely the uncontrollable fuss of life, in shops and cars and cafés, even though the nightmare quality is enhanced by the weirdness of almost everybody Lise encounters – Mrs Fiedke, for instance, and the dangerous macrobiotic crank. Perhaps all this detail is irrelevant to her prime purpose, as she evidently believes; but she will discover in her last moments that she cannot control even the central event of her life. It is part of her tragedy that she cannot impose the terms of her own death; and the closing words of the book insist that it is truly tragic, awakening (in all but policemen): 'fear and pity, pity and fear'.

The Driver's Seat is among the most perfectly composed of modern novellas. By reason of its terrible subject and its unremitting onslaught on the reader's sensibility it stands a little apart from most of the other works. *Not to Disturb* appeared in the following year, and is fascinating in a quite different manner – a novel contemplating, in a comic spirit, the oddity of there being such things as stories and story-tellers who, within sometimes unacknowledged limits, can control action and out-come. Five more novels, which must here be passed over, inter-vened before the publication of *The Only Problem* in 1984.

Dame Muriel had long been a student of the Book of Job. She published an article on 'The Mystery of Job's Suffering' in 1955, and drew the title of her first novel, *The Comforters*, from the Bible story. What is the mystery of Job's suffering? It is clearly untrue to say, with the comforters, that he deserved it. Why, given that God is good and also omnipotent, should there be suffering, anyway? This may be regarded as the big-gest, or only, problem. One answer, offered with great subtlety by Leibniz and ridiculed by Voltaire, is that this is the best of all possible worlds. Harvey, the protagonist in this novel, can-not accept such explanations; nor can Dame Muriel. Harvey thinks that if God permits suffering he must, 'by the logic of his omnipotence, be the author of it'. And all problems are, in the end, part of that greater problem.

Harvey is rich. He ends his marriage without undue suffer-ing, and buys a house and then a château in France in order to have enough peace to work on his Job book. His choice of location is dictated by his wish to go to Epinal as often as he likes to see a painting by Georges de La Tour called 'Job Visited by His Wife'. The Bible credits Job's wife with only one sentence: 'Dost thou still retain thine integrity? curse God, and die.' Job tells her not to speak as foolish women do, and goes on scratching his sores with a potsherd. But the painting, unlike any other of the same subject, shows Job's wife to be beautiful and tender, so Harvey wonders at the discrepancy between the biblical text and the picture.

In fact the subject of the painting, dated about 1640, was long thought to be 'The Clothing of the Naked'. The female figure, being Compassion personified, is not at all bad-tempered; and looks rather like the angel in another of De La Tour's works, the 'Angel Appearing to St Joseph'. The subject of the picture was identified, and the present title attached to it, as late as 1935. Only then did art historians begin to see the woman's face, assumed for centuries to be angelic, as in fact angry and cruel.

My own view, which is not Spark's, is that De La Tour was working from the Vulgate Latin text of the Bible. Its author, St Jerome, was well aware that in the Hebrew text 'bless God' was a euphemism for 'curse God', which no scribe would write. But the Roman Catholic Church did not take the course followed by the vernacular translators (including the English) and render 'bless' as 'curse'. Consequently a painter or his patron might read the passage in the Bible and see Job's wife as a tender though foolish woman, who, unable to bear his misery, advises Job to make his peace with God and seek a good end. The antithetical and more usual interpretation makes the woman gloat as if possessed by Satan: 'Are you still going to be righteous? If you're going to die, curse God and get it off your chest first. It will do you good.'

However, Spark's Harvey is right to conclude that 'it was impossible not to wonder what the artist actually means'. His difficulty is compounded by the fact that the woman in the picture resembles his discarded wife Effie, who also resembles her sister Ruth. The mystery of Job's suffering becomes deeper and deeper as Effie's illegal adventures cause Harvey more and more trouble. It seems to Harvey that God comes out of the argument very badly with his boasting and shouting and bribery: if Job will admit he is vile he shall have back his sheep and camels and asses and seven sons and three daughters, one of them named Keren-happuch, which means Eye-Paint. (This last is a detail one would not expect Spark to miss, or indeed fail to repeat.)

One of the reporters who plague Harvey because of his wife's misdeeds is an old Swede, who alone of all the company knows what the Book of Job is. He asks Harvey whether to feel perfectly innocent while you are guilty in the eyes of the world is to find oneself in the position of Job. Harvey, ignoring such parallels as that of the comforters who beset him – Ruth, Nathan, Stewart – denies that he is so situated; he is not covered with boils, and so on. He adds that Job's problem was ignorance; nobody tried to explain his suffering to him. Job says he wants 'to reason with God', but God won't 'come out like a man and state his case'. Since the Book of Job is so hostile to God the real wonder is how it ever got into the Bible.

It is 'the pivotal book of the Bible', yet there is nothing 'moral' about it.

Typically, this central argument is set in the midst of a Sparkian plot of shoplifting, holdups, love affairs, Californian communes and other forms of human mess and muddle. But the point remains that all these problems are aspects of 'the only problem worth discussing'.

*

In the twenty years since the publication of *The Only Problem* Spark has produced four more novels and an autobiography. Another novel is said to be in preparation. All have, or will have, that amused, sceptical, satirical attitude to what she once called 'the ridiculous nature of reality'; and all offer an image of life in the world that is virtually unique though perfectly reasonable – a quality that greatly enhances what we may surely take to be its permanent value.

Frank Kermode

SELECT BIBLIOGRAPHY

CHEYETTE, BRYAN: *Muriel Spark*, Northcote House, 2000.
KEMP, PETER: *Muriel Spark*, Paul Elek, 1974.

CHRONOLOGY

_____

DATE	AUTHOR'S LIFE	LITERARY CONTEXT
1918	Muriel Sarah Camberg is born in Edinburgh, second child of Bernard Camberg, an engineer from a family of Jewish/ Lithuanian origin, and Cissy Camberg, *née* Uezzell, from Hertfordshire.	1918 Strachey: *Eminent Victorians*. West: *The Return of the Soldier*. Hopkins: *Poems* (posth.). Brooke: *Poems* (posth.).
		1920 Lawrence: *Women in Love*. Mansfield: *Bliss*. Wharton: *The Age of Innocence*. Pound: *Hugh Selwyn Mauberley*. 1921 Huxley: *Crome Yellow*. Pirandello: *Six Characters in Search of an Author*. 1922 Joyce: *Ulysses*. Eliot: *The Waste Land*. West: *The Judge*. Mansfield: *The Garden Party*.
1923	Begins education in the infant/ junior department of James Gillespie's High School for Girls in Edinburgh.	
		1924 Ford: *Parade's End* (to 1928). Forster: *A Passage to India*. 1925 Woolf: *Mrs Dalloway*. Kafka: *The Trial*. Fitzgerald: *The Great Gatsby*.
1926		
1927	Aged 9, Muriel rewrites Robert Browning's *The Pied Piper of Hamelin*.	1927 Woolf: *To the Lighthouse*. Proust: *In Search of Lost Time* (posth.). Cather: *Death Comes for the Archbishop*.
1928		1928 Lawrence: *Lady Chatterley's Lover*. Yeats: *The Tower*. Waugh: *Decline and Fall*.

1918 In January the suffrage bill is passed, giving women over 30 the right to vote. World War 1 ends (11 November). Civil war in Russia (to 1921).

1920 League of Nations formed. Prohibition in US.

1921 Irish Free State is established.

1922 Civil war in Ireland. Establishment of USSR, Stalin General Secretary of Communist Party Central Committee. Mussolini marches on Rome: Fascist government formed in Italy.

1923 Hyper-inflation in Germany. Munich *putsch* by Nazis fails. Nationalist revolution in Turkey under Mustafa Kemal.

1924 Ramsay Macdonald forms first Labour government in Britain (January–November). Death of Lenin.

1925 Welsh Nationalist party, *Plaid Cymru*, founded. Locarno conference. *New Yorker* magazine started.

1926 General Strike in Britain.
1927 Lindberg flies the Atlantic.

1928 National Party of Scotland founded. Women over 21 are given the right to vote. Stalin's first Five Year Plan in USSR.

DATE	AUTHOR'S LIFE	LITERARY CONTEXT
1929–30	Muriel is taught for two years by Christina Kay, a brilliant teacher who later serves as an inspiration for the character of Miss Jean Brodie. In 1930 she moves up to the senior school.	1929 Green: *Living*. Bowen: *The Last September*. West: *Harriet Hume*. Hemingway: *A Farewell to Arms*. 1930 Coward: *Private Lives*. Waugh: *Vile Bodies*.
1932	Awarded first prize in an Edinburgh schools' poetry competition to mark the centenary of the death of Sir Walter Scott.	1932 Waugh: *Black Mischief*. Huxley: *Brave New World*.
		1933 Orwell: *Down and Out in Paris and London*. Fitzgerald: *Tender is the Night*. 1934 Waugh: *A Handful of Dust*. Rhys: *Voyage in the Dark*. Céline: *Death on the Instalment Plan*.
1935–7	Leaves school and enrols for précis-writing course at Heriot-Watt College. Teaches at a private school to finance a secretarial course, and works as a PA to the owner of a department store in Princes Street.	1935 Compton-Burnett: *A House and its Head*. 1936 Stevie Smith: *Novel on Yellow Paper*. Auden: *Look, Stranger!* Isherwood: *Mr Norris Changes Trains*.
1937–8	Muriel becomes engaged to Sydney Oswald Spark, who is about to take up a teaching post in Southern Rhodesia. She sails out to join him and they marry in September 1937. Their son, Robin, is born in 1938. The couple separate shortly afterwards.	1937 Christie: *Death on the Nile*. 1938 Greene: *Brighton Rock*. Waugh: *Scoop*. Nabokov: *The Gift*. Bowen: *The Death of the Heart*. Sartre: *Nausea*.
1939–44	Muriel shares a flat in Bulawayo and works as a secretary. She continues to write poetry.	1939 Joyce: *Finnegans Wake*. Steinbeck:*The Grapes of Wrath*. 1940 Hemingway: *For Whom the Bell Tolls*.
		1941 Joyce and Woolf die. Brecht: *Mother Courage*. O'Neill: *Long Day's Journey into Night*. Coward: *Blithe Spirit*. 1942 Camus: *The Outsider*. MacCarthy: *The Company She Keeps*.

CHRONOLOGY

1929 Collapse of the New York stock exchange. Worldwide depression follows. First use of term *apartheid* in South Africa.

1930 Nazis win seats from moderates in German elections. Gandhi begins campaign of civil disobedience in India.
1932 Oswald Mosley founds British Union of Fascists. Unemployment in Britain reaches 2,947,000. Unemployed marchers clash with police in London.

1933 Hitler becomes German Chancellor. Churchill first warns of German rearmament. Roosevelt announces 'New Deal' in the US.

1934 Hitler becomes German Führer.

1935 Nuremberg Laws depriving Jews of German citizenship.

1936 Spanish Civil War (to 1939). Italian forces occupy Abyssinia. Hitler and Mussolini form Rome–Berlin Axis. Stalin's Great Purge of the Communist Party (to 1938). George V dies. Abdication crisis. Jarrow march.

1937 Japanese invasion of China.
1938 Germany annexes Austria; Munich crisis. Italian manifesto: statement of Fascist racialist ideology. Estimated that one-third of British families live below the poverty line.

1939 Italian troops invade Albania. Germans occupy Czechoslovakia. Nazi–Soviet Pact; Hitler invades Poland. Outbreak of World War II.
1940 Resignation of Chamberlain. Coalition ministry under Winston Churchill (to 1945). Expeditionary force evacuated from Dunkirk. Fall of France and Battle of Britain. Home Guard formed. Rationing introduced.
1941 Germans invade Russia. Japanese attack on Pearl Harbor.

1942 North African campaign.

MURIEL SPARK

DATE	AUTHOR'S LIFE	LITERARY CONTEXT
1944–5	Having finally obtained a divorce, Muriel returns to England on a troop ship. She heads for London, in order to experience the war, and lodges at the Helena Club, original of the May of Teck Club in *The Girls of Slender Means*. She finds war work in the Political Intelligence department of the Foreign Office, based at Woburn.	1944 Eliot: *Four Quartets*. Compton-Burnett: *Elders and Betters*. 1945 Orwell: *Animal Farm*. Waugh: *Brideshead Revisited*. Green: *Loving*. Mitford: *The Pursuit of Love*. Borges: *Fictions*.
1947	After a spell on the quarterly magazine, *Argentor*, Spark becomes General Secretary of the Poetry Society, and Editor of *Poetry Review* until 1949.	1947 Camus: *The Plague*. Compton-Burnett: *Manservant and Maidservant*.
1948		1948 Greene: *The Heart of the Matter*. Paton: *Cry, the Beloved Country*.
1949	Works for the magazine *European Affairs* (to 1951). Co-writes with Derek Stanford *A Tribute to Wordsworth*.	1949 Beauvoir: *The Second Sex*. Orwell: *Nineteen Eighty-Four*. Bowen: *The Heat of the Day*. Miller: *Death of a Salesman*. 1950 Lessing: *The Grass is Singing*.
1951	'The Seraph and the Zambesi' wins a short story competition running in the *Observer*. *Child of Light*, a biography of Mary Wollstonecraft Shelley, is published.	1951 Greene: *The End of the Affair*. Yourcenar: *Memoirs of Hadrian*. Salinger: *The Catcher in the Rye*.
1952	*The Fanfarlo and Other Verse.*	1952 Waugh: *Sword of Honour Trilogy* (to 1961). Pym: *Excellent Women*. Dylan Thomas: *Collected Poems*.
1953	*Emily Brontë: Her Life and Work* (with Derek Stanford). Biography of John Masefield. Reading the theological works of John Henry Newman.	1953 Bellow: *The Adventures of Augie March*. Pym: *Jane and Prudence*. Beckett: *Waiting for Godot*. Robbe-Grillet: *The Erasers*.
1954	Spark is received into the Catholic Church and begins work on her first novel.	1954 Golding: *The Lord of the Flies*. Amis: *Lucky Jim*.

CHRONOLOGY

1944 Allied landings in Normandy. Liberation of Paris.

1945 Mussolini shot by partisans. Unconditional surrender of Germany and suicide of Hitler. Atomic bombs detonated over Hiroshima and Nagasaki. End of World War II. Labour government under Attlee. Establishment of United Nations. Death of Roosevelt.

1947 Marshall Plan: US gives aid for European postwar recovery. Beginning of Cold War. Indian Independence Act. Edinburgh Festival is launched. Christian Dior's New Look.

1948 State of Israel established. Soviet blockade of Berlin and allied airlift. Communist coup in Czechoslovakia. South African government adopts *apartheid* as official policy. Assassination of Gandhi.
1949 Federal Republic of Germany established. Communist revolution in China.

1951 Defection of Burgess and Maclean. McCarthy's anti-Communist Committee of Enquiry active in the US.

1952 Accession of Elizabeth II. Eisenhower is elected US President. Britain produces its first atomic bomb. The Mau Mau are active in Kenya.

1953 European Court of Human Rights set up in Strasbourg. Hillary and Tenzing reach the summit of Everest.

1954 Vietnam War begins. Nasser gains power in Egypt.

DATE	AUTHOR'S LIFE	LITERARY CONTEXT
1955		1955: Nabokov: *Lolita*. Highsmith: *The Talented Mr Ripley*. 1956 Macaulay: *The Towers of Trebizond*. West: *The Fountain Overflows*.
1957	*The Comforters* is published. Spark is able to give up part-time secretarial work and devote herself full-time to writing.	1957 Pasternak: *Doctor Zhivago*. Pinter: *The Birthday Party*. Hughes: *The Hawk in the Rain*. Stevie Smith: *Not Waving, but Drowning*. Waugh: *The Ordeal of Gilbert Pinfold*.
1958	*Robinson*. *The Go Away Bird* (stories).	1958 Murdoch: *The Bell*. Betjeman: *Collected Poems*. Pym: *A Glass of Blessings*.
1959	*Memento Mori*.	
1960	*The Ballad of Peckham Rye*. *The Bachelors*.	1960 Updike: *Rabbit, Run*.
1961	*The Prime of Miss Jean Brodie* is published and widely acclaimed. It is turned into a play and subsequently filmed.	1961 Naipaul: *A House for Mr Biswas*. Heller: *Catch-22*
1962	*Doctors of Philosophy* (play). William Shawn, Editor of *The New Yorker*, gives Spark an office to write in. Here she produces her next two novels.	1962 Nabokov: *Pale Fire*. Burgess: *A Clockwork Orange*. Lessing: *The Golden Notebook*. Solzhenitsyn: *One Day in the Life of Ivan Denisovich*. Bassani: *The Garden of the Finzi-Contini*.
1963	*The Girls of Slender Means*.	1963 Plath: *The Bell Jar*. McCarthy: *The Group*. Le Carré: *The Spy Who Came in from the Cold*.
1965	*The Mandelbaum Gate*.	1965 Pinter: *The Homecoming*. Drabble: *The Millstone*. Robbe-Grillet: *For a New Novel*.
1966	*The Brontë Letters*. Spark is awarded the James Tait Black Memorial Prize for *The Mandelbaum Gate*.	1966 Brooke-Rose: *Such*. Rhys: *Wide Sargasso Sea*. West: *The Birds Fall Down*.

CHRONOLOGY

DATE	AUTHOR'S LIFE	LITERARY CONTEXT
1967	*Collected Poems I. Collected Stories I.* Awarded an OBE. Spark moves to Italy, visiting Rome many times.	1967 Márquez: *One Hundred Years of Solitude.* Carter: *The Magic Toyshop.* Jennings: *Collected Poems.*
1968	*The Public Image.* *The Very Fine Clock.*	1968 Solzhenitsyn: *Cancer Ward.* Stoppard: *The Real Inspector Hound.* Brooke-Rose: *Between.*
1969		1969 Drabble: *The Waterfall.* First Booker Prize for fiction awarded in Britain.
1970	*The Driver's Seat.*	
1971	*Not to Disturb.*	1971 Weldon: *Down Among the Women.*
1972		1972 Stoppard: *Jumpers.* Drabble: *The Needle's Eye.*
1973	*The Hothouse by the East River.*	1973 Murdoch: *The Black Prince.* Greene: *The Honorary Consul.*
1974	*The Abbess of Crewe,* a satirical treatment of the Watergate scandal.	1974 Larkin: *High Windows.* Stoppard: *Travesties.* Gordimer: *The Conservationists.*
1975		1975 Levi: *The Periodic Table.* Stevie Smith: *Collected Poems.* Jhabvala: *Heat and Dust.*
1976	*The Takeover.*	
1978		1978 Greene: *The Human Factor.* Murdoch: *The Sea, The Sea.* Byatt: *The Virgin in the Garden.* Penelope Fitzgerald: *The Bookshop.* Yourcenar: *The Abyss.*
1979	*Territorial Rights.*	1979 Calvino: *If on a winter's night a traveller.* Kundera: *The Book of Laughter and Forgetting.* Penelope Fitzgerald: *Offshore.* Gordimer: *Burger's Daughter.*
1980		1980 Burgess: *Earthly Powers.* Golding: *Rites of Passage.* Desai: *Clear Light of Day.* Bowen: *Collected Stories.* McCarthy: *Cannibals and Missionaries.*
1981	*Loitering with Intent.*	1981 Rushdie: *Midnight's Children.* Yourcenar: *Anna, Soror.*

CHRONOLOGY

1967 Arab–Israeli Six Day War. Nigerian civil war.

1968 Student unrest throughout Europe and the US. Soviet-led invasion of Czechoslovakia. Assassination of Martin Luther King. Nixon US President.

1969 Americans land first man on the moon. British troops assume responsibility for security in Northern Ireland.

1972 Bloody Sunday in Northern Ireland. Direct rule imposed by Britain.

1973 Miners' strike. Energy crisis prompts state of emergency in Britain.

1974 Resignation of Nixon following Watergate scandal.

1975 End of Vietnam war. USSR and western powers sign Helsinki agreement.

1976 Death of Mao Tse-Tung. Sadam Hussein becomse President of Iraq. Carter elected US President. Soweto massacre in South Africa.
1978 Camp David agreement between Carter (USA), Begin (Israel) and Sadat (Egypt).

1979 Winter of Discontent in Britain. Strike of public sector workers, including dustmen and grave-diggers. Margaret Thatcher becomes first woman Prime Minister in Britain. British rule in Zimbabwe (former Rhodesia) formally ends. Soviet forces invade Afghanistan. Iran hostage crisis (to 1981). Carter and Brezhnev sign SALT-2.

1980 Over 2 million people are unemployed in Britain, a level not reached since the 1930s. Many thousands of these are teenagers or young people. Lech Walesa leads strikes in Gdansk, Poland. Iran–Iraq war (to 1988).

1981 Race riots in Liverpool and London. Reagan becomes US President. President Sadat assassinated.

DATE	AUTHOR'S LIFE	LITERARY CONTEXT
1982	*Bang-bang You're Dead* (stories). *Going up to Sotheby's* (poems).	1982 Walker: *The Color Purple.* Levi: *If Not Now, When?* Márquez: *Chronicle of a Death Foretold.*
1984	*The Only Problem.*	1984 Carter: *Nights at the Circus.* Barnes: *Flaubert's Parrot.* Brookner: *Hotel du Lac.* Heaney: *Station Island.*
1985	*The Stories of Muriel Spark.*	1985 Márquez: *Love in the Time of Cholera.* Winterson: *Oranges are not the only Fruit.* Murdoch: *The Good Apprentice.*
1986		1986 DeLillo: *The End Zone.* Levi: *The Drowned and the Saved.*
1987		1987 Attwood: *The Handmaid's Tale.* Winterson: *Sexing the Cherry.* Morrison: *Beloved.*
1988	*A Far Cry from Kensington.*	1988 Rushdie: *The Satanic Verses.* Carey: *Oscar and Lucinda.* Barnes: *A History of the World in $10\frac{1}{2}$ Chapters.* Larkin: *Collected Poems.*
1989	D.Litt., Edinburgh.	1989 Ishiguro: *The Remains of the Day.* M. Amis: *London Fields.* Trevor: *The Silence in the Garden.*
1990	*Symposium.* Spark is awarded the Sunday Times Award for Literary Excellence.	1990 Byatt: *Possession.* Penelope Fitzgerald: *The Gate of Angels.* Kureishi: *The Buddha of Suburbia.* Updike: *Rabbit at Rest.* 1991 Márquez: *The General in his Labyrinth.* Okri: *The Famished Road.* Trevor: *Two Lives*
1992	The author publishes her autobiography, *Curriculum Vitae.* Ingersoll Foundation T. S. Eliot Award (USA).	1992 Byatt: *Angels and Insects.* Ondaatje: *The English Patient.*

CHRONOLOGY

DATE	AUTHOR'S LIFE	LITERARY CONTEXT
1993	*Omnibus I. The Essence of the Brontës. The French Window and The Small Telephone* (children's). Muriel Spark is made a Dame.	
1994	*Omnibus II. The Collected Stories.*	1994 Trevor: *Felicia's Journey.*
1995		1995 M. Amis: *The Information.* Murdoch: *Jackson's Dilemma.* Atkinson: *Behind the Scenes at the Museum.* Penelope Fitzgerald: *The Blue Flower.*
1996	*Reality and Dreams* (Scottish Arts Council Award). *Omnibus III.*	1996 Attwood: *Alias Grace.* Byatt: *Babel Tower.* Bainbridge: *Every Man for Himself.* Drabble: *The Witch of Exmoor.*
1997	*Open to the Public* (stories). *Omnibus IV.* Muriel Spark is awarded the David Cohen British Literature Prize for a lifetime's achievement.	1997 McEwan: *Enduring Love.* Arundhati Roy: *The God of Small Things.* A.L. Kennedy: *Original Bliss.*
1998	Gold Pen Award, PEN International.	1998 Iris Murdoch and Ted Hughes die. Hughes: *Birthday Letters.* McEwan: *Amsterdam.* Bainbridge: *Master Georgie.*
1999	D.Litt., Oxford.	
2000	*Aiding and Abetting.*	2000 Attwood: *The Blind Assassin.* Roth: *The Human Stain.*
2001	*The Complete Short Stories.* The Editorial Board of the Catholic Book Club grants Spark the Campion Award. D.Litt., London.	2001 Lessing: *The Sweetest Dream.* McEwan: *Atonement.*
2002	Boccacio Prize for European Literature (Italy)	
2003	*Ghost Stories.*	
2004	*All the Poems of Muriel Spark. The Finishing School* (novel).	2004 Lessing: *The Grandmothers.*

CHRONOLOGY

1993 Palestinian leader Arafat and Israeli Prime Minister Rabin sign peace agreement in the US. Maastricht Treaty (creating European Union) ratified.

1994 Mandela and ANC sweep to victory in South African elections. Civil war in Rwanda. Russian military action against Chechen Republic. IRA ceasefire announced. The Channel Tunnel is opened. Tony Blair becomes leader of the Labour Party, hailing the advent of 'New Labour'.
1995 Rabin is assassinated.

1996 A huge bomb blast in Canary Wharf, London, brings to an end the uneasy truce in Northern Ireland. President Clinton re-elected.

1997 Tony Blair elected Prime Minister (first Labour government since 1979). Princess Diana is killed in a car accident in Paris.

1998 The *Washington Post* discloses a sexual liaison between President Clinton and a White House intern. Northern Ireland Referendum accepts the Good Friday Agreement; an assembly is elected. Omagh Bomb in August kills 29 people. Clinton orders air strikes against Iraq.

1999 Serbs attack ethnic Albanians in Kosovo; US leads NATO in bombing of Belgrade.
2000 Milosevic's regime in the former Yugoslavia collapses. George W. Bush is elected President of the US, although there is some controversy surrounding the election results.
2001 Al-Qaeda terrorist attacks of 9/11. US and allied military action against the Taliban in Afghanistan.

2003 Iraq weapons crisis. American and British troops invade Iraq.

THE PRIME OF
MISS JEAN BRODIE

CHAPTER 1

THE BOYS, AS they talked to the girls from Marcia Blaine School, stood on the far side of their bicycles holding the handlebars, which established a protective fence of bicycle between the sexes, and the impression that at any moment the boys were likely to be away.

The girls could not take off their panama hats because this was not far from the school gates and hatlessness was an offence. Certain departures from the proper set of the hat on the head were overlooked in the case of fourth-form girls and upwards so long as nobody wore their hat at an angle. But there were other subtle variants from the ordinary rule of wearing the brim turned up at the back and down at the front. The five girls, standing very close to each other because of the boys, wore their hats each with a definite difference.

These girls formed the Brodie set. That was what they had been called even before the headmistress had given them the name, in scorn, when they had moved from the Junior to the Senior school at the age of twelve. At that time they had been immediately recognizable as Miss Brodie's pupils, being vastly informed on a lot of subjects irrelevant to the authorized curriculum, as the headmistress said, and useless to the school as a school. These girls were discovered to have heard of the Buchmanites and Mussolini, the Italian Renaissance painters, the advantages to the skin of cleansing cream and witch-hazel over honest soap and water, and the word 'menarche'; the interior decoration of the London house of the author of *Winnie-the-Pooh* had been described to them, as had the love lives of Charlotte Brontë and of Miss Brodie herself.

They were aware of the existence of Einstein and the arguments of those who considered the Bible to be untrue. They knew the rudiments of astrology but not the date of the Battle of Flodden or the capital of Finland. All of the Brodie set, save one, counted on its fingers, as had Miss Brodie, with accurate results more or less.

By the time they were sixteen, and had reached the fourth form, and loitered beyond the gates after school, and had adapted themselves to the orthodox régime, they remained unmistakably Brodie, and were all famous in the school, which is to say they were held in suspicion and not much liking. They had no team spirit and very little in common with each other outside their continuing friendship with Jean Brodie. She still taught in the Junior department. She was held in great suspicion.

Marcia Blaine School for Girls was a day school which had been partially endowed in the middle of the nineteenth century by the wealthy widow of an Edinburgh book-binder. She had been an admirer of Garibaldi before she died. Her manly portrait hung in the great hall, and was honoured every Founder's Day by a bunch of hard-wearing flowers such as chrysanthemums or dahlias. These were placed in a vase beneath the portrait, upon a lectern which also held an open Bible with the text underlined in red ink, 'O where shall I find a virtuous woman, for her price is above rubies.'

The girls who loitered beneath the tree, shoulder to shoulder, very close to each other because of the boys, were all famous for something. Now, at sixteen, Monica Douglas was a prefect, famous mostly for mathematics which she could do in her brain, and for her anger which, when it was lively enough, drove her to slap out to right and left. She had a very red nose, winter and summer, long dark plaits, and fat, peg-like legs. Since she had turned sixteen, Monica wore her panama hat rather higher on her head than normal, perched as if it were too small and as if she knew she looked grotesque in any case.

4

Rose Stanley was famous for sex. Her hat was placed quite unobtrusively on her blonde short hair, but she dented in the crown on either side.

Eunice Gardiner, small, neat, and famous for her spritely gymnastics and glamorous swimming, had the brim of her hat turned up at the front and down at the back.

Sandy Stranger wore it turned up all round and as far back on her head as it could possibly go; to assist this, she had attached to her hat a strip of elastic which went under the chin. Sometimes Sandy chewed this elastic and when it was chewed down she sewed on a new piece. She was merely notorious for her small, almost non-existent, eyes, but she was famous for her vowel sounds which, long ago in the long past, in the Junior school, had enraptured Miss Brodie. 'Well, come and recite for us please, because it has been a tiring day.'

> 'She left the web, she left the loom,
> She made three paces thro' the room,
> She saw the water-lily bloom,
> She saw the helmet and the plume,
> She look'd down to Camelot.'

'It lifts one up,' Miss Brodie usually said, passing her hand outwards from her breast towards the class of ten-year-old girls who were listening for the bell which would release them. 'Where there is no vision,' Miss Brodie had assured them, 'the people perish. Eunice, come and do a somersault in order that we may have comic relief.'

But now, the boys with their bicycles were cheerfully insulting Jenny Gray about her way of speech which she had got from her elocution classes. She was going to be an actress. She was Sandy's best friend. She wore her hat with the front brim bent sharply downwards; she was the prettiest and most graceful girl of the set, and this was her fame. 'Don't be a lout,

Andrew,' she' said with her uppish tone. There were three Andrews among the five boys, and these three Andrews now started mimicking Jenny: 'Don't be a lout, Andrew,' while the girls laughed beneath their bobbing panamas.

Along came Mary Macgregor, the last member of the set, whose fame rested on her being a silent lump, a nobody whom everybody could blame. With her was an outsider, Joyce Emily Hammond, the very rich girl, their delinquent, who had been recently sent to Blaine as a last hope, because no other school, no governess, could manage her. She still wore the green uniform of her old school. The others wore deep violet. The most she had done, so far, was to throw paper pellets sometimes at the singing master. She insisted on the use of her two names, Joyce Emily. This Joyce Emily was trying very hard to get into the famous set, and thought the two names might establish her as a something, but there was no chance of it and she could not see why.

Joyce Emily said, 'There's a teacher coming out,' and nodded towards the gates.

Two of the Andrews wheeled their bicycles out on to the road and departed. The other three boys remained defiantly, but looking the other way as if they might have stopped to admire the clouds on the Pentland Hills. The girls crowded round each other as if in discussion. 'Good afternoon,' said Miss Brodie when she approached the group. 'I haven't seen you for some days. I think we won't detain these young men and their bicycles. Good afternoon, boys.' The famous set moved off with her, and Joyce, the new delinquent, followed. 'I think I haven't met this new girl,' said Miss Brodie, looking closely at Joyce. And when they were introduced she said: 'Well, we must be on our way, my dear.'

Sandy looked back as Joyce Emily walked, and then skipped, leggy and uncontrolled for her age, in the opposite direction, and the Brodie set was left to their secret life as it had been six years ago in their childhood.

'I am putting old heads on your young shoulders,' Miss Brodie had told them at that time, 'and all my pupils are the crème de la crème.'

Sandy looked with her little screwed-up eyes at Monica's very red nose and remembered this saying as she followed the set in the wake of Miss Brodie.

'I should like you girls to come to supper tomorrow night,' Miss Brodie said. 'Make sure you are free.'

'The Dramatic Society...' murmured Jenny.

'Send an excuse,' said Miss Brodie. 'I have to consult you about a new plot which is afoot to force me to resign. Needless to say, I shall not resign.' She spoke calmly as she always did in spite of her forceful words.

Miss Brodie never discussed her affairs with the other members of the staff, but only with those former pupils whom she had trained up in her confidence. There had been previous plots to remove her from Blaine, which had been foiled.

'It has been suggested again that I should apply for a post at one of the progressive schools, where my methods would be more suited to the system than they are at Blaine. But I shall not apply for a post at a crank school. I shall remain at this education factory. There needs must be a leaven in the lump. Give me a girl at an impressionable age, and she is mine for life.'

The Brodie set smiled in understanding of various kinds.

Miss Brodie forced her brown eyes to flash as a meaningful accompaniment to her quiet voice. She looked a mighty woman with her dark Roman profile in the sun. The Brodie set did not for a moment doubt that she would prevail. As soon expect Julius Caesar to apply for a job at a crank school as Miss Brodie. She would never resign. If the authorities wanted to get rid of her she would have to be assassinated.

'Who are the gang, this time?' said Rose, who was famous for sex-appeal.

'We shall discuss tomorrow night the persons who oppose me,' said Miss Brodie. 'But rest assured they shall not succeed.'

'No,' said everyone. 'No, of course they won't.'

'Not while I am in my prime,' she said. 'These years are still the years of my prime. It is important to recognize the years of one's prime, always remember that. Here is my tram-car. I dare say I'll not get a seat. This is nineteen-thirty-six. The age of chivalry is past.'

Six years previously, Miss Brodie had led her new class into the garden for a history lesson underneath the big elm. On the way through the school corridors they passed the headmistress's study. The door was wide open, the room was empty.

'Little girls,' said Miss Brodie, 'come and observe this.'

They clustered round the open door while she pointed to a large poster pinned with drawing-pins on the opposite wall within the room. It depicted a man's big face. Underneath were the words 'Safety First'.

'This is Stanley Baldwin who got in as Prime Minister and got out again ere long,' said Miss Brodie. 'Miss Mackay retains him on the wall because she believes in the slogan "Safety First". But Safety does not come first. Goodness, Truth and Beauty come first. Follow me.'

This was the first intimation, to the girls, of an odds between Miss Brodie and the rest of the teaching staff. Indeed, to some of them, it was the first time they had realized it was possible for people glued together in grown-up authority to differ at all. Taking inward note of this, and with the exhilarating feeling of being in on the faint smell of row, without being endangered by it, they followed dangerous Miss Brodie into the secure shade of the elm.

Often, that sunny autumn, when the weather permitted, the small girls took their lessons seated on three benches arranged about the elm.

'Hold up your books,' said Miss Brodie quite often that autumn, 'prop them up in your hands, in case of intruders. If there are any intruders, we are doing our history lesson . . . our poetry . . . English grammar.'

The small girls held up their books with their eyes not on them, but on Miss Brodie.

'Meantime I will tell you about my last summer holiday in Egypt . . . I will tell you about care of the skin, and of the hands . . . about the Frenchman I met in the train to Biarritz . . . and I must tell you about the Italian paintings I saw. Who is the greatest Italian painter?'

'Leonardo da Vinci, Miss Brodie.'

'That is incorrect. The answer is Giotto, he is my favourite.'

Some days it seemed to Sandy that Miss Brodie's chest was flat, no bulges at all, but straight as her back. On other days her chest was breast-shaped and large, very noticeable, something for Sandy to sit and peer at through her tiny eyes while Miss Brodie on a day of lessons indoors stood erect, with her brown head held high, staring out of the window like Joan of Arc as she spoke.

'I have frequently told you, and the holidays just past have convinced me, that my prime has truly begun. One's prime is elusive. You little girls, when you grow up, must be on the alert to recognize your prime at whatever time of your life it may occur. You must then live it to the full. Mary, what have you got under your desk, what are you looking at?'

Mary sat lump-like and too stupid to invent something. She was too stupid ever to tell a lie; she didn't know how to cover up.

'A comic, Miss Brodie,' she said.

'Do you mean a comedian, a droll?'

Everyone tittered.

'A comic paper,' said Mary.

'A comic paper, forsooth. How old are you?'

'Ten, ma'am.'

'You are too old for comic papers at ten. Give it to me.'

Miss Brodie looked at the coloured sheets. '*Tiger Tim's* forsooth,' she said, and threw it into the waste-paper basket. Perceiving all eyes upon it she lifted it out of the basket, tore it up beyond redemption and put it back again.

'Attend to me, girls. One's prime is the moment one was born for. Now that my prime has begun – Sandy, your attention is wandering. What have I been talking about?'

'Your prime, Miss Brodie.'

'If anyone comes along,' said Miss Brodie, 'in the course of the following lesson, remember that it is the hour for English grammar. Meantime I will tell you a little of my life when I was younger than I am now, though six years older than the man himself.'

She leaned against the elm. It was one of the last autumn days when the leaves were falling in little gusts. They fell on the children who were thankful for this excuse to wriggle and for the allowable movements in brushing the leaves from their hair and laps.

'Season of mists and mellow fruitfulness. I was engaged to a young man at the beginning of the War but he fell on Flanders' Field,' said Miss Brodie. 'Are you thinking, Sandy, of doing a day's washing?'

'No, Miss Brodie.'

'Because you have got your sleeves rolled up. I won't have to do with girls who roll up the sleeves of their blouses, however fine the weather. Roll them down at once, we are civilized beings. He fell the week before Armistice was declared. He fell like an autumn leaf, although he was only twenty-two years of age. When we go indoors we shall look on the map at Flanders, and the spot where my lover was laid before you were born. He was poor. He came from Ayrshire, a countryman, but a hard-working and clever scholar. He said, when he asked me to marry him, "We shall have to drink water and walk slow." That was Hugh's country way of expressing that we would live quietly. We shall drink water and walk slow. What does the saying signify, Rose?'

'That you would live quietly, Miss Brodie,' said Rose Stanley who six years later had a great reputation for sex.

The story of Miss Brodie's felled fiancé was well on its way when the headmistress, Miss Mackay, was seen to approach across the lawn. Tears had already started to drop from Sandy's little pig-like eyes and Sandy's tears now affected her friend Jenny, later famous in the school for her beauty, who gave a sob and groped up the leg of her knickers for her handkerchief. 'Hugh was killed,' said Miss Brodie, 'a week before the Armistice. After that there was a general election and people were saying "Hang the Kaiser!" Hugh was one of the Flowers of the Forest, lying in his grave.' Rose Stanley had now begun to weep. Sandy slid her wet eyes sideways, watching the advance of Miss Mackay, head and shoulders forward, across the lawn.

'I am come to see you and I have to be off,' she said. 'What are you little girls crying for?'

'They are moved by a story I have been telling them. We are having a history lesson,' said Miss Brodie, catching a falling leaf neatly in her hand as she spoke.

'Crying over a story at ten years of age!' said Miss Mackay to the girls who had stragglingly risen from the benches, still dazed with Hugh the warrior. 'I am only come to see you and I must be off. Well, girls, the new term has begun. I hope you all had a splendid summer holiday and I look forward to seeing your splendid essays on how you spent them. You shouldn't be crying over history at the age of ten. My word!'

'You did well,' said Miss Brodie to the class, when Miss Mackay had gone, 'not to answer the question put to you. It is well, when in difficulties, to say never a word, neither black nor white. Speech is silver but silence is golden. Mary, are you listening? What was I saying?'

Mary Macgregor, lumpy, with merely two eyes, a nose and a mouth like a snowman, who was later famous for being stupid and always to blame and who, at the age of twenty-three, lost her life in a hotel fire, ventured, 'Golden.'

'What did I say was golden?'

Mary cast her eyes around her and up above. Sandy whispered, 'The falling leaves.'

'The falling leaves,' said Mary.

'Plainly,' said Miss Brodie, 'you were not listening to me. If only you small girls would listen to me I would make of you the crème de la crème.'

CHAPTER 2

MARY MACGREGOR, ALTHOUGH she lived into her twenty-fourth year, never quite realized that Jean Brodie's confidences were not shared with the rest of the staff and that her love story was given out only to her pupils. She had not thought much about Jean Brodie, certainly never disliked her, when, a year after the outbreak of the Second World War, she joined the Wrens, and was clumsy and incompetent, and was much blamed. On one occasion of real misery – when her first and last boy-friend, a corporal whom she had known for two weeks, deserted her by failing to turn up at an appointed place and failing to come near her again – she thought back to see if she had ever really been happy in her life; it occurred to her then that the first years with Miss Brodie, sitting listening to all those stories and opinions which had nothing to do with the ordinary world, had been the happiest time of her life. She thought this briefly, and never again referred her mind to Miss Brodie, but had got over her misery, and had relapsed into her habitual slow bewilderment, before she died while on leave in Cumberland in a fire in the hotel. Back and forth along the corridors ran Mary Macgregor, through the thickening smoke. She ran one way; then, turning, the other way; and at either end the blast furnace of the fire met her. She heard no screams, for the roar of the fire drowned the screams; she gave no scream, for the smoke was choking her. She ran into somebody on her third turn, stumbled and died. But at the beginning of the nineteen-thirties, when Mary Macgregor was ten, there she was sitting blankly among Miss Brodie's pupils. 'Who has spilled ink on the floor – was it you, Mary?'

'I don't know, Miss Brodie.'

'I dare say it was you. I've never come across such a clumsy girl. And if you can't take an interest in what I am saying, please try to look as if you do.'

These were the days that Mary Macgregor, on looking back, found to be the happiest days of her life.

Sandy Stranger had a feeling at the time that they were supposed to be the happiest days of her life, and on her tenth birthday she said so to her best friend Jenny Gray who had been asked to tea at Sandy's house. The speciality of the feast was pineapple cubes with cream, and the speciality of the day was that they were left to themselves. To Sandy the unfamiliar pineapple had the authentic taste and appearance of happiness and she focused her small eyes closely on the pale gold cubes before she scooped them up in her spoon, and she thought the sharp taste on her tongue was that of a special happiness, which was nothing to do with eating, and was different from the happiness of play that one enjoyed unawares. Both girls saved the cream to the last, then ate it in spoonfuls.

'Little girls, you are going to be the crème de la crème,' said Sandy, and Jenny spluttered her cream into her handkerchief.

'You know,' Sandy said, 'these are supposed to be the happiest days of our lives.'

'Yes, they are always saying that,' Jenny said. 'They say, make the most of your schooldays because you never know what lies ahead of you.'

'Miss Brodie says prime is best,' Sandy said.

'Yes, but she never got married like our mothers and fathers.'

'They don't have primes,' said Sandy.

'They have sexual intercourse,' Jenny said.

The little girls paused, because this was still a stupendous thought, and one which they had only lately lit upon; the very phrase and its meaning were new. It was quite unbelievable. Sandy said, then, 'Mr Lloyd had a baby last week. He must

14

have committed sex with his wife.' This idea was easier to cope with and they laughed screamingly into their pink paper napkins. Mr Lloyd was the Art master to the Senior girls.

'Can you *see* it happening?' Jenny whispered.

Sandy screwed her eyes even smaller in the effort of seeing with her mind. 'He would be wearing his pyjamas,' she whispered back.

The girls rocked with mirth, thinking of one-armed Mr Lloyd, in his solemnity, striding into school.

Then Jenny said, 'You do it on the spur of the moment. That's how it happens.'

Jenny was a reliable source of information, because a girl employed by her father in his grocer shop had recently been found to be pregnant, and Jenny had picked up some fragments of the ensuing fuss. Having confided her finds to Sandy, they had embarked on a course of research which they called 'research', piecing together clues from remembered conversations illicitly overheard, and passages from the big dictionaries.

'It all happens in a flash,' Jenny said. 'It happened to Teenie when she was out walking at Puddocky with her boy-friend. Then they had to get married.'

'You would think the urge would have passed by the time she got her *clothes* off,' Sandy said. By 'clothes' she definitely meant to imply knickers, but 'knickers' was rude in this scientific context.

'Yes, that's what I can't understand,' said Jenny.

Sandy's mother looked round the door and said, 'Enjoying yourselves, darlings?' Over her shoulder appeared the head of Jenny's mother. 'My word,' said Jenny's mother, looking at the tea-table, 'they've been tucking in!'

Sandy felt offended and belittled by this; it was as if the main idea of the party had been the food.

'What would you like to do now?' Sandy's mother said.

Sandy gave her mother a look of secret ferocity which meant: you promised to leave us all on our own, and a promise is a promise, you know it's very bad to break a promise to a child, you might ruin all my life by breaking your promise, it's my birthday.

Sandy's mother backed away bearing Jenny's mother with her. 'Let's leave them to themselves,' she said. 'Just enjoy yourselves, darlings.'

Sandy was sometimes embarrassed by her mother being English and calling her 'darling', not like the mothers of Edinburgh who said 'dear'. Sandy's mother had a flashy winter coat trimmed with fluffy fox fur like the Duchess of York's, while the other mothers wore tweed or, at the most, musquash that would do them all their days.

It had been raining and the ground was too wet for them to go and finish digging the hole to Australia, so the girls lifted the tea-table with all its festal relics over to the corner of the room. Sandy opened the lid of the piano stool and extracted a notebook from between two sheaves of music. On the first page of the notebook was written,

The Mountain Eyrie
by
Sandy Stranger and Jenny Gray

This was a story, still in the process of composition, about Miss Brodie's lover, Hugh Carruthers. He had not been killed in the war, that was a mistake in the telegram. He had come back from the war and called to inquire for Miss Brodie at school, where the first person whom he encountered was Miss Mackay, the headmistress. She had informed him that Miss Brodie did not desire to see him, she loved another. With a bitter, harsh laugh, Hugh went and made his abode in a mountain eyrie, where, wrapped in a leather jacket, he had been discovered one day by Sandy and Jenny. At the present stage in the story Hugh was holding Sandy captive but Jenny had escaped by night and was attempting to find her way down the mountainside in the dark. Hugh was preparing to pursue her.

Sandy took a pencil from a drawer in the sideboard and continued:

'Hugh!' Sandy beseeched him, 'I swear to you before all I hold sacred that Miss Brodie has never loved another, and she awaits you below, praying and hoping in her prime. If you will let Jenny go, she will bring back your lover Jean Brodie to you and you will see her with your own eyes and hold her in your arms after these twelve long years and a day.'

His black eye flashed in the lamplight of the hut. 'Back, girl!' he cried, 'and do not bar my way. Well do I know that yon girl Jenny will report my whereabouts to my mocking erstwhile fiancée. Well do I know that you are both spies sent by her that she might mock. Stand back from the door, I say!'

'Never!' said Sandy, placing her young lithe body squarely in front of the latch and her arm through the bolt. Her large eyes flashed with an azure light of appeal.

Sandy handed the pencil to Jenny. 'It's your turn,' she said.

Jenny wrote: With one movement he flung her to the farthest end of the hut and strode out into the moonlight and his strides made light of the drifting snow.

'Put in about his boots,' said Sandy.

Jenny wrote: His high boots flashed in the moonlight.

'There are too many moonlights,' Sandy said, 'but we can sort that later when it comes to publication.'

'Oh, but it's a secret, Sandy!' said Jenny.

'I know that,' Sandy said. 'Don't worry, we won't publish it till our prime.'

'Do you think Miss Brodie ever had sexual intercourse with Hugh?' said Jenny.

'She would have had a baby, wouldn't she?'

'I don't know.'

'I don't think they did anything like that,' said Sandy. 'Their love was above all that.'

'Miss Brodie said they clung to each other with passionate abandon on his last leave.'

'I don't think they took their clothes off, though,' Sandy said, 'do you?'

'No. I can't see it,' said Jenny.

'I wouldn't like to have sexual intercourse,' Sandy said.

'Neither would I. I'm going to marry a pure person.'

'Have a toffee.'

They ate their sweets, sitting on the carpet. Sandy put some coal on the fire and the light spurted up, reflecting on Jenny's ringlets. 'Let's be witches by the fire, like we were at Hallowe'en.'

They sat in the twilight eating toffees and incanting witches' spells. Jenny said, 'There's a Greek god at the museum standing up with nothing on. I saw it last Sunday afternoon but I was with Auntie Kate and I didn't have a chance to *look* properly.'

'Let's go to the museum next Sunday,' Sandy said. 'It's research.'

'Would you be allowed to go alone with me?'

Sandy, who was notorious for not being allowed to go out and about without a grown-up person, said, 'I don't think so. Perhaps we could get someone to take us.'

'We could ask Miss Brodie.'

Miss Brodie frequently took the little girls to the art galleries and museums, so this seemed feasible.

'But suppose,' said Sandy, 'she won't let us look at the statue if it's naked.'

'I don't think she would notice that it was naked,' Jenny said. 'She just wouldn't see its thingummyjig.'

'I know,' said Sandy. 'Miss Brodie's above all that.'

It was time for Jenny to go home with her mother, all the way in the tram-car through the haunted November twilight of Edinburgh across the Dean Bridge. Sandy waved from the window, and wondered if Jenny, too, had the feeling of leading a double life, fraught with problems that even a millionaire did not have to face. It was well known that millionaires led double lives. The evening paper rattlesnaked its way through the letter box and there was suddenly a six-o'clock feeling in the house.

Miss Brodie was reciting poetry to the class at a quarter to four, to raise their minds before they went home. Miss Brodie's eyes were half shut and her head was thrown back:

> 'In the stormy east wind straining,
> The pale yellow woods were waning,
> The broad stream in his banks complaining,
> Heavily the low sky raining
> > Over tower'd Camelot.'

Sandy watched Miss Brodie through her little pale eyes, screwed them smaller and shut her lips tight.

Rose Stanley was pulling threads from the girdle of her gym tunic. Jenny was enthralled by the poem, her lips were parted, she was never bored. Sandy was never bored, but she had to lead a double life of her own in order never to be bored.

> Down she came and found a boat
> Beneath a willow left afloat,
> And round about the prow she wrote
> > *The Lady of Shalott.*

'By what means did your Ladyship write these words?' Sandy inquired in her mind with her lips shut tight.

'There was a pot of white paint and a brush which happened to be standing upon the grassy verge,' replied the

Lady of Shalott graciously. 'It was left there no doubt by some heedless member of the Unemployed.'

'Alas, and in all that rain!' said Sandy for want of something better to say, while Miss Brodie's voice soared up to the ceiling, and curled round the feet of the Senior girls upstairs.

The Lady of Shalott placed a white hand on Sandy's shoulder and gazed at her for a space. 'That one so young and beautiful should be so ill-fated in love!' she said in low sad tones.

'What can be the meaning of these words?' cried Sandy in alarm, with her little eyes screwed on Miss Brodie and her lips shut tight.

Miss Brodie said: 'Sandy, are you in pain?'

Sandy looked astonished.

'You girls,' said Miss Brodie, 'must learn to cultivate an expression of composure. It is one of the best assets of a woman, an expression of composure, come foul, come fair. Regard the Mona Lisa over yonder!'

All heads turned to look at the reproduction which Miss Brodie had brought back from her travels and pinned on the wall. Mona Lisa in her prime smiled in steady composure even though she had just come from the dentist and her lower jaw was swollen.

'She is older than the rocks on which she sits. Would that I had been given charge of you girls when you were seven. I sometimes fear it's too late, now. If you had been mine when you were seven you would have been the crème de la crème. Sandy, come and read some stanzas and let us hear your vowel sounds.'

Sandy, being half-English, made the most of her vowels, it was her only fame. Rose Stanley was not yet famous for sex, and it was not she but Eunice Gardiner who had approached Sandy and Jenny with a Bible, pointing out the words, 'The babe leapt in her womb'. Sandy and Jenny said she was dirty and threatened to tell on her. Jenny was already famous for her prettiness, and she had a sweet voice, so that Mr Lowther, who came to teach singing, would watch her admiringly as she sang 'Come see where golden-hearted spring...'; and he twitched her ringlets, the more daringly since Miss Brodie always stayed with her pupils during the singing lesson. He twitched her ringlets and looked at Miss Brodie like a child showing off its tricks and almost as if testing Miss Brodie to see if she were at all willing to conspire in his un-Edinburgh conduct.

Mr Lowther was small, with a long body and short legs. His hair and moustache were red-gold. He curled his hand round the back of his ear and inclined his head towards each girl to test her voice. 'Sing ah!'

'Ah!' sang Jenny, high and pure as the sea maiden of the Hebrides whom Sandy had been talking about. But her eyes swivelled over to catch Sandy's.

Miss Brodie ushered the girls from the music room and, gathering them about her, said, 'You girls are my vocation. If I were to receive a proposal of marriage tomorrow from the Lord Lyon King-of-Arms I would decline it. I am dedicated to you in my prime. Form a single file, now, please, and walk with your heads up, *up*, like Sybil Thorndike, a woman of noble mien.'

Sandy craned back her head, pointed her freckled nose in the air and fixed her little pig-like eyes on the ceiling as she walked along in the file.

'What are you doing, Sandy?'

'Walking like Sybil Thorndike, ma'am.'

'One day, Sandy, you will go too far.'

Sandy looked hurt and puzzled.

'Yes,' said Miss Brodie, 'I have my eye upon you, Sandy. I observe a frivolous nature. I fear you will never belong to life's élite or, as one might say, the crème de la crème.'

When they had returned to the classroom Rose Stanley said, 'I've got ink on my blouse.'

'Go to the science room and have the stain removed; but remember it is very bad for the tussore.'

Sometimes the girls would put a little spot of ink on a sleeve of their tussore silk blouses so that they might be sent to the science room in the Senior school. There a thrilling teacher, a Miss Lockhart, wearing a white overall, with her grey short hair set back in waves from a tanned and weathered golfer's face, would pour a small drop of white liquid from a large jar on to a piece of cotton wool. With this she would dab the ink-spot on the sleeve, silently holding the girl's arm, intently absorbed in the task. Rose Stanley went to the science room with her inky blouse only because she was bored, but Sandy and Jenny got ink on their blouses at discreet intervals of four weeks, so that they could go and have their arms held by Miss Lockhart who seemed to carry six inches of pure air around her person wherever she moved in that strange-smelling room. This long room was her natural setting and she had lost something of her quality when Sandy saw her walking from the school in her box-pleat tweeds over to her sports car like an ordinary teacher. Miss Lockhart in the science room was to Sandy something apart, surrounded by three lanes of long benches set out with jars half-full of coloured crystals and powders and liquids, ochre and bronze and metal grey and cobalt blue, glass vessels of curious shapes, bulbous, or with pipe-like stems. Only once when Sandy went to the science room was there a lesson in progress. The older girls, big girls, some with bulging chests, were standing in couples at the benches, with gas jets burning before them. They held a glass tube full of green stuff in their hands and were dancing the tube in the flame, dozens of dancing green tubes and flames, all along the benches. The bare winter top branches of the trees brushed the windows of this long room, and beyond that was the cold winter sky with a huge red sun. Sandy, on that occasion, had the presence of mind to remember that her schooldays were supposed to be the happiest days of her life and she took the compelling news back

THE PRIME OF MISS JEAN BRODIE

to Jenny that the Senior school was going to be marvellous and Miss Lockhart was beautiful.

'All the girls in the science room were doing just as they liked,' said Sandy, 'and that's what they were supposed to be doing.'

'We do a lot of what we like in Miss Brodie's class,' Jenny said. 'My mummy says Miss Brodie gives us too much freedom.'

'She's not supposed to give us freedom, she's supposed to give us lessons,' said Sandy. 'But the science class is supposed to be free, it's allowed.'

'Well, I like being in Miss Brodie's,' Jenny said.

'So do I,' Sandy said. 'She takes an interest in our general knowledge, my mother says.'

All the same, the visits to the science room were Sandy's most secret joy, and she calculated very carefully the intervals between one ink-spot and another, so that there should be no suspicion on Miss Brodie's part that the spots were not an accident. Miss Lockhart would hold her arm and carefully dab the ink-stain on her sleeve while Sandy stood enthralled by the long room which was this science teacher's rightful place, and by the lawful glamour of everything there. It was on the occasion when Rose Stanley, after the singing lesson, was sent to the science room to get ink off her blouse that Miss Brodie told her class,

'You must be more careful with your ink. I can't have my girls going up and down to the science room like this. We must keep our good name.'

She added, 'Art is greater than science. Art comes first, and then science.'

The large map had been rolled down over the blackboard because they had started the geography lesson. Miss Brodie turned with her pointer to show where Alaska lay. But she turned again to the class and said: 'Art and religion first; then philosophy; lastly science. That is the order of the great subjects of life, that's their order of importance.'

This was the first winter of the two years that this class spent with Miss Brodie. It had turned nineteen-thirty-one. Miss Brodie had already selected her favourites, or rather those whom she could trust; or rather those whose parents she could trust not to lodge complaints about the more advanced and seditious aspects of her educational policy, these parents being either too enlightened to complain or too unenlightened, or too awed by their good fortune in getting their girls' education at endowed rates, or too trusting to question the value of what their daughters were learning at this school of sound reputation. Miss Brodie's special girls were taken home to tea and bidden not to tell the others, they were taken into her confidence, they understood her private life and her feud with the headmistress and the allies of the headmistress. They learned what troubles in her career Miss Brodie had encountered on their behalf. 'It is for the sake of you girls – my influence, now, in the years of my prime.' This was the beginning of the Brodie set. Eunice Gardiner was so quiet at first, it was difficult to see why she had been drawn in by Miss Brodie. But eventually she cut capers for the relief and amusement of the tea-parties, doing cartwheels on the carpet. 'You are an Ariel,' said Miss Brodie. Then Eunice began to chatter. She was not allowed to do cartwheels on Sundays, for in many ways Miss Brodie was an Edinburgh spinster of the deepest dye. Eunice Gardiner did somersaults on the mat only at Saturday gatherings before high teas, or afterwards on Miss Brodie's kitchen linoleum, while the other girls were washing up and licking honey from the depleted comb off their fingers as they passed it over to be put away in the food cupboard. It was twenty-eight years after Eunice did the splits in Miss Brodie's flat that she, who had become a nurse and married a doctor, said to her husband one evening:

'Next year when we go for the Festival –'

'Yes?'

She was making a wool rug, pulling at a different stitch.

'Yes?' he said.

'When we go to Edinburgh,' she said, 'remind me while we're there to go and visit Miss Brodie's grave.'

'Who was Miss Brodie?'

'A teacher of mine, she was full of culture. She was an Edinburgh Festival all on her own. She used to give us teas at her flat and tell us about her prime.'

'Prime what?'

'Her prime of life. She fell for an Egyptian courier once, on her travels, and came back and told us all about it. She had a few favourites. I was one of them. I did the splits and made her laugh, you know.'

'I always knew your upbringing was a bit peculiar.'

'But she wasn't mad. She was as sane as anything. She knew exactly what she was doing. She told us all about her love life, too.'

'Let's have it then.'

'Oh, it's a long story. She was just a spinster. I must take flowers to her grave – I wonder if I could find it?'

'When did she die?'

'Just after the war. She was retired by then. Her retirement was rather a tragedy, she was forced to retire before time. The head never liked her. There's a long story attached to Miss Brodie's retirement. She was betrayed by one of her own girls, we were called the Brodie set. I never found out which one betrayed her.'

It is time now to speak of the long walk through the old parts of Edinburgh where Miss Brodie took her set, dressed in their deep violet coats and black velour hats with the green and white crest, one Friday in March when the school's central heating system had broken down and everyone else had been muffled up and sent home. The wind blew from the icy Forth and the sky was loaded with forthcoming snow. Mary Macgregor walked with Sandy because Jenny had gone home. Monica Douglas, later famous for being able to do real mathematics in her head, and for her anger, walked behind them with her dark red face, broad nose and dark pigtails falling from her black hat and her legs already shaped like pegs in their black wool stockings. By her side walked Rose Stanley, tall and blonde with a yellow-pale skin, who had not yet won her reputation for sex, and whose conversation was all about trains, cranes, motor cars, Meccanos, and other boys' affairs. She was not interested in the works of engines or the constructive powers of the Meccanos, but she knew their names, the variety of colours in which they came, the makes of motor cars and their horse-power, the various prices of the Meccano sets. She was also an energetic climber of walls and trees. And although these concerns at Rose Stanley's eleventh year marked her as a tomboy, they did not go deep into her femininity and it was her superficial knowledge of these topics alone, as if they had been a conscious preparation, which stood her in good stead a few years later with the boys.

With Rose walked Miss Brodie, head up, like Sybil Thorndike, her nose arched and proud. She wore her loose brown tweed coat with the beaver collar tightly buttoned, her brown felt hat with the brim up at one side and down at the other. Behind Miss Brodie, last in the group, little Eunice Gardiner who, twenty-eight years later, said of Miss Brodie, 'I must visit her grave', gave a skip between each of her walking steps as if she might even break into pirouettes on the pavement, so that Miss Brodie, turning round, said from time to time, 'Now, Eunice!' And, from time to time again, Miss Brodie would fall behind to keep Eunice company.

Sandy, who had been reading *Kidnapped*, was having a conversation with the hero, Alan Breck, and was glad to be with Mary Macgregor because it was not necessary to talk to Mary.

'Mary, you may speak quietly to Sandy.'

'Sandy won't talk to me,' said Mary who later, in that hotel fire, ran hither and thither till she died.

'Sandy cannot talk to you if you are so stupid and disagreeable. Try to wear an agreeable expression at least, Mary.'

'Sandy, you must take this message o'er the heather to the Macphersons,' said Alan Breck. 'My life depends upon it, and the Cause no less.'

'I shall never fail you, Alan Breck,' said Sandy. 'Never.'

'Mary,' said Miss Brodie, from behind, 'please try not to lag behind Sandy.'

Sandy kept pacing ahead, fired on by Alan Breck whose ardour and thankfulness, as Sandy prepared to set off across the heather, had reached touching proportions.

Mary tried to keep up with her. They were crossing the Meadows, a gusty expanse of common land, glaring green under the snowy sky. Their destination was the Old Town, for Miss Brodie had said they should see where history had been lived; and their route had brought them to the Middle Meadow Walk.

Eunice, unaccompanied at the back, began to hop to a rhyme which she repeated to herself:

> Edinburgh, Leith,
> Portobello, Musselburgh
> *And* Dalkeith.

Then she changed to the other foot.

> Edinburgh, Leith . . .

Miss Brodie turned round and hushed her, then called forward to Mary Macgregor who was staring at an Indian student who was approaching,

'Mary, don't you *want* to walk tidily?'

27

'Mary,' said Sandy, 'stop staring at the brown man.'

The nagged child looked numbly at Sandy and tried to quicken her pace. But Sandy was walking unevenly, in little spurts forward and little halts, as Alan Breck began to sing to her his ditty before she took to the heather to deliver the message that was going to save Alan's life. He sang:

> This is the song of the sword of Alan:
> The smith made it,
> The fire set it;
> Now it shines in the hands of Alan Breck.

Then Alan Breck clapped her shoulder and said, 'Sandy, you are a brave lass and want nothing in courage that any King's man might possess.'

'Don't walk so fast,' mumbled Mary.

'You aren't walking with your head up,' said Sandy. 'Keep it up, up.'

Then suddenly Sandy wanted to be kind to Mary Macgregor, and thought of the possibilities of feeling nice from being nice to Mary instead of blaming her. Miss Brodie's voice from behind was saying to Rose Stanley, 'You are all heroines in the making. Britain must be a fit country for heroines to live in. The League of Nations . . . ' The sound of Miss Brodie's presence, just when it was on the tip of Sandy's tongue to be nice to Mary Macgregor, arrested the urge. Sandy looked back at her companions, and understood them as a body with Miss Brodie for the head. She perceived herself, the absent Jenny, the ever-blamed Mary, Rose, Eunice, and Monica, all in a frightening little moment, in unified compliance to the destiny of Miss Brodie, as if God had willed them to birth for that purpose.

She was even more frightened then, by her temptation to be nice to Mary Macgregor, since by this action she would separate herself, and be lonely, and blameable in a more dreadful way than Mary who, although officially the faulty one, was at least inside Miss Brodie's category of heroines in the making. So, for good fellowship's sake, Sandy said to Mary, 'I wouldn't be walking with *you* if Jenny was here.' And Mary said, 'I know.' Then Sandy started to hate herself again and to nag on and on at Mary, with the feeling that if you did a thing a lot of times, you made it into a right thing. Mary started to cry, but quietly, so that Miss Brodie could not see. Sandy was unable to cope and decided to stride on and be a married lady having an argument with her husband:

'Well, Colin, it's rather hard on a woman when the lights have fused and there isn't a man in the house.'

'Dearest Sandy, *how* was I to know . . .'

As they came to the end of the Meadows a group of Girl Guides came by. Miss Brodie's brood, all but Mary, walked past with eyes ahead. Mary stared at the dark blue big girls with their regimented vigorous look and broader accents of speech than the Brodie girls used when in Miss Brodie's presence. They passed, and Sandy said to Mary, 'It's rude to stare.' And Mary said, 'I wasn't staring.' Meanwhile Miss Brodie was being questioned by the girls behind on the question of the Brownies and the Girl Guides, for quite a lot of the other girls in the Junior School were Brownies.

'For those who like that sort of thing,' said Miss Brodie in her best Edinburgh voice, 'that is the sort of thing they like.'

So Brownies and Guides were ruled out. Sandy recalled Miss Brodie's admiration for Mussolini's marching troops, and the picture she had brought back from Italy showing the triumphant march of the black uniforms in Rome.

'These are the fascisti,' said Miss Brodie, and spelt it out. 'What are these men, Rose?'

'The fascisti, Miss Brodie.'

They were dark as anything and all marching in the straightest of files, with their hands raised at the same angle,

MURIEL SPARK

while Mussolini stood on a platform like a gym teacher or a Guides mistress and watched them. Mussolini had put an end to unemployment with his fascisti and there was no litter in the streets. It occurred to Sandy, there at the end of the Middle Meadow Walk, that the Brodie set was Miss Brodie's fascisti, not to the naked eye, marching along, but all knit together for her need and in another way, marching along. That was all right, but it seemed, too, that Miss Brodie's disapproval of the Girl Guides had jealousy in it, there was an inconsistency, a fault. Perhaps the Guides were too much of a rival fascisti, and Miss Brodie could not bear it. Sandy thought she might see about joining the Brownies. Then the group-fright seized her again, and it was necessary to put the idea aside, because she loved Miss Brodie.

'We make good company for each other, Sandy,' said Alan Breck, crunching beneath his feet the broken glass among the blood on the floor of the ship's roundhouse. And taking a knife from the table, he cut off one of the silver buttons from his coat. 'Wherever you show that button,' he said, 'the friends of Alan Breck will come around you.'

'We turn to the right,' said Miss Brodie.

They approached the Old Town which none of the girls had properly seen before, because none of their parents was so historically minded as to be moved to conduct their young into the reeking network of slums which the Old Town constituted in those years. The Canongate, The Grassmarket, The Lawnmarket, were names which betokened a misty region of crime and desperation: 'Lawnmarket Man Jailed.' Only Eunice Gardiner and Monica Douglas had already traversed the High Street on foot on the Royal Mile from the Castle or Holyrood. Sandy had been taken to Holyrood in an uncle's car and had seen the bed, too short and too broad, where Mary Queen of Scots had slept, and the tiny room, smaller than their own scullery at home, where the Queen had played cards with Rizzio.

Now they were in a great square, the Grassmarket, with the Castle, which was in any case everywhere, rearing between a big gap in the houses where the aristocracy used to live. It was Sandy's first experience of a foreign country, which intimates itself by its new smells and shapes and its new poor. A man sat on the icy-cold pavement; he just sat. A crowd of children, some without shoes, were playing some fight game, and some boys shouted after Miss Brodie's violet-clad company, with words that the girls had not heard before, but rightly understood to be obscene. Children and women with shawls came in and out of the dark closes. Sandy found she was holding Mary's hand in her bewilderment, all the girls were holding hands, while Miss Brodie talked of history. Into the High Street, and 'John Knox,' said Miss Brodie, 'was an embittered man. He could never be at ease with the gay French Queen. We of Edinburgh owe a lot to the French. We are Europeans.' The smell was amazingly terrible. In the middle of the road farther up the High Street a crowd was gathered. 'Walk past quietly,' said Miss Brodie.

A man and a woman stood in the midst of the crowd which had formed a ring round them. They were shouting at each other and the man hit the woman twice across the head. Another woman, very little, with cropped black hair, a red face and a big mouth, came forward and took the man by the arm. She said:

'I'll be your man.'

From time to time throughout her life Sandy pondered this, for she was certain that the little woman's words were 'I'll be your man', not 'I'll be your woman', and it was never explained.

And many times throughout her life Sandy knew with a shock, when speaking to people whose childhood had been in Edinburgh, that there were other people's Edinburghs quite different from hers, and with which she held only the names of districts and streets and monuments in common.

Similarly, there were other people's nineteen-thirties. So that, in her middle age, when she was at last allowed all those visitors to the convent – so many visitors being against the Rule, but a special dispensation was enforced on Sandy because of her Treatise – when a man said, 'I must have been at school in Edinburgh at the same time as you, Sister Helena,' Sandy, who was now some years Sister Helena of the Transfiguration, clutched the bars of the grille as was her way, and peered at him through her little faint eyes and asked him to describe his schooldays and his school, and the Edinburgh he had known. And it turned out, once more, that his was a different Edinburgh from Sandy's. His school, where he was a boarder, had been cold and grey. His teachers had been supercilious Englishmen, 'or near-Englishmen', said the visitor 'with third-rate degrees'. Sandy could not remember ever having questioned the quality of her teachers' degrees, and the school had always been lit with the sun or, in winter, with a pearly north light. 'But Edinburgh,' said the man, 'was a beautiful city, more beautiful then than it is now. Of course, the slums have been cleared. The Old Town was always my favourite. We used to love to explore the Grassmarket and so on. Architecturally speaking, there is no finer sight in Europe.'

'I was once taken for a walk through the Canongate,' Sandy said, 'but I was frightened by the squalor.'

'Well, it was the 'thirties,' said the man. 'Tell me, Sister Helena, what would you say was your greatest influence during the 'thirties? I mean, during your teens. Did you read Auden and Eliot?'

'No,' said Sandy.

'We boys were very keen on Auden and that group of course. We wanted to go and fight in the Spanish Civil War. On the Republican side, of course. Did you take sides in the Spanish Civil War at your school?'

'Well, not exactly,' said Sandy. 'It was all different for us.'

'You weren't a Catholic then, of course?'

'No,' said Sandy.

'The influences of one's teens are very important,' said the man.

'Oh yes,' said Sandy, 'even if they provide something to react against.'

'What was your biggest influence, then, Sister Helena? Was it political, personal? Was it Calvinism?'

'Oh no,' said Sandy. 'But there was a Miss Jean Brodie in her prime.' She clutched the bars of the grille as if she wanted to escape from the dim parlour beyond, for she was not composed like the other nuns who sat, when they received their rare visitors, well back in the darkness with folded hands. But Sandy always leaned forward and peered, clutching the bars with both hands, and the other sisters remarked it and said that Sister Helena had too much to bear from the world since she had published her psychological book which was so unexpectedly famed. But the dispensation was forced upon Sandy, and she clutched the bars and received the choice visitors, the psychologists and the Catholic seekers, and the higher journalist ladies and the academics who wanted to question her about her odd psychological treatise on the nature of moral perception, called 'The Transfiguration of the Commonplace'.

'We will not go into St Giles's,' said Miss Brodie, 'because the day draws late. But I presume you have all been to St Giles's Cathedral?'

They had nearly all been in St Giles's with its tattered blood-stained banners of the past. Sandy had not been there, and did not want to go. The outsides of old Edinburgh churches frightened her, they were of such dark stone, like presences almost the colour of the Castle rock, and were built so warningly with their upraised fingers.

Miss Brodie had shown them a picture of Cologne Cathedral, like a wedding cake, which looked as if it had been built for pleasure and festivities, and parties given by the Prodigal Son in his early career. But the insides of Scottish churches were more reassuring because during the services they contained people, and no ghosts at all. Sandy, Rose Stanley and Monica Douglas were of believing though not church-going families. Jenny Gray and Mary Macgregor were Presbyterians and went to Sunday School. Eunice Gardiner was Episcopalian and claimed that she did not believe in Jesus, but in the Father, Son and Holy Ghost. Sandy, who believed in ghosts, felt that the Holy Ghost was a feasible proposition. The whole question was, during this winter term, being laid open by Miss Brodie who, at the same time as adhering to the strict Church of Scotland habits of her youth, and keeping the Sabbath, was now, in her prime, attending evening classes in comparative religion at the University. So her pupils heard all about it, and learned for the first time that some honest people did not believe in God, nor even Allah. But the girls were set to study the Gospels with diligence for their truth and goodness, and to read them aloud for their beauty.

Their walk had brought them into broad Chambers Street. The group had changed its order, and was now walking three abreast, with Miss Brodie in front between Sandy and Rose. 'I am summoned to see the headmistress at morning break on Monday,' said Miss Brodie. 'I have no doubt Miss Mackay wishes to question my methods of instruction. It has happened before. It will happen again. Meanwhile, I follow my principles of education and give of my best in my prime. The word "education" comes from the root e from ex, out, and duco, I lead. It means a leading out. To me education is a leading out of what is already there in the pupil's soul. To Miss Mackay it is a putting in of something that is not there, and that is not what I call education, I call it intrusion, from the Latin root prefix in meaning in and the stem trudo, I thrust. Miss Mackay's method is to thrust a lot of information into the pupil's head; mine is a leading out of knowledge, and that is true education as is proved by the root meaning. Now Miss Mackay has accused me of putting ideas into my girls' heads, but in fact that is *her* practice and mine is quite the opposite. Never let it be said that I put ideas into your heads. What is the meaning of education, Sandy?'

'To lead out,' said Sandy who was composing a formal invitation to Alan Breck, a year and a day after their breathtaking flight through the heather.

Miss Sandy Stranger requests the pleasure of Mr Alan Breck's company at dinner on Tuesday the 6th of January at 8 o'clock.

That would surprise the hero of *Kidnapped* coming unexpectedly from Sandy's new address in the lonely harbour house on the coast of Fife – described in a novel by the daughter of John Buchan – of which Sandy had now by devious means become the mistress. Alan Breck would arrive in full Highland dress. Supposing that passion struck upon them in the course of the evening and they were swept away into sexual intercourse? She saw the picture of it happening in her mind, and Sandy could not stand for this spoiling. She argued with herself, surely people have time to *think*, they have to stop to think while they are taking their clothes off, and if they stop to think, how can they be swept away?

'That is a Citroën,' said Rose Stanley about a motor car that had passed by. 'They are French.'

'Sandy, dear, don't rush. Take my hand,' said Miss Brodie. 'Rose, your mind is full of motor cars. There is nothing wrong with motor cars, of course, but there are higher things. I'm sure Sandy's mind is not on motor cars, she is paying attention to my conversation like a well-mannered girl.'

And if people take their clothes off in front of each other, thought Sandy, it is so rude, they are bound to be put off their passion for a moment. And if they are put off just for a single moment, *how* can they be swept away in the urge? If it all happens in a flash . . .

Miss Brodie said, 'So I intend simply to point out to Miss Mackay that there is a radical difference in our principles of education. Radical is a word pertaining to roots – Latin *radix*, a root. We differ at root, the headmistress and I, upon the question whether we are employed to educate the minds of girls or to intrude upon them. We have had this argument before, but Miss Mackay is not, I may say, an outstanding logician. A logician is one skilled in logic. Logic is the art of reasoning. What is logic, Rose?'

'To do with reasoning, ma'am,' said Rose, who later, while still in her teens, was to provoke Miss Brodie's amazement and then her awe and finally her abounding enthusiasm for the role which Rose then appeared to be enacting: that of a great lover, magnificently elevated above the ordinary run of lovers, above the moral laws, Venus incarnate, something set apart. In fact, Rose was not at the time in question engaged in the love affair which Miss Brodie thought she was, but it seemed so, and Rose was famous for sex. But in her mere eleventh year, on the winter's walk, Rose was taking note of the motor cars and Miss Brodie had not yet advanced far enough into her prime to speak of sex except by veiled allusion, as when she said of her warrior lover, 'He was a pure man', or when she read from James Hogg's poem 'Bonnie Kilmeny',

'Kilmeny was pure as pure could be'

and added, 'Which is to say, she did not go to the glen in order to mix with men.'

'When I see Miss Mackay on Monday morning,' said Miss Brodie, 'I shall point out that by the terms of my employment my methods cannot be condemned unless they can be proved to be in any part improper or subversive, and so long as the girls are in the least equipped for the end-of-term examination. I trust you girls to work hard and try and scrape through, even if you learn up the stuff and forget it next day. As for impropriety, it could never be imputed to me except by some gross distortion on the part of a traitor. I do not think ever to be betrayed. Miss Mackay is younger than I am and higher salaried. That is by accident. The best qualifications available at the University in my time were inferior to those open to Miss Mackay. That is why she holds the senior position. But her reasoning power is deficient, and so I have no fears for Monday.'

'Miss Mackay has an awfully red face, with the veins all showing,' said Rose.

'I can't permit that type of remark to pass in my presence, Rose,' said Miss Brodie, 'for it would be disloyal.'

They had come to the end of Lauriston Place, past the fire station, where they were to get on a tram-car to go to tea with Miss Brodie in her flat at Churchhill. A very long queue of men lined this part of the street. They were without collars, in shabby suits. They were talking and spitting and smoking little bits of cigarette held between middle finger and thumb.

'We shall cross here,' said Miss Brodie and herded the set across the road.

Monica Douglas whispered, 'They are the Idle.'

'In England they are called the Unemployed. They are waiting to get their dole from the labour bureau,' said Miss Brodie. 'You must all pray for the Unemployed, I will write you out the special prayer for them. You all know what the dole is?'

Eunice Gardiner had not heard of it.

'It is the weekly payment made by the State for the relief of the Unemployed and their families. Sometimes they go and spend their dole on drink before they go home, and their children starve. They are our brothers. Sandy, stop staring at once. In Italy the unemployment problem has been solved.'

Sandy felt that she was not staring across the road at the endless queue of brothers, but that it was pulling her eyes towards it. She felt once more very frightened. Some of the men looked over at the girls, but without seeing them. The girls had reached the tram stop. The men were talking and spitting a great deal. Some were laughing with hacking laughs merging into coughs and ending up with spits.

As they waited for the tram-car Miss Brodie said, 'I had lodgings in this street when first I came to Edinburgh as a student. I must tell you a story about the landlady, who was very frugal. It was her habit to come to me every morning to ask what I would have for breakfast, and she spoke like this: "Wud ye have a red herrin? – no ye wouldn't. Could ye eat a boilt egg? – no ye couldn't." The result was, I never had but bread and butter to my breakfast all the time I was in those lodgings, and very little of that.'

The laughter of the girls met that of the men opposite, who had now begun to file slowly by fits and starts into the labour bureau. Sandy's fear returned as soon as she had stopped laughing. She saw the slow jerkily moving file tremble with life, she saw it all of a piece like one dragon's body which had no right to be in the city and yet would not go away and was unslayable. She thought of the starving children. This was a relief to her fear. She wanted to cry as she always did when she saw a street singer or a beggar. She wanted Jenny to be there, because Jenny cried easily about poor children. But the snaky creature opposite started to shiver in the cold and made Sandy tremble again. She turned and said to Mary Macgregor who had brushed against her sleeve, 'Stop pushing.'

'Mary, dear, you mustn't push,' said Miss Brodie.

'I wasn't pushing,' said Mary.

In the tram-car Sandy excused herself from tea with Miss Brodie on the plea that she thought she had a cold coming on. Indeed she shivered. She wanted at that moment to be warmly at home, outside which even the corporate Brodie set lived in a colder sort of way.

But later, when Sandy thought of Eunice doing somersaults and splits on Miss Brodie's kitchen linoleum while the other girls washed up, she rather wished she had gone to tea at Miss Brodie's after all. She took out her secret notebook from between the sheets of music and added a chapter to 'The Mountain Eyrie', the true love story of Miss Jean Brodie.

CHAPTER 3

THE DAYS PASSED and the wind blew from the Forth.

It is not to be supposed that Miss Brodie was unique at this point of her prime; or that (since such things are relative) she was in any way off her head. She was alone, merely, in that she taught in a school like Marcia Blaine's. There were legions of her kind during the nineteen-thirties, women from the age of thirty and upward, who crowded their war-bereaved spinsterhood with voyages of discovery into new ideas and energetic practices in art or social welfare, education or religion. The progressive spinsters of Edinburgh did not teach in schools, especially in schools of traditional character like Marcia Blaine's School for Girls. It was in this that Miss Brodie was, as the rest of the staff spinsterhood put it, a trifle out of place. But she was not out of place amongst her own kind, the vigorous daughters of dead or enfeebled merchants, of ministers of religion, University professors, doctors, big warehouse owners of the past, or the owners of fisheries who had endowed these daughters with shrewd wits, high-coloured cheeks, constitutions like horses, logical educations, hearty spirits and private means. They could be seen leaning over the democratic counters of Edinburgh grocers' shops arguing with the Manager at three in the afternoon on every subject from the authenticity of the Scriptures to the question what the word 'guaranteed' on a jam-jar really meant. They went to lectures, tried living on honey and nuts, took lessons in German and then went walking in Germany; they bought caravans and went off with them into the hills among the lochs; they played the guitar, they supported all the new little theatre companies; they took lodgings in the slums and, distributing pots of paint, taught their neighbours the arts of simple interior decoration; they preached the inventions of Marie Stopes; they attended the meetings of the Oxford Group and put Spiritualism to their hawk-eyed test. Some assisted in the Scottish Nationalist Movement; others, like Miss Brodie, called themselves Europeans and Edinburgh a European capital, the city of Hume and Boswell.

They were not, however, committee women. They were not school-teachers. The committee spinsters were less enter-prising and not at all rebellious, they were sober church-goers and quiet workers. The school-mistresses were of a still more orderly type, earning their keep, living with aged parents and taking walks on the hills and holidays at North Berwick.

But those of Miss Brodie's kind were great talkers and feminists and, like most feminists, talked to men as man-to-man.

'I tell you this, Mr Geddes, birth control is the only answer to the problem of the working class. A free issue to every household . . . '

And often in the thriving grocers' shops at three in the afternoon:

'Mr Logan, Elder though you are, I am a woman in my prime of life, so you can take it from me that you get a sight more religion out of Professor Tovey's Sunday concerts than you do out of your kirk services.'

And so, seen in this light, there was nothing outwardly odd about Miss Brodie. Inwardly was a different matter, and it remained to be seen, towards what extremities her nature worked her. Outwardly she differed from the rest of the teaching staff in that she was still in a state of fluctuating development, whereas they had only too understandably not trusted themselves to change their minds, particularly on ethical questions, after the age of twenty. There was nothing Miss Brodie could not yet learn, she boasted of it. And it was not a static Miss Brodie who told her girls, 'These are the years of my prime. You are benefiting by my prime', but one whose nature was growing under their eyes, as the girls themselves were under formation. It extended, this prime of Miss Brodie's, still in the making when the girls were well on in their teens. And the principles governing the end of her prime would have astonished herself at the beginning of it.

The summer holidays of nineteen-thirty-one marked the first anniversary of the launching of Miss Brodie's prime. The year to come was in many ways the sexual year of the Brodie set, who were now turned eleven and twelve: it was a crowded year of stirring revelations. In later years, sex was only one of the things in life. That year it was everything.

The term opened vigorously as usual. Miss Brodie stood bronzed before her class and said, 'I have spent most of my summer holidays in Italy once more, and a week in London, and I have brought back a great many pictures which we can pin on the wall. Here is a Cimabue. Here is a larger formation of Mussolini's fascisti, it is a better view of them than that of last year's picture. They are doing splendid things as I shall tell you later. I went with my friends for an audience with the Pope. My friends kissed his ring but I thought it proper only to bend over it. I wore a long black gown with a lace mantilla, and looked magnificent. In London my friends who are well-to-do – their small girl has two nurses, or nannies as they say in England – took me to visit A. A. Milne. In the hall was hung a reproduction of Botticelli's *Primavera* which means the Birth of Spring. I wore my silk dress with the large red poppies which is just right for my colouring. Mussolini is one of the greatest men in the world, far more so than Ramsay MacDonald, and his fascisti –'

'Good morning, Miss Brodie. Good morning, sit down, girls,' said the headmistress who had entered in a hurry, leaving the door wide open.

Miss Brodie passed behind her with her head up, up, and shut the door with the utmost meaning.

'I have only just looked in,' said Miss Mackay, 'and I have to be off. Well, girls, this is the first day of the new session. Are we downhearted? No. You girls must work hard this year at every subject and pass your qualifying examination with flying colours. Next year you will be in the Senior school, remember. I hope you've all had a nice summer holiday, you all look nice and brown. I hope in due course of time to read your essays on how you spent them.'

When she had gone Miss Brodie looked hard at the door for a long time. A girl, not of her set, called Judith, giggled. Miss Brodie said to Judith, 'That will do.' She turned to the blackboard and rubbed out with her duster the long division sum she always kept on the blackboard in case of intrusions from outside during any arithmetic periods when Miss Brodie should happen not to be teaching arithmetic. When she had done this she turned back to the class and said, 'Are we downhearted no, are we downhearted no. As I was saying, Mussolini has performed feats of magnitude and unemployment is even farther abolished under him than it was last year. I shall be able to tell you a great deal this term. As you know, I don't believe in talking down to children, you are capable of grasping more than is generally appreciated by your elders. Education means a leading out, from *e*, out and *duco*, I lead. Qualifying examination or no qualifying examination, you will have the benefit of my experiences in Italy. In Rome I saw the Forum and I saw the Colosseum where the gladiators died and the slaves were thrown to the lions. A vulgar American remarked to me, "It looks like a mighty fine quarry." They talk nasally. Mary, what does to talk nasally mean?'

Mary did not know.

'Stupid as ever,' said Miss Brodie. 'Eunice?'

'Through your nose,' said Eunice.

43

'Answer in a complete sentence, please,' said Miss Brodie. 'This year I think you should all start answering in complete sentences, I must try to remember this rule. Your correct answer is "To talk nasally means to talk through one's nose". The American said, "It looks like a mighty fine quarry." Ah, it was there the gladiators fought. "Hail Caesar!" they cried. "These about to die salute thee!"'

Miss Brodie stood in her brown dress like a gladiator with raised arm and eyes flashing like a sword. 'Hail Caesar!' she cried again, turning radiantly to the window light, as if Caesar sat there. 'Who opened the window?' said Miss Brodie dropping her arm.

Nobody answered.

'Whoever has opened the window has opened it too wide,' said Miss Brodie. 'Six inches is perfectly adequate. More is vulgar. One should have an innate sense of these things. We ought to be doing history at the moment according to the time-table. Get out your history books and prop them up in your hands. I shall tell you a little more about Italy. I met a young poet by a fountain. Here is a picture of Dante meeting Beatrice – it is pronounced Beatri*chay* in Italian which makes the name very beautiful – on the Ponte Vecchio. He fell in love with her at that moment. Mary, sit up and don't slouch. It was a sublime moment in a sublime love. By whom was the picture painted?'

Nobody knew.

'It was painted by Rossetti. Who was Rossetti, Jenny?'

'A painter,' said Jenny.

Miss Brodie looked suspicious.

'And a genius,' said Sandy, to come to Jenny's rescue.

'A friend of – ?' said Miss Brodie.

'Swinburne,' said a girl.

Miss Brodie smiled. 'You have not forgotten,' she said, looking round the class. 'Holidays or no holidays. Keep your history books propped up in case we have any further intruders.' She looked disapprovingly towards the door and lifted her fine dark Roman head with dignity. She had often told the girls that her dead Hugh had admired her head for its Roman appearance.

'Next year,' she said, 'you will have the specialists to teach you history and mathematics and languages, a teacher for this and a teacher for that, a period of forty-five minutes for this and another for that. But in this your last year with me you will receive the fruits of my prime. They will remain with you all your days. First, however, I must mark the register for today before we forget. There are two new girls. Stand up the two new girls.'

They stood up with wide eyes while Miss Brodie sat down at her desk.

'You will get used to our ways. What religions are you?' said Miss Brodie with her pen poised on the page while, outside in the sky, the gulls from the Firth of Forth wheeled over the school and the green and golden tree-tops swayed towards the windows.

> 'Come autumn sae pensive, in yellow and gray,
> And soothe me wi' tidings o' nature's decay

– Robert Burns,' said Miss Brodie when she had closed the register. 'We are now well into the nineteen-thirties. I have four pounds of rosy apples in my desk, a gift from Mr Lowther's orchard, let us eat them now while the coast is clear – not but what the apples do not come under my own jurisdiction, but discretion is ... discretion is ... Sandy?'

'The better part of valour, Miss Brodie.' Her little eyes looked at Miss Brodie in a slightly smaller way.

Even before the official opening of her prime Miss Brodie's colleagues in the Junior school had been gradually turning against her. The teaching staff of the Senior school was indifferent or mildly amused, for they had not yet felt the impact of the Brodie set; that was to come the following year, and even then these senior mistresses were not unduly irritated by the effects of what they called Miss Brodie's experimental methods. It was in the Junior school, among the lesser paid and lesser qualified women, with whom Miss Brodie had daily dealings, that indignation seethed. There were two exceptions on the staff, who felt neither resentment nor indifference towards Miss Brodie, but were, on the contrary, her supporters on every count. One of these was Mr Gordon Lowther, the singing master for the whole school, Junior and Senior. The other was Mr Teddy Lloyd, the Senior girls' art master. They were the only men on the staff. Both were already a little in love with Miss Brodie, for they found in her the only sex-bestirred object in their daily environment, and although they did not realize it, both were already beginning to act as rivals for her attention. But so far, they had not engaged her attention as men, she knew them only as supporters, and was proudly grateful. It was the Brodie set who discerned, before she did, and certainly these men did, that Mr Lowther and Mr Lloyd were at pains to appear well, each in his exclusive right before Miss Brodie.

To the Brodie set Gordon Lowther and Teddy Lloyd looked rather like each other until habitual acquaintance proved that they looked very different. Both were red-gold in colouring. Teddy Lloyd, the art master, was by far the better-shaped, the better-featured and the more sophisticated. He was said to be half Welsh, half English. He spoke with a hoarse voice as if he had bronchitis all the time. A golden forelock of his hair fell over his forehead into his eyes. Most wonderful of all, he had only one arm, the right, with which he painted. The other was a sleeve tucked into his pocket. He had lost the contents of the sleeve in the Great War.

Miss Brodie's class had only once had an opportunity to size him up closely, and then it was in a dimmed light, for the blinds of the art room had been drawn to allow Mr Lloyd to show his lantern slides. They had been marched into the art room by Miss Brodie, who was going to sit with the girls on the end of a bench, when the art master came forward with a chair for her held in his one hand and presented in a special way with a tiny inflection of the knees, like a flunkey. Miss Brodie seated herself nobly like Britannia with her legs apart under her loose brown skirt which came well over her knees. Mr Lloyd showed his pictures from an exhibition of Italian art in London. He had a pointer with which he indicated the design of the picture in accompaniment to his hoarse voice. He said nothing of what the pictures represented, only followed each curve and line as the artist had left it off – perhaps at the point of an elbow – and picked it up – perhaps at the edge of a cloud or the back of a chair. The ladies of the *Primavera*, in their netball-playing postures, provided Mr Lloyd with much pointer work. He kept on passing the pointer along the lines of their bottoms which showed through the drapery. The third time he did this a collective quiver of mirth ran along the front row of girls, then spread to the back rows. They kept their mouths shut tight against these convulsions, but the tighter their lips, the more did the little gusts of humour escape through their noses. Mr Lloyd looked round with offended exasperation.

'It is obvious,' said Miss Brodie, 'that these girls are not of cultured homes and heritage. The Philistines are upon us, Mr Lloyd.'

The girls, anxious to be of cultured and sexless antecedents, were instantly composed by the shock of this remark. But immediately Mr Lloyd resumed his demonstration of artistic form, and again dragged his pointer all round the draped private parts of one of Botticelli's female subjects, Sandy affected to have a fit of spluttering coughs, as did several

47

girls behind her. Others groped under their seat as if looking for something they had dropped. One or two frankly leaned against each other and giggled with hands to their helpless mouths.

'I am surprised at *you*, Sandy,' said Miss Brodie. 'I thought you were the leaven in the lump.'

Sandy looked up from her coughs with a hypocritical blinking of her eyes. Miss Brodie, however, had already fastened on Mary Macgregor who was nearest to her. Mary's giggles had been caused by contagion, for she was too stupid to have any sex-wits of her own, and Mr Lloyd's lesson would never have affected her unless it had first affected the rest of the class. But now she was giggling openly like a dirty-minded child of an uncultured home. Miss Brodie grasped Mary's arm, jerked her to her feet and propelled her to the door where she thrust her outside and shut her out, returning as one who had solved the whole problem. As indeed she had, for the violent action sobered the girls and made them feel that, in the official sense, an unwanted ring-leader had been apprehended and they were no longer in the wrong.

As Mr Lloyd had now switched his equipment to a depiction of the Madonna and Child, Miss Brodie's action was the more appreciated, for no one in the class would have felt comfortable at being seized with giggles while Mr Lloyd's pointer was tracing the outlines of this sacred subject. In fact, they were rather shocked that Mr Lloyd's hoarse voice did not change its tone in the slightest for this occasion, but went on stating what the painter had done with his brush; he was almost defiant in his methodical tracing of lines all over the Mother and the Son. Sandy caught his glance towards Miss Brodie as if seeking her approval for his very artistic attitude and Sandy saw her smile back as would a goddess with superior understanding smile to a god away on the mountain tops.

It was not long after this that Monica Douglas, later famous for mathematics and anger, claimed that she had seen

Mr Lloyd in the act of kissing Miss Brodie. She was very definite about it in her report to the five other members of the Brodie set. There was a general excited difficulty in believing her.

'When?'

'Where?'

'In the art room after school yesterday.'

'What were you doing in the art room?' said Sandy who took up the role of cross-examiner.

'I went to get a new sketch pad.'

'Why? You haven't finished your old sketch pad yet.'

'I have,' said Monica.

'When did you use up your old sketch pad?'

'Last Saturday afternoon when you were playing golf with Miss Brodie.'

It was true that Jenny and Sandy had done nine holes on the Braid Hills course with Miss Brodie on the previous Saturday, while the rest of the Brodie set wandered afield to sketch.

'Monica used up all her book. She did the Tee Woods from five angles,' said Rose Stanley in verification.

'What part of the art room were they standing in?' Sandy said.

'The far side,' Monica said. 'I know he had his arm round her and was kissing her. They jumped apart when I opened the door.'

'Which arm?' Sandy snapped.

'The right of course, he hasn't got a left.'

'Were you inside or outside the room when you saw them?' Sandy said.

'Well, in and out. I *saw* them, I tell you.'

'What did they say?' Jenny said.

'They didn't see me,' said Monica. 'I just turned and ran away.'

'Was it a long and lingering kiss?' Sandy demanded, while Jenny came closer to hear the answer.

Monica cast the corner of her eye up to the ceiling as if doing mental arithmetic. Then when her calculation was finished she said, 'Yes it was.'

'How do you know if you didn't stop to see how long it was?'

'I know,' said Monica, getting angry, 'by the bit that I did see. It was a small bit of a good long kiss that I saw, I could tell it by his arm being round her, and –'

'I don't believe all this,' Sandy said squeakily, because she was excited and desperately trying to prove the report true by eliminating the doubts. 'You must have been dreaming,' she said.

Monica pecked with the fingers of her right hand at Sandy's arm, and pinched the skin of it with a nasty half turn. Sandy screamed. Monica, whose face was becoming very red, swung the attaché case which held her books, so that it hit the girls who stood in its path and made them stand back from her.

'She's losing her temper,' said Eunice Gardiner, skipping.

'I don't believe what she says,' said Sandy, desperately trying to visualize the scene in the art room and to goad factual Monica into describing it with due feeling.

'I believe it,' said Rose. 'Mr Lloyd is an artist and Miss Brodie is artistic too.'

Jenny said, 'Didn't they see the door opening?'

'Yes,' said Monica, 'they jumped apart as I opened the door.'

'How did you know they didn't see you?' Sandy said.

'I got away before they turned round. They were standing at the far end of the room beside the still-life curtain.' She went to the classroom door and demonstrated her quick get-away. This was not dramatically satisfying to Sandy who went out of the classroom, opened the door, looked, opened her eyes in a startled way, gasped and retreated in a flash. She seemed satisfied by her experimental re-enactment but it so delighted her friends that she repeated it. Miss Brodie came up from behind her on her fourth performance which had reached a state of extreme flourish.

'What are you doing, Sandy?' said Miss Brodie.

'Only playing,' said Sandy, photographing this new Miss Brodie with her little eyes.

The question of whether Miss Brodie was actually capable of being kissed and of kissing occupied the Brodie set till Christmas. For the war-time romance of her life had presented to their minds a Miss Brodie of hardly flesh and blood, since that younger Miss Brodie belonged to the prehistory of before their birth. Sitting under the elm last autumn, Miss Brodie's story of 'when I was a girl' had seemed much less real, and yet more believable than this report by Monica Douglas. The Brodie set decided to keep the incident to themselves lest, if it should spread to the rest of the class, it should spread wider still and eventually to someone's ears who would get Monica Douglas into trouble.

There was, indeed, a change in Miss Brodie. It was not merely that Sandy and Jenny, recasting her in their minds, now began to try to imagine her as someone called 'Jean'. There was a change in herself. She wore newer clothes and with them a glowing amber necklace which was of such real amber that, as she once showed them, it had magnetic properties when rubbed and then applied to a piece of paper.

The change in Miss Brodie was best discerned by comparison with the other teachers in the Junior school. If you looked at them and then looked at Miss Brodie it was more possible to imagine her giving herself up to kissing.

Jenny and Sandy wondered if Mr Lloyd and Miss Brodie had gone further that day in the art room, and had been swept away by passion. They kept an eye on Miss Brodie's stomach to see if it showed signs of swelling. Some days, if they were bored, they decided it had begun to swell. But on Miss Brodie's entertaining days they found her stomach as flat as

ever and at these times even agreed together that Monica
Douglas had been telling a lie.

The other Junior school teachers said good morning to Miss
Brodie, these days, in a more than Edinburgh manner, that is to
say it was gracious enough, and not one of them omitted to say
good morning at all; but Sandy, who had turned eleven,
perceived that the tone of 'morning' in good morning made
the word seem purposely to rhyme with 'scorning', so that
these colleagues of Miss Brodie's might just as well have said
'I scorn you' instead of good morning. Miss Brodie's reply was
more than ever anglicized in its accent than was its usual proud
wont. 'Good mawning,' she replied, in the corridors, flattening
their scorn beneath the chariot wheels of her superiority, and
deviating her head towards them no more than an insulting
half-inch. She held her head up, up, as she walked, and often,
when she reached and entered her own classroom, permitted
herself to sag gratefully against the door for an instant. She did
not frequent the staff common rooms in the free periods
when her class was taking its singing or sewing lessons, but
accompanied them.

Now the two sewing teachers were somewhat apart from
the rest of the teaching staff and were not taken seriously. They
were the two younger sisters of a third, dead, eldest sister
whose guidance of their lives had never been replaced. Their
names were Miss Ellen and Miss Alison Kerr; they were
incapable of imparting any information whatsoever, so flustered were they, with their fluffed-out hair, dry blue-grey skins
and birds' eyes; instead of teaching sewing they took each girl's
work in hand, one by one, and did most of it for her. In the
worst cases they unstitched what had been done and did it
again, saying 'This'll not do', or 'That's never a run and fell
seam'. The sewing sisters had not as yet been induced to judge
Miss Brodie since they were by nature of the belief that their
scholastic colleagues were above criticism. Therefore the
sewing lessons were a great relaxation to all, and Miss Brodie

in the time before Christmas used the sewing period each week to read *Jane Eyre* to her class who, while they listened, pricked their thumbs as much as was bearable so that interesting little spots of blood might appear on the stuff they were sewing, and it was even possible to make blood-spot designs.

The singing lessons were far different. Some weeks after the report of her kissing in the art room it gradually became plain that Miss Brodie was agitated before, during, and after the singing lessons. She wore her newest clothes on singing days.

Sandy said to Monica Douglas, 'Are you sure it was Mr Lloyd who kissed her? Are you sure it wasn't Mr Lowther?'

'It was Mr Lloyd,' said Monica, 'and it was in the art room, not the music room. What would Mr Lowther have been doing in the art room?'

'They look alike, Mr Lloyd and Mr Lowther,' Sandy said.

Monica's anger was rising in her face. 'It was Mr Lloyd with his one arm round her,' she said. 'I saw them. I'm sorry I ever told you. Rose is the only one that believes me.'

Rose Stanley believed her, but this was because she was indifferent. She was the least of all the Brodie set to be excited by Miss Brodie's love affairs, or by anyone else's sex. And it was always to be the same. Later, when she was famous for sex, her magnificently appealing qualities lay in the fact that she had no curiosity about sex at all, she never reflected upon it. As Miss Brodie was to say, she had instinct.

'Rose is the only one who believes me,' said Monica Douglas.

When she visited Sandy at the nunnery in the late nineteen-fifties, Monica said, 'I really did see Teddy Lloyd kiss Miss Brodie in the art room one day.'

'I know you did,' said Sandy.

She knew it even before Miss Brodie had told her so one day after the end of the war, when they sat in the Braid Hills Hotel eating sandwiches and drinking tea which

Miss Brodie's rations at home would not run to. Miss Brodie sat shrivelled and betrayed in her long-preserved dark musquash coat. She had been retired before time. She said, 'I am past my prime.'

'It was a good prime,' said Sandy.

They looked out of the wide windows at the little Braid Burn trickling through the fields and at the hills beyond, so austere from everlasting that they had never been capable of losing anything by the war.

'Teddy Lloyd was greatly in love with me, as you know,' said Miss Brodie, 'and I with him. It was a great love. One day in the art room he kissed me. We never became lovers, not even after you left Edinburgh, when the temptation was strongest.'

Sandy stared through her little eyes at the hills.

'But I renounced him,' said Miss Brodie. 'He was a married man. I renounced the great love of my prime. We had everything in common, the artistic nature.'

She had reckoned on her prime lasting till she was sixty. But this, the year after the war, was in fact Miss Brodie's last and fifty-sixth year. She looked older than that, she was suffering from an internal growth. This was her last year in the world and in another sense it was Sandy's.

Miss Brodie sat in her defeat and said, 'In the late autumn of nineteen-thirty-one – are you listening, Sandy?'

Sandy took her eyes from the hills.

In the late autumn of nineteen-thirty-one Miss Brodie was away from school for two weeks. It was understood she had an ailment. The Brodie set called at her flat after school with flowers and found no one at home. On inquiring at school next day they were told she had gone to the country to stay with a friend until she was better.

In the meantime Miss Brodie's class was dispersed, and squashed in among the classes of her colleagues. The Brodie set stuck together and were placed with a gaunt woman who was, in fact, a Miss Gaunt from the Western Isles who wore a knee-length skirt made from what looked like grey blanket stuff; this had never been smart even in the knee-length days; Rose Stanley said it was cut short for economy. Her head was very large and bony. Her chest was a slight bulge flattened by a bust bodice, and her jersey was a dark forbidding green. She did not care at all for the Brodie set who were stunned by a sudden plunge into industrious learning and very put out by Miss Gaunt's horrible sharpness and strict insistence on silence throughout the day.

'Oh dear,' said Rose out loud one day when they were settled to essay writing, 'I can't remember how you spell "possession". Are there two "s"s or – ?'

'A hundred lines of *Marmion*,' Miss Gaunt flung at her.

The black-marks book which eventually reflected itself on the end-of-term reports, was heavily scored with the names of the Brodie set by the end of the first week. Apart from inquiring their names for this purpose Miss Gaunt did not trouble to remember them. 'You, girl,' she would say to every Brodie face. So dazed were the Brodie girls that they did not notice the omission during that week of their singing lesson which should have been on Wednesday.

On Thursday they were herded into the sewing room in the early afternoon. The two sewing teachers, Miss Alison and Miss Ellen Kerr, seemed rather cowed by gaunt Miss Gaunt, and applied themselves briskly to the sewing machines which they were teaching the girls to use. The shuttle of the sewing machines went up and down, which usually caused Sandy and Jenny to giggle, since at that time everything that could conceivably bear a sexual interpretation immediately did so to them. But the absence of Miss Brodie and the presence of Miss Gaunt had a definite subtracting effect from the sexual significance of everything, and the trepidation of the two sewing sisters contributed to the effect of grim realism.

Miss Gaunt evidently went to the same parish church as the Kerr sisters, to whom she addressed remarks from time to time while she embroidered a tray cloth.

'My brothurr . . . ' she kept saying, 'my brothurr says . . . '

Miss Gaunt's brother was apparently the minister of the parish, which accounted for the extra precautions Miss Alison and Miss Ellen were taking about their work today, with the result that they got a lot of the sewing mixed up.

'My brothurr is up in the morning at five-thirty . . . My brothurr organized a . . . '

Sandy was thinking of the next instalment of *Jane Eyre* which Miss Brodie usually enlivened this hour by reading. Sandy had done with Alan Breck and had taken up with Mr Rochester, with whom she now sat in the garden.

'You are afraid of me, Miss Sandy.'

'You talk like the Sphinx, sir, but I am not afraid.'

'You have such a grave, quiet manner, Miss Sandy – you are going?'

'It has struck nine, sir.'

A phrase of Miss Gaunt's broke upon the garden scene: 'Mr Lowther is not at school this week.'

'So I hear,' Miss Alison said.

'It seems he will be away for another week at least.'

'Is he ill?'

'I understand so, unfortunately,' said Miss Gaunt.

'Miss Brodie is ailing, too,' said Miss Ellen.

'Yes,' said Miss Gaunt. 'She too is expected to be absent for another week.'

'What is the trouble?'

'That I couldn't say,' said Miss Gaunt. She stuck her needle in and out of her embroidery. Then she looked up at the sisters. 'It may be Miss Brodie has the same complaint as Mr Lowther,' she said.

Sandy saw her face as that of the housekeeper in *Jane Eyre*, watching her carefully and knowingly as she entered the house, late, from the garden where she had been sitting with Mr Rochester.

'Perhaps Miss Brodie is having a love affair with Mr Lowther,' Sandy said to Jenny, merely in order to break up the sexless gloom that surrounded them.

'But it was Mr Lloyd who kissed her. She must be in love with Mr Lloyd or she wouldn't have let him kiss her.'

'Perhaps she's working it off on Mr Lowther. Mr Lowther isn't married.'

It was a fantasy worked up between them, in defiance of Miss Gaunt and her forbidding brother, and it was understood in that way. But Sandy, remembering Miss Gaunt's expression as she remarked 'It may be Miss Brodie has the same complaint as Mr Lowther', was suddenly not sure that the suggestion was not true. For this reason she was more reticent than Jenny about the details of the imagined love affair. Jenny whispered, 'They go to bed. Then he puts out the light. Then their toes touch. And then Miss Brodie . . . Miss Brodie . . . ' She broke into giggles.

'Miss Brodie yawns,' said Sandy in order to restore decency, now that she suspected it was all true.

'No, Miss Brodie says "Darling". She says –'

'Quiet,' whispered Sandy, 'Eunice is coming.'

Eunice Gardiner approached the table where Jenny and Sandy sat, grabbed the scissors and went away. Eunice had lately taken a religious turn and there was no talking about sex in front of her. She had stopped hopping and skipping. The phase did not last long, but while it did she was nasty and not to be trusted. When she was well out of the way Jenny resumed:

'Mr Lowther's legs are shorter than Miss Brodie's, so I suppose she winds hers round his, and –'

'Where does Mr Lowther live, do you know?' Sandy said.

'At Cramond. He's got a big house with a housekeeper.'

In that year after the war when Sandy sat with Miss Brodie in the window of the Braid Hills Hotel and brought her eyes back from the hills to show she was listening, Miss Brodie said:

'I renounced Teddy Lloyd. But I decided to enter into a love affair, it was the only cure. My love for Teddy was an obsession, he was the love of my prime. But in the autumn of nineteen-thirty-one I entered an affair with Gordon Lowther, he was a bachelor and it was more becoming. That is the truth and there is no more to say. Are you listening, Sandy?'

'Yes, I'm listening.'

'You look as if you were thinking of something else, my dear. Well, as I say, that is the whole story.'

Sandy was thinking of something else. She was thinking that it was not the whole story.

'Of course the liaison was suspected. Perhaps you girls knew about it. You, Sandy, had a faint idea . . . but nobody could prove what was between Gordon Lowther and myself. It was never proved. It was not on those grounds that I was betrayed. I should like to know who betrayed me. It is incredible that it should have been one of my own girls. I often wonder if it was poor Mary. Perhaps I should have been nicer to Mary. Well, it was tragic about Mary, I picture that fire, that poor girl. I can't see how Mary could have betrayed me, though.'

'She had no contact with the school after she left,' Sandy said.

'I wonder, was it Rose who betrayed me?'

The whine in her voice – ' . . . betrayed me, betrayed me' – bored and afflicted Sandy. It is seven years, thought Sandy, since I betrayed this tiresome woman. What does she mean by 'betray'? She was looking at the hills as if to see there the first and unbetrayable Miss Brodie, indifferent to criticism as a crag.

After her two weeks' absence Miss Brodie returned to tell her class that she had enjoyed an exciting rest and a well-earned one. Mr Lowther's singing class went on as usual and he beamed at Miss Brodie as she brought them proudly into the music room with their heads up, up. Miss Brodie now played the accompaniment, sitting very well at the piano and sometimes, with a certain sadness of countenance, richly taking the second soprano in 'How sweet is the shepherd's sweet lot', and other melodious preparations for the annual concert. Mr Lowther, short-legged, shy and golden-haired, no longer played with Jenny's curls. The bare branches brushed the windows and Sandy was almost as sure as could be that the singing master was in love with Miss Brodie and that Miss Brodie was in love with the art master. Rose Stanley had not yet revealed her potentialities in the working-out of Miss Brodie's passion for one-armed Teddy Lloyd, and Miss Brodie's prime still flourished unbetrayed.

It was impossible to imagine Miss Brodie sleeping with Mr Lowther, it was impossible to imagine her in a sexual context at all, and yet it was impossible not to suspect that such things were so.

During the Easter term Miss Mackay, the headmistress, had the girls in to tea in her study in small groups and, later, one by one. This was a routine of inquiry as to their intentions for the Senior school, whether they would go on the Modern side or whether they would apply for admission to the Classical.

Miss Brodie had already prompted them as follows: 'I am not saying anything against the Modern side. Modern and Classical, they are equal, and each provides for a function in life. You must make your free choice. Not everyone is capable of a Classical education. You must make your choice quite freely.' So that the girls were left in no doubt as to Miss Brodie's contempt for the Modern side.

From among her special set only Eunice Gardiner stood out to be a Modern, and that was because her parents wanted her to take a course in domestic science and she herself wanted the extra scope for gymnastics and games which the Modern side offered. Eunice, preparing arduously for Confirmation, was still a bit too pious for Miss Brodie's liking. She now refused to do somersaults outside of the gymnasium, she wore lavender water on her handkerchief, declined a try of Rose Stanley's aunt's lipstick, was taking a suspiciously healthy interest in international sport and, when Miss Brodie herded her set to the Empire Theatre for their first and last opportunity to witness the dancing of Pavlova, Eunice was absent, she had pleaded off because of something else she had to attend which she described as 'a social'.

'Social what?' said Miss Brodie, who always made difficulties about words when she scented heresy.

'It's in the Church Hall, Miss Brodie.'

'Yes, yes, but social what? Social is an adjective and you are using it as a noun. If you mean a social gathering, by all means attend your social gathering and we shall have our own social gathering in the presence of the great Anna Pavlova, a dedicated woman who, when she appears on the stage, makes the other dancers look like elephants. By all means attend your social gathering. We shall see Pavlova doing the death of the Swan, it is a great moment in eternity.'

All that term she tried to inspire Eunice to become at least a pioneer missionary in some deadly and dangerous zone of the earth, for it was intolerable to Miss Brodie that any of her girls should grow up not largely dedicated to some vocation. 'You will end up as a Girl Guide leader in a suburb like Corstorphine,' she said warningly to Eunice, who was in fact secretly attracted to this idea and who lived in Corstorphine. The term was filled with legends of Pavlova and her dedicated habits, her wild fits of temperament and her intolerance of the second-rate. 'She screams at the chorus,' said Miss Brodie, 'which is permissible in a great artist. She speaks English fluently, her accent is charming. Afterwards she goes home to meditate upon the swans which she keeps on a lake in the grounds.'

'Sandy,' said Anna Pavlova, 'you are the only truly dedicated dancer, next to me. Your dying Swan is perfect, such a sensitive, final tap of the claw upon the floor of the stage . . . '

'I know it,' said Sandy (in considered preference to 'Oh, I do my best'), as she relaxed in the wings.

Pavlova nodded sagely and gazed into the middle distance with the eyes of tragic exile and of art. 'Every artist knows,' said Pavlova, 'is it not so?' Then, with a voice desperate with the menace of hysteria, and a charming accent, she declared, 'I have never been understood. Never. Never.'

Sandy removed one of her ballet shoes and cast it casually to the other end of the wings where it was respectfully retrieved by a member of the common chorus. Pausing before she removed the other shoe, Sandy said to Pavlova, 'I am sure I understand you.'

'It is true,' exclaimed Pavlova, clasping Sandy's hand, 'because you are an artist and will carry on the torch.'

Miss Brodie said: 'Pavlova contemplates her swans in order to perfect her swan dance, she studies them. That is true dedication. You must all grow up to be dedicated women as I have dedicated myself to you.'

A few weeks before she died, when, sitting up in bed in the nursing home, she learned from Monica Douglas that Sandy had gone to a convent, she said: 'What a waste. That is not the sort of dedication I meant. Do you think she has done this to annoy me? I begin to wonder if it was not Sandy who betrayed me.'

The headmistress invited Sandy, Jenny and Mary to tea just before the Easter holidays and asked them the usual questions about what they wanted to do in the Senior school and whether they wanted to do it on the Modern or the Classical side. Mary Macgregor was ruled out of the Classical side because her marks did not reach the required standard. She seemed despondent on hearing this.

'Why do you want so much to go on the Classical side, Mary? You aren't cut out for it. Don't your parents realize that?'

'Miss Brodie prefers it.'

'It has nothing to do with Miss Brodie,' said Miss Mackay, settling her great behind more firmly in her chair. 'It is a question of your marks or what you and your parents think. In your case, your marks don't come up to the standard.'

When Jenny and Sandy opted for Classical, she said: 'Because Miss Brodie prefers it, I suppose. What good will Latin and Greek be to you when you get married or take a job? German would be more useful.'

But they stuck out for Classical, and when Miss Mackay had accepted their choice she transparently started to win over the girls by praising Miss Brodie. 'What we would do without Miss Brodie, I don't know. There is always a difference about Miss Brodie's girls, and the last two years I may say a *marked* difference.'

Then she began to pump them. Miss Brodie took them to the theatre, the art galleries, for walks, to Miss Brodie's flat for tea? How kind of Miss Brodie. 'Does Miss Brodie pay for all your theatre tickets?'

'Sometimes,' said Mary.

'Not for all of us every time,' said Jenny.

'We go up to the gallery,' Sandy said.

'Well, it is most kind of Miss Brodie. I hope you are appreciative.'

'Oh, yes,' they said, united and alert against anything unfavourable to the Brodie idea which the conversation might be leading up to. This was not lost on the headmistress.

'That's splendid,' she said. 'And do you go to concerts with Miss Brodie? Miss Brodie is very musical, I believe?'

'Yes,' said Mary, looking at her friends for a lead.

'We went to the opera with Miss Brodie last term to see *La Traviata*,' said Jenny.

'Miss Brodie is musical?' said Miss Mackay again, addressing Sandy and Jenny.

'We saw Pavlova,' said Sandy.

'Miss Brodie is musical?' said Miss Mackay.

'I think Miss Brodie is more interested in art, ma'am,' said Sandy.

'But music is a form of art.'

'Pictures and drawings, I mean,' said Sandy.

'Very enlightening,' said Miss Mackay. 'Do you girls take piano lessons?'

They all said yes.

'From whom? From Mr Lowther?'

They answered variously, for Mr Lowther's piano lessons were not part of the curriculum and these three girls had private arrangements for the piano at home. But now, at the mention of Mr Lowther, even slow-minded Mary suspected what Miss Mackay was driving at.

'I understand Miss Brodie plays the piano for your singing lessons. So what makes you think she prefers art to music, Sandy?'

'Miss Brodie told us so. Music is an interest to her but art is a passion, Miss Brodie said.'

'And what are *your* cultural interests? I'm sure you are too young to have passions.'

'Stories, ma'am,' Mary said.

'Does Miss Brodie tell you stories?'

'Yes,' said Mary.

'What about?'

'History,' said Jenny and Sandy together, because it was a question they had foreseen might arise one day and they had prepared the answer with a brain-racking care for literal truth.

Miss Mackay paused and looked at them in the process of moving the cake from the table to the tray; their reply had plainly struck her as being on the ready side.

She asked no further questions, but made the following noteworthy speech:

'You are very fortunate in Miss Brodie. I could wish your arithmetic papers had been better. I am always impressed by Miss Brodie's girls in one way or another. You will have to work hard at ordinary humble subjects for the qualifying examination. Miss Brodie is giving you an excellent preparation for the Senior school. Culture cannot compensate for lack of hard knowledge. I am happy to see you are devoted to Miss Brodie. Your loyalty is due to the school rather than to any one individual.'

Not all of this conversation was reported back to Miss Brodie.

'We told Miss Mackay how much you liked art,' said Sandy, however.

'I do indeed,' said Miss Brodie, 'but "like" is hardly the word; pictorial art is my passion.'

'That's what I said,' said Sandy.

Miss Brodie looked at her as if to say, as in fact she had said twice before, 'One day, Sandy, you will go too far for my liking.'

'Compared to music,' said Sandy, blinking up at her with her little pig-like eyes.

Towards the end of the Easter holidays, to crown the sex-laden year, Jenny, out walking alone, was accosted by a man joyfully exposing himself beside the Water of Leith. He said, 'Come and look at this.'

'At what?' said Jenny, moving closer, thinking to herself he had picked up a fallen nestling from the ground or had discovered a strange plant. Having perceived the truth, she escaped unharmed and unpursued though breathless, and was presently surrounded by solicitous, horrified relations and was coaxed to sip tea well sugared against the shock. Later in the day, since the incident had been reported to the police, came a wonderful policewoman to question Jenny.

These events contained enough exciting possibilities to set the rest of the Easter holidays spinning like a top and to last out the whole of the summer term. The first effect on Sandy was an adverse one, for she had been on the point of obtaining permission to go for walks alone in just such isolated spots as that in which Jenny's encounter had taken place. Sandy was now still forbidden lone walks, but this was a mere by-effect of the affair. The rest brought nothing but good. The subject fell under two headings: first, the man himself and the nature of what he had exposed to view, and secondly the policewoman.

The first was fairly quickly exhausted.

'He was a horrible creature,' said Jenny.

'A terrible beast,' said Sandy.

The question of the policewoman was inexhaustible, and although Sandy never saw her, nor at that time any police-woman (for these were in the early days of the women police), she quite deserted Alan Breck and Mr Rochester and all the heroes of fiction for the summer term, and fell in love with the unseen policewoman who had questioned Jenny; and in this way she managed to keep alive Jenny's enthusiasm too.

'What did she look like? Did she wear a helmet?'

'No, a cap. She had short, fair, curly hair curling under the cap. And a dark blue uniform. She said, "Now tell me all about it."'

'And what did you say?' said Sandy for the fourth time.

For the fourth time Jenny replied: 'Well, I said, "The man was walking along under the trees by the bank, and he was holding something in his hand. And then when he saw me he laughed out loud and said, come and look at this. I said, at what? And I went a bit closer and I saw..." – but I couldn't tell the policewoman what I saw, could I? So the policewoman said to me, "You saw something nasty?" And I said "yes". Then she asked me what the man was like, and...'

But this was the same story all over again. Sandy wanted new details about the policewoman, she looked for clues.

Jenny had pronounced the word 'nasty' as 'nesty', which was unusual for Jenny.

'Did she say "nasty" or "nesty"?' said Sandy on this fourth telling.

'Nesty.'

This gave rise to an extremely nasty feeling in Sandy and it put her off the idea of sex for months. All the more as she disapproved of the pronunciation of the word, it made her flesh creep, and she plagued Jenny to change her mind and agree that the policewoman had pronounced it properly.

'A lot of people say nesty,' said Jenny.

'I know, but I don't like them. They're neither one thing nor another.'

It bothered Sandy a great deal, and she had to invent a new speaking-image for the policewoman. Another thing that troubled her was that Jenny did not know the policewoman's name, or even whether she was addressed as 'constable', 'sergeant', or merely 'miss'. Sandy decided to call her Sergeant Anne Grey. Sandy was Anne Grey's right-hand woman in the Force, and they were dedicated to eliminate sex from Edinburgh and environs. In the Sunday newspapers, to which Sandy had free access, the correct technical phrases were to be found, such as 'intimacy took place' and 'plaintiff was in a certain condition'. Females who were up for sex were not called 'Miss' or 'Mrs', they were referred to by their surnames: 'Willis was remanded in custody . . . ' 'Roebuck', said Counsel, 'was discovered to be in a certain condition.'

So Sandy pushed her dark blue police force cap to the back of her head and sitting on a stile beside Sergeant Anne Grey watched the spot between the trees by the Water of Leith where the terrible beast had appeared who had said 'Look at this' to Jenny, but where, in fact, Sandy never was.

'And another thing,' said Sandy, 'we've got to find out more about the case of Brodie and whether she is yet in a certain condition as a consequence of her liaison with Gordon

Lowther, described as singing master, Marcia Blaine School for Girls.'

'Intimacy has undoubtedly taken place,' said Sergeant Anne, looking very nice in her dark uniform and short-cropped curls blondely fringing her cap. She said, 'All we need are a few incriminating documents.'

'Leave all that to me, Sergeant Anne,' said Sandy, because she was at that very time engaged with Jenny in composing the love correspondence between Miss Brodie and the singing master. Sergeant Anne pressed Sandy's hand in gratitude; and they looked into each other's eyes, their mutual understanding too deep for words.

At school after the holidays the Water of Leith affair was kept a secret between Jenny and Sandy, for Jenny's mother had said the story must not be spread about. But it seemed natural that Miss Brodie should be told in a spirit of sensational confiding.

But something made Sandy say to Jenny on the first afternoon of the term: 'Don't tell Miss Brodie.'

'Why?' said Jenny.

Sandy tried to work out the reason. It was connected with the undecided state of Miss Brodie's relationship to cheerful Mr Lowther, and with the fact that she had told her class, first thing: 'I have spent Easter at the little Roman village of Cramond.' That was where Mr Lowther lived all alone in a big house with a housekeeper.

'Don't tell Miss Brodie,' said Sandy.

'Why?' said Jenny.

Sandy made a further effort to work out her reasons. They were also connected with something that had happened in the course of the morning, when Miss Brodie, wanting a supply of drawing books and charcoal to start the new term, sent Monica Douglas to fetch them from the art room, then called her back, and sent Rose Stanley instead. When Rose returned, laden with drawing books and boxes of chalks, she was followed by

Teddy Lloyd, similarly laden. He dumped his books and asked Miss Brodie if she had enjoyed her holiday. She gave him her hand, and said she had been exploring Cramond, one should not neglect these little nearby seaports.

'I shouldn't have thought there was much to *explore* at Cramond,' said Mr Lloyd, smiling at her with his golden forelock falling into his eye.

'It has quite a lot of charm,' she said. 'And did you go away at all?'

'I've been painting,' he said in his hoarse voice. 'Family portraits.'

Rose had been stacking the drawing books into their cupboard and now she had finished. As she turned, Miss Brodie put her arm round Rose's shoulder and thanked Mr Lloyd for his help, as if she and Rose were one.

'N'tall,' said Mr Lloyd, meaning 'Not at all', and went away. It was then Jenny whispered, 'Rose has changed in the holidays, hasn't she?'

This was true. Her fair hair was cut shorter and was very shiny. Her cheeks were paler and thinner, her eyes less wide open, set with the lids half-shut as if she were posing for a special photograph.

'Perhaps she has got the Change,' said Sandy. Miss Brodie called it the Menarche but so far when they tried to use this word amongst themselves it made them giggle and feel shy.

Later in the afternoon after school, Jenny said: 'I'd better tell Miss Brodie about the man I met.'

Sandy replied, 'Don't tell Miss Brodie.'

'Why not?' said Jenny.

Sandy tried, but could not think why not, except to feel an unfinished quality about Miss Brodie and her holiday at Cramond, and her sending Rose to Mr Lloyd. So she said, 'The policewoman said to try to forget what happened. Perhaps Miss Brodie would make you remember it.'

Jenny said, 'That's what I think, too.'

And so they forgot the man by the Water of Leith and remembered the policewoman more and more as the term wore on.

During the last few months of Miss Brodie's teaching she made herself adorable. She did not exhort or bicker and even when hard pressed was irritable only with Mary Macgregor. That spring she monopolized with her class the benches under the elm from which could be seen an endless avenue of dark pink May trees, and heard the trotting of horses in time to the turning wheels of light carts returning home empty by a hidden lane from their early morning rounds. Not far off, like a promise of next year, a group of girls from the Senior school were doing first-form Latin. Once, the Latin mistress was moved by the spring of the year to sing a folk-song to fit the clip-clop of the ponies and carts, and Miss Brodie held up her index finger with delight so that her own girls should listen too.

> Nundinarum adest dies,
> Mulus ille nos vehet.
> Eie, curre, mule, mule,
> I tolutari gradu.

That spring Jenny's mother was expecting a baby, there was no rain worth remembering, the grass, the sun and the birds lost their self-centred winter mood and began to think of others. Miss Brodie's old love story was newly embroidered, under the elm, with curious threads: it appeared that while on leave from the war, her late fiancé had frequently taken her out sailing in a fishing boat and that they had spent some of their merriest times among the rocks and pebbles of a small seaport. 'Sometimes Hugh would sing, he had a rich tenor voice. At other times he fell silent and would set up his easel and paint. He was very talented at both arts, but I think the painter was the real Hugh.'

This was the first time the girls had heard of Hugh's artistic leanings. Sandy puzzled over this and took counsel with Jenny, and it came to them both that Miss Brodie was making her new love story fit the old. Thereafter the two girls listened with double ears, and the rest of the class with single.

Sandy was fascinated by this method of making patterns with facts, and was divided between her admiration for the technique and the pressing need to prove Miss Brodie guilty of misconduct.

'What about those incriminating documents?' said Sergeant Anne Grey in her jolly friendly manner. She really was very thrilling.

Sandy and Jenny completed the love correspondence between Miss Brodie and the singing master at half-term. They were staying in the small town of Crail on the coast of Fife with Jenny's aunt who showed herself suspicious of their notebook: and so they took it off to a neighbouring village along the coast by bus, and sat at the mouth of a cave to finish the work. It had been a delicate question how to present Miss Brodie in both a favourable and an unfavourable light, for now, as their last term with Miss Brodie drew to a close, nothing less than this was demanded.

That intimacy had taken place was to be established. But not on an ordinary bed. That had been a thought suitable only for the enlivening of a sewing period, but Miss Brodie was entitled to something like a status. They placed Miss Brodie on the lofty lion's back of Arthur's Seat, with only the sky for roof and bracken for a bed. The broad parkland rolled away beneath her gaze to the accompanying flash and crash of a thunder-storm. It was here that Gordon Lowther, shy and smiling, small with a long body and short legs, his red-gold hair and mous-tache, found her.

'Took her,' Jenny had said when they had first talked it over.

'Took her – well, no. She gave herself to him.'

'She gave herself to him,' Jenny said, 'although she would fain have given herself to another.'

The last letter in the series, completed at mid-term, went as follows:

My Own Delightful Gordon,

Your letter has moved me deeply as you may imagine. But alas, I must ever decline to be Mrs Lower. My reasons are two-fold. I am dedicated to my Girls as is Madame Pavlova, and there is another in my life whose mutual love reaches out to me beyond the bounds of Time and Space. He is Teddy Lloyd! Intimacy has never taken place with him. He is married to another. One day in the art room we melted into each other's arms and knew the truth. But I was proud of giving myself to you when you came and took me in the bracken on Arthur's Seat while the storm raged about us. If I am in a certain condition I shall place the infant in the care of a worthy shepherd and his wife, and we can discuss it calmly as platonic acquaintances. I may permit misconduct to occur again from time to time as an outlet because I am in my Prime. We can also have many a breezy day in the fishing boat at sea.

I wish to inform you that your housekeeper fills me with anxiety like John Knox. I fear she is rather narrow, which arises from an ignorance of culture and the Italian scene. Pray ask her not to say 'You know your way up' when I call at your house at Cramond. She should take me up and show me in. Her knees are not stiff. She is only pretending that they are.

I love to hear you singing 'Hey Johnnie Cope'. But were I to receive a proposal of marriage tomorrow from the Lord Lyon King-of-Arms I would decline it.

Allow me, in conclusion, to congratulate you warmly upon your sexual intercourse, as well as your singing.

With fondest joy,
Jean Brodie

When they had finished writing this letter they read the whole correspondence from beginning to end. They were undecided then whether to cast this incriminating document out to sea or to bury it. The act of casting things out to sea from the shore was, as they knew, more difficult than it sounded. But Sandy found a damp hole half-hidden by a stone at the back of the cave and they pressed into it the notebook containing the love correspondence of Miss Jean Brodie, and never saw it again. They walked back to Crail over the very springy turf full of fresh plans and fondest joy.

CHAPTER 4

'I HAVE ENOUGH gunpowder in this jar to blow up this school,' said Miss Lockhart in even tones.

She stood behind her bench in her white linen coat, with both hands on a glass jar three-quarters full of a dark grey powder. The extreme hush that fell was only what she expected, for she always opened the first science lesson with these words and with the gunpowder before her, and the first science lesson was no lesson at all, but a naming of the most impressive objects in the science room. Every eye was upon the jar. Miss Lockhart lifted it and placed it carefully in a cupboard which was filled with similar jars full of different coloured crystals and powders.

'These are bunsen burners, this is a test-tube, this is a pipette, that's a burette, that is a retort, a crucible ... '

Thus she established her mysterious priesthood. She was quite the nicest teacher in the Senior school. But they were all the nicest teachers in the school. It was a new life altogether, almost a new school. Here were no gaunt mistresses like Miss Gaunt, those many who had stalked past Miss Brodie in the corridors saying 'good morning' with predestination in their smiles. The teachers here seemed to have no thoughts of anyone's personalities apart from their speciality in life, whether it was mathematics, Latin or science. They treated the new first-formers as if they were not real, but only to be dealt with, like symbols of algebra, and Miss Brodie's pupils found this refreshing at first. Wonderful, too, during the first week was the curriculum of dazzling new subjects, and the rushing to and from room to room to keep to the time-table.

Their days were now filled with unfamiliar shapes and sounds which were magically dissociated from ordinary life, the great circles and triangles of geometry, the hieroglyphics of Greek on the page and the curious hisses and spits some of the Greek sounds made from the teacher's lips – 'psst . . . psooch . . . '

A few weeks later, when meanings appeared from among these sighs and sounds, it was difficult to remember the party-game effect of that first week, and that Greek had ever made hisses and spits or that 'mensarum' had sounded like something out of nonsense verse. The Modern side, up to the third form, was distinguished from the Classical only by modern or ancient languages. The girls on the Modern side were doing German and Spanish, which, when rehearsed between periods, made the astonishing noises of foreign stations got in passing on the wireless. A mademoiselle with black frizzy hair, who wore a striped shirt with real cufflinks, was pronouncing French in a foreign way which never really caught on. The science room smelt unevenly of the Canongate on that day of the winter's walk with Miss Brodie, the bunsen burners, and the sweet autumnal smoke that drifted in from the first burning leaves. Here in the science room – strictly not to be referred to as a laboratory – lessons were called experiments, which gave everyone the feeling that not even Miss Lockhart knew what the result might be, and anything might occur between their going in and coming out and the school might blow up.

Here, during that first week, an experiment was conducted which involved magnesium in a test-tube which was made to tickle a bunsen flame. Eventually, from different parts of the room, great white magnesium flares shot out of the test-tubes and were caught in larger glass vessels which waited for the purpose. Mary Macgregor took fright and ran along a single lane between two benches, met with a white flame, and ran back to meet another brilliant tongue of fire. Hither and thither she ran in panic between the benches until she was caught and induced to calm down, and she was told not to be so stupid by Miss Lockhart, who already had learned the exasperation of looking at Mary's face, its two eyes, nose and mouth, with nothing more to say about it.

Once, in later years, when Sandy was visited by Rose Stanley, and they fell to speaking of dead Mary Macgregor, Sandy said,

'When any ill befalls me I wish I had been nicer to Mary.'

'How were we to know?' said Rose.

And Miss Brodie, sitting in the window of the Braid Hills Hotel with Sandy, had said: 'I wonder if it was Mary Macgregor betrayed me? Perhaps I should have been kinder to Mary.'

The Brodie set might easily have lost its identity at this time, not only because Miss Brodie had ceased to preside over their days which were now so brisk with the getting of knowledge from unsoulful experts, but also because the headmistress intended them to be dispersed.

She laid a scheme and it failed. It was too ambitious, it aimed at ridding the school of Miss Brodie and breaking up the Brodie set in the one stroke.

She befriended Mary Macgregor, thinking her to be gullible and bribable, and underrating her stupidity. She remembered that Mary had, in common with all Miss Brodie's girls, applied to go on the Classical side, but had been refused. Now Miss Mackay changed her mind and allowed her to take at least Latin. In return she expected to be informed concerning Miss Brodie. But as the only reason that Mary had wanted to learn Latin was to please Miss Brodie, the headmistress got no further. Give the girl tea as she might, Mary simply did not understand what was required of her and thought all the teachers were in league together, Miss Brodie and all.

'You won't be seeing much of Miss Brodie,' said Miss Mackay, 'now that you are in the Senior school.'

'I see,' said Mary, taking the remark as an edict rather than a probing question.

Miss Mackay laid another scheme and the scheme undid her. There was a highly competitive house system in the Senior school, whose four houses were named Holyrood, Melrose, Argyll and Biggar. Miss Mackay saw to it that the Brodie girls were as far as possible placed in different houses. Jenny was put in Holyrood, Sandy with Mary Macgregor in Melrose, Monica and Eunice went into Argyll and Rose Stanley into Biggar. They were therefore obliged to compete with each other in every walk of life within the school and on the wind-swept hockey fields which lay like the graves of the martyrs exposed to the weather in an outer suburb. It was the team spirit, they were told, that counted now, every house must go all out for the Shield and turn up on Saturday mornings to yell encouragement to the house. Inter-house friendships must not suffer, of course, but the team spirit . . .

This phrase was enough for the Brodie set who, after two years at Miss Brodie's, had been well directed as to its meaning.

'Phrases like "the team spirit" are always employed to cut across individualism, love and personal loyalties,' she had said. 'Ideas like "the team spirit"', she said, 'ought not to be enjoined on the female sex, especially if they are of that dedicated nature whose virtues from time immemorial have been utterly opposed to the concept. Florence Nightingale knew nothing of the team spirit, her mission was to save life regardless of the team to which it belonged. Cleopatra knew nothing of the team spirit if you read your Shakespeare. Take Helen of Troy. And the Queen of England, it is true she attends international sport, but she has to, it is all empty show, she is concerned only with the King's health and antiques. Where would the team spirit have got Sybil Thorndike? *She* is the great actress and the rest of the cast have got the team spirit. Pavlova . . . '

Perhaps Miss Brodie had foreseen this moment of the future when her team of six should be exposed to the appeal of four different competing spirits, Argyll, Melrose, Biggar and

Holyrood. It was impossible to know how much Miss Brodie planned by deliberation, or how much she worked by instinct alone. However, in this, the first test of her strength, she had the victory. Not one of the senior house-prefects personified an argument to touch Sybil Thorndike and Cleopatra. The Brodie set would as soon have entered the Girl Guides as the team spirit. Not only they, but at least ten other girls who had passed through Brodie hands kept away from the playing grounds except under compulsion. No one, save Eunice Gardiner, got near to being put in any team to try her spirit upon. Everyone agreed that Eunice was so good on the field, she could not help it.

On most Saturday afternoons Miss Brodie entertained her old set to tea and listened to their new experiences. Herself, she told them, she did not think much of her new pupils' potentialities, and she described some of her new little girls and made the old ones laugh, which bound her set together more than ever and made them feel chosen. Sooner or later she inquired what they were doing in the art class, for now the girls were taught by golden-locked, one-armed Teddy Lloyd.

There was always a great deal to tell about the art lesson. Their first day, Mr Lloyd found difficulty in keeping order. After so many unfamiliar packed hours and periods of different exact subjects, the girls immediately felt the relaxing nature of the art room, and brimmed over with relaxation. Mr Lloyd shouted at them in his hoarse voice to shut up. This was most bracing.

He was attempting to explain the nature and appearance of an ellipse by holding up a saucer in his one right hand, high above his head, then lower. But his romantic air and his hoarse 'Shut up' had produced a reaction of giggles varying in tone and pitch.

'If you girls don't shut up I'll smash this saucer to the floor,' he said.

They tried but failed to shut up.

77

He smashed the saucer to the floor.

Amid the dead silence which followed he picked on Rose Stanley and indicating the fragments of saucer on the floor, he said, 'You with the profile – pick this up.'

He turned away and went and did something else at the other end of the long room for the rest of the period, while the girls looked anew at Rose Stanley's profile, marvelled at Mr Lloyd's style, and settled down to drawing a bottle set up in front of a curtain. Jenny remarked to Sandy that Miss Brodie really had good taste.

'He has an artistic temperament, of course,' said Miss Brodie when she was told about the saucer. And when she heard that he had called Rose 'you with the profile', she looked at Rose in a special way, while Sandy looked at Miss Brodie.

The interest of Sandy and Jenny in Miss Brodie's lovers had entered a new phase since they had buried their last composition and moved up to the Senior school. They no longer saw everything in a sexual context, it was now rather a question of plumbing the deep heart's core. The world of pure sex seemed years away. Jenny had turned twelve. Her mother had recently given birth to a baby boy, and the event had not moved them even to speculate upon its origin.

'There's not much time for sex research in the Senior school,' Sandy said.

'I feel I'm past it,' said Jenny. This was strangely true, and she did not again experience her early sense of erotic wonder in life until suddenly one day when she was nearly forty, an actress of moderate reputation married to a theatrical manager. It happened she was standing with a man whom she did not know very well outside a famous building in Rome, waiting for the rain to stop. She was surprised by a reawakening of that same buoyant and airy discovery of sex, a total sensation which it was impossible to say was physical or mental, only that it contained the lost and guileless delight of her eleventh year. She supposed herself to have fallen in love with the man, who might, she thought, have been moved towards her in his own way out of a world of his own, the associations of which were largely unknown to her. There was nothing whatever to be done about it, for Jenny had been contentedly married for sixteen years past; but the concise happening filled her with astonishment whenever it came to mind in later days, and with a sense of the hidden possibilities in all things.

'Mr Lowther's housekeeper,' said Miss Brodie one Saturday afternoon, 'has left him. It is most ungrateful, that house at Cramond is easily run. I never cared for her as you know. I think she resented my position as Mr Lowther's friend and confidante, and seemed dissatisfied by my visits. Mr Lowther is composing some music for song at the moment. He ought to be encouraged.'

The next Saturday she told the girls that the sewing sisters, Miss Ellen and Miss Alison Kerr, had taken on the temporary task of housekeepers to Mr Lowther, since they lived near Cramond.

'I think those sisters are inquisitive,' Miss Brodie remarked. 'They are too much in with Miss Gaunt and the Church of Scotland.'

On Saturday afternoons an hour was spent on her Greek lessons, for she had insisted that Jenny and Sandy should teach her Greek at the same time as they learned it. 'There is an old tradition for this practice,' said Miss Brodie. 'Many families in the olden days could afford to send but one child to school, whereupon that one scholar of the family imparted to the others in the evening what he had learned in the morning. I have long wanted to know the Greek language, and this scheme will also serve to impress your knowledge on your own minds. John Stuart Mill used to rise at dawn to learn Greek at the age of five, and what John Stuart Mill could do as an infant at dawn, I too can do on a Saturday afternoon in my prime.'

She progressed in Greek, although she was somewhat muddled about the accents, being differently informed by Jenny and Sandy who took turns to impart to her their weekly intake of the language. But she was determined to enter and share the new life of her special girls, and what she did not regard as humane of their new concerns, or what was not within the scope of her influence, she scorned.

She said: 'It is witty to say that a straight line is the shortest distance between two points, or that a circle is a plane figure bounded by one line, every point of which is equidistant from a fixed centre. It is plain witty. Everyone knows what a straight line and a circle are.'

When, after the examinations at the end of the first term, she looked at the papers they had been set, she read some of the more vulnerable of the questions aloud with the greatest contempt: 'A window cleaner carries a uniform 60-lb ladder 15 ft long, at one end of which a bucket of water weighing 40 lb is hung. At what point must he support the ladder to carry it horizontally? Where is the c.g. of his load?' Miss Brodie looked at the paper, after reading out this question, as if to indicate that she could not believe her eyes. Many a time she gave the girls to understand that the solution to such problems would be quite useless to Sybil Thorndike, Anna Pavlova and the late Helen of Troy.

But the Brodie set were on the whole still dazzled by their new subjects. It was never the same in later years when the languages of physics and chemistry, algebra and geometry had lost their elemental strangeness and formed each an individual department of life with its own accustomed boredom, and become hard work. Even Monica Douglas, who later developed such a good brain for mathematics, was plainly never so thrilled with herself as when she first subtracted x from y and the result from a; she never afterwards looked so happy.

Rose Stanley sliced a worm down the middle with the greatest absorption during her first term's biology, although in two terms' time she shuddered at the thought and had dropped the subject. Eunice Gardiner discovered the Industrial Revolution, its rights and wrongs, to such an extent that the history teacher, a vegetarian communist, had high hopes of her which were dashed within a few months when Eunice reverted to reading novels based on the life of Mary Queen of Scots. Sandy, whose handwriting was bad, spent hours forming the Greek characters in neat rows in her notebooks while Jenny took the same pride in drawing scientific apparatus for her chemistry notes. Even stupid Mary Macgregor amazed herself by understanding Caesar's Gallic Wars which as yet made no demands on her defective imagination and the words of which were easier to her than English to spell and pronounce, until suddenly one day it appeared, from an essay she had been obliged to write, that she believed the document to date from the time of Samuel Pepys; and then Mary was established in the wrong again, being tortured with probing questions, and generally led on to confess to the mirth-shaken world her notion that Latin and shorthand were one.

Miss Brodie had a hard fight of it during those first few months when the Senior school had captivated her set, displaying as did the set that capacity for enthusiasm which she herself had implanted. But, having won the battle over the team spirit, she did not despair. It was evident even then that her main concern was lest the girls should become personally attached to any one of the senior teachers, but she carefully refrained from direct attack because the teachers themselves seemed so perfectly indifferent to her brood.

By the summer term, the girls' favourite hours were those spent unbrainfully in the gymnasium, swinging about on parallel bars, hanging upside down on wall bars or climbing ropes up to the ceiling, all competing with agile Eunice to heave themselves up by hands, knees, and feet like monkeys climbing a tropical creeper, while the gym teacher, a thin grey-haired little wire, showed them what to do and shouted each order in a broad Scots accent interspersed by her short cough, on account of which she was later sent to a sanatorium in Switzerland.

By the summer term, to stave off the onslaughts of boredom, and to reconcile the necessities of the working day with their love for Miss Brodie, Sandy and Jenny had begun to apply their new-found knowledge to Miss Brodie in a merry fashion. 'If Miss Brodie was weighed in air and then in water...' And, when Mr Lowther seemed not quite himself at the singing lesson, they would remind each other that an immersed Jean Brodie displaces its own weight of Gordon Lowther.

Presently, in the late spring of nineteen-thirty-three, Miss Brodie's Greek lessons on a Saturday afternoon came to an end, because of the needs of Mr Lowther who, in his house at Cramond which the girls had not yet seen, was being catered for quite willingly by those sewing mistresses, Miss Ellen and Miss Alison Kerr. Living on the coast nearby, it was simple for them to go over turn by turn and see to Mr Lowther after school hours, and prepare his supper and lay out provision for his breakfast; it was not only simple, it was enjoyable to be doing good, and it was also profitable in a genteel way. On Saturdays either Miss Ellen or Miss Alison would count his laundry and keep house for him. On some Saturday mornings both were busy for him; Miss Ellen supervised the woman who came to clean while Miss Alison did the week's shopping. They never had been so perky or useful in their lives before, and especially not since the eldest sister had died, who had always told them what to do with their spare time as it cropped up, so that Miss Alison could never get used to being called Miss Kerr and Miss Ellen could never find it in her to go and get a book from the library, wanting the order from the late Miss Kerr.

But the minister's sister, gaunt Miss Gaunt, was secretly taking over the dead sister's office. As it became known later, Miss Gaunt approved of their arrangement with Gordon Lowther and encouraged them to make it a permanent one for their own good and also for private reasons connected with Miss Brodie.

Up to now, Miss Brodie's visits to Mr Lowther had taken place on Sundays. She always went to church on Sunday mornings, she had a rota of different denominations and sects which included the Free Churches of Scotland, the Established Church of Scotland, the Methodist and the Episcopalian churches and any other church outside the Roman Catholic pale which she might discover. Her disapproval of the Church of Rome was based on her assertions that it was a church of superstition, and that only people who did not want to think for themselves were Roman Catholics. In some ways, her attitude was a strange one, because she was by temperament suited only to the Roman Catholic Church; possibly it could have embraced, even while it disciplined, her soaring and diving spirit, it might even have normalized her. But perhaps this was the reason that she shunned it, lover of Italy though she was, bringing to her support a rigid Edinburgh-born side of herself when the Catholic Church was in question, although this side was not otherwise greatly in evidence. So she went round the various non-Roman churches instead, hardly ever missing a Sunday morning. She was not in any doubt, she let everyone know she was in no doubt, that God was on her side whatever her course, and so she experienced no difficulty or sense of hypocrisy in worship while at the same time she went to bed with the singing master. Just as an excessive sense of guilt can drive people to excessive action, so was Miss Brodie driven to it by an excessive lack of guilt.

The side-effects of this condition were exhilarating to her special girls in that they in some way partook of the general absolution she had assumed to herself, and it was only in retrospect that they could see Miss Brodie's affair with

Mr Lowther for what it was, that is to say, in a factual light. All the time they were under her influence she and her actions were outside the context of right and wrong. It was twenty-five years before Sandy had so far recovered from a creeping vision of disorder that she could look back and recognize that Miss Brodie's defective sense of self-criticism had not been without its beneficent and enlarging effects; by which time Sandy had already betrayed Miss Brodie and Miss Brodie was laid in her grave.

It was after morning church on Sundays that Miss Brodie would go to Cramond, there to lunch and spend the afternoon with Mr Lowther. She spent Sunday evenings with him also, and more often than not the night, in a spirit of definite duty, if not exactly martyrdom, since her heart was with the renounced teacher of art.

Mr Lowther, with his long body and short legs, was a shy fellow who smiled upon nearly everyone from beneath his red-gold moustache, and who won his own gentle way with nearly everybody, and who said little and sang much.

When it became certain that the Kerr sisters had taken over permanently the housekeeping for this bashful, smiling bachelor, Miss Brodie fancied he was getting thin. She announced this discovery just at a time when Jenny and Sandy had noticed a slimmer appearance in Miss Brodie and had begun to wonder, since they were nearly thirteen and their eyes were more focused on such points, if she might be physically beautiful or desirable to men. They saw her in a new way, and decided she had a certain deep romantic beauty, and that she had lost weight through her sad passion for Mr Lloyd, and this noble undertaking of Mr Lowther in his place, and that it suited her.

Now Miss Brodie was saying: 'Mr Lowther is looking thin these days. I have no faith in those Kerr sisters, they are skimping him, they have got skimpy minds. The supplies of food they leave behind on Saturdays are barely sufficient to see him through Sunday, let alone the remainder of the week. If only Mr Lowther could be persuaded to move from that big house and take a flat in Edinburgh, he would be so much easier to look after. He needs looking after. But he will not be persuaded. It is impossible to persuade a man who does not disagree, but smiles.'

She decided to supervise the Kerr sisters on their Saturdays at Cramond when they prepared for Mr Lowther's domestic week ahead. 'They get well paid for it,' said Miss Brodie. 'I shall go over and see that they order the right stuff, and sufficient.' It might have seemed an audacious proposition, but the girls did not think of it this way. They heartily urged Miss Brodie to descend upon the Kerrs and to interfere, partly in anticipation of some eventful consequence, and partly because Mr Lowther would somehow smile away any fuss; and the Kerr sisters were fairly craven; and, above all, Miss Brodie was easily the equal of both sisters together, she was the square on the hypotenuse of a right-angled triangle and they were only the squares on the other two sides.

The Kerr sisters took Miss Brodie's intrusion quite meekly, and that they were so unquestioning about any authority which imposed itself upon them was the very reason why they also did not hesitate later on to answer the subsequent questions of Miss Gaunt. Meantime Miss Brodie set about feeding Mr Lowther up, and, since this meant her passing Saturday afternoons at Cramond, the Brodie set was invited to go, two by two, one pair every week, to visit her in Mr Lowther's residence, where he smiled and patted their hair or pulled pretty Jenny's ringlets, looking meanwhile for reproof or approval, or some such thing, at brown-eyed Jean Brodie. She gave them tea while he smiled; and he frequently laid down his cup and saucer, went and sat at the piano and burst into song. He sang:

'March, march, Ettrick and Teviotdale,
Why the de'il dinna ye march *forward* in order?

85

March, march, Eskdale and Liddesdale,
All the Blue Bonnets are bound for the Border.'

At the end of the song he would smile his overcome and bashful smile and take his teacup again, looking up under his ginger eyebrows at Jean Brodie to see what she felt about him at the current moment. She was Jean to him, a fact that none of the Brodie set thought proper to mention to anyone.

She reported to Sandy and Jenny: 'I made short work of those Kerr sisters. They were starving him. Now it is I who see to the provisions. I am a descendant, do not forget, of Willie Brodie, a man of substance, a cabinet maker and designer of gibbets, a member of the Town Council of Edinburgh and a keeper of two mistresses who bore him five children between them. Blood tells. He played much dice and fighting cocks. Eventually he was a wanted man for having robbed the Excise Office – not that he needed the money, he was a night burglar only for the sake of the danger in it. Of course, he was arrested abroad and was brought back to the Tolbooth prison, but that was mere chance. He died cheerfully on a gibbet of his own devising in seventeen-eighty-eight. However all this may be, it is the stuff I am made of, and I have brooked and shall brook no nonsense from Miss Ellen and Miss Alison Kerr.'

Mr Lowther sang:

'O mother, mother, make my bed,
O make it soft and narrow,
For my true love died for me today.
I'll die for him tomorrow.'

Then he looked at Miss Brodie. She was, however, looking at a chipped rim of a teacup. 'Mary Macgregor must have chipped it,' she said. 'Mary was here last Sunday with Eunice and they washed up together. Mary must have chipped it.'

Outside on the summer lawn the daisies sparkled. The lawn spread wide and long, one could barely see the little wood at the end of it and even the wood belonged to Mr Lowther, and the fields beyond. Shy, musical and gentle as he was, Mr Lowther was a man of substance.

Now Sandy considered Miss Brodie not only to see if she was desirable, but also to find out if there was any element of surrender about her, since this was the most difficult part of the affair to realize. She had been a dominant presence rather than a physical woman like Norma Shearer or Elizabeth Bergner. Miss Brodie was now forty-three and this year when she looked so much thinner than when she had stood in the classroom or sat under the elm, her shape was pleasanter, but it was still fairly large compared with Mr Lowther's. He was slight and he was shorter than Miss Brodie. He looked at her with love and she looked at him severely and possessively.

By the end of the summer term, when the Brodie set were all turned, or nearly turned, thirteen, Miss Brodie questioned them in their visiting pairs each week about their art lesson. The girls always took a close interest in Teddy Lloyd's art classes and in all he did, making much of details, so as to provide happy conversation with Miss Brodie when their turn came to visit her at Gordon Lowther's house at Cramond.

It was a large gabled house with a folly-turret. There were so many twists and turns in the wooded path leading up from the road, and the front lawn was so narrow, that the house could never be seen from the little distance that its size demanded and it was necessary to crane one's neck upward to see the turret at all. The back of the house was quite plain. The rooms were large and gloomy with Venetian blinds. The banisters began with a pair of carved lions' heads and carried up and up, round and round, as far as the eye could reach. All the furniture was large and carved, dotted with ornaments of silver and rose-coloured glass. The library on the ground floor where

Miss Brodie entertained them held a number of glass bookcases so dim in their interiors that it was impossible to see the titles of the books without peering close. A grand piano was placed across one corner of the room, and on it, in summer, stood a bowl of roses.

This was a great house to explore and on days when Miss Brodie was curiously occupied in the kitchen with some enormous preparation for the next day's eating – in those months when her obsession with Mr Lowther's food had just begun – the girls were free to roam up the big stairs, hand-in-hand with awe, and to open the doors and look into the dust-sheeted bedrooms and especially into two rooms that people had forgotten to furnish properly, one of which had nothing in it but a large desk, not even a carpet, the other of which was empty except for an electric light bulb and a large blue jug. These rooms were icy cold, whatever the time of year. On their descending the stairs after these expeditions, Mr Lowther would often be standing waiting for them, shyly smiling in the hall with his hands clasped together as if he hoped that everything was to their satisfaction. He took roses from the bowl and presented one each to the girls before they went home.

Mr Lowther never seemed quite at home in his home, although he had been born there. He always looked at Miss Brodie for approval before he touched anything or opened a cupboard as if, really, he was not allowed to touch without permission. The girls decided that perhaps his mother, now four years dead, had kept him under all his life, and he was consequently unable to see himself as master of the house.

He sat silently and gratefully watching Miss Brodie entertain the two girls whose turn it was to be there, when she had already started on her project of fattening him up which was to grow to such huge proportions that her food-supplying mania was the talk of Miss Ellen and Miss Alison Kerr, and so of the Junior school. One day, when Sandy and Jenny were on the visiting rota, she gave Mr Lowther, for tea alone, an admirable lobster salad, some sandwiches of liver paste, cake and tea, followed by a bowl of porridge and cream. These were served to him on a tray for himself alone, you could see he was on a special diet. Sandy was anxious to see if Mr Lowther would manage the porridge as well as everything else. But he worked his way through everything with impassive obedience while she questioned the girls: 'What are you doing in the art class just now?'

'We're at work on the poster competition.'

'Mr Lloyd – is he well?'

'Oh yes, he's great fun. He showed us his studio two weeks ago.'

'Which studio, where? At his house?' – although Miss Brodie knew perfectly well.

'Yes, it's a great long attic, it –'

'Did you meet his wife, what was she like? What did she say, did she give you tea? What are the children like, what did you do when you got there? . . . '

She did not attempt to conceal from her munching host her keen interest in the art master. Mr Lowther's eyes looked mournful as he ate on. Sandy and Jenny knew that similar questions had been pressed upon Mary Macgregor and Eunice Gardiner the previous week, and upon Rose Stanley and Monica Douglas the week before. But Miss Brodie could not hear enough versions of the same story if it involved Teddy Lloyd, and now that the girls had been to his house – a large and shabby, a warm and unconventional establishment in the north of Edinburgh – Miss Brodie was in a state of high excitement by very contact with these girls who had lately breathed Lloyd air.

'How many children?' said Miss Brodie, her teapot poised.

'Five, I think,' said Sandy.

'Six, I think,' said Jenny, 'counting the baby.'

'There are lots of babies,' said Sandy.

'Roman Catholics, of course,' said Miss Brodie, addressing this to Mr Lowther.

'But the littlest baby,' said Jenny, 'you've forgotten to count the wee baby. That makes six.'

Miss Brodie poured tea and cast a glance at Gordon Lowther's plate.

'Gordon,' she said, 'a cake.'

He shook his head and said softly, as if soothing her, 'Oh, no, no.'

'Yes, Gordon. It is full of goodness.' And she made him eat a Chester cake, and spoke to him in a slightly more Edinburgh way than usual, so as to make up to him by both means for the love she was giving to Teddy Lloyd instead of to him.

'You must be fattened up, Gordon,' she said. 'You must be two stone the better before I go on my holidays.'

He smiled as best he could at everyone in turn, with his drooped head and slowly moving jaws. Meanwhile Miss Brodie said:

'And Mrs Lloyd — is she a woman, would you say, in her prime?'

'Perhaps not yet,' said Sandy.

'Well, Mrs Lloyd may be past it,' Jenny said. 'It's difficult to say with her hair being long on her shoulders. It makes her look young although she may not be.'

'She looks really like as if she won't have any prime,' Sandy said.

'The word "like" is redundant in that sentence. What is Mrs Lloyd's Christian name?'

'Deirdre,' said Jenny, and Miss Brodie considered the name as if it were new to her although she had heard it last week from Mary and Eunice, and the week before that from Rose and Monica and so had Mr Lowther. Outside, light rain began to fall on Mr Lowther's leaves.

'Celtic,' said Miss Brodie.

Sandy loitered at the kitchen door waiting for Miss Brodie to come for a walk by the sea. Miss Brodie was doing something to an enormous ham prior to putting it into a huge pot. Miss Brodie's new ventures into cookery in no way diminished her previous grandeur, for everything she prepared for Gordon Lowther seemed to be large, whether it was family-sized puddings to last him out the week, or joints of beef or lamb, or great angry-eyed whole salmon.

'I must get this on for Mr Lowther's supper,' she said to Sandy, 'and see that he gets his supper before I go home tonight.'

She always so far kept up the idea that she went home on these week-end nights and left Mr Lowther alone in the big house. So far the girls had found no evidence to the contrary, nor were they ever to do so; a little later Miss Ellen Kerr was brought to the headmistress by Miss Gaunt to testify to having found Miss Brodie's nightdress under a pillow of the double bed on which Mr Lowther took his sleep. She had found it while changing the linen; it was the pillow on the far side of the bed, nearest the wall, under which the nightdress had been discovered folded neatly.

'How do you know the nightdress was Miss Brodie's?' demanded Miss Mackay, the sharp-minded woman, who smelt her prey very near and yet saw it very far. She stood with a hand on the back of her chair, bending forward full of ears.

'One must draw one's own conclusions,' said Miss Gaunt.

'I am addressing Miss Ellen.'

'Yes, one must draw one's own conclusions,' said Miss Ellen, with her tight-drawn red-veined cheeks looking shiny and flustered. 'It was crêpe de Chine.'

'It is non-proven,' said Miss Mackay, sitting down to her desk. 'Come back to me,' she said, 'if you have proof positive. What did you do with the garment? Did you confront Miss Brodie with it?'

'Oh, no, Miss Mackay,' said Miss Ellen.

'You should have confronted her with it. You should have said, "Miss Brodie, come here a minute, can you explain this?" That's what you should have said. Is the nightdress still there?'

'Oh, no, it's gone.'

'She's that brazen,' said Miss Gaunt.

All this was conveyed to Sandy by the headmistress herself at that subsequent time when Sandy looked at her distastefully through her little eyes and, evading the quite crude question which the coarse-faced woman asked her, was moved by various other considerations to betray Miss Brodie.

'But I must organize the dear fellow's food before I go home tonight,' Miss Brodie said in the summer of nineteen-thirty-three while Sandy leaned against the kitchen door with her legs longing to be running along the sea shore. Jenny came and joined her, and together they waited upon Miss Brodie, and saw on the vast old kitchen table the piled-up provisions of the morning's shopping. Outside on the dining-room table stood large bowls of fruit with boxes of dates piled on top of them, as if this were Christmas and the kitchen that of a holiday hotel.

'Won't all this give Mr Lowther a stoppage?' Sandy said to Jenny.

'Not if he eats his greens,' said Jenny.

While they waited for Miss Brodie to dress the great ham like the heroine she was, there came the sound of Mr Lowther at the piano in the library singing rather slowly and mournfully:

'All people that on earth do dwell,
    Sing to the Lord with cheerful voice.
  Him serve with mirth, his praise forth tell,
    Come ye before him and rejoice.'

Mr Lowther was the choir-master and an Elder of the church, and had not yet been quietly advised to withdraw from these offices by Mr Gaunt the minister, brother of Miss Gaunt, following the finding of the nightdress under the pillow next to his.

Presently, as she put the ham on a low gas and settled the lid on the pot Miss Brodie joined in the psalm richly, contralto-wise, giving the notes more body:

> 'O enter then his gates with praise,
>   Approach with joy His courts unto.'

The rain had stopped and was only now hanging damply within the salt air. All along the sea front Miss Brodie questioned the girls, against the rhythm of the waves, about the appointments of Teddy Lloyd's house, the kind of tea they got, how vast and light was the studio, and what was said.

'He looked very romantic in his own studio,' Sandy said.

'How was that?'

'I think it was his having only one arm,' said Jenny.

'But he always has only one arm.'

'He did more than usual with it,' said Sandy.

'He was waving it about,' Jenny said. 'There was a lovely view from the studio window. He's proud of it.'

'The studio is in the attic, I presume?'

'Yes, all along the top of the house. There is a new portrait he has done of his family, it's a little bit amusing, it starts with himself, very tall, then his wife. Then all the little children graded downwards to the baby on the floor, it makes a diagonal line across the canvas.'

'What makes it amusing?' said Miss Brodie.

'They are all facing square and they all look serious,' Sandy said. 'You are supposed to laugh at it.'

Miss Brodie laughed a little at this. There was a wonderful sunset across the distant sky, reflected in the sea, streaked with blood and puffed with avenging purple and gold as if the end of the world had come without intruding on everyday life.

'There's another portrait,' Jenny said, 'not finished yet, of Rose.'

'He has been painting Rose?'

'Yes.'

'Rose has been sitting for him?'

'Yes, for about a month.'

Miss Brodie was very excited. 'Rose didn't mention this,' she said.

Sandy halted. 'Oh, I forgot. It was supposed to be a surprise. You aren't supposed to know.'

'What, the portrait, I am to see it?'

Sandy looked confused, for she was not sure how Rose had meant her portrait to be a surprise to Miss Brodie.

Jenny said, 'Oh, Miss Brodie, it is the fact that she's sitting for Mr Lloyd that she wanted to keep for a surprise.' Sandy realized, then, that this was right.

'Ah,' said Miss Brodie, well pleased. 'That is thoughtful of Rose.'

Sandy was jealous, because Rose was not supposed to be thoughtful.

'What is she wearing for her portrait?' said Miss Brodie.

'Her gym tunic,' Sandy said.

'Sitting sideways,' Jenny said.

'In profile,' said Miss Brodie.

Miss Brodie stopped a man to buy a lobster for Mr Lowther. When this was done she said:

'Rose is bound to be painted many times. She may well sit for Mr Lloyd on future occasions, she is one of the crème de la crème.'

It was said in an inquiring tone. The girls understood she was trying quite hard to piece together a whole picture from their random remarks.

Jenny accordingly let fall, 'Oh, yes, Mr Lloyd wants to paint Rose in red velvet.'

And Sandy added, 'Mrs Lloyd has a bit of red velvet to put around her, they were trying it round her.'

'Are you to return?' said Miss Brodie.

'Yes, all of us,' Sandy said. 'Mr Lloyd thinks we're a jolly nice set.'

'Have you not thought it remarkable,' said Miss Brodie, 'that it is you six girls that Mr Lloyd has chosen to invite to his studio?'

'Well, we're a set,' said Jenny.

'Has he invited any other girls from the school?' – but Miss Brodie knew the answer.

'Oh, no, only us.'

'It is because you are mine,' said Miss Brodie. 'I mean of my stamp and cut, and I am in my prime.'

Sandy and Jenny had not given much thought to the fact of the art master's inviting them as a group. Indeed, there was something special in his acceptance of the Brodie set. There was a mystery here to be worked out, and it was clear that when he thought of them he thought of Miss Brodie.

'He always asks about you,' Sandy said to Miss Brodie, 'as soon as he sees us.'

'Yes, Rose did tell me that,' said Miss Brodie.

Suddenly, like migrating birds, Sandy and Jenny were of one mind for a run and without warning they ran along the pebbly beach into the air which was full of sunset, returning to Miss Brodie to hear of her forthcoming summer holiday when she was going to leave the fattened-up Mr Lowther, she was afraid, to fend for himself with the aid of the Misses Kerr, and was going abroad, not to Italy this year but to Germany, where Hitler was become Chancellor, a prophet-figure like Thomas Carlyle, and more reliable than Mussolini; the German brown-shirts, she said, were exactly the same as the Italian black, only more reliable.

Jenny and Sandy were going to a farm for the summer holidays, where in fact the name of Miss Brodie would not very much be on their lips or in their minds after the first two weeks, and instead they would make hay and follow the sheep about. It was always difficult to realize during term times that the world of Miss Brodie might be half forgotten, as were the worlds of the school houses, Holyrood, Melrose, Argyll and Biggar.

'I wonder if Mr Lowther would care for sweetbreads done with rice,' Miss Brodie said.

CHAPTER 5

'WHY, IT'S LIKE Miss Brodie!' said Sandy. 'It's terribly like Miss Brodie.' Then, perceiving that what she had said had accumulated a meaning between its passing her lips and reaching the ears of Mr and Mrs Lloyd, she said, 'Though of course it's Rose, it's more like Rose, it's terribly like Rose.'

Teddy Lloyd shifted the new portrait so that it stood in a different light. It still looked like Miss Brodie.

Deirdre Lloyd said, 'I haven't met Miss Brodie, I think. Is she fair?'

'No,' said Teddy Lloyd in his hoarse way, 'she's dark.'

Sandy saw that the head on the portrait was fair, it was Rose's portrait all right. Rose was seated in profile by a window in her gym dress, her hands palm-downwards, one on each knee. Where was the resemblance to Miss Brodie? It was the profile perhaps; it was the forehead, perhaps; it was the type of stare from Rose's blue eyes, perhaps, which was like the dominating stare from Miss Brodie's brown. The portrait was very like Miss Brodie.

'It's Rose, all right,' Sandy said, and Deirdre Lloyd looked at her.

'Do you like it?' said Teddy Lloyd.

'Yes, it's lovely.'

'Well, that's all that matters.'

Sandy continued looking at it through her very small eyes, and while she was doing so Teddy Lloyd drew the piece of sheeting over the portrait with a casual flip of his only arm.

Deirdre Lloyd had been the first woman to dress up as a peasant whom Sandy had ever met, and peasant women were to be fashionable for the next thirty years or more. She wore a fairly long full-gathered dark skirt, a bright green blouse with the sleeves rolled up, a necklace of large painted wooden beads, and gipsy-looking ear-rings. Round her waist was a bright red wide belt. She wore dark brown stockings and sandals of dark green suede. In this, and various other costumes of similar kind, Deirdre was depicted on canvas in different parts of the studio. She had an attractive near-laughing voice. She said:

'We've got a new one of Rose. Teddy, show Sandy the new one of Rose.'

'It isn't quite at a stage for looking at.'

'Well, what about Red Velvet? Show Sandy that – Teddy did a splendid portrait of Rose last summer, we swathed her in red velvet, and we've called it Red Velvet.'

Teddy Lloyd had brought out a canvas from behind a few others. He stood it in the light on an easel. Sandy looked at it with her tiny eyes which it was astonishing that anyone could trust.

The portrait was like Miss Brodie. Sandy said, 'I like the colours.'

'Does it resemble Miss Brodie?' said Deirdre Lloyd with her near-laughter.

'Miss Brodie is a woman in her prime,' said Sandy, 'but there is a resemblance now you mention it.'

Deirdre Lloyd said: 'Rose was only fourteen at the time; it makes her look very mature, but indeed she is very mature.'

The swathing of crimson velvet was so arranged that it did two things at once, it made Rose look one-armed like the artist himself, and it showed the curves of her breast to be more developed than they were, even now, when Rose was fifteen. Also, the picture was like Miss Brodie, and this was the main thing about it and the main mystery. Rose had a large-boned pale face. Miss Brodie's bones were small, although her eyes, nose and mouth were large. It was difficult to see how Teddy Lloyd had imposed the dark and Roman face of Miss Brodie on that of pale Rose, but he had done so.

Sandy looked again at the other recent portraits in the studio, Teddy Lloyd's wife, his children, some unknown sitters. They were none of them like Miss Brodie.

Then she saw a drawing lying on top of a pile on the work-table. It was Miss Brodie leaning against a lamp post in the Lawnmarket with a working-woman's shawl around her; on looking closer it proved to be Monica Douglas with the high cheekbones and long nose. Sandy said:

'I didn't know Monica sat for you.'

'I've done one or two preliminary sketches. Don't you think that setting's rather good for Monica? Here's one of Eunice in her harlequin outfit, I thought she looked rather well in it.'

Sandy was vexed. These girls, Monica and Eunice, had not said anything to the others about their being painted by the art master. But now they were all fifteen there was a lot they did not tell each other. She looked more closely at this picture of Eunice.

Eunice had worn the harlequin dress for a school perform-ance. Small and neat and sharp-featured as she was, in the portrait she looked like Miss Brodie. In amongst her various bewilderments Sandy was fascinated by the economy of Teddy Lloyd's method, as she had been four years earlier by Miss Brodie's variations on her love story, when she had attached to her first, war-time lover the attributes of the art master and the singing master who had then newly entered her orbit. Teddy Lloyd's method of presentation was similar, it was economical, and it always seemed afterwards to Sandy that where there was a choice of various courses, the most economical was the best, and that the course to be taken was the most expedient and most suitable at the time for all the objects in hand.

She acted on this principle when the time came for her to betray Miss Brodie.

Jenny had done badly in her last term's examinations and was mostly, these days, at home working up her subjects. Sandy had the definite feeling that the Brodie set, not to mention Miss Brodie herself, was getting out of hand. She thought it perhaps a good thing that the set might split up.

From somewhere below one of the Lloyd children started to yell, and then another, and then a chorus. Deirdre Lloyd disappeared with a swing of her peasant skirt to see to all her children. The Lloyds were Catholics and so were made to have a lot of children by force.

'One day,' said Teddy Lloyd as he stacked up his sketches before taking Sandy down to tea, 'I would like to do all you Brodie girls, one by one and then all together.' He tossed his head to move back the golden lock of his hair from his eye. 'It would be nice to do you all together,' he said, 'and see what sort of a group portrait I could make of you.'

Sandy thought this might be an attempt to keep the Brodie set together at the expense of the newly glimpsed individuality of its members. She turned on him in her new manner of sudden irritability and said, 'We'd look like one big Miss Brodie, I suppose.'

He laughed in a delighted way and looked at her more closely, as if for the first time. She looked back just as closely through her little eyes, with the near-blackmailing insolence of her knowledge. Whereupon he kissed her long and wetly. He said in his hoarse voice, 'That'll teach you to look at an artist like that.'

She started to run to the door, wiping her mouth dry with the back of her hand, but he caught her with his one arm and said: 'There's no need to run away. You're just about the ugliest little thing I've ever seen in my life.' He walked out and left her standing in the studio, and there was nothing for her to do but to follow him downstairs. Deirdre Lloyd's voice called from the sitting-room. 'In here, Sandy.'

She spent most of the tea time trying to sort out her preliminary feelings in the matter, which was difficult because of the children who were present and making demands on the guest. The eldest boy, who was eight, turned on the wireless and began to sing in mincing English tones, 'Oh play to me, Gipsy' to the accompaniment of Henry Hall's band. The other three children were making various kinds of din. Above this noise Deirdre Lloyd requested Sandy to call her Deirdre rather than Mrs Lloyd. And so Sandy did not have much opportunity to discover how she was feeling inside herself about Teddy Lloyd's kiss and his words, and to decide whether she was insulted or not. He now said, brazenly, 'And you can call me Teddy outside of school.' Amongst themselves, in any case, the girls called him Teddy the Paint. Sandy looked from one to the other of the Lloyds.

'I've heard such a lot about Miss Brodie from the girls,' Deirdre was saying. 'I really must ask her to tea. D'you think she'd like to come?'

'No,' said Teddy.

'Why?' said Deirdre, not that it seemed to matter, she was so languid and long-armed, lifting the plate of biscuits from the table and passing them round without moving from the low stool on which she sat.

'You kids stop that row or you leave the room,' Teddy declared.

'Bring Miss Brodie to tea,' Deirdre said to Sandy.

'She won't come,' Teddy said, ' – will she, Sandy?'

'She's awfully busy,' Sandy said.

'Pass me a fag,' said Deirdre.

'Is she still looking after Lowther?' said Teddy.

'Well, yes, a bit –'

'Lowther,' said Teddy, waving his only arm, 'must have a way with women. He's got half the female staff of the school looking after him. Why doesn't he employ a house-keeper? He's got plenty of money, no wife, no kids, no rent to pay, it's his own house. Why doesn't he get a proper housekeeper?'

'I think he likes Miss Brodie,' Sandy said.

'But what does she see in him?'

'He sings to her,' Sandy said, suddenly sharp.

Deirdre laughed. 'Miss Brodie sounds a bit queer, I must say. What age is she?'

'Jean Brodie,' said Teddy, 'is a magnificent woman in her prime.' He got up, tossing back his lock of hair, and left the room.

Deirdre blew a cloud of reflective smoke and stubbed out her cigarette, and Sandy said she would have to go now.

Mr Lowther had caused Miss Brodie a good deal of worry in the past two years. There had been a time when it seemed he might be thinking of marrying Miss Alison Kerr, and another time when he seemed to favour Miss Ellen, all the while being in love with Miss Brodie herself, who refused him all but her bed-fellowship and her catering.

He tired of food, for it was making him fat and weary and putting him out of voice. He wanted a wife to play golf with and to sing to. He wanted a honeymoon on the Hebridean island of Eigg, near Rum, and then to return to Cramond with the bride.

In the midst of this dissatisfaction had occurred Ellen Kerr's finding of a nightdress of quality folded under the pillow next to Mr Lowther's in that double bed on which, to make matters worse, he had been born.

Still Miss Brodie refused him. He fell into a melancholy mood upon his retirement from the offices of choir-master and Elder, and the girls thought he brooded often upon the possibility that Miss Brodie could not take to his short legs, and was all the time pining for Teddy Lloyd's long ones.

Most of this Miss Brodie obliquely confided in the girls as they grew from thirteen to fourteen and from fourteen to fifteen. She did not say, even obliquely, that she slept with the singing master, for she was still testing them out to see whom she could trust, as it would be her way to put it. She did not want any alarming suspicions to arise in the minds of their parents. Miss Brodie was always very careful to impress the parents of her set and to win their approval and gratitude. So she confided according to what seemed expedient at the time, and was in fact now on the look-out for a girl amongst her set in whom she could confide entirely, whose curiosity was greater than her desire to make a sensation outside, and who, in the need to gain further confidences from Miss Brodie, would never betray what had been gained. Of necessity there had to be but one girl; two would be dangerous. Almost shrewdly, Miss Brodie fixed on Sandy, and even then it was not of her own affairs that she spoke.

In the summer of nineteen-thirty-five the whole school was forced to wear rosettes of red, white and blue ribbons in the lapels of its blazers, because of the Silver Jubilee. Rose Stanley lost hers and said it was probably in Teddy Lloyd's studio. This was not long after Sandy's visit to the art master's residence.

'What are you doing for the summer holidays, Rose?' said Miss Brodie.

'My father's taking me to the Highlands for a fortnight. After that, I don't know. I suppose I'll be sitting for Mr Lloyd off and on.'

'Good,' said Miss Brodie.

Miss Brodie started to confide in Sandy after the next summer holidays. They played rounds of golf in the sunny early autumn after school.

'All my ambitions,' said Miss Brodie, 'are fixed on yourself and Rose. You will not speak of this to the other girls, it would cause envy. I had hopes of Jenny, she is so pretty; but Jenny has become insipid, don't you think?'

This was a clever question, because it articulated what was already growing in Sandy's mind. Jenny had bored her this last year, and it left her lonely.

'Don't you think?' said Miss Brodie, towering above her, for Sandy was playing out of a bunker. Sandy gave a hack with her niblick and said, 'Yes, a bit,' sending the ball in a little backward half-circle.

'And I had hopes of Eunice,' Miss Brodie said presently, 'but she seems to be interested in some boy she goes swimming with.'

Sandy was not yet out of the bunker. It was sometimes difficult to follow Miss Brodie's drift when she was in her prophetic moods. One had to wait and see what emerged. In the meantime she glanced up at Miss Brodie who was standing on the crest of the bunker which was itself on a crest of the hilly course. Miss Brodie looked admirable in her heather-blue tweed with the brown of a recent holiday in Egypt still warming her skin. Miss Brodie was gazing out over Edinburgh as she spoke.

Sandy got out of the bunker. 'Eunice,' said Miss Brodie, 'will settle down and marry some professional man. Perhaps I have done her some good. Mary, well Mary. I never had any hopes of Mary. I thought, when you were young children, that Mary might be something. She was a little pathetic. But she's really a most irritating girl, I'd rather deal with a rogue than a fool. Monica will get her B.Sc. with honours I've no doubt, but she has no spiritual insight, and of course that's why she's –'

Miss Brodie was to drive off now and she had decided to stop talking until she had measured her distance and swiped her ball. Which she did. '– that's why she has a bad temper, she understands nothing but signs and symbols and calculations. Nothing infuriates people more than their own lack of spiritual insight, Sandy, that is why the Moslems are so placid, they are full of spiritual insight. My dragoman in Egypt would not have it that Friday was their Lord's Day. "Every day is the Lord's day," he said to me. I thought that very profound, I felt humbled. We had already said our farewells on the day before my departure, Sandy, but lo and behold when I was already seated in the train, along the platform came my dragoman with a beautiful bunch of flowers for me. He had true dignity. Sandy, you will never get anywhere by hunching over your putter, hold your shoulders back and bend from the waist. He was a very splendid person with a great sense of his bearing.'

They picked up their balls and walked to the next tee. 'Have you ever played with Miss Lockhart?' Sandy said.

'Does she play golf?'

'Yes, rather well.' Sandy had met the science mistress surprisingly on the golf course one Saturday morning playing with Gordon Lowther.

'Good shot, Sandy. I know very little of Miss Lockhart,' said Miss Brodie. 'I leave her to her jars and gases. They are all gross materialists, these women in the Senior school, they all belong to the Fabian Society and are pacifists. That's the sort of thing Mr Lowther, Mr Lloyd and myself are up against when we are not up against the narrow-minded, half-educated crowd in the junior departments. Sandy, I'll swear you are short-sighted, the way you peer at people. You must get spectacles.'

'I'm not,' said Sandy irritably, 'it only seems so.'

'It's unnerving,' said Miss Brodie. 'Do you know, Sandy dear, all my ambitions are for you and Rose. You have got insight, perhaps not quite spiritual, but you're a deep one, and Rose has got instinct, Rose has got instinct.'

'Perhaps not quite spiritual,' said Sandy.

'Yes,' said Miss Brodie, 'you're right. Rose has got a future by virtue of her instinct.'

'She has an instinct how to sit for her portrait,' said Sandy.

'That's what I mean by your insight,' said Miss Brodie. 'I ought to know, because my prime has brought me instinct and insight, both.'

Fully to savour her position, Sandy would go and stand outside St Giles's Cathedral or the Tolbooth, and contemplate these emblems of a dark and terrible salvation which made the fires of the damned seem very merry to the imagination by contrast, and much preferable. Nobody in her life, at home or at school, had ever spoken of Calvinism except as a joke that had once been taken seriously. She did not at the time understand that her environment had not been on the surface peculiar to the place, as was the environment of the Edinburgh social classes just above or, even more, just below her own. She had no experience of social class at all. In its outward forms her fifteen years might have been spent in any suburb of any city in the British Isles; her school, with its alien house system, might have been in Ealing. All she was conscious of now was that some quality of life peculiar to Edinburgh and nowhere else had been going on unbeknown to her all the time, and however undesirable it might be, she felt deprived of it; however undesirable, she desired to know what it was, and to cease to be protected from it by enlightened people.

In fact, it was the religion of Calvin of which Sandy felt deprived, or rather a specified recognition of it. She desired this birthright; something definite to reject. It pervaded the place in proportion as it was unacknowledged. In some ways the most real and rooted people whom Sandy knew were Miss Gaunt and the Kerr sisters who made no evasions about their belief that God had planned for practically everybody before they were born a nasty surprise when they died. Later, when Sandy read John Calvin, she found that although popular conceptions of Calvinism were sometimes mistaken, in this particular there was no mistake, indeed it was but a mild understanding of the case, he having made it God's pleasure to implant in certain people an erroneous sense of joy and salvation, so that their surprise at the end might be the nastier.

Sandy was unable to formulate these exciting propositions; nevertheless she experienced them in the air she breathed, she sensed them in the curiously defiant way in which the people she knew broke the Sabbath, and she smelt them in the excesses of Miss Brodie in her prime. Now that she was allowed to go about alone, she walked round the certainly forbidden quarters of Edinburgh to look at the blackened monuments and hear the unbelievable curses of drunken men and women, and comparing their faces with the faces from Morningside and Merchiston with which she was familiar, she saw, with stabs of new and exciting Calvinistic guilt, that there was not much difference.

In this oblique way, she began to sense what went to the makings of Miss Brodie who had elected herself to grace in so particular a way and with more exotic suicidal enchantment than if she had simply taken to drink like other spinsters who couldn't stand it any more.

It was plain that Miss Brodie wanted Rose with her instinct to start preparing to be Teddy Lloyd's lover, and Sandy with her insight to act as informant on the affair. It was to this end that Rose and Sandy had been chosen as the crème de la crème. There was a whiff of sulphur about the idea which fascinated Sandy in her present mind. After all, it was only an idea. And there was no pressing hurry in the matter, for Miss Brodie liked to take her leisure over the unfolding of her plans, most of her joy deriving from the preparation, and moreover, even if these plans were as clear to her own mind as they were to Sandy's, the girls were too young. All the same, by the time the girls were sixteen Miss Brodie was saying to her set at large: 'Sandy will make an excellent Secret Service agent, a great spy'; and to Sandy alone she had started saying: 'Rose will be a great lover. She is above the common moral code, it does not apply to her.

This is a fact which it is not expedient for anyone to hear about who is not endowed with insight.'

For over a year Sandy entered into the spirit of this plan, for she visited the Lloyds' frequently, and was able to report to Miss Brodie how things were going with the portraits of Rose which so resembled Miss Brodie.

'Rose,' said Miss Brodie, 'is like a heroine from a novel by D. H. Lawrence. She has got instinct.'

But in fact the art master's interest in Rose was simply a professional one, she was a good model; Rose had an instinct to be satisfied with this role, and in the event it was Sandy who slept with Teddy Lloyd and Rose who carried back the information.

It was some time before these things came to pass, and meanwhile Miss Brodie was neglecting Mr Lowther at Cramond and spending as much time as possible with Rose and Sandy discussing art, and then the question of sitting for an artist, and Rose's future as a model, and the necessity for Rose to realize the power she had within her, it was a gift and she an exception to all the rules, she was the exception that proved the rule. Miss Brodie was too cautious to be more precise and Rose only half-guessed at Miss Brodie's meaning, for she was at this time, as Sandy knew, following her instinct and becoming famous for sex among the schoolboys who stood awkwardly with their bicycles at a safe distance from the school gates. Rose was greatly popular with these boys, which was the only reason why she was famed for sex, although she did not really talk about sex, far less indulge it. She did everything by instinct, she even listened to Miss Brodie as if she agreed with every word.

'When you are seventeen or eighteen, Rose, you will come to the moment of your great fulfilment.'

'Yes, honestly I think so, Miss Brodie.'

Teddy Lloyd's passion for Jean Brodie was greatly in evidence in all the portraits he did of the various members of the Brodie set. He did them in a group during one summer term, wearing their panama hats each in a different way, each hat adorning, in a magical transfiguration, a different Jean Brodie under the forms of Rose, Sandy, Jenny, Mary, Monica and Eunice. But mostly it was Rose, because she was instinctively a good model and Teddy Lloyd paid her five shillings a sitting, which Rose found useful, being addicted to the cinema.

Sandy felt warmly towards Miss Brodie at those times when she saw how she was misled in her idea of Rose. It was then that Miss Brodie looked beautiful and fragile, just as dark heavy Edinburgh itself could suddenly be changed into a floating city when the light was a special pearly white and fell upon one of the gracefully fashioned streets. In the same way Miss Brodie's masterful features became clear and sweet to Sandy when viewed in the curious light of the woman's folly, and she never felt more affection for her in her later years than when she thought upon Miss Brodie as silly.

But Miss Brodie as the leader of the set, Miss Brodie as a Roman matron, Miss Brodie as an educational reformer were still prominent. It was not always comfortable, from the school point of view, to be associated with her. The lack of team spirit alone, the fact that the Brodie set preferred golf to hockey or netball if they preferred anything at all, were enough to set them apart, even if they had not dented in the crowns of their hats and tilted them backwards or forwards. It was impossible for them to escape from the Brodie set because they were the Brodie set in the eyes of the school. Nominally, they were members of Holyrood, Melrose, Argyll and Biggar, but it had been well known that the Brodie set had no team spirit and did not care which house won the shield. They were not allowed to care. Their disregard had now become an institution, to be respected like the house system itself. For their own part, and without this reputation, the six girls would have gone each her own way by the time she was in the fourth form and had reached the age of sixteen.

But it was irrevocable, and they made the most of it, and saw that their position was really quite enviable. Everyone thought the Brodie set had more fun than anyone else, what with visits to Cramond, to Teddy Lloyd's studio, to the theatre and teas with Miss Brodie. And indeed it was so. And Miss Brodie was always a figure of glamorous activity even in the eyes of the non-Brodie girls.

Miss Brodie's struggles with the authorities on account of her educational system were increasing throughout the years, and she made it a moral duty for her set to rally round her each time her battle reached a crisis. Then she would find them, perhaps, loitering with the bicycle boys after school, and the bicycles would rapidly bear the boys away, and they would be bidden to supper the following evening.

They went to the tram-car stop with her. 'It has been suggested again that I should apply for a post at one of the progressive, that is to say, crank schools. I shall not apply for a post at a crank school. I shall remain at this education factory where my duty lies. There needs must be a leaven in the lump. Give me a girl at an impressionable age and she is mine for life. The gang who oppose me shall not succeed.'

'No,' said everyone. 'No, of course they won't.'

The headmistress had not quite given up testing the girls of the Brodie set to see what they knew. In her frustration she sometimes took reprisals against them when she could do so under the guise of fair play, which was not often.

'If they do not try to unseat me on the grounds of my educational policy, they attempt personal calumny,' said Miss Brodie one day. 'It is unfortunate, but true, that there have been implications against my character in regard to my relations with poor Mr Lowther. As you girls well know, I have given much of my energy to Mr Lowther's health. I am fond of Mr Lowther. Why not? Are we not bidden to love one another? I am Gordon Lowther's closest friend, his confidante. I have neglected him of late I am afraid, but still I have been all things to Gordon Lowther, and I need only lift my little finger and he would be at my side. This relationship has been distorted . . . '

It was some months, now, that Miss Brodie had neglected the singing master, and the girls no longer spent Saturday afternoons at Cramond. Sandy assumed that the reason why Miss Brodie had stopped sleeping with Gordon Lowther was that her sexual feelings were satisfied by proxy; and Rose was predestined to be the lover of Teddy Lloyd. 'I have had much calumny to put up with on account of my good offices at Cramond,' said Miss Brodie. 'However, I shall survive it. If I wished I could marry him tomorrow.'

The morning after this saying, the engagement of Gordon Lowther to Miss Lockhart, the science teacher, was announced in *The Scotsman*. Nobody had expected it. Miss Brodie was greatly taken aback and suffered untimely, for a space, from a sense of having been betrayed. But she seemed to recall herself to the fact that the true love of her life was Teddy Lloyd whom she had renounced; and Gordon Lowther had merely been useful. She subscribed with the rest of the school to the china tea-set which was presented to the couple at the last assembly of the term. Mr Lowther made a speech in which he called them 'you girlies', glancing shyly from time to time at Miss Brodie who was watching the clouds through the window. Sometimes he looked towards his bride to be, who stood quietly by the side of the headmistress half-way up the hall waiting till he should be finished and they could join him on the platform. He had confidence in Miss Lockhart, as everyone did, she not only played golf well and drove a car, she could also blow up the school with her jar of gunpowder and would never dream of doing so.

Miss Brodie's brown eyes were fixed on the clouds, she looked quite beautiful and frail, and it occurred to Sandy that she had possibly renounced Teddy Lloyd only because she was aware that she could not keep up this beauty; it was a quality in her that came and went.

Next term, when Mr Lowther returned from his honeymoon on the island of Eigg, Miss Brodie put her spare energy into her plan for Sandy and Rose, with their insight and instinct; and what energy she had to spare from that she now put into political ideas.

CHAPTER 6

MISS MACKAY, THE headmistress, never gave up pumping the Brodie set. She knew it was useless to do so directly, her approach was indirect, in the hope that they would be tricked into letting fall some piece of evidence which could be used to enforce Miss Brodie's retirement. Once a term, the girls went to tea with Miss Mackay.

But in any case there was now very little they could say without implicating themselves. By the time their friendship with Miss Brodie was of seven years' standing, it had worked itself into their bones, so that they could not break away without, as it were, splitting their bones to do so.

'You still keep up with Miss Brodie?' said Miss Mackay, with a gleaming smile. She had new teeth.

'Oh, yes, rather...'

'Yes, oh yes, from time to time...'

Miss Mackay said to Sandy confidentially when her turn came round – because she treated the older girls as equals, which is to say, as equals definitely wearing school uniform – 'Dear Miss Brodie, she sits on under the elm, telling her remarkable life story to the junior children. I mind when Miss Brodie first came to the school, she was a vigorous young teacher, but now –' She sighed and shook her head. She had a habit of putting the universal wise saws into Scots dialect to make them wiser. Now she said, 'What canna be cured maun be endured. But I fear Miss Brodie is past her best. I doubt her class will get through its qualifying examination this year. But don't think I'm criticizing Miss Brodie. She likes her wee drink, I'm sure. After all, it's nobody's business, so long as it doesn't affect her work and you girls.'

'She doesn't drink,' said Sandy, 'except for sherry on her birthday, half a bottle between the seven of us.'

Miss Mackay could be observed mentally scoring drink off her list of things against Miss Brodie. 'Oh, that's all I meant,' said Miss Mackay.

The Brodie girls, now that they were seventeen, were able to detach Miss Brodie from her aspect of teacher. When they conferred amongst themselves on the subject they had to admit, at last, and without doubt, that she was really an exciting woman as a woman. Her eyes flashed, her nose arched proudly, her hair was still brown, and coiled matriarchally at the nape of her neck. The singing master, well satisfied as he was with Miss Lockhart, now Mrs Lowther and lost to the school, would glance at Miss Brodie from under his ginger eyebrows with shy admiration and memories whenever he saw her.

One of her greatest admirers was the new girl called Joyce Emily Hammond who had been sent to Blaine School as a last hope, having been obliged to withdraw from a range of expensive schools north and south of the border, because of her alleged delinquency which so far had not been revealed, except once or twice when she had thrown paper pellets at Mr Lowther and succeeded only in hurting his feelings. She insisted on calling herself Joyce Emily, was brought to school in the morning by a chauffeur in a large black car, though she was obliged to make her own way home; she lived in a huge house with a stables in the near environs of Edinburgh. Joyce Emily's parents, wealthy as they were, had begged for a trial period to elapse before investing in yet another set of school uniform clothing for their daughter. So Joyce Emily still went about in dark green, while the rest wore deep violet, and she boasted five sets of discarded colours hanging in her wardrobe at home besides such relics of governesses as a substantial switch of hair cut off by Joyce Emily's own hand, a post office savings book belonging to a governess called Miss Michie, and the charred remains of a pillow-case upon which the head of yet another governess called Miss Chambers had been resting when Joyce Emily had set fire to it.

The rest of the girls listened to her chatter, but in general she was disapproved of not only because of her green stockings and skirt, her shiny car and chauffeur, but because life was already exceedingly full of working for examinations and playing for the shield. It was the Brodie set to which Joyce Emily mostly desired to attach herself, perceiving their individualism; but they, less than anybody, wanted her. With the exception of Mary Macgregor, they were, in fact, among the brightest girls in the school, which was somewhat a stumbling-block to Miss Mackay in her efforts to discredit Miss Brodie.

The Brodie set, moreover, had outside interests. Eunice had a boy-friend with whom she practised swimming and diving. Monica Douglas and Mary Macgregor went slum-visiting together with bundles of groceries, although Mary was reported to be always making remarks like, 'Why don't they eat cake?' (What she actually said was, 'Well, why don't they send their clothes to the laundry?' when she heard complaints of the prohibitive price of soap.) Jenny was already showing her dramatic talent and was all the time rehearsing for something in the school dramatic society. Rose modelled for Teddy Lloyd and Sandy occasionally joined her, and was watchful, and sometimes toyed with the idea of inducing Teddy Lloyd to kiss her again just to see if it could be done by sheer looking at him insolently with her little eyes. In addition to these activities the Brodie set were meeting Miss Brodie by twos and threes, and sometimes all together after school. It was at this time, in nineteen-thirty-seven, that she was especially cultivating Rose, and questioning Sandy, and being answered as to the progress of the great love affair presently to take place between Rose and the art master.

So that they had no time to do much about a delinquent whose parents had dumped her on the school by their influence, even if she was apparently a delinquent in name only. Miss Brodie, however, found time to take her up. The Brodie girls slightly resented this but were relieved that they were not obliged to share the girl's company, and that Miss Brodie took her to tea and the theatre on her own.

One of Joyce Emily's boasts was that her brother at Oxford had gone to fight in the Spanish Civil War. This dark, rather mad girl wanted to go too, and to wear a white blouse and black skirt and march with a gun. Nobody had taken this seriously. The Spanish Civil War was something going on outside in the newspapers and only once a month in the school debating society. Everyone, including Joyce Emily, was anti-Franco if they were anything at all.

One day it was realized that Joyce Emily had not been at school for some days, and soon someone else was occupying her desk. No one knew why she had left until, six weeks later, it was reported that she had run away to Spain and had been killed in an accident when the train she was travelling in had been attacked. The school held an abbreviated form of remembrance service for her.

Mary had gone to be a shorthand typist and Jenny had gone to a school of dramatic art. Only four remained of the Brodie set for the last year. It was hardly like being at school at all, there was so much free time, so many lectures and so much library research outside the school building for the sixth-form girls that it was just a matter of walking in and out. They were deferred to and consulted, and had the feeling that they could, if they wished, run the place.

Eunice was to do modern languages, although she changed her mind a year later and became a nurse. Monica was destined for science, Sandy for psychology. Rose had hung on, not for any functional reason, but because her father thought she should get the best out of her education, even if she was only going to the art school later on, or at the worst, become a model for artists or dress designers. Rose's father played a big part in her life, he was a huge widower, as handsome in his masculine way as was Rose in her feminine, proudly professing himself a cobbler; that was to say, he now owned an extensive shoe-making business. Some years ago, on meeting Miss Brodie he had immediately taken a hearty male interest in her, as so many men did, not thinking her to be ridiculous as might have been expected; but she would have none of Mr Stanley, for he was hardly what she would call a man of culture. She thought him rather carnal. The girls, however, had always guiltily liked Rose's father. And Rose, instinctive as she undoubtedly was, followed her instinct so far as to take on his hard-headed and merry carnality, and made a good marriage soon after she left school. She shook off Miss Brodie's influence as a dog shakes pond-water from its coat.

Miss Brodie was not to know that this would be, and meantime Rose was inescapably famous for sex and was much sought after by sixth-form schoolboys and first-year university students. And Miss Brodie said to Sandy: 'From what you tell me I should think that Rose and Teddy Lloyd will soon be lovers.' All at once Sandy realized that this was not all theory and a kind of Brodie game, in the way that so much of life was unreal talk and game-planning, like the prospects of a war and other theories that people were putting about in the air like pigeons, and one said, 'Yes, of course, it's inevitable.' But this was not theory; Miss Brodie meant it. Sandy looked at her, and perceived that the woman was obsessed by the need for Rose to sleep with the man she herself was in love with; there was nothing new in the idea, it was the reality that was new. She thought of Miss Brodie eight years ago sitting under the elm tree telling her first simple love story and wondered to what extent it was Miss Brodie who had developed complications throughout the years, and to what extent it was her own conception of Miss Brodie that had changed.

During the year past Sandy had continued seeing the Lloyds. She went shopping with Deirdre Lloyd and got herself a folkweave shirt like Deirdre's. She listened to their conversation, at the same time calculating their souls by signs and symbols, as was the habit in those days of young persons who had read books of psychology when listening to older persons who had not. Sometimes, on days when Rose was required to pose naked, Sandy sat with the painter and his model in the studio, silently watching the strange mutations of the flesh on the canvas as they represented an anonymous nude figure, and at the same time resembled Rose, and more than this, resembled Miss Brodie. Sandy had become highly interested in the painter's mind, so involved with Miss Brodie as it was, and not accounting her ridiculous.

'From what you tell me I should think that Rose and Teddy Lloyd will soon be lovers.' Sandy realized that Miss Brodie meant it. She had told Miss Brodie how peculiarly all his portraits reflected her. She had said so again and again, for Miss Brodie loved to hear it. She had said that Teddy Lloyd wanted to give up teaching and was preparing an exhibition, and was encouraged in this course by art critics and discouraged by the thought of his large family.

'I am his Muse,' said Miss Brodie. 'But I have renounced his love in order to dedicate my prime to the young girls in my care. I am his Muse but Rose shall take my place.'

She thinks she is Providence, thought Sandy, she thinks she is the God of Calvin, she sees the beginning and the end. And Sandy thought, too, the woman is an unconscious lesbian. And many theories from the books of psychology categorized Miss Brodie, but failed to obliterate her image from the canvases of one-armed Teddy Lloyd.

When she was a nun, sooner or later one and the other of the Brodie set came to visit Sandy, because it was something to do, and she had written her book of psychology, and everyone likes to visit a nun, it provides a spiritual sensation, a catharsis to go home with, especially if the nun clutches the bars of the grille. Rose came, now long since married to a successful businessman who varied in his line of business from canned goods to merchant banking. They fell to talking about Miss Brodie.

'She talked a lot about dedication,' said Rose, 'but she didn't mean your sort of dedication. But don't you think she was dedicated to her girls in a way?'

'Oh yes, I think she was,' said Sandy.

'Why did she get the push?' said Rose. 'Was it sex?'

'No, politics.'

'I didn't know she bothered about politics.'

'It was only a side line,' Sandy said, 'but it served as an excuse.'

Monica Douglas came to visit Sandy because there was a crisis in her life. She had married a scientist and in one of her fits of anger had thrown a live coal at his sister. Whereupon the scientist demanded a separation, once and for all.

'I'm not much good at that sort of problem,' said Sandy. But Monica had not thought she would be able to help much, for she knew Sandy of old, and persons known of old can never be of much help. So they fell to talking of Miss Brodie.

'Did she ever get Rose to sleep with Teddy Lloyd?' said Monica.

'No,' said Sandy.

'Was she in love with Teddy Lloyd herself?'

'Yes,' said Sandy, 'and he was in love with her.'

'Then it was a real renunciation in a way,' said Monica.

'Yes, it was,' said Sandy. 'After all, she was a woman in her prime.'

'You used to think her talk about renunciation was a joke,' said Monica.

'So did you,' said Sandy.

In the summer of nineteen-thirty-eight, after the last of the Brodie set had left Blaine, Miss Brodie went to Germany and

Austria, while Sandy read psychology and went to the Lloyds' to sit for her own portrait. Rose came and kept them company occasionally.

When Deirdre Lloyd took the children into the country Teddy had to stay on in Edinburgh because he was giving a summer course at the art school. Sandy continued to sit for her portrait twice a week, and sometimes Rose came and sometimes not.

One day when they were alone, Sandy told Teddy Lloyd that all his portraits, even that of the littlest Lloyd baby, were now turning out to be likenesses of Miss Brodie, and she gave him her insolent blackmailing stare. He kissed her as he had done three years before when she was fifteen, and for the best part of five weeks of the summer they had a love affair in the empty house, only sometimes answering the door to Rose, but at other times letting the bell scream on.

During that time he painted a little, and she said: 'You are still making me look like Jean Brodie.' So he started a new canvas, but it was the same again.

She said: 'Why are you obsessed with that woman? Can't you see she's ridiculous?'

He said, yes, he could see Jean Brodie was ridiculous. He said, would she kindly stop analysing his mind, it was unnatural in a girl of eighteen.

Miss Brodie telephoned for Sandy to come to see her early in September. She had returned from Germany and Austria which were now magnificently organized. After the war Miss Brodie admitted to Sandy, as they sat in the Braid Hills Hotel, 'Hitler *was* rather naughty,' but at this time she was full of her travels and quite sure the new régime would save the world. Sandy was bored, it did not seem necessary that the world should be saved, only that the poor people in the streets and slums of Edinburgh should be relieved. Miss Brodie said there would be no war. Sandy never had thought so, anyway. Miss Brodie came to the point: 'Rose tells me you have become his lover.'

'Yes, does it matter which one of us it is?'

'Whatever possessed you?' said Miss Brodie in a very Scottish way, as if Sandy had given away a pound of marmalade to an English duke.

'He interests me,' said Sandy.

'Interests you, forsooth,' said Miss Brodie. 'A girl with a mind, a girl with insight. He is a Roman Catholic and I don't see how you can have to do with a man who can't think for himself. Rose was suitable. Rose has instinct but no insight.'

Teddy Lloyd continued reproducing Jean Brodie in his paintings. 'You have instinct,' Sandy told him, 'but no insight, or you would see that the woman isn't to be taken seriously.'

'I know she isn't,' he said. 'You are too analytical and irritable for your age.'

The family had returned and their meetings were dangerous and exciting. The more she discovered him to be still in love with Jean Brodie, the more she was curious about the mind that loved the woman. By the end of the year it happened that she had quite lost interest in the man himself, but was deeply absorbed in his mind, from which she extracted, among other things, his religion as a pith from a husk. Her mind was as full of his religion as a night sky is full of things visible and invisible. She left the man and took his religion and became a nun in the course of time.

But that autumn, while she was still probing the mind that invented Miss Brodie on canvas after canvas, Sandy met Miss Brodie several times. She was at first merely resigned to Sandy's liaison with the art master. Presently she was exultant, and presently again inquired for details, which she did not get.

'His portraits still resemble me?' said Miss Brodie.

'Yes, very much,' said Sandy.

'Then all is well,' said Miss Brodie. 'And after all, Sandy,' she said, 'you are destined to be the great lover, although I would not have thought it. Truth is stranger than fiction. I wanted Rose for him, I admit, and sometimes I regretted urging young Joyce Emily to go to Spain to fight for Franco, she would have done admirably for him, a girl of instinct, a —'

'Did she go to fight for Franco?' said Sandy.

'That was the intention. I made her see sense. However, she didn't have the chance to fight at all, poor girl.'

When Sandy returned, as was expected of her, to see Miss Mackay that autumn, the headmistress said to this rather difficult old girl with the abnormally small eyes, 'You'll have been seeing something of Miss Brodie, I hope. You aren't forgetting your old friends, I hope.'

'I've seen her once or twice,' said Sandy.

'I'm afraid she put ideas into your young heads,' said Miss Mackay with a knowing twinkle, which meant that now Sandy had left school it would be all right to talk openly about Miss Brodie's goings-on.

'Yes, lots of ideas,' Sandy said.

'I wish I knew what some of them were,' said Miss Mackay, slumping a little and genuinely worried. 'Because it is still going on, I mean class after class, and now she has formed a new set, and they are so out of key with the rest of the school, Miss Brodie's set. They are precocious. Do you know what I mean?'

'Yes,' said Sandy. 'But you won't be able to pin her down on sex. Have you thought of politics?'

Miss Mackay turned her chair so that it was nearly square with Sandy's. This was business.

'My dear,' she said, 'what do you mean? I didn't know she was attracted by politics.'

'Neither she is,' said Sandy, 'except as a side interest. She's a born Fascist, have you thought of that?'

'I shall question her pupils on those lines and see what emerges, if that is what you advise, Sandy. I had no idea you felt so seriously about the state of world affairs, Sandy, and I'm more than delighted –'

'I'm not really interested in world affairs,' said Sandy, 'only in putting a stop to Miss Brodie.'

It was clear the headmistress thought this rather unpleasant of Sandy. But she did not fail to say to Miss Brodie, when the time came, 'It was one of your own girls who gave me the tip, one of your set, Miss Brodie.'

Sandy was to leave Edinburgh at the end of the year and when she said goodbye to the Lloyds she looked round the studio at the canvases on which she had failed to put a stop to Miss Brodie. She congratulated Teddy Lloyd on the economy of his method. He congratulated her on the economy of hers, and Deirdre looked to see whatever did he mean? Sandy thought, if he knew about my stopping of Miss Brodie, he would think me more economical still. She was more fuming, now, with Christian morals, than John Knox.

Miss Brodie was forced to retire at the end of the summer term of nineteen-thirty-nine, on the grounds that she had been teaching Fascism. Sandy, when she heard of it, thought of the marching troops of black shirts in the pictures on the wall. By now she had entered the Catholic Church, in whose ranks she had found quite a number of Fascists much less agreeable than Miss Brodie.

'Of course,' said Miss Brodie when she wrote to tell Sandy the news of her retirement, 'this political question was only an excuse. They tried to prove personal immorality against me on many occasions and failed. My girls were always reticent on these matters. It was my educational policy they were up against which had reached its perfection in my prime. I was dedicated to my girls, as you know. But they used this political excuse as a weapon. What hurts and amazes me most of all is the fact, if Miss Mackay is to be believed, that it was one of my own set who betrayed me and put the inquiry in motion.

'You will be astonished. I can write to you of this, because you of all my set are exempt from suspicion, you had no *reason* to betray me. I think first of Mary Macgregor. Perhaps Mary has nursed a grievance, in her stupidity of mind, against me – she is such an exasperating young woman. I think of Rose. It may be that Rose resented my coming first with Mr L. Eunice – I cannot think it could be Eunice, but I did frequently have to come down firmly on her commonplace ideas. She wanted to be a Girl Guide, you remember. She was attracted to the Team Spirit – could it be that Eunice bore a grudge? Then there is Jenny. Now you know Jenny, how she went *off* and was never the same after she wanted to be an actress. She became so dull. Do you think she minded my telling her that she would never be a Fay Compton, far less a Sybil Thorndike? Finally, there is Monica. I half incline to suspect Monica. There is very little Soul behind the mathematical brain, and it may be that, in a fit of rage against that Beauty, Truth and Goodness which was beyond her grasp, she turned and betrayed me.

'You, Sandy, as you see, I exempt from suspicion, since you had no reason whatsoever to betray me, indeed you have had the best part of me in my confidences and in the man I love. Think, if you can, who it could have been. I must know which one of you betrayed me . . .'

Sandy replied like an enigmatic Pope: 'If you did not betray us it is impossible that you could have been betrayed by us. The word betrayed does not apply . . .'

She heard again from Miss Brodie at the time of Mary Macgregor's death, when the girl ran hither and thither in the hotel fire and was trapped by it. 'If this is a judgment on poor Mary for betraying me, I am sure I would not have wished . . .'

'I'm afraid', Jenny wrote, 'Miss Brodie is past her prime. She keeps wanting to know who betrayed her. It isn't at all like the old Miss Brodie; she was always so full of fight.'

Her name and memory, after her death, flitted from mouth to mouth like swallows in summer, and in winter they were gone. It was always in summer time that the Brodie set came to visit Sandy, for the nunnery was deep in the country.

When Jenny came to see Sandy, who now bore the name Sister Helena of the Transfiguration, she told Sandy about her sudden falling in love with a man in Rome and there being nothing to be done about it. 'Miss Brodie would have liked to know about it,' she said, 'sinner as she was.'

'Oh, she was quite an innocent in her way,' said Sandy, clutching the bars of the grille.

Eunice, when she came, told Sandy, 'We were at the Edinburgh Festival last year. I found Miss Brodie's grave, I put some flowers on it. I've told my husband all the stories about her, sitting under the elm and all that; he thinks she was marvellous fun.'

'So she was, really, when you think of it.'

'Yes, she was,' said Eunice, 'when she was in her prime.'

Monica came again. 'Before she died,' she said, 'Miss Brodie thought it was you who betrayed her.'

'It's only possible to betray where loyalty is due,' said Sandy.

'Well, wasn't it due to Miss Brodie?'

'Only up to a point,' said Sandy.

And there was that day when the inquiring young man came to see Sandy because of her strange book of psychology, 'The Transfiguration of the Commonplace', which had brought so many visitors that Sandy clutched the bars of her grille more desperately than ever.

'What were the main influences of your schooldays, Sister Helena? Were they literary or political or personal? Was it Calvinism?'

Sandy said: 'There was a Miss Jean Brodie in her prime.'

THE GIRLS OF SLENDER MEANS

For Alan Maclean

CHAPTER 1

LONG AGO IN 1945 all the nice people in England were poor, allowing for exceptions. The streets of the cities were lined with buildings in bad repair or in no repair at all, bomb-sites piled with stony rubble, houses like giant teeth in which decay had been drilled out, leaving only the cavity. Some bomb-ripped buildings looked like the ruins of ancient castles until, at a closer view, the wallpapers of various quite normal rooms would be visible, room above room, exposed, as on a stage, with one wall missing; sometimes a lavatory chain would dangle over nothing from a fourth- or fifth-floor ceiling; most of all the staircases survived, like a new art-form, leading up and up to an unspecified destination that made unusual demands on the mind's eye. All the nice people were poor; at least, that was a general axiom, the best of the rich being poor in spirit.

There was absolutely no point in feeling depressed about the scene, it would have been like feeling depressed about the Grand Canyon or some event of the earth outside everybody's scope. People continued to exchange assurances of depressed feelings about the weather or the news, or the Albert Memorial which had not been hit, not even shaken, by any bomb from first to last.

The May of Teck Club stood obliquely opposite the site of the Memorial, in one of a row of tall houses which had endured, but barely; some bombs had dropped nearby, and in a few back gardens, leaving the buildings cracked on the outside and shakily hinged within, but habitable for the time being. The shattered windows had been replaced with new

129

glass rattling in loose frames. More recently, the bituminous black-out paint had been removed from landing and bathroom windows. Windows were important in that year of final reckoning; they told at a glance whether a house was inhabited or not; and in the course of the past years they had accumulated much meaning, having been the main danger-zone between domestic life and the war going on outside: everyone had said, when the sirens sounded, 'Mind the windows. Keep away from the windows. Watch out for the glass.'

The May of Teck Club had been three times window-shattered since 1940, but never directly hit. There the windows of the upper bedrooms overlooked the dip and rise of tree-tops in Kensington Gardens across the street, with the Albert Memorial to be seen by means of a slight craning and twist of the neck. These upper bedrooms looked down on the opposite pavement on the park side of the street, and on the tiny people who moved along in neat-looking singles and couples, pushing little prams loaded with pin-head babies and provisions, or carrying little dots of shopping bags. Everyone carried a shopping bag in case they should be lucky enough to pass a shop that had a sudden stock of something off the rations.

From the lower-floor dormitories the people in the street looked larger, and the paths of the park were visible. All the nice people were poor, and few were nicer, as nice people come, than these girls at Kensington who glanced out of the windows in the early mornings to see what the day looked like, or gazed out on the green summer evenings, as if reflecting on the months ahead, on love and the relations of love. Their eyes gave out an eager-spirited light that resembled near-genius, but was youth merely. The first of the Rules of Constitution, drawn up at some remote and innocent Edwardian date, still applied more or less to them:

The May of Teck Club exists for the Pecuniary Convenience and Social Protection of Ladies of Slender Means below the age of Thirty

Years, who are obliged to reside apart from their Families in order to follow an Occupation in London.

As they realized themselves in varying degrees, few people alive at the time were more delightful, more ingenious, more movingly lovely, and, as it might happen, more savage, than the girls of slender means.

*

'I've got something to tell you,' said Jane Wright, the woman columnist.

At the other end of the telephone, the voice of Dorothy Markham, owner of the flourishing model agency, said, 'Darling, where have you been?' She spoke, by habit since her débutante days, with the utmost enthusiasm of tone.

'I've got something to tell you. Do you remember Nicholas Farringdon? Remember he used to come to the old May of Teck just after the war, he was an anarchist and poet sort of thing. A tall man with –'

'The one that got on to the roof to sleep out with Selina?'

'Yes, Nicholas Farringdon.'

'Oh rather. Has he turned up?'

'No, he's been martyred.'

'What–ed?'

'Martyred in Haiti. Killed. Remember he became a Brother –'

'But I've just been to Tahiti, it's marvellous, everyone's marvellous. Where did you hear it?'

'Haiti. There's a news paragraph just come over Reuters. I'm sure it's the same Nicholas Farringdon because it says a missionary, former poet. I nearly died. I knew him well, you know, in those days. I expect they'll hush it all up, about those days, if they want to make a martyr story.'

'How did it happen, is it gruesome?'

'Oh, I don't know, there's only a paragraph.'

'You'll have to find out more through your grapevine. I'm shattered. I've got heaps to tell you.'

*

The Committee of Management wishes to express surprise at the Members' protest regarding the wall-paper chosen for the drawing-room. The Committee wishes to point out that Members' residential fees do not meet the running expenses of the Club. The Committee regrets that the spirit of the May of Teck Foundation has apparently so far deteriorated that such a protest has been made. The Committee refers Members to the terms of the Club's Foundation.

Joanna Childe was a daughter of a country rector. She had a good intelligence and strong obscure emotions. She was training to be a teacher of elocution and, while attending a school of drama, already had pupils of her own. Joanna Childe had been drawn to this profession by her good voice and love of poetry which she loved rather as it might be assumed a cat loves birds; poetry, especially the declamatory sort, excited and possessed her; she would pounce on the stuff, play with it quivering in her mind, and when she had got it by heart, she spoke it forth with devouring relish. Mostly, she indulged the habit while giving elocution lessons at the club where she was highly thought of for it. The vibrations of Joanna's elocution voice from her room or from the recreation room where she frequently rehearsed, were felt to add tone and style to the establishment when boy-friends called. Her taste in poetry became the accepted taste of the club. She had a deep feeling for certain passages in the authorized version of the Bible, besides the Book of Common Prayer, Shakespeare and Gerard Manley Hopkins, and had newly discovered Dylan Thomas. She was not moved by the poetry of Eliot and Auden, except for the latter's lyric:

> Lay your sleeping head, my love,
> Human on my faithless arm;

Joanna Childe was large, with light shiny hair, blue eyes and deep-pink cheeks. When she read the notice signed by Lady Julia Markham, chairwoman of the committee, she stood with the other young women round the green baize board and was given to murmur:

'He rageth, and again he rageth, because he knows his time is short.'

It was not known to many that this was a reference to the Devil, but it caused amusement. She had not intended it so. It was not usual for Joanna to quote anything for its aptitude, and at conversational pitch.

Joanna, who was now of age, would henceforth vote conservative in the elections, which at that time in the May of Teck Club was associated with a desirable order of life that none of the members was old enough to remember from direct experience. In principle they all approved of what the committee's notice stood for. And so Joanna was alarmed by the amused reaction to her quotation, the hearty laugh of understanding that those days were over when the members of anything whatsoever might not raise their voices against the drawing-room wall-paper. Principles regardless, everyone knew that the notice was plain damned funny. Lady Julia must be feeling pretty desperate.

'He rageth and again he rageth, because he knows his time is short.'

Little dark Judy Redwood who was a shorthand typist in the Ministry of Labour said, 'I've got a feeling that as members we're legally entitled to a say in the administration. I must ask Geoffrey.' This was the man Judy was engaged to. He was still in the forces, but had qualified as a solicitor before being called up. His sister, Anne Baberton, who stood with the notice-board group, said, 'Geoffrey would be the last person I would

consult.' Anne Baberton said this to indicate that she knew
Geoffrey better than Judy knew him; she said it to indicate
affectionate scorn; she said it because it was the obvious thing
for a nicely brought-up sister to say, since she was proud of
him; and besides all this, there was an element of irritation in
her words, 'Geoffrey would be the last person I would consult', for she knew there was no point in members taking up
this question of the drawing-room wall-paper.

Anne trod out her cigarette-end contemptuously on the
floor of the large entrance hall with its pink and grey Victorian
tiles. This was pointed to by a thin middle-aged woman, one of
the few older, if not exactly the earliest members. She said,
'One is not permitted to put cigarette-ends on the floor.' The
words did not appear to impress themselves on the ears of the
group, more than the ticking of the grandfather clock behind
them. But Anne said, 'Isn't one permitted to spit on the floor,
even?' 'One certainly isn't,' said the spinster. 'Oh, I thought
one was,' said Anne.

The May of Teck Club was founded by Queen Mary
before her marriage to King George the Fifth, when she was
Princess May of Teck. On an afternoon between the engagement and the marriage, the Princess had been induced to come
to London and declare officially open the May of Teck Club
which had been endowed by various gentle forces of wealth.

None of the original Ladies remained in the club. But three
subsequent members had been permitted to stay on past the
stipulated age-limit of thirty, and were now in their fifties, and
had resided at the May of Teck Club since before the First
World War at which time, they said, all members had been
obliged to dress for dinner.

Nobody knew why these three women had not been asked
to leave when they had reached the age of thirty. Even the
warden and committee did not know why the three remained.
It was now too late to turn them out with decency. It was too
late even to mention to them the subject of their continuing

residence. Successive committees before 1939 had decided that the three older residents might, in any case, be expected to have a good influence on the younger ones.

During the war the matter had been left in abeyance, since the club was half empty; in any case members' fees were needed, and bombs were then obliterating so much and so many in the near vicinity that it was an open question whether indeed the three spinsters would remain upright with the house to the end. By 1945 they had seen much coming of new girls and going of old, and were generally liked by the current batch, being subject to insults when they interfered in anything, and intimate confidences when they kept aloof. The confidences seldom represented the whole truth, particularly those revealed by the young women who occupied the top floor. The three spinsters were, through the ages, known and addressed as Collie (Miss Coleman), Greggie (Miss Macgregor) and Jarvie (Miss Jarman). It was Greggie who had said to Anne by the notice-board:

'One isn't permitted to put cigarette-ends on the floor.'

'Isn't one permitted to spit on the floor, even?'

'No, one isn't.'

'Oh, I thought one was.'

Greggie affected an indulgent sigh and pushed her way through the crowd of younger members. She went to the open door, set in a wide porch, to look out at the summer evening like a shopkeeper waiting for custom. Greggie always behaved as if she owned the club.

The gong was about to sound quite soon. Anne kicked her cigarette-stub into a dark corner.

Greggie called over her shoulder, 'Anne, here comes your boy-friend.'

'On time, for once,' said Anne, with the same pretence of scorn that she had adopted when referring to her brother Geoffrey: 'Geoffrey would be the last person I would consult.' She moved, with her casual hips, towards the door.

A square-built high-coloured young man in the uniform of an English captain came smiling in. Anne stood regarding him as if he was the last person in the world she would consult.

'Good evening,' he said to Greggie as a well-brought-up man would naturally say to a woman of Greggie's years standing in the doorway. He made a vague nasal noise of recognition to Anne, which if properly pronounced would have been 'Hallo'. She said nothing at all by way of greeting. They were nearly engaged to be married.

'Like to come in and see the drawing-room wall-paper?' Anne said then.

'No, let's get cracking.'

Anne went to get her coat off the banister where she had slung it. He was saying to Greggie, 'Lovely evening, isn't it?'

Anne returned with her coat slung over her shoulder. 'Bye, Greggie,' she said. 'Good-bye,' said the soldier. Anne took his arm.

'Have a nice time,' said Greggie.

The dinner-gong sounded and there was a scuffle of feet departing from the notice-board and a scamper of feet from the floors above.

    *

On a summer night during the previous week the whole club, forty-odd women, with any young men who might happen to have called that evening, had gone like swift migrants into the dark cool air of the park, crossing its wide acres as the crow flies in the direction of Buckingham Palace, there to express themselves along with the rest of London on the victory in the war with Germany. They clung to each other in twos and threes, fearful of being trampled. When separated, they clung to, and were clung to by, the nearest person. They became members of a wave of the sea, they surged and sang until, at every half-hour interval, a light flooded the tiny distant balcony of the Palace and four small straight digits appeared upon it: the King, the Queen, and the two Princesses. The royal family raised their right arms, their hands fluttered as in a slight breeze, they were three candles in uniform and one in the recognizable fur-trimmed folds of the civilian queen in war-time. The huge organic murmur of the crowd, different from anything like the voice of animate matter but rather more a cataract or a geological disturbance, spread through the parks and along the Mall. Only the St John Ambulance men, watchful beside their vans, had any identity left. The royal family waved, turned to go, lingered and waved again, and finally disappeared. Many strange arms were twined round strange bodies. Many liaisons, some permanent, were formed in the night, and numerous infants of experimental variety, delightful in hue of skin and racial structure, were born to the world in the due cycle of nine months after. The bells pealed. Greggie observed that it was something between a wedding and a funeral on a world scale.

The next day everyone began to consider where they personally stood in the new order of things.

Many citizens felt the urge, which some began to indulge, to insult each other, in order to prove something or to test their ground.

The government reminded the public that it was still at war. Officially this was undeniable, but except to those whose relations lay in the Far-Eastern prisons of war, or were stuck in Burma, that war was generally felt to be a remote affair.

A few shorthand typists at the May of Teck Club started to apply for safer jobs – that is to say, in private concerns, not connected with the war like the temporary Ministries where many of them had been employed.

Their brothers and men friends in the forces, not yet demobilized, by a long way, were talking of vivid enterprises for the exploitation of peace, such as buying a lorry and building up from it a transport business.

*

'I've got something to tell you,' said Jane.

'Just a minute till I shut the door. The kids are making a row,' Anne said. And presently, when she returned to the telephone, she said, 'Yes, carry on.'

'Do you remember Nicholas Farringdon?'

'I seem to remember the name.'

'Remember I brought him to the May of Teck in 1945, he used to come often for supper. He got mixed up with Selina.'

'Oh, Nicholas. The one who got up on the roof? What a long time ago that was. Have you seen him?'

'I've just seen a news item that's come over Reuters. He's been killed in a local rising in Haiti.'

'Really? How awful! What was he doing there?'

'Well, he became a missionary or something.'

'No!'

'Yes. It's terribly tragic. I knew him well.'

'Ghastly. It brings everything back. Have you told Selina?'

'Well, I haven't been able to get her. You know what Selina's like these days, she won't answer the phone personally, you have to go through thousands of secretaries or whatever they are.'

'You could get a good story for your paper out of it, Jane,' Anne said.

'I know that. I'm just waiting to get more details. Of course it's all those years ago since I knew him, but it would be an interesting story.'

*

Two men – poets by virtue of the fact that the composition of
poetry was the only consistent thing they had so far done –
beloved of two May of Teck girls and, at the moment, of
nobody else, sat in their corduroy trousers in a café in
Bayswater with their silent listening admirers and talked
about the new future as they flicked the page-proofs of an
absent friend's novel. A copy of *Peace News* lay on the table
between them. One of the men said to the other:

And now what will become of us without Barbarians? Those people
were some sort of a solution.

And the other smiled, bored-like, but conscious that very few
in all the great metropolis and its tributary provinces were as
yet privy to the source of these lines. This other who smiled
was Nicholas Farringdon, not yet known or as yet at all likely
to be.

'Who wrote that?' said Jane Wright, a fat girl who
worked for a publisher and who was considered to be
brainy but somewhat below standard, socially, at the May of
Teck.

Neither man replied.

'Who wrote that?' Jane said again.

The poet nearest her said, through his thick spectacles,
'An Alexandrian poet.'

'A new poet?'

'No, but fairly new to this country.'

'What's his name?'

He did not reply. The young men had started talking again.
They talked about the decline and fall of the anarchist movement on the island of their birth in terms of the personalities
concerned. They were bored with educating the girls for this
evening.

CHAPTER 2

JOANNA CHILDE WAS giving elocution lessons to Miss Harper, the cook, in the recreation room. When she was not giving lessons she was usually practising for her next examination. The house frequently echoed with Joanna's rhetoric. She got six shillings an hour from her pupils, five shillings if they were May of Teck members. Nobody knew what her arrangements were with Miss Harper, for at that time all who kept keys of food-cupboards made special arrangements with all others. Joanna's method was to read each stanza herself first and make her pupil repeat it.

Everyone in the drawing-room could hear the loud lesson in progress beating out the stresses and throbs of *The Wreck of the Deutschland*.

> The frown of his face
> Before me, the hurtle of hell
> Behind, where, where was a, where was a place?

The club was proud of Joanna Childe, not only because she chucked up her head and recited poetry, but because she was so well built, fair and healthy looking, the poetic essence of tall, fair rectors' daughters who never used a scrap of make-up, who had served tirelessly day and night in parish welfare organizations since leaving school early in the war, who before that had been Head Girl and who never wept that anyone knew or could imagine, being stoical by nature.

What had happened to Joanna was that she had fallen in love with a curate on leaving school. It had come to nothing. Joanna had decided that this was to be the only love of her life.

She had been brought up to hear, and later to recite,

> ...Love is not love ⌐
> Which alters when it alteration finds,
> Or bends with the remover to remove:

All her ideas of honour and love came from the poets. She was vaguely acquainted with distinctions and sub-distinctions of human and divine love, and their various attributes, but this was picked up from rectory conversations when theologically-minded clerics came to stay; it was in a different category of instruction from ordinary household beliefs such as the axiom, 'People are holier who live in the country', and the notion that a nice girl should only fall in love once in her life.

It seemed to Joanna that her longing for the curate must have been unworthy of the name of love, had she allowed a similar longing, which she began to feel, for the company of a succeeding curate, more suitable and even handsomer, to come to anything. Once you admit that you can change the object of a strongly-felt affection, you undermine the whole structure of love and marriage, the whole philosophy of Shakespeare's sonnet: this had been the approved, though unspoken, opinion of the rectory and its mental acres of upper air. Joanna pressed down her feelings for the second curate and worked them off in tennis and the war effort. She had not encouraged the second curate at all but brooded silently upon him until the Sunday she saw him standing in the pulpit and announce his sermon upon the text:

... if thy right eye offend thee, pluck it out, and cast it from thee: for it is profitable for thee that one of thy members should perish, and not that thy whole body should be cast into hell.

And if thy right hand offend thee, cut it off, and cast it from thee: for it is profitable for thee that one of thy members should perish, and not that thy whole body should be cast into hell.

It was the evening service. Many young girls from the district had come, some of them in their service uniforms. One particular Wren looked up at the curate, her pink cheeks touched by the stained-glass evening light; her hair curled lightly upwards on her Wren hat. Joanna could hardly imagine a more handsome man than this second curate. He was newly ordained, and was shortly going into the Air Force. It was spring, full of preparations and guesses, for the second front was to be established against the enemy, some said in North Africa, some said Scandinavia, the Baltic, France. Meantime, Joanna listened attentively to the young man in the pulpit, she listened obsessively. He was dark and tall, his eyes were deep under his straight black brows, he had a chiselled look. His wide mouth suggested to Joanna generosity and humour, that type of generosity and humour special to the bishop sprouting within him. He was very athletic. He had made it as clear that he wanted Joanna as the former curate had not. Like the rector's eldest daughter that she was, Joanna sat in her pew without seeming to listen in any particular way to this attractive fellow. She did not turn her face towards him as the pretty Wren was doing. The right eye and the right hand, he was saying, means that which we hold most precious. What the scripture meant, he said, was that if anything we hold most dear should prove an offence – as you know, he said, the Greek word here was σχὰνδαλον, frequently occurring in Scripture in the connotation of scandal, offence, stumbling-block, as when St Paul said . . . The rustics who predominated in the congregation looked on with their round moveless eyes. Joanna decided to pluck out her right eye, cut off her right hand, this looming offence to the first love, this stumbling-block, the adorable man in the pulpit.

'For it is profitable for thee that one of thy members should perish, and not that thy whole body should be cast into hell,' rang the preacher's voice. 'Hell of course,' he said, 'is a negative concept. Let us put it more positively. More positively, the text should read, "It is better to enter maimed into the Kingdom of Heaven than not to enter at all."' He hoped to publish this sermon one day in a Collected Sermons, for he was as yet inexperienced in many respects, although he later learned some reality as an Air Force chaplain.

Joanna, then, had decided to enter maimed into the Kingdom of Heaven. By no means did she look maimed. She got a job in London and settled at the May of Teck Club. She took up elocution in her spare time. Then, towards the end of the war, she began to study and make a full-time occupation of it. The sensation of poetry replaced the sensation of the curate and she took on pupils at six shillings an hour pending her diploma.

> The wanton troopers riding by
> Have shot my fawn, and it will die.

Nobody at the May of Teck Club knew her precise history, but it was generally assumed to be something emotionally heroic. She was compared to Ingrid Bergman, and did not take part in the argument between members and staff about the food, whether it contained too many fattening properties, even allowing for the necessities of war-time rationing.

CHAPTER 3

LOVE AND MONEY were the vital themes in all the bedrooms and dormitories. Love came first, and subsidiary to it was money for the upkeep of looks and the purchase of clothing coupons at the official black-market price of eight coupons for a pound.

The house was a spacious Victorian one, and very little had been done to change its interior since the days when it was a private residence. It resembled in its plan most of the women's hostels, noted for cheapness and tone, which had flourished since the emancipation of women had called for them. No one at the May of Teck Club referred to it as a hostel, except in moments of low personal morale such as was experienced by the youngest members only on being given the brush-off by a boy-friend.

The basement of the house was occupied by kitchens, the laundry, the furnace and fuel-stores.

The ground floor contained staff offices, the dining-room, the recreation room and, newly papered in a mud-like shade of brown, the drawing-room. This resented wall-paper had unfortunately been found at the back of a cupboard in huge quantities, otherwise the walls would have remained grey and stricken like everyone else's.

Boy-friends were allowed to dine as guests at a cost of two-and-sixpence. It was also permitted to entertain in the recreation room, on the terrace which led out from it, and in the drawing-room whose mud-brown walls appeared so penitential in tone at that time – for the members were not to know that within a few years many of them would be lining the walls of their own homes with paper of a similar colour, it then having become smart.

Above this, on the first floor, where, in the former days of private wealth, an enormous ballroom had existed, an enormous dormitory now existed. This was curtained off into numerous cubicles. Here lived the very youngest members, girls between the ages of eighteen and twenty who had not long moved out of the cubicles of school dormitories throughout the English countryside, and who understood dormitory life from start to finish. The girls on this floor were not yet experienced in discussing men. Everything turned on whether the man in question was a good dancer and had a sense of humour. The Air Force was mostly favoured, and a DFC was an asset. A Battle of Britain record aged a man in the eyes of the first-floor dormitory, in the year 1945. Dunkirk, too, was largely something that their fathers had done. It was the air heroes of the Normandy landing who were popular, lounging among the cushions in the drawing-room. They gave full entertainment value:

'Do you know the story of the two cats that went to Wimbledon? – Well, one cat persuaded another to go to Wimbledon to watch the tennis. After a few sets one cat said to the other, "I must say, I'm bloody bored. I honestly can't see why you're so interested in this game of tennis." And the other cat replied, "Well, my father's in the racquet!"'

'No!' shrieked the girls, and duly doubled up.

'But that's not the end of the story. There was a colonel sitting behind these two cats. He was watching the tennis because the war was on and so there wasn't anything for him to do. Well, this colonel had his dog with him. So when the cats started talking to each other the dog turned to the colonel and said, "Do you hear those two cats in front of us?" "No, shut up," said the colonel, "I'm concentrating on the game." "All right," said the dog – very happy this dog, you know –

"I only thought you might be interested in a couple of cats that can talk."'

'Really,' said the voice of the dormitory later on, a twittering outburst, 'what a wizard sense of humour!' They were like birds waking up instead of girls going to bed, since 'Really, what a wizard sense of humour' would be the approximate collective euphony of the birds in the park five hours later, if anyone was listening.

On the floor above the dormitory were the rooms of the staff and the shared bedrooms of those who could afford shared bedrooms rather than a cubicle. Those who shared, four or two to a room, tended to be young women in transit, or temporary members looking for flats and bed-sitting rooms. Here, on the second floor, two of the elder spinsters, Collie and Jarvie, shared a room as they had done for eight years, since they were saving money now for their old age.

But on the floor above that, there seemed to have congregated, by instinctive consent, most of the celibates, the old maids of settled character and various ages, those who had decided on a spinster's life, and those who would one day do so but had not yet discerned the fact for themselves.

This third-floor landing had contained five large bedrooms, now partitioned by builders into ten small ones. The occupants ranged from prim and pretty young virgins who would never become fully-wakened women, to bossy ones in their late twenties who were too wide-awake ever to surrender to any man. Greggie, the third of the elder spinsters, had her room on this floor. She was the least prim and the kindest of the women there.

On this floor was the room of a mad girl, Pauline Fox, who was wont to dress carefully on certain evenings in the long dresses which were swiftly and temporarily reverted to in the years immediately following the war. She also wore long white gloves, and her hair was long, curling over her shoulders.

On these evenings she said she was going to dine with the famous actor, Jack Buchanan. No one disbelieved her outright, and her madness was undetected.

Here, too, was Joanna Childe's room from which she could be heard practising her elocution at times when the recreation room was occupied.

> All the flowers of the spring
> Meet to perfume our burying;

At the top of the house, on the fourth floor, the most attractive, sophisticated and lively girls had their rooms. They were filled with deeper and deeper social longings of various kinds, as peace-time crept over everyone. Five girls occupied the five top rooms. Three of them had lovers in addition to men-friends with whom they did not sleep but whom they cultivated with a view to marriage. Of the remaining two, one was almost engaged to be married, and the other was Jane Wright, fat but intellectually glamorous by virtue of the fact that she worked for a publisher. She was on the look-out for a husband, meanwhile being mixed up with young intellectuals.

Nothing but the roof-tops lay above this floor, now in-accessible by the trap-door in the bathroom ceiling – a mere useless square since it had been bricked up long ago before the war after a girl had been attacked by a burglar or a lover who had entered by it – attacked or merely confronted unex-pectedly, or found in bed with him as some said; as the case might be, he left behind him a legend of many screams in the night and the skylight had been henceforth closed to the public. Workmen who, from time to time, were called in to do something up above the house had to approach the roof from the attic of a neighbouring hotel. Greggie claimed to know all about the story, she knew everything about the club. Indeed it was Greggie who, inspired by a shaft of remembrance, had directed the warden to the hoard of mud-coloured wall-paper in the cupboard which now defiled the walls of the drawing-room and leered in the sunlight at everyone. The top-floor girls had often thought it might be a good idea to sunbathe on the flat portion of the roof and had climbed up on chairs to see about the opening of the trap-door. But it would not budge, and Greggie had once more told them why. Greggie produced a better version of the story every time.

'If there was a fire, we'd be stuck,' said Selina Redwood who was exceedingly beautiful.

'You've obviously been taking no notice of the emergency instructions,' Greggie said. This was true. Selina was seldom in to dinner and so she had never heard them. Four times a year the emergency instructions were read out by the warden after dinner, on which nights no guests were allowed. The top floor was served for emergency purposes by a back staircase leading down two flights to the perfectly sound fire-escape, and by the fire-equipment which lay around everywhere in the club. On these evenings of no guests the members were also reminded about putting things down lavatories, and the difficulties of plumbing systems in old houses, and of obtaining plumbers these days. They were reminded that they were expected to put everything back in place after a dance had been held in the club. Why some members unfortunately just went off to night clubs with their men-friends and left everything to others, said the warden, she simply did not know.

Selina had missed all this, never having been in to dinner on the warden's nights. From her window she could see, level with the top floor of the house, and set back behind the chimney pots, the portion of flat roof, shared by the club with the hotel next door, which would have been ideal for sunbathing. There was no access to any part of the roof from the bedroom windows, but one day she noticed that it was accessible from the lavatory window, a narrow slit made narrower by the fact that the wall in which it was set had been sub-divided at some point in the house's history when the wash-rooms had been put in. One had to climb upon the lavatory seat to see the roof. Selina measured the window. The aperture was seven inches wide by fourteen inches long. It opened casement-wise.

'I believe I could get through the lavatory window,' she said to Anne Baberton who occupied the room opposite hers.

'Why do you want to get through the lavatory window?' said Anne.

'It leads out to the roof. There's only a short jump from the window.'

Selina was extremely slim. The question of weight and measurement was very important on the top floor. The ability or otherwise to wriggle sideways through the lavatory window would be one of those tests that only went to prove the club's food policy to be unnecessarily fattening.

'Suicidal,' said Jane Wright who was miserable about her fatness and spent much of her time in eager dread of the next meal, and in making resolutions what to eat of it and what to leave, and in making counter-resolutions in view of the fact that her work at the publisher's was essentially mental, which meant that her brain had to be fed more than most people's.

Among the five top-floor members only Selina Redwood and Anne Baberton could manage to wriggle through the lavatory window, and Anne only managed it naked, having made her body slippery with margarine. After the first attempt, when she had twisted her ankle on the downward leap and grazed her skin on the return clamber, Anne said she would in future use her soap ration to facilitate the exit. Soap was as tightly rationed as margarine but more precious, for margarine was fattening, anyway. Face cream was too expensive to waste on the window venture.

Jane Wright could not see why Anne was so concerned about her one inch and a half on the hips more than Selina's, since Anne was already slender and already fixed up for marriage. She stood on the lavatory seat and threw out Anne's faded green dressing-gown for her to drape round her slippery body and asked what it was like out there. The two other girls on the floor were away for the week-end on this occasion.

Anne and Selina were peeping over the edge of the flat roof at a point where Jane could not see them. They returned to report that they had looked down on the back garden where Greggie was holding her conducted tour of the premises for the benefit of two new members. She had been showing them the spot where the bomb had fallen and failed to go off, and had been removed by a bomb-squad, during which operation everyone had been obliged to leave the house. Greggie had also been showing them the spot where, in her opinion, an unexploded bomb still lay.

The girls got themselves back into the house.

'Greggie and her sensations': Jane felt she could scream. She added, 'Cheese pie for supper tonight, guess how many calories?'

The answer, when they looked up the chart, was roughly 350 calories. 'Followed by stewed cherries,' said Jane, '94 calories normal helping unless sweetened by saccharine, in which case 64 calories. We've had over a thousand calories today already. It's always the same on Sundays. The bread-and-butter pudding alone was –'

'I didn't eat the bread-and-butter pudding,' said Anne. 'Bread-and-butter pudding is suicidal.'

'I only eat a little bit of everything,' Selina said. 'I feel starved all the time, actually.'

'Well, I'm doing brain-work,' said Jane.

Anne was walking about the landing sponging off all the margarine. She said, 'I've had to use up soap and margarine as well.'

'I can't lend you any soap this month,' Selina said. Selina had a regular supply of soap from an American Army officer who got it from a source of many desirable things, called the

PX. But she was accumulating a hoard of it, and had stopped lending.

Anne said, 'I don't want your bloody soap. Just don't ask for the taffeta, that's all.'

By this she meant a Schiaparelli taffeta evening dress which had been given to her by a fabulously rich aunt, after one wearing. This marvellous dress, which caused a stir wherever it went, was shared by all the top floor on special occasions, excluding Jane whom it did not fit. For lending it out Anne got various returns, such as free clothing coupons or a half-used piece of soap.

Jane went back to her brain-work and shut the door with a definite click. She was rather tyrannous about her brain-work, and made a fuss about other people's wirelesses on the landing, and about the petty-mindedness of these haggling bouts that took place with Anne when the taffeta dress was wanted to support the rising wave of long-dress parties.

'You can't wear it to the Milroy. It's been twice to the Milroy . . . it's been to Quaglino's, Selina wore it to Quags, it's getting known all over London.'

'But it looks altogether different on me, Anne. You can have a whole sheet of sweet-coupons.'

'I don't want your bloody sweet-coupons. I give all mine to my grandmother.'

Then Jane would put out her head. 'Stop being so petty-minded and stop screeching. I'm doing brain-work.'

Jane had one smart thing in her wardrobe, a black coat and skirt made out of her father's evening clothes. Very few dinner jackets in England remained in their original form after the war. But this looted outfit of Jane's was too large for anyone to borrow; she was thankful for that, at least. The exact nature of her brain-work was a mystery to the club because, when asked about it, she reeled off fast an explanation of extreme and alien detail about costing, printers, lists, manuscripts, galleys and contracts.

'Well, Jane, you ought to get paid for all that extra work you do.'

'The world of books is essentially disinterested,' Jane said. She always referred to the publishing business as 'The world of books'. She was always hard up, so presumably ill paid. It was because she had to be careful of her shillings for the meter which controlled the gas-fire in her room that she was unable, so she said, to go on a diet during the winter, since one had to keep warm as well as feed one's brain.

Jane received from the club, on account of her brain-work and job in publishing, a certain amount of respect which was socially offset by the arrival in the front hall, every week or so, of a pale, thin foreigner, decidedly in his thirties, with dandruff on his dark overcoat, who would ask in the office for Miss Jane Wright, always adding, 'I wish to see her privately, please.' Word also spread round from the office that many of Jane's incoming telephone calls were from this man.

'Is that the May of Teck Club?'

'Yes.'

'May I speak to Miss Wright privately, please?'

At one of these moments the secretary on duty said to him, 'All the members' calls are private. We don't listen in.'

'Good. I would know if you did, I wait for the click before I speak. Kindly remember.'

Jane had to apologize to the office for him. 'He's a foreigner. It's in connexion with the world of books. It isn't my fault.'

But another and more presentable man from the world of books had lately put in an appearance for Jane. She had brought him into the drawing-room and introduced him to Selina, Anne, and the mad girl Pauline Fox who dressed up for Jack Buchanan on her lunatic evenings.

This man, Nicholas Farringdon, had been rather charming, though shy. 'He's thoughtful,' Jane said. 'We think him brilliant but he's still feeling his way in the world of books.'

'Is he something in publishing?'

'Not at the moment. He's still feeling his way. He's writing something.'

Jane's brain-work was of three kinds. First, and secretly, she wrote poetry of a strictly non-rational order, in which occurred, in about the proportion of cherries in a cherry-cake, certain words that she described as 'of a smouldering nature', such as loins and lovers, the root, the rose, the seawrack and the shroud. Secondly, also secretly, she wrote letters of a friendly tone but with a business intention, under the auspices of the pale foreigner. Thirdly, and more openly, she sometimes did a little work in her room which overlapped from her day's duties at the small publisher's office.

She was the only assistant at Huy Throvis-Mew Ltd. Huy Throvis-Mew was the owner of the firm, and Mrs Huy Throvis-Mew was down as a director on the letter heading. Huy Throvis-Mew's private name was George Johnson, or at least it had been so for some years, although a few very old friends called him Con and older friends called him Arthur or Jimmie. However, he was George in Jane's time, and she would do anything for George, her white-bearded employer. She parcelled up the books, took them to the post or delivered them, answered the telephone, made tea, minded the baby when George's wife, Tilly, wanted to go and queue for fish, entered the takings into ledgers, entered two different versions of the petty cash and office expenses into two sets of books, and generally did a small publisher's business. After a year George allowed her to do some of the detective work on new authors, which he was convinced was essential to the publishing trade, and to find out their financial circumstances and psycho-logically weak points so that he could deal with them to a publisher's best advantage.

Like the habit of changing his name after a number of years, which he had done only in the hope that his luck would turn with it, this practice of George's was fairly innocent, in that he

never really succeeded in discovering the whole truth about an
author, or in profiting by his investigations at all. Still, it was his
system, and its plot-formation gave him a zest for each day's
work. Formerly George had done these basic investigations
himself, but lately he had begun to think he might have more
luck by leaving the new author to Jane. A consignment of
books, on their way to George, had recently been seized at the
port of Harwich and ordered to be burnt by the local magis-
trates on the grounds of obscenity, and George was feeling
unlucky at this particular time.

Besides, it saved him all the expense and nervous exhaustion
involved in the vigilant lunching with unpredictable writers,
and feeling his way with them as to whether their paranoia
exceeded his. It was better altogether to let them talk to
Jane in a café, or bed, or wherever she went with them.
It was nerve-racking enough to George to wait for her report.
He fancied that many times in the past year she had saved
him from paying out more ready money for a book than
necessary – as when she had reported a dire need for ready
cash, or when she had told George exactly what part of
the manuscript he should find fault with – it was usually the
part in which the author took a special pride – in order
to achieve the minimum resistance, if not the total collapse,
of the author.

George had obtained a succession of three young wives on
account of his continuous eloquence to them on the subject of
the world of books, which they felt was an elevating one – he
had deserted the other two, not they him – and he had not yet
been declared bankrupt although he had undergone in the
course of the years various tangled forms of business recon-
struction which were probably too much for the nerves of his
creditors to face legally, since none ever did.

George took a keen interest in Jane's training in the hand-
ling of a writer of books. Unlike his fireside eloquence to his
wife Tilly, his advice to Jane in the office was furtive, for he

half believed, in the twilight portion of his mind, that authors were sly enough to make themselves invisible and be always floating under the chairs of publishers' offices.

'You see, Jane,' said George, 'these tactics of mine are an essential part of the profession. All the publishers do it. The big firms do it too, they do it automatically. The big fellows can afford to do it automatically, they can't afford to acknowledge all the facts like me, too much face to lose. I've had to work out every move for myself and get everything clear in my mind where authors are concerned. In publishing, one is dealing with a temperamental raw material.'

He went over to the corner curtain which concealed a coat-rail, and pulled aside the curtain. He peered within, then closed the curtain again and continued, 'Always think of authors as your raw material, Jane, if you're going to stay in the world of books.' Jane took this for fact. She had now been given Nicholas Farringdon to work on. George had said he was a terrible risk. Jane judged his age to be just over thirty. He was known only as a poet of small talent and an anarchist of dubious loyalty to that cause; but even these details were not at first known to Jane. He had brought to George a worn-out-looking sheaf of typewritten pages, untidily stacked in a brown folder. The whole was entitled *The Sabbath Notebooks*.

Nicholas Farringdon differed in some noticeable respects from the other writers she had come across. He differed, unnoticeably so far, in that he knew he was being worked on. But meantime she observed he was more arrogant and more impatient than other authors of the intellectual class. She noticed he was more attractive.

She had achieved some success with the very intellectual author of *The Symbolism of Louisa May Alcott*, which George was now selling very well and fast in certain quarters, since it had a big lesbian theme. She had achieved some success with Rudi Bittesch, the Rumanian who called on her frequently at the club.

But Nicholas had produced a more upsetting effect than usual on George, who was moreover torn between his attraction to a book he could not understand and his fear of its failure. George handed him over to Jane for treatment and meanwhile complained nightly to Tilly that he was in the hands of a writer, lazy, irresponsible, insufferable and cunning.

Inspired by a brain-wave, Jane's first approach to a writer had been, 'What is your raison d'être?' It had worked marvellously. She tried it on Nicholas Farringdon when he called to the office about his manuscript one day when George was 'at a meeting', which was to say, hiding in the back office. 'What is your raison d'être, Mr Farringdon?'

He frowned at her in an abstract sort of way, as if she were a speaking machine that had gone wrong.

Inspired by another brain-wave Jane invited him to dine at the May of Teck Club. He accepted with a special modesty, plainly from concern for his book. It had been rejected by ten publishers already, as had most of the books that came to George.

His visit put Jane up in the estimation of the club. She had not expected him to react so eagerly to everything. Sipping black Nescafé in the drawing-room with Jane, Selina, dark little Judy Redwood and Anne, he had looked round with a faint, contented smile. Jane had chosen her companions for the evening with the instinct of an experimental procuress which, when she perceived the extent of its success, she partly regretted and partly congratulated herself on, since she had not been sure from various reports whether Nicholas preferred men, and now she concluded that he at least liked both sexes. Selina's long unsurpassable legs arranged themselves diagonally from the deep chair where she lolled in the distinct attitude of being the only woman present who could afford to loll. There was something about Selina's lolling which gave her a queenly eminence. She visibly appraised Nicholas, while he continued to glance here and there at the several groups of chattering girls in other parts of the room. The terrace doors stood wide open to the cool night and presently from the recreation room there came, by way of the terrace, the sound of Joanna in the process of an elocution lesson.

> I thought of Chatterton, the marvellous Boy,
> The sleepless Soul that perished in his pride;
> Of Him who walked in glory and in joy
> Following his plough, along the mountain-side;
> By our own spirits are we deified:
> We Poets in our youth begin in gladness;
> But thereof come in the end despondency and madness.

'I wish she would stick to *The Wreck of the Deutschland*,' Judy Redwood said. 'She's marvellous with Hopkins.'

Joanna's voice was saying, 'Remember the stress on Chatterton and the slight pause to follow.'

Joanna's pupil recited:

> I thought of Chatterton, the marvellous Boy...

*

The excitement over the slit window went on for the rest of the afternoon. Jane's brain-work proceeded against the background echoes of voices from the large wash-room where the lavatories were. The two other occupants of the top floor had returned, having been to their homes in the country for the week-end: Dorothy Markham, the impoverished niece of Lady Julia Markham who was chairwoman of the club's management committee, and Nancy Riddle, one of the club's many clergymen's daughters. Nancy was trying to overcome her Midlands accent, and took lessons in elocution from Joanna with this end in view.

Jane, at her brain-work, heard from the direction of the wash-room the success of Dorothy Markham's climb through the window. Dorothy's hips were thirty-six and a half inches; her bust measurement was only thirty-one, a fact which did not dismay her, as she intended to marry one of three young men out of her extensive acquaintance who happened to find themselves drawn to boyish figures, and although she did not know about such things as precisely as did her aunt, Dorothy knew well enough that her hipless and breastless shape would always attract the sort of young man who felt at home with it. Dorothy could emit, at any hour of the day or night, a waterfall of débutante chatter, which rightly gave the impression that on any occasion between talking, eating and sleeping, she did not think, except in terms of these phrase-ripples of hers: 'Filthy lunch.' 'The most gorgeous wedding.' 'He actually raped her, she was amazed.' 'Ghastly film.' 'I'm desperately well, thanks, how are you?'

Her voice from the wash-room distracted Jane: 'Oh hell, I'm black with soot, I'm absolutely filthington.' She opened Jane's door without knocking and put in her head. 'Got any soapyjo?' It was some months before she was to put her head round Jane's door and announce, 'Filthy luck. I'm preggers. Come to the wedding.'

Jane said, on being asked for the use of her soap, 'Can you lend me fifteen shillings till next Friday?' It was her final resort for getting rid of people when she was doing brain-work.

Evidently, from the sound of things, Nancy Riddle was stuck in the window. Nancy was getting hysterical. Finally, Nancy was released and calmed, as was betokened by the gradual replacement of Midlands vowels with standard English ones issuing from the wash-room.

Jane continued with her work, describing her effort to herself as pressing on regardless. All the club, infected by the Air Force idiom current amongst the dormitory virgins, used this phrase continually.

She had put aside Nicholas's manuscript for the time being, as it was a sticky proposition; she had not yet, in fact, grasped the theme of the book, as was necessary before deciding on a significant passage to cast doubt upon, although she had already thought of the comment she would recommend George to make: 'Don't you think this part is a bit derivative?' Jane had thought of it in a brain-wave.

She had put the book aside. She was at work, now, on some serious spare-time work for which she was paid. This came into the department of her life that had to do with Rudi Bittesch whom she hated, at this stage in her life, for his unattractive appearance. He was too old for her, besides everything else. When in a depressed state of mind, she found it useful to remember that she was only twenty-two, for the fact cheered her up. She looked down Rudi's list of famous authors and their respective addresses to see who still remained to be done. She took a sheet of writing paper and wrote her great-aunt's address in the country, followed by the date. She then wrote:

Dear Mr Hemingway,
    I am addressing this letter to you care of your publisher in the confidence that it will be sent on to you.

This was an advisable preliminary, Rudi said, because sometimes publishers were instructed to open authors' letters and throw them away if not of sufficient business importance, but this approach, if it got into the publishers' hands, 'might touch their heart'. The rest of the letter was entirely Jane's province. She paused to await a small brain-wave, and after a moment continued:

I am sure you receive many admiring letters, and have hesitated to add yet another to your post-bag. But since my release from prison, where I have been for the past two years and four months, I have felt more and more that I want you to know how much your novels

159

meant to me during that time. I had few visitors. My allotted weekly hours of leisure were spent in the Library. It was unheated alas, but I did not notice the cold as I read on. Nothing I read gave me so much courage to face the future and to build a new future on my release as *For Whom the Bell Tolls*. The novel gave me back my faith in life.

I just want you to know this, and to say 'Thank you'.

Yours sincerely

(Miss) J. Wright.

PS. This is not a begging letter. I assure you I would return any money that was sent to me.

If this succeeded in reaching him it might bring a hand-written reply. The prison letter and the asylum letter were more liable to bring replies in the author's own hand than any other type of letter, but one had to choose an author 'with heart', as Rudi said. Authors without heart seldom replied at all, and if they did it was a typewritten letter. For a typewritten letter signed by the author, Rudi paid two shillings if the autograph was scarce, but if the author's signature was available everywhere, and the letter a mere formal acknowledgement, Rudi paid nothing. For a letter in the author's own handwriting Rudi paid five shillings for the first page and a shilling thereafter. Jane's ingenuity was therefore awakened to the feat of composing the sort of letters which would best move the recipient to reply in total holograph.

Rudi paid for the writing paper and the postage. He told her he only wanted the letters 'for sentimental purpose of my collection'. She had seen his collection. But she assumed that he was collecting them with an eye to their increasing value year by year.

'If I write myself it does not ring true; I do not get interesting replies. By the way, my English is not like the English of an English girl.'

She would have made her own collection if only she had not needed the ready money, and could afford to save up the letters for the future.

'Never ask for money in your letters,' Rudi had warned her. 'Do not mention the subject of money. It makes criminal offence under false pretences.' However, she had the brain-wave of adding her postscript, to make sure.

Jane had worried, at first, lest she should be found out and get into some sort of trouble. Rudi reassured her. 'You say you only make a joke. It is not criminal. Who would check up on you, by the way? Do you think Bernard Shaw is going to write and make questions about you from the old aunt? Bernard Shaw is a Name.'

Bernard Shaw had in fact proved disappointing. He had sent a typewritten postcard:

Thank you for your letter in praise of my writings. As you say they have consoled you in your misfortunes, I shall not attempt to gild the lily by my personal comments. As you say you desire no money I shall not press upon you my holograph signature which has some cash value. G.B.S.

The initials, too, had been typed.

Jane learned by experience. Her illegitimate-child letter brought a sympathetic reply from Daphne du Maurier, for which Rudi paid his price. With some authors a scholarly question about the underlying meaning worked best. One day, on a brain-wave, she wrote to Henry James at the Athenaeum Club.

'That was foolish of you because James is dead, by the way,' Rudi said.

'Do you want a letter from an author called Nicholas Farringdon?' she said.

'No, I have known Nicholas Farringdon, he's no good, he is not likely to be a Name ever. What has he written?'

'A book called *The Sabbath Notebooks*.'

'Is it religious?'

'Well, he calls it political philosophy. It's just a lot of notes and thoughts.'

'It smells religious. He will finish up as a reactionary Catholic, to obey the Pope. Already I have predicted this before the war.'

'He's jolly good-looking.'

She hated Rudi. He was not at all attractive. She addressed and stamped her letter to Ernest Hemingway and ticked off his name on the list, writing the date beside it. The girls' voices had disappeared from the wash-room. Anne's wireless was singing:

> There were angels dining at the Ritz
> And a nightingale sang in Berkeley Square.

It was twenty minutes past six. There was time for one more letter before supper. Jane looked down the list.

Dear Mr Maugham,
  I am addressing this letter to you at your club . . .

Jane paused for thought. She ate a square of chocolate to keep her brain going till supper-time. The prison letter might not appeal to Maugham. Rudi had said he was cynical about human nature. On a brain-wave she recalled that he had been a doctor. It might be an idea to make up a sanatorium letter . . . She had been ill for two years and four months with tuberculosis. After all, this disease was not attributable to human nature, there was nothing in it to be cynical about. She regretted having eaten the chocolate, and put the rest of the bar right at the back of a shelf in her cupboard where it was difficult to reach, as if hiding it from a child. The rightness of this action and the wrongness of her having eaten any at all were confirmed by Selina's voice from Anne's room. Anne had turned off the wireless and they had been talking. Selina would probably be stretched out on Anne's bed in her languid manner. This became certain as Selina began to repeat, slowly and solemnly, the Two Sentences.

The Two Sentences were a simple morning and evening exercise prescribed by the Chief Instructress of the Poise Course which Selina had recently taken, by correspondence, in twelve lessons for five guineas. The Poise Course believed strongly in auto-suggestion and had advised, for the mainten-ance of poise in the working woman, a repetition of the following two sentences twice a day:

Poise is perfect balance, an equanimity of body and mind, complete composure whatever the social scene. Elegant dress, immaculate grooming, and perfect deportment all contribute to the attainment of self-confidence.

Even Dorothy Markham stopped her chatter for a few seconds every morning at eight-thirty and evening at six-thirty, in respect for Selina's Sentences. All the top floor was respectful. It had cost five guineas. The two floors below were indifferent. But the dormitories crept up on the landings to listen, they could hardly believe their ears, and saved up each word with savage joy to make their boy-friends in the Air Force laugh like a drain, which was how laughter was de-scribed in those circles. At the same time, the dormitory girls were envious of Selina, knowing in their hearts they would never quite be in the Selina class where looks were concerned.

The Sentences were finished by the time Jane had shoved her remaining piece of chocolate well out of sight and range. She returned to the letter. She had TB. She gave a frail cough and looked round the room. It contained a wash-basin, a bed, a chest-of-drawers, a cupboard, a table and lamp, a wicker chair, a hard chair, a bookcase, a gas-fire and a meter-box with a slot to measure the gas, shilling by shilling. Jane felt she might easily be in a room in a sanatorium.

'One last time,' said Joanna's voice from the floor below. She was now rehearsing Nancy Riddle, who was at this moment managing her standard English vowels very well.

'And again,' said Joanna. 'We've just got time before supper.
I'll read the first stanza, then you follow on.'

> At the top of the house the apples are laid in rows,
> And the skylight lets the moonlight in, and those
> Apples are deep-sea apples of green. There goes
> A cloud on the moon in the autumn night.

CHAPTER 4

IT WAS JULY 1945, three weeks before the general election.

> They are lying in rows there, under the gloomy beams;
> On the sagging floor; they gather the silver streams
> Out of the moon, those moonlit apples of dreams
> And quiet is the steep stair under.

'I wish she would stick to *The Wreck of the Deutschland*.'
'Do you? I rather like *Moonlit Apples*.'

We come now to Nicholas Farringdon in his thirty-third year. He was said to be an anarchist. No one at the May of Teck Club took this seriously as he looked quite normal; that is to say, he looked slightly dissipated, like the disappointing son of a good English family that he was. That each of his brothers — two accountants and one dentist – said of him from the time he left Cambridge in the mid 1930s, 'Nicholas is a bit of a misfit, I'm afraid,' would not have surprised anyone.

Jane Wright applied for information about him to Rudi Bittesch who had known Nicholas throughout the 1930s. 'You don't bother with him. He is a mess by the way,' Rudi said. 'I know him well, he is a good friend of mine.' From Rudi she gathered that before the war he had been always undecided whether to live in England or France, and whether he preferred men or women, since he alternated between passionate intervals with both. Also, he could never make up his mind between suicide and an equally drastic course of action known as Father D'Arcy. Rudi explained that the latter was a

Jesuit philosopher who had the monopoly for converting the English intellectuals. Nicholas was a pacifist up to the outbreak of war, Rudi said, then he joined the Army. Rudi said, 'I have met him one day in Piccadilly wearing his uniform, and he said to me the war has brought him peace. Next thing he is psycho-analysed out of the Army, a wangle, and he is working for the Intelligence. The anarchists have given him up but he calls himself an anarchist, by the way.'

Far from putting Jane against Nicholas Farringdon, the scraps of his history that came to her by way of Rudi gave him an irresistible heroism in her mind, and, through her, in the eyes of the top-floor girls.

'He must be a genius,' said Nancy Riddle.

Nicholas had a habit of saying 'When I'm famous . . .' when referring to the remote future, with the same cheerful irony that went into the preface of the bus conductor on the No. 73 route to his comments on the law of the land: 'When I come to power . . .'

Jane showed Rudi *The Sabbath Notebooks*, so entitled because Nicholas had used as an epigraph the text 'The Sabbath was made for Man, not Man for the Sabbath'.

'George must be out of his mind to publish this,' Rudi said when he brought it back to Jane. They sat in the recreation room at the other end of which, cornerwise by the open French window, a girl was practising scales on the piano with as much style as she could decently apply to the scales. The music-box tinkle was far enough away, and sufficiently dispersed by the Sunday morning sounds from the terrace, not to intrude too strongly on Rudi's voice, as he read out, in his foreign English, small passages from Nicholas's book in order to prove something to Jane. He did this as a cloth merchant, perhaps wishing to persuade a customer to buy his best quality of goods, might first produce samples of inferior stuff, feel it, invite comment, shrug, and toss it away. Jane was convinced that Rudi was right in his judgement of what he was reading, but she was really more fascinated by what small glimpses of Nicholas Farringdon's personality she got from Rudi's passing remarks. Nicholas was the only presentable intellectual she had met.

'It is not bad, not good,' said Rudi, putting his head this way, that way, as he said it. 'It is mediocrity. I recall he composed this in 1938 when he had a freckled bed-mate of the female sex; she was an anarchist and pacifist. Listen, by the way . . . ' He read out:

X is writing a history of anarchism. Anarchism properly has no history in the sense that X intends – i.e. in the sense of continuity and development. It is a spontaneous movement of people in par-ticular times and circumstances. A history of anarchism would not be in the nature of political history, it would be analogous to a history of the heart-beat. One may make new discoveries about it, one may compare its reactions under varying conditions, but there is nothing new of itself.

Jane was thinking of the freckled girl-friend whom Nicholas had slept with at the time, and she almost fancied they had taken *The Sabbath Notebooks* to bed together. 'What happened to his girl-friend?' Jane said. 'There is nothing wrong with this,' Rudi said, referring to what he had just read, 'but it is not so magnificent a great truth that he should like a great man place it on the page, by the way, in a paragraph alone. He makes *pensées* as he is too lazy to write the essay. Listen . . . '

Jane said, 'What happened to the girl?'

'She went to prison for pacifism maybe, I don't know. If I would be George I would not touch this book. Listen . . . '

Every communist has a fascist frown; every fascist has a communist smile.

'Ha!' said Rudi.

'I thought that was a very profound bit,' Jane said, as it was the only bit she could remember.

'That is why he writes it in, he counts that the bloody book has got to have a public, so he puts in some little bit of aphorism, very clever, that a girl like you likes to hear, by the way. It means nothing, this, where is the meaning?' Most of Rudi's last words were louder-sounding than he had intended, as the girl at the piano had paused for rest.

'There's no need to get excited,' said Jane loudly.

The girl at the piano started a new set of rippling tinkles.

'We move to the drawing-room,' said Rudi.

'No, everyone's in the drawing-room this morning,' Jane said. 'There's not a quiet corner in the drawing-room.' She did not particularly want to display Rudi to the rest of the club.

Up and down the scales went the girl at the piano. From a window above, Joanna, fitting in an elocution lesson with Miss Harper, the cook, in the half-hour before the Sunday joint was ready to go in the oven, said, 'Listen:'

> Ah! Sun-flower! weary of time,
> Who countest the steps of the Sun;
> Seeking after that sweet golden clime,
> Where the traveller's journey is done;

'Now try it,' said Joanna. 'Very slowly on the third line. Think of a sweet golden clime as you say it.'

> Ah! Sun-flower! ...

The dormitory girls who had spilled out of the drawing-room on to the terrace chattered like a parliament of fowls. The little notes of the scales followed one another obediently. 'Listen,' said Rudi:

Everyone should be persuaded to remember how far, and with what a pathetic thump, the world has fallen from grace, that it needs must appoint politicians for its keepers, that its emotions, whether of consolation at breakfast-time or fear in the evening . . .

Rudi said, 'You notice his words, that he says the world has fallen from grace? This is the reason that he is no anarchist, by the way. They chuck him out when he talks like a son of the Pope. This man is a mess that he calls himself an anarchist; the anarchists do not make all that talk of original sin, so forth; they permit only anti-social tendencies, unethical conduct, so forth. Nick Farringdon is a diversionist, by the way.'

'Do you call him Nick?' Jane said.

'Sometimes in the pubs, The Wheatsheaf and The Gargoyle, so on, he was Nick in those days. Except there was a barrow-boy called him Mr Farringdon. Nicholas said to him, "Look, I wasn't christened Mister," but was no good; the barrow-boy was his friend, by the way.'

'Once more,' said Joanna's voice.

Ah! Sun-flower! weary of time,

'Listen,' said Rudi:

Nevertheless, let our moment or opportunity be stated. We do not need a government. We do not need a House of Commons. Parliament should dissolve forever. We could manage very well in our movement towards a complete anarchist society, with our great but powerless institutions: we could manage with the monarchy as an example of the dignity inherent in the free giving and receiving of precedence and favour without power; the churches for the spiritual needs of the people; the House of Lords for purposes of debate and recommendation; and the universities for consultation. We do not need institutions with power. The practical affairs of society could be dealt with locally by the Town, Borough, and Village Councils. International affairs could be conducted by variable representatives in a non-professional capacity. We do not need professional politicians with an eye to power. The grocer, the doctor, the cook, should serve their country for a term as men serve on a jury. We can be ruled by the corporate will of men's hearts alone. It is Power that is defunct, not as we are taught, the powerless institutions.

'I ask you a question,' Rudi said. 'It is a simple question. He wants monarchy, he wants anarchism. What does he want? These two are enemies in all of history. Simple answer is, he is a mess.'

'How old was the barrow-boy?' Jane said.

'And again,' said Joanna's voice from the upper window.

Dorothy Markham had joined the girls on the sunny terrace. She was telling a hunting story. ' . . . the only one time I've been thrown, it shook me to the core. What a brute!'

'Where did you land?'

'Where do you think?'

The girl at the piano stopped and folded her scale-sheet with seemly concentration.

'I go,' said Rudi, looking at his watch. 'I have an appointment to meet a contact for a drink.' He rose and once more, before he handed over the book, flicked through the typewritten pages. He said, sadly, 'Nicholas is a friend of mine, but I regret to say he's a non-contributive thinker, by the way. Come here, listen to this:'

There is a kind of truth in the popular idea of an anarchist as a wild man with a home-made bomb in his pocket. In modern times this bomb, fabricated in the back workshops of the imagination, can only take one effective form: Ridicule.

Jane said, ' "Only take" isn't grammatical, it should be "take only". I'll have to change that, Rudi.'

*

So much for the portrait of the martyr as a young man as it was suggested to Jane on a Sunday morning between armistice and armistice, in the days of everyone's poverty, in 1945. Jane, who lived to distort it in many elaborate forms, at the time merely felt she was in touch with something reckless, intellectual, and Bohemian by being in touch with Nicholas. Rudi's contemptuous attitude bounded back upon himself in her estimation. She felt she knew too much about Rudi to respect him; and was presently astonished to find that there was indeed a sort of friendship between himself and Nicholas, lingering on from the past.

Meantime, Nicholas touched lightly on the imagination of the girls of slender means, and they on his. He had not yet slept on the roof with Selina on the hot summer nights – he gaining access from the American-occupied attic of the hotel next door, and she through the slit window – and he had not yet witnessed that action of savagery so extreme that it forced him involuntarily to make an entirely unaccustomed gesture, the signing of the cross upon himself. At this time Nicholas still worked for one of those left-hand departments of the Foreign Office, the doings of which the right-hand did not know. It came under Intelligence. After the Normandy landing he had been sent on several missions to France. Now there was very little left for his department to do except wind-up. Winding-up was arduous, it involved the shuffling of papers and people from office to office; particularly it involved considerable shuffling between the British and American Intelligence pockets in London. He had a bleak furnished room at Fulham. He was bored.

*

'I've got something to tell you, Rudi,' said Jane.
    'Hold on please, I have a customer.'

'I'll ring you back later, then, I'm in a hurry. I only wanted to tell you that Nicholas Farringdon's dead. Remember that book of his he never published – he gave you the manuscript. Well, it might be worth something now, and I thought –'

'Nick's dead? Hold on please, Jane. I have a customer waiting here to buy a book. Hold on.'

'I'll ring you later.'

*

Nicholas came, then, to dine at the club.

> I thought of Chatterton, the marvellous Boy,
> The sleepless Soul that perished in his Pride;

'Who is that?'

'It's Joanna Childe, she teaches elocution, you must meet her.'

The twittering movements at other points in the room, Joanna's singular voice, the beautiful aspects of poverty and charm amongst these girls in the brown-papered drawing-room, Selina, furled like a long soft sash, in her chair, came to Nicholas in a gratuitous flow. Months of boredom had subdued him to intoxication by an experience which, at another time, might itself have bored him.

Some days later he took Jane to a party to meet the people she longed to meet, young male poets in corduroy trousers and young female poets with waist-length hair, or at least females who typed the poetry and slept with the poets, it was nearly the same thing. Nicholas took her to supper at Bertorelli's; then he took her to a poetry reading at a hired meeting-house in the Fulham Road; then he took her on to a party with some of the people he had collected from the reading. One of the poets who was well thought of had acquired a job at Associated

News in Fleet Street, in honour of which he had purchased a pair of luxurious pigskin gloves; he displayed these proudly. There was an air of a resistance movement against the world at this poetry meeting. Poets seemed to understand each other with a secret instinct, almost a kind of pre-arrangement, and it was plain that the poet with the gloves would never show off these poetic gloves so frankly, or expect to be understood so well in relation to them, at his new job in Fleet Street or anywhere else, as here.

Some were men demobilized from the non-combatant corps. Some had been unfit for service for obvious reasons – a nervous twitch of the facial muscles, bad eyesight, or a limp. Others were still in battle dress. Nicholas had been out of the Army since the month after Dunkirk, from which he had escaped with a wound in the thumb; his release from the Army had followed a mild nervous disorder in the month after Dunkirk.

Nicholas stood noticeably aloof at the poets' gathering, but although he greeted his friends with a decided reserve, it was evident that he wanted Jane to savour her full joy of it. In fact, he wanted her to invite him again to the May of Teck Club, as dawned on her later in the evening.

The poets read their poems, two each, and were applauded. Some of these poets were to fail and fade into a no-man's-land of Soho public houses in a few years' time, and become the familiar messes of literary life. Some, with many talents, faltered, in time, from lack of stamina, gave up and took a job in advertising or publishing, detesting literary people above all. Others succeeded and became paradoxes; they did not always continue to write poetry, or even poetry exclusively.

One of these young poets, Ernest Claymore, later became a mystical stockbroker of the 1960s, spending his week-days urgently in the City, three week-ends each month at his country cottage – an establishment of fourteen rooms, where he ignored his wife and, alone in his study, wrote Thought – and

one week-end a month in retreat at a monastery. In the 1960s
Ernest Claymore read a book a week in bed before sleep, and
sometimes addressed a letter to the press about a book review:
'Sir, Maybe I'm dim. I have read your review of . . .'; he was to
publish three short books of philosophy which everyone could
easily understand indeed; at the moment in question, the
summer of 1945, he was a dark-eyed young poet at the poetry
recital, and had just finished reading, with husky force, his
second contribution:

> I in my troubled night of the dove clove brightly my
> Path from the tomb of love incessantly to redress my
> Articulate womb, that new and necessary rose, exposing my . . .

He belonged to the Cosmic school of poets. Jane, perceiving that he was orthosexual by definition of his manner and
appearance, was uncertain whether to cultivate him for future
acquaintance or whether to hang on to Nicholas. She managed
to do both, since Nicholas brought along this dark husky poet,
this stockbroker to be, to the party which followed, and there
Jane was able to make a future assignment with him before
Nicholas drew her aside to inquire further into the mysterious
life of the May of Teck Club.

'It's just a girls' hostel,' she said, 'that's all it boils down to.'

Beer was served in jam-jars, which was an affectation of the
highest order, since jam-jars were at that time in shorter supply
than glasses and mugs. The house where the party was held was
in Hampstead. There was a stifling crowd. The hosts, Nicholas
said, were communist intellectuals. He led her up to a bedroom where they sat on the edge of an unmade bed and
looked, with philosophical exhaustion on Nicholas's side,
and on hers the enthusiasm of the neophyte Bohemian, at
the bare boards of the floor. The people of the house, said
Nicholas, were undeniably communist intellectuals, as one
could see from the variety of dyspepsia remedies on the

bathroom shelf. He said he would point them out to her on the way downstairs when they rejoined the party. By no means, said Nicholas, did the hosts expect to meet their guests at this party. 'Tell me about Selina,' said Nicholas.

Jane's dark hair was piled on top of her head. She had a large face. The only attractive thing about her was her youth and those mental areas of inexperience she was not yet conscious of. She had forgotten for the time being that her job was to reduce Nicholas's literary morale as far as possible, and was treacherously behaving as if he were the genius that, before the week was out, he claimed to be in the letter he got her to forge for him in Charles Morgan's name. Nicholas had decided to do everything nice for Jane, except sleep with her, in the interests of two projects: the publication of his book and his infiltration of the May of Teck Club in general and Selina in particular. 'Tell me more about Selina.' Jane did not then, or at any time, realize that he had received from his first visit to the May of Teck Club a poetic image that teased his mind and pestered him for details as he now pestered Jane. She knew nothing of his boredom and social discontent. She did not see the May of Teck Club as a microcosmic ideal society; far from it. The beautiful heedless poverty of a Golden Age did not come into the shilling meter life which any sane girl would regard only as a temporary one until better opportunities occurred.

> A damsel with a dulcimer
> In a vision once I saw:
> It was an Abyssinian maid,

The voice had wafted with the night breeze into the drawing-room. Nicholas said, now, 'Tell me about the elocution teacher.'

'Oh, Joanna – you must meet her.'

'Tell me about the borrowing and lending of clothes.'

Jane pondered as to what she could barter for this information which he seemed to want. The party downstairs was going on without them. The bare boards under her feet and the patchy walls seemed to hold out no promise of becoming memorable by tomorrow. She said, 'We've got to discuss your book some time. George and I've got a list of queries.'

Nicholas lolled on the unmade bed and casually thought he would probably have to plan some defence measures with George. His jam-jar was empty. He said, 'Tell me more about Selina. What does she do apart from being secretary to a pansy?'

Jane was not sure how drunk she was, and could not bring herself to stand up, this being the test. She said, 'Come to lunch on Sunday.' Sunday lunch for a guest was two-and-sixpence extra; she felt she might be taken to more of these parties by Nicholas, among the inner circle of the poets of today; but she supposed he wanted to take Selina out, and that was that; she thought he would probably want to sleep with Selina, and as Selina had slept with two men already, Jane did not envisage any obstacle. It made her sad to think, as she did, that the whole rigmarole of his interest in the May of Teck Club, and the point of their sitting in this bleak room, was his desire to sleep with Selina. She said, 'What bits would you say were the most important?'

'What bits?'

'Your book,' she said. '*The Sabbath Notebooks*. George is looking for a genius. It must be you.'

'It's all important.' He formed the plan immediately of forging a letter from someone crudely famous to say it was a work of genius. Not that he believed it to be so one way or the other, the idea of such an unspecific attribute as genius not being one on which his mind was accustomed to waste its time. However, he knew a useful word when he saw it, and, perceiving the trend of Jane's question, made his plan. He said, 'Tell me again that delightful thing Selina repeats about poise.'

'Poise is perfect balance, an equanimity of body and mind, complete composure whatever the social scene. Elegant dress, immaculate . . . Oh, Christ,' she said, 'I'm tired of picking crumbs of meat out of the shepherd's pie, picking with a fork to get the little bits of meat separated from the little bits of potato. You don't know what it's like trying to eat enough to live on and at the same time avoid fats and carbohydrates.'

Nicholas kissed her tenderly. He felt there might be a sweetness in Jane, after all, for nothing reveals a secret sweetness so much as a personal point of misery bursting out of a phlegmatic creature.

Jane said, 'I've got to feed my brain.'

He said he would try to get her a pair of nylon stockings from the American with whom he worked. Her legs were bare and dark-haired. There and then he gave her six clothing coupons out of his coupon book. He said she could have his next week's egg. She said, 'You need your egg for your brain.'

'I have breakfast at the American canteen,' he said. 'We have eggs there, and orange juice.'

She said she would take his egg. The egg-ration was one a week at this time, it was the beginning of the hardest period of food-rationing, since the liberated countries had now to be supplied. Nicholas had a gas-ring in his bed-sitting room on which he cooked his supper when he was at home and remembered about supper. He said, 'You can have all my tea, I drink coffee. I get it from the Americans.'

She said she would be glad of his tea. The tea-ration was two ounces one week and three ounces the next, alternately. Tea was useful for bartering purposes. She felt she would really have to take the author's side, where Nicholas was concerned, and somehow hoodwink George. Nicholas was a true artist and had some feelings. George was only a publisher. She would have to put Nicholas wise to George's fault-finding technique of business.

'Let's go down,' Nicholas said.

The door opened and Rudi Bittesch stood watching them for a moment. Rudi was always sober.

'Rudi!' said Jane with unusual enthusiasm. She was glad to be seen to know somebody in this milieu who had not been introduced by Nicholas. It was a way of showing that she belonged to it.

'Well, well,' Rudi said. 'How are you doing these days, Nick, by the way?'

Nicholas said he was on loan to the Americans.

Rudi laughed like a cynical uncle and said, himself he too could have worked for the Americans if he had wanted to sell out.

'Sell out what?' Nicholas said.

'My integrity to work only for peace,' said Rudi. 'By the way, come and join the party and forget it.'

On the way down he said to Nicholas, 'You're publishing a book with Throvis–Mew? I hear this news by Jane.'

Jane said quickly, in case Rudi should reveal that he had already seen the book, 'It's a sort of anarchist book.'

Rudi said to Nicholas, 'You still like anarchism, by the way?'

'But not anarchists by and large, by the way,' Nicholas said.

    *

'How has he died, by the way?' said Rudi.

'He was martyred, they say,' said Jane.

'In Haiti? How is this?'

'I don't know much, except what I get from the news sources. Reuters says a local rising. Associated News has a bit that's just come in . . . I was thinking of that manuscript *The Sabbath Notebooks*.'

'I have it still. If he is famous by his death, I find it. How has he died . . . ?'

'I can't hear you, it's a rotten line . . .

'I say I can't hear, Rudi . . . '

'How has he died . . . By what means?'

'It will be worth a lot of money, Rudi.'

'I find it. This line is bad by the way, can you hear me? How has he died . . . ?'

' . . . a hut . . . '

'I can't hear . . . '

' . . . in a valley . . . '

'Speak loud.'

' . . . in a clump of palms . . . deserted . . . it was market day, everyone had gone to market.'

'I find it. There is maybe a market for this Sabbath book. They make a cult of him, by the way?'

'He was trying to interfere with their superstitions, they said. They're getting rid of a lot of Catholic priests.'

'I can't hear a word. I ring you tonight, Jane. We meet later.'

CHAPTER 5

SELINA CAME INTO the drawing-room wearing a high hoop-brimmed blue hat and shoes with high block wedges; these fashions from France, it was said, were symbols of the Resistance. It was late on Sunday morning. She had been for a seemly walk along the pathways of Kensington Gardens with Greggie.

Selina took off her hat and laid it on the sofa beside her. She said, 'I've got a guest for lunch, Felix.' Felix was Colonel G. Felix Dobell who was head of a branch of the American Intelligence Service which occupied the top floor of the hotel next door to the club. He had been among a number of men invited to one of the club's dances, and there had selected Selina for himself.

Jane said, 'I'm having Nicholas Farringdon for lunch.'

'But he was here during the week.'

'Well, he's coming again. I went to a party with him.'

'Good,' said Selina. 'I like him.'

Jane said, 'Nicholas works with the American Intelligence. He probably knows your Colonel.'

It was found that the men had not met. They shared a table for four with the two girls, who waited on them, fetching the food from the hatch. Sunday lunch was the best meal of the week. Whenever one of the girls rose to fetch and carry, Felix Dobell half-rose in his chair, then sat down again, for courtesy. Nicholas lolled like an Englishman possessed of *droits de seigneur* while the two girls served him.

The warden, a tall grey-skinned woman habitually dressed in grey, made a brief announcement that 'the Conservative

MP was coming to give a pre-election discussion' on the following Tuesday.

Nicholas smiled widely so that his long dark face became even more good-looking. He seemed to like the idea of *giving* a discussion, and said so to the Colonel who amiably agreed with him. The Colonel seemed to be in love with the entire club, Selina being the centre and practical focus of his feelings in this respect. This was a common effect of the May of Teck Club on its male visitors, and Nicholas was enamoured of the entity in only one exceptional way, that it stirred his poetic sense to a point of exasperation, for at the same time he discerned with irony the process of his own thoughts, how he was imposing upon this society an image incomprehensible to itself.

The grey warden's conversational voice could be heard addressing grey-haired Greggie who sat with her at table, 'You see, Greggie, I can't be everywhere in the club at once.'

Jane said to her companions, 'That's the one fact that makes life bearable for us.'

'That is a very original idea,' said the American Colonel, but he was referring to something that Nicholas had said before Jane had spoken, when they were discussing the political outlook of the May of Teck Club. Nicholas had offered: 'They should be told not to vote at all, I mean persuaded not to vote at all. We could do without the government. We could manage with the monarchy, the House of Lords, the . . . '

Jane looked bored, as she had several times read this bit in the manuscript, and she rather wanted to discuss personalities, which always provided her with more real pleasure than any impersonal talk, however light and fantastic, although she did not yet admit this fact in her aspiring brain. It was not till Jane had reached the apex of her career as a reporter and interviewer for the largest of women's journals that she found her right role in life, while still incorrectly subscribing to a belief that she was capable of thought – indeed, was demonstrating a capacity for it. But now she sat at table with Nicholas and longed for him to stop talking to the Colonel about the happy possibilities inherent in the delivery of political speeches to the May of Teck girls, and the different ways in which they might be corrupted. Jane felt guilty about her boredom. Selina laughed with poise when Nicholas said, next, 'We could do without a central government. It's bad for us, and what's worse, it's bad for the politicians . . .' but that he was as serious about this as it was possible for his self-mocking mind to be about anything, seemed to be apparent to the Colonel, who amazingly assured Nicholas, 'My wife Gareth also is a member of the Guild of Ethical Guardians in our town. She's a hard worker.'

Nicholas, reminding himself that poise was perfect balance, accepted this statement as a rational response. 'Who are the Ethical Guardians?' said Nicholas.

'They stand for the ideal of purity in the home. They keep a special guard on reading material. Many homes in our town will not accept literature unstamped by the Guardians' crest of honour.'

Nicholas now saw that the Colonel had understood him to hold ideals, and had connected them with the ideals of his wife Gareth, these being the only other ideals he could immediately lay hands on. It was the only explanation. Jane wanted to put everything straight. She said, 'Nicholas is an anarchist.'

'Ah no, Jane,' said the Colonel. 'That's being a bit hard on your author-friend.'

Selina had already begun to realize that Nicholas held unorthodox views about things to the point where they might be regarded as crackpot by the sort of people she was used to. She felt his unusualness was a weakness, and this weakness in an attractive man held desirability for her. There were two other men of her acquaintance who were vulnerable in some way. She was not perversely interested in this fact, so far as she felt no urge to hurt them; if she did so, it was by accident. What she liked about these men was that neither of them wished to possess her entirely. She slept with them happily because of this. She had another man-friend, a businessman of thirty-five, still in the Army, very wealthy, not weak. He was altogether possessive; Selina thought she might marry him eventually. In the meantime she looked at Nicholas as he conversed in this mad sequence with the Colonel, and thought she could use him.

They sat in the drawing-room and planned the afternoon which had developed into a prospective outing for four in the Colonel's car. By this time he had demanded to be called Felix.

He was about thirty-two. He was one of Selina's weak men. His weakness was an overwhelming fear of his wife, so that he took great pains not to be taken unawares in bed with Selina on their country week-ends, even although his wife was in California. As he locked the door of the bedroom Felix would say, very worried, 'I wouldn't like to hurt Gareth,' or some such thing. The first time he did this Selina looked through the bathroom door, tall and beautiful with wide eyes, she looked at Felix to see what was the matter with him. He was still anxious and tried the door again. On the late Sunday mornings, when the bed was already uncomfortable with breakfast crumbs, he would sometimes fall into a muse and be far away. He might then say, 'I hope there's no way Gareth could come by knowledge of this hideout.' And so he was one of those who did not want to possess Selina entirely; and being beautiful and liable to provoke possessiveness, she found this all right provided the man was attractive to sleep with and be out with, and was a good dancer. Felix was blond with an appearance of reserved nobility which he must have inherited. He seldom said anything very humorous, but was willing to be gay. On this Sunday afternoon in the May of Teck Club he proposed to drive to Richmond, which was a long way by car from Knightsbridge in those days when petrol was so scarce that nobody went driving for pleasure except in an American's car, in the vague mistaken notion that their vehicles were supplied by 'American' oil, and so were not subject to the conscience of

British austerity or the reproachful question about the necessity of the journey displayed at all places of public transport.

Jane, observing Selina's long glance of perfect balance and equanimity resting upon Nicholas, immediately foresaw that she would be disposed in the front seat with Felix while Selina stepped, with her arch-footed poise, into the back, where Nicholas would join her; and she foresaw that this arrangement would come about with effortless elegance. She had no objection to Felix, but she could not hope to win him for herself, having nothing to offer a man like Felix. She felt she had a certain something, though small, to offer Nicholas, this being her literary and brain-work side which Selina lacked. It was in fact a misunderstanding of Nicholas – she vaguely thought of him as a more attractive Rudi Bittesch – to imagine he would receive more pleasure and reassurance from a literary girl than simply a girl. It was the girl in Jane that had moved him to kiss her at the party; she might have gone further with Nicholas without her literary leanings. This was a mistake she continued to make in her relations with men, inferring from her own preference for men of books and literature their preference for women of the same business. And it never really occurred to her that literary men, if they like women at all, do not want literary women but girls.

But Jane was presently proved right in her prediction about the seating arrangements in the car; and it was her repeated accuracy of intuition in such particulars as these which gave her confidence in her later career as a prophetic gossip-columnist.

Meantime the brown-lined drawing-room began to chirp into life as the girls came in from the dining-room bearing trays of coffee cups. The three spinsters, Greggie, Collie, and Jarvie, were introduced to the guests, as was their accustomed right. They sat in hard chairs and poured coffee for the young loungers. Collie and Jarvie were known to be in the process of a religious quarrel, but they made an effort to conceal their differences for the occasion. Jarvie, however, was agitated by the fact that her coffee cup had been filled too full by Collie. She laid the cup and swimming saucer on a table a little way behind her, and ignored it significantly. She was dressed to go out, with gloves, bag, and hat. She was presently going to take her Sunday-school class. The gloves were made of a stout green-brown suède. Jarvie smoothed them out on her lap, then fluttered her fingers over the cuffs, turning them back. They revealed the utility stamp, two half-moons facing the same way, which was the mark of price-controlled clothes and which, on dresses, where the mark was merely stamped on a tape sewn on the inside, everyone removed. Jarvie surveyed her gloves' irremovable utility mark with her head at a slight angle, as if considering some question connected with it. She then smoothed out the gloves again and jerkily adjusted her spectacles. Jane felt in a great panic to get married. Nicholas, on hearing that Jarvie was about to go to teach a Sunday-school class, was solicitous to inquire about it.

'I think we had better drop the subject of religion,' Jarvie said, as if in conclusion of an argument long in progress. Collie said, 'I thought we *had* dropped it. What a lovely day for Richmond!'

Selina slouched elegantly in her chair, untouched by the threat of becoming a spinster, as she would never be that sort of spinster, anyway. Jane recalled the beginning of the religious quarrel overheard on all floors, since it had taken place in the echoing wash-room on the second landing. Collie had at first accused Jarvie of failing to clean the sink after using it to wash up her dishes of stuff, which she surreptitiously cooked on her gas-ring where only kettles were lawfully permitted. Then, ashamed of her outburst, Collie had more loudly accused Jarvie of putting spiritual obstacles in her path 'just when you know I'm growing in grace'. Jarvie had then said something scornful about the Baptists as opposed to the true spirit of the Gospels. This religious row, with elaborations, had now lasted more than two weeks but the women were doing their best to conceal it.

Collie now said to Jarvie, 'Are you going to waste your coffee with the milk in it?' This was a moral rebuke, for milk was on the ration. Jarvie turned, smoothed, patted and pulled straight the gloves on her lap and breathed in and out. Jane wanted to tear off her clothes and run naked into the street, screaming. Collie looked with disapproval at Jane's bare fat knees.

Greggie, who had very little patience with the two other elder members, had been winning her way with Felix, and had enquired what went on 'up there, next door', meaning in the hotel, the top floor of which the American Intelligence was using, the lower floors being strangely empty and forgotten by the requisitioners.

'Ah, you'd be surprised, ma'am,' Felix said.

Greggie said she must show the men round the garden before they set off for Richmond. The fact that Greggie did practically all the gardening detracted from its comfort for the rest of the girls. Only the youngest and happiest girls could feel justified in using it to sit about in, as it was so much Greggie's toiled-at garden. Only the youngest and happiest could walk on the grass with comfort; they were not greatly given to scruples and consideration for others, by virtue of their unblighted spirits.

Nicholas had noticed a handsome bright-cheeked fair-haired girl standing, drinking down her coffee fairly quickly. She left the room with graceful speed when she had drunk her coffee.

Jane said, 'That's Joanna Childe who does elocution.'

Later, in the garden, while Greggie was conducting her tour, they heard Joanna's voice. Greggie was displaying her various particular items, rare plants reared from stolen cuttings, these being the only objects that Greggie would ever think of stealing. She boasted, like a true gardening woman, of her thefts and methods of acquiring snips of other people's rare plants. The sound of Joanna's afternoon pupil lilted down from her room.

Nicholas said, 'The voice is coming from up there, now. Last time, it came from the ground floor.'

'She uses her own room at week-ends when the recreation room is used a lot. We're very proud of Joanna.'

Joanna's voice followed her pupil's.

Greggie said, 'This hollow shouldn't be there. It's where the bomb dropped. It just missed the house.'

'Were you in the house at the time?' said Felix.

'I was,' said Greggie, 'I was in bed. Next moment I was on the floor. All the windows were broken. And it's my suspicion there was a second bomb that didn't go off. I'm almost sure I saw it drop as I picked myself up off the floor. But the disposal squad found only the one bomb and removed it. Anyway, if there's a second it must have died a natural death by now. I'm talking about the year 1942.'

Felix said, with his curious irrelevancy, 'My wife Gareth talks of coming over here with UNRRA. I wonder if she could put up at your club in transit for a week or two? I have to be back and forth, myself. She would be lonely in London.'

'It would have been lying underneath the hydrangeas on the right if I was correct,' Greggie said.

> The sea of faith
> Was once, too, at the full, and round earth's shore
> Lay like the folds of a bright girdle furled.
> But now I only hear
> Its melancholy, long, withdrawing roar,
> Retreating, to the breath
> Of the night-wind, down the vast edges drear
> And naked shingles of the world.

'We'd better be on our way to Richmond,' Felix said.

'We're awfully proud of Joanna,' said Greggie.

'A fine reader.'

'No, she recites from memory. But her pupils read, of course. It's elocution.'

Selina gracefully knocked some garden mud off her wedge shoes on the stone step, and the party moved inside.

The girls went to get ready. The men disappeared in the dark little downstairs cloakroom.

'That is a fine poem,' said Felix, for Joanna's voices were here, too, and the lesson had moved to *Kubla Khan*.

Nicholas almost said, 'She is orgiastical in her feeling for poetry. I can hear it in her voice,' but refrained in case the Colonel should say 'Really?' and he should go on to say, 'Poetry takes the place of sex for her, I think.'

'Really? She looked sexually fine to me.'

Which conversation did not take place, and Nicholas kept it for his notebooks.

They waited in the hall till the girls came down. Nicholas read the notice-board, advertising second-hand clothes for sale, or in exchange for clothing coupons. Felix stood back, a refrainer from such intrusions on the girls' private business, but tolerant of the other man's curiosity. He said, 'Here they come.'

The number and variety of muted noises-off were considerable. Laughter went on behind the folded doors of the first-floor dormitory. Someone was shovelling coal in the cellar, having left open the green baize door which led to those quarters. The telephone desk within the office rang distantly shrill with boy-friends, and various corresponding buzzes on the landings summoned the girls to talk. The sun broke through as the forecast had promised.

> Weave a circle round him thrice,
> And close your eyes with holy dread,
> For he on honey-dew hath fed,
> And drunk the milk of Paradise.

CHAPTER 6

'DEAR DYLAN THOMAS,' wrote Jane.

Downstairs, Nancy Riddle, who had finished her elocution lesson, was attempting to discuss with Joanna Childe the common eventualities arising from being a clergyman's daughter.

'My father's always in a filthy temper on Sundays. Is yours?'

'No, he's rather too occupied.'

'Father goes on about the Prayer Book. I must say, I agree with him there. It's out of date.'

'Oh, I think the Prayer Book's wonderful,' said Joanna. She had the Book of Common Prayer practically by heart, including the Psalms – especially the Psalms – which her father repeated daily at Matins and Evensong in the frequently empty church. In former years at the rectory Joanna had attended these services every day, and had made the responses from her pew, as it might be on 'Day 13', when her father would stand in his lofty meekness, robed in white over black, to read:

Let God arise, and let his enemies be scattered:

whereupon without waiting for pause Joanna would respond:

let them also that hate him flee before him.

The father continued:

Like as the smoke vanisheth, so shalt thou drive them away:

And Joanna came in swiftly:

> and like as wax melteth at the fire, so let the ungodly perish at the presence of God.

And so on had circled the Psalms, from Day 1 to Day 31 of the months, morning and evening, in peace and war; and often the first curate, and then the second curate, took over the office, uttering as it seemed to the empty pews, but by faith to the congregations of the angels, the Englishly rendered intentions of the sweet singer of Israel.

Joanna lit the gas-ring in her room in the May of Teck Club and put on the kettle. She said to Nancy Riddle:

'The Prayer Book is wonderful. There was a new version got up in 1928, but Parliament put it out. Just as well, as it happened.'

'What's the Prayer Book got to do with them?'

'It's within their jurisdiction funnily enough.'

'I believe in divorce,' Nancy said.

'What's that got to do with the Prayer Book?'

'Well, it's all connected with the C. of E. and all the arguing.'

Joanna mixed some powdered milk carefully with water from the tap and poured the mixture upon two cups of tea. She passed a cup to Nancy and offered saccharine tablets from a small tin box. Nancy took one tablet, dropped it in her tea, and stirred it. She had recently got involved with a married man who talked of leaving his wife.

Joanna said, 'My father had to buy a new cloak to wear over his cassock at funerals, he always catches cold at funerals. That means no spare coupons for me this year.'

Nancy said, 'Does he wear a cloak? He must be High. My father wears an overcoat; he's Low to Middle, of course.'

*

All through the first three weeks of July Nicholas wooed Selina and at the same time cultivated Jane and others of the May of Teck Club.

The sounds and sights impinging on him from the hall of the club intensified themselves, whenever he called, into one sensation, as if with a will of their own. He thought of the lines:

> Let us roll all our strength, and all
> Our sweetness up into one ball;

And I would like, he thought, to teach Joanna that poem or rather demonstrate it; and he made spasmodic notes of all this on the back pages of his *Sabbath* manuscript.

Jane told him everything that went on in the club. 'Tell me more,' he said. She told him things, in her clever way of intuition, which fitted his ideal of the place. In fact, it was not an unjust notion, that it was a miniature expression of a free society, that it was a community held together by the graceful attributes of a common poverty. He observed that at no point did poverty arrest the vitality of its members but rather nourished it. Poverty differs vastly from want, he thought.

*

'Hallo, Pauline?'

'Yes?'

'It's Jane.'

'Yes?'

'I've got something to tell you. What's the matter?'

'I was resting.'

'Sleeping?'

'No, resting. I've just got back from the psychiatrist, he makes me rest after every session. I've got to lie down.'

'I thought you were finished with the psychiatrist. Are you not very well again?'

'This is a new one. Mummy found him, he's marvellous.'

'Well, I just wanted to tell you something, can you listen? Do you remember Nicholas Farringdon?'

'No, I don't think so. Who's he?'

'Nicholas . . . remember that last time on the roof at the May of Teck . . . Haiti, in a hut . . . among some palms, it was market day, everyone had gone to the market centre. Are you listening?'

*

We are in the summer of 1945 when he was not only enamoured of the May of Teck Club as an aesthetic and ethical conception of it, lovely frozen image that it was, but he presently slept with Selina on the roof.

> The mountains look on Marathon
>   And Marathon looks on the sea;
> And musing there an hour alone,
>   I dream'd that Greece might still be free;
> For standing on the Persians' grave,
> I could not deem myself a slave.

Joanna needs to know more life, thought Nicholas, as he loitered in the hall on one specific evening, but if she knew life she would not be proclaiming these words so sexually and matriarchally as if in the ecstatic act of suckling a divine child.

> At the top of the house the apples are laid in rows.

She continued to recite as he loitered in the hall. No one was about. Everyone was gathered somewhere else, in the drawing-room or in the bedrooms, sitting round wireless sets, tuning in to some special programme. Then one wireless, and another, roared forth louder by far than usual from the upper floors; others tuned in to the chorus, justified in the din by the voice of Winston Churchill. Joanna ceased. The wirelesses spoke forth their simultaneous Sinaitic predictions of what fate would befall the freedom-loving electorate should it vote for Labour in the forthcoming elections. The wirelesses suddenly started to reason humbly:

We shall have Civil Servants...

The wirelesses changed their tones, they roared:

No longer civil...

Then they were sad and slow:

No longer...
    ...servants.

Nicholas imagined Joanna standing by her bed, put out of business as it were, but listening, drawing it into her blood-stream. As in a dream of his own that depicted a dream of hers, he thought of Joanna in this immovable attitude, given up to the cadences of the wireless as if it did not matter what was producing them, the politician or herself. She was a proclaiming statue in his mind.

A girl in a long evening dress slid in the doorway, furtively. Her hair fell round her shoulders in a brown curl. Through the bemused mind of the loitering, listening man went the fact of a girl slipping furtively into the hall; she had a meaning, even if she had no meaningful intention.

She was Pauline Fox. She was returning from a taxi-ride round the park at the price of eight shillings. She had got into the taxi and told the driver to drive round, round anywhere, just drive. On such occasions the taxi-drivers suspected at first that she was driving out to pick up a man, then as the taxi circled the park and threepences ticked up on the meter, the drivers suspected she was mad, or even, perhaps, one of those foreign royalties still exiled in London: and they concluded one or the other when she ordered them back to the door to which she had summoned them by carefully pre-arranged booking. It was dinner with Jack Buchanan which Pauline held as an immovable idea to be established as fact at the May of Teck Club. In the day-time she worked in an office and was normal. It was dinner with Jack Buchanan that prevented her from dining with any other man, and caused her to wait in the hall for half an hour after the other members had gone to the dining-room, and to return surreptitiously half an hour later when nobody, or few, were about.

At times, when Pauline had been seen returning within so short a time, she behaved quite convincingly.

'Goodness, back already, Pauline! I thought you'd gone out to dinner with –'

'Oh! Don't talk to me. We've had a row.' Pauline, with one hand holding a handkerchief to her eye, and the other lifting the hem of her dress, would run sobbing up the stairs to her room.

'She must have had a row with Jack Buchanan again. Funny she never brings Jack Buchanan here.'

'Do you believe it?'

'What?'

'That she goes out with Jack Buchanan?'

'Well, I've wondered.'

Pauline looked furtive, and Nicholas cheerfully said to her, 'Where have *you* been?'

She came and gazed into his face and said, 'I've been to dinner with Jack Buchanan.'

'You've missed Churchill's speech.'

'I know.'

'Did Jack Buchanan get rid of you the moment you had finished your dinner?'

'Yes. He did. We had a row.'

She shook back her shining hair. For this evening, she had managed to borrow the Schiaparelli dress. It was made of taffeta, with small side panniers stuck out with cleverly curved pads over the hips. It was coloured dark blue, green, orange and white in a floral pattern as from the Pacific Islands.

He said, 'I don't think I've ever seen such a gorgeous dress.'

'Schiaparelli,' she said.

He said, 'Is it the one you swap amongst yourselves?'

'Who told you that?'

'You look beautiful,' he replied.

She picked up the rustling skirt and floated away up the staircase.

Oh, girls of slender means!

The election speech having come to an end, everybody's wireless was turned off for a space, as if in reverence to what had just passed through the air.

He approached the office door which stood open. The office was still empty. The warden came up behind him, having deserted her post for the duration of the speech.

'I'm still waiting for Miss Redwood.'

'I'll ring her again. No doubt she's been listening to the speech.'

Selina came down presently. Poise is perfect balance, an equanimity of body and mind. Down the staircase she floated, as it were even more realistically than had the sad communer with the spirit of Jack Buchanan a few moments ago floated up it. It might have been the same girl, floating upwards in a Schiaparelli rustle of silk with a shining hood of hair, and floating downwards in a slim skirt with a white-spotted blue blouse, her hair now piled high. The normal

noises of the house began to throb again. 'Good-evening,' said
Nicholas.

> And all my days are trances,
>   And all my nightly dreams
> Are where thy dark eye glances,
>   And where thy footstep gleams –
> In what ethereal dances,
>   By what eternal streams!

'Now repeat,' said Joanna's voice.

'Come on then,' said Selina, stepping ahead of him into
the evening light like a racer into the paddock, with a high
disregard of all surrounding noises.

CHAPTER 7

'HAVE YOU GOT a shilling for the meter?' said Jane.

'Poise is perfect balance, an equanimity of body and mind, complete composure whatever the social scene. Elegant dress, immaculate grooming, and perfect deportment all contribute to the attainment of self-confidence.'

'Have you got a shilling for two sixpences?'

'No. Anne's got a key that opens the meters, though.'

'Anne, are you in? What about a loan of the key?'

'If we all start using it too often we'll be found out.'

'Only this once. I've got brain-work to do.'

Now sleeps the crimson petal, now the white . . .

*

Selina sat, not yet dressed, on the edge of Nicholas's bed. She had a way of glancing sideways beneath her lashes that gave her command of a situation which might otherwise place her in a weakness.

She said, 'How can you bear to live here?'

He said, 'It does till one finds a flat.'

In fact he was quite content with his austere bed-sitting room. With the reckless ambition of a visionary, he pushed his passion for Selina into a desire that she, too, should accept and exploit the outlines of poverty in her life. He loved her as he loved his native country. He wanted Selina to be an ideal society personified amongst her bones, he wanted her beautiful limbs to obey her mind and heart like intelligent men and women, and for these to possess the same grace and beauty as her body. Whereas Selina's desires were comparatively humble, she only wanted, at that particular moment, a packet of hair-grips which had just then disappeared from the shops for a few weeks.

It was not the first instance of a man taking a girl to bed with the aim of converting her soul, but he, in great exasperation, felt that it was, and poignantly, in bed, willed and willed the awakening of her social conscience. After which, he sighed softly into his pillow with a limp sense of achievement, and presently rose to find, with more exasperation than ever, that he had not in the least conveyed his vision of perfection to the girl. She sat on the bed and glanced around beneath her lashes. He was experienced in girls sitting on his bed, but not in girls as cool as Selina about their beauty, and such beauty as hers. It was incredible to him that she should not share with him an understanding of the lovely attributes of dispossession and poverty, her body was so austere and economically furnished.

She said, 'I don't know how you can live in this place, it's like a cell. Do you cook on that thing?' She meant the gas grill.

He said, while it dawned upon him that his love affair with Selina remained a love affair on his side only, 'Yes, of course. Would you like some bacon and egg?'

'Yes,' she said, and started to dress.

He took hope again, and brought out his rations. She was accustomed to men who got food from the black market.

'After the twenty-second of this month,' said Nicholas, 'we are to get two and a half ounces of tea – two ounces one week and three ounces the next.'

'How much do we get now?'

'Two ounces every week. Two ounces of butter; margarine, four ounces.'

She was amused. She laughed for a long time. She said, 'You sound so funny.'

'Christ, so I do!' he said.

'Have you used all your clothing coupons?'

'No, I've got thirty-four left.'

He turned the bacon in the pan. Then, on a sudden thought, he said, 'Would you like some clothing coupons?'

'Oh yes, please.'

He gave her twenty, ate some bacon with her, and took her home in a taxi.

He said, 'I've arranged about the roof.'

She said, 'Well, see and arrange about the weather.'

'We can go to the pictures if it's raining,' he said.

*

He had arranged to have access to the roof through the top floor of the hotel next door, occupied as it was by American Intelligence, which organization he served in another part of London. Colonel Dobell, who, up to ten days ago, would have opposed this move, now energetically supported it. The reason for this was that his wife Gareth was preparing to join him in London and he was anxious to situate Selina in another context, as he put it.

In the north of California, up a long drive, Mrs G. Felix Dobell had not only resided, but held meetings of the Guardians of Ethics. Now she was coming to London, for she said that a sixth sense told her Felix was in need of her presence there.

Now sleeps the crimson petal, now the white . . .

Nicholas greatly desired to make love to Selina on the roof, it needs must be on the roof. He arranged everything as precisely as a practised incendiary.

The flat roof of the club, accessible only by the slit window on the top floor, was joined to a similar flat roof of the neighbouring hotel by a small gutter. The hotel had been requisitioned and its rooms converted into offices for the use of the American Intelligence. Like many other requisitioned premises in London, it had been overcrowded with personnel during the war in Europe, and now was practically un-occupied. Only the top floor of this hotel, where uniformed men worked mysteriously day and night, and the ground floor, which was guarded day and night by two American servicemen, and served by night- and day-porters who worked the lift, were in use. Nobody could enter this house without a pass. Nicholas obtained a pass quite easily, and he also by means of a few words and a glance obtained the ambivalent permission of Colonel Dobell, whose wife was already on her journey, to move into a large attic office which was being used as a typing pool. Nicholas was given a courtesy desk there. This attic had a hatch door leading to the flat roof.

*

The weeks had passed, and since in the May of Teck Club they were weeks of youth in the ethos of war, they were capable of accommodating quick happenings and reversals, rapid forma-tions of intimate friendships, and a range of lost and discovered loves that in later life and in peace would take years to happen, grow, and fade. The May of Teck girls were nothing if not economical. Nicholas, who was past his youth, was shocked at heart by their week-by-week emotions.

'I thought you said she was in love with the boy.'

'So she was.'

'Well, wasn't it only last week he died? You said he died of dysentery in Burma.'

'Yes I know. But she met this naval type on Monday, she's madly in love with him.'

'She can't be in love with him,' said Nicholas.

'Well, they've got a lot in common she says.'

'A lot in common? It's only Wednesday now.'

> Like one, that on a lonesome road
> Doth walk in fear and dread,
> And having once turned round, walks on,
> And turns no more his head;
> Because he knows a frightful fiend
> Doth close behind him tread.

'Joanna's marvellous at that one, I love it.'
'Poor Joanna.'
'Why do you say poor Joanna?'
'Well, she never gets any fun, no men-friends.'
'She's terribly attractive.'
'Frightfully attractive. Why doesn't someone do something about Joanna?'

*

Jane said, 'Look here, Nicholas, there's something you ought to know about Huy Throvis-Mew as a firm and George himself as a publisher.'

They were sitting in the offices of Throvis-Mew, high above Red Lion Square; but George was out.

'He's a crook,' said Nicholas.

'Well, that would be putting it a bit strongly,' she said.

'He's a crook with subtleties.'

'It's not quite that, either. It's a psychological thing about George. He's got to get the better of an author.'

'I know that,' Nicholas said. 'I had a long emotional letter from him making a lot of complaints about my book.'

'He wants to break down your confidence, you see, and then present you with a rotten contract to sign. He finds out the author's weak spot. He always attacks the bit the author likes best. He –'

'I know that,' said Nicholas.

'I'm only telling you because I like you,' Jane said. 'In fact, it's part of my job to find out the author's weak spot, and report to George. But I like you, and I'm telling you all this because –'

'You and George,' said Nicholas, 'draw me a tiny bit closer to understanding the Sphinx's inscrutable smile. And I'll tell you another fact.'

Beyond the grimy window rain fell from a darkening sky on the bomb-sites of Red Lion Square. Jane had looked out in an abstract pose before making her revelation to Nicholas. She now actually noticed the scene, it made her eyes feel miserable and her whole life appeared steeped in equivalent misery. She was disappointed in life, once more.

'I'll tell you another fact,' said Nicholas. 'I'm a crook too. What are you crying for?'

'I'm crying for myself,' said Jane. 'I'm going to look for another job.'

'Will you write a letter for me?'

'What sort of a letter?'

'A crook-letter. From Charles Morgan to myself. Dear Mr Farringdon, When first I received your manuscript I was tempted to place it aside for my secretary to return to you with some polite excuse. But as happy chance would have it, before passing your work to my secretary, I flicked over the pages and my eyes lit on . . . '

'Lit on what?' said Jane.

'I'll leave that to you. Only choose one of the most concise and brilliant passages when you come to write the letter. That will be difficult, I admit, since all are equally brilliant. But choose the piece you like best. Charles Morgan is to say he read that one piece, and then the whole, avidly, from start to finish. He is to say it's a work of genius. He congratulates me on a work of genius, you realize. Then I show the letter to George.'

Jane's life began to sprout once more, green with possibility. She recalled that she was only twenty-three, and smiled.

'Then I show the letter to George,' Nicholas said, 'and I tell him he can keep his contract and –'

George arrived. He looked busily at them both. Simultaneously, he took off his hat, looked at his watch, and said to Jane, 'What's the news?'

Nicholas said, 'Ribbentrop is captured.'

George sighed.

'No news,' said Jane. 'Nobody's rung at all. No letters, nobody's been, nobody's rung us up. Don't worry.'

George went into his inner office. He came out again immediately.

'Did you get my letter?' he said to Nicholas.

'No,' said Nicholas, 'which letter?'

'I wrote, let me see, the day before yesterday, I think. I wrote –'

'Oh, that letter,' said Nicholas. 'Yes, I believe I did receive a letter.'

George went away into his inner office.

Nicholas said to Jane, in a good, loud voice, that he was going for a stroll in the park now that the rain had stopped, and that it was lovely having nothing to do but dream beautiful dreams all the day long.

'Yours very sincerely and admiringly, Charles Morgan,' wrote Jane. She opened the door of her room and shouted, 'Turn down the wireless a bit, I've got to do some brain-work before supper.'

On the whole, they were proud of Jane's brain-work and her connexion with the world of books. They turned down all the wirelesses on the landing.

She read over the first draft of the letter, then very carefully began again, making an authentic-looking letter in a small but mature hand such as Charles Morgan might use. She had no idea what Charles Morgan's handwriting looked like; and had no reason to find out, since George would certainly not know either, and was not to be allowed to retain the document. She had an address at Holland Park which Nicholas had supplied. She wrote this at the top of her writing paper, hoping that it looked all right, and assuring herself that it did since many nice people did not attempt to have their letter-heads printed in war-time and thus make unnecessary demands on the nation's labour.

She had finished by the time the supper-bell rang. She folded the letter with meticulous neatness, having before her eyes the pencil-line features of Charles Morgan's photograph. Jane calculated that this letter by Charles Morgan which she had just written was worth at least fifty pounds to Nicholas. George would be in a terrible state of conflict when he saw it. Poor Tilly, George's wife, had told her that when George was persecuted by an author, he went on and on about it for hours.

Nicholas was coming to the club after supper to spend the evening, having at last persuaded Joanna to give a special recital of *The Wreck of the Deutschland*. It was to be recorded on a tape-machine that Nicholas had borrowed from the news-room of a Government office.

Jane joined the throng in its descent to supper. Only Selina loitered above, finishing off her evening's disciplinary recitation:

. . . Elegant dress, immaculate grooming, and perfect deportment all contribute to the attainment of self-confidence.

The warden's car stopped piercingly outside as the girls reached the lower floor. The warden drove a car as she would have driven a man had she possessed one. She strode, grey, into her office and shortly afterwards joined them in the dining-room, banging on the water-jug with her fork for silence, as she always did when about to make an announcement. She announced that an American visitor, Mrs G. Felix Dobell, would address the club on Friday evening on the subject, 'Western Woman: her Mission'. Mrs Dobell was a leading member of the Guardians of Ethics and had recently come to join her husband who was serving with the United States Intelligence Service stationed in London.

After supper Jane was struck by a sense of her treachery to the establishment of Throvis-Mew, and to George with whom she was paid to conspire in the way of business. She was fond of old George, and began to reflect on his kindly qualities. Without the slightest intention of withdrawing from her conspiracy with Nicholas, she gazed at the letter she had written and wondered what to do about her feelings. She decided to telephone to his wife, Tilly, and have a friendly chat about something.

Tilly was delighted. She was a tiny redhead of lively intelligence and small information, whom George kept well apart from the world of books, being experienced in wives. To Tilly, this was a great deprivation, and she loved nothing better than to keep in touch, through Jane, with the book business and to hear Jane say, 'Well, Tilly, it's a question of one's raison d'être.' George tolerated this friendship, feeling that it established himself with Jane. He relied on Jane. She understood his ways.

Jane was usually bored by Tilly, who, although she had not exactly been a cabaret dancer, imposed on the world of books, whenever she was given the chance, a high leg-kicker's spirit which played on Jane's nerves, since she herself was newly awed by the gravity of literature in general. She felt Tilly was altogether too frivolous about the publishing and writing scene, and moreover failed to realize this fact. But her heart in its treachery now swelled with an access of warmth for Tilly. She telephoned and invited her to supper on Friday. Jane had already calculated that, if Tilly should be a complete bore, they would be able to fill in an hour with Mrs G. Felix Dobell's

lecture. The club was fairly eager to see Mrs Dobell, having
already seen a certain amount of her husband as Selina's escort,
rumoured to be her lover. 'There's a talk on Friday by an
American woman on the Western Woman's Mission, but we
won't listen to that, it would be a bore,' Jane said, contradict-
ing her resolution in her effusive anxiety to sacrifice anything,
anything to George's wife, now that she had betrayed and was
about to deceive George.

Tilly said, 'I always love the May of Teck. It's like being
back at school.' Tilly always said that, it was infuriating.

*

Nicholas arrived early with his tape-recorder, and sat in the
recreation room with Joanna, waiting for the audience to drift
in from supper. She looked to Nicholas very splendid and
Nordic, as from a great saga.

'Have you lived here long?' said Nicholas sleepily, while he
admired her big bones. He was sleepy because he had spent
most of the previous night on the roof with Selina.

'About a year. I daresay I'll die here,' she said with the
conventional contempt of all members for the club.

He said, 'You'll get married.'

'No, no.' She spoke soothingly, as to a child who had just
been prevented from spooning jam into the stew.

A long shriek of corporate laughter came from the floor
immediately above them. They looked at the ceiling and
realized that the dormitory girls were as usual exchanging
those RAF anecdotes which needed an audience hilariously
drunken, either with alcohol or extreme youth, to give
them point.

Greggie had appeared, and cast her eyes up to the laughter as
she came towards Joanna and Nicholas. She said, 'The sooner
that dormitory crowd gets married and gets out of the club, the
better. I've never known such a rowdy dormitory crowd in all

my years in the club. Not a farthing's worth of intelligence between them.'

Collie arrived and sat down next to Nicholas. Greggie said, 'I was saying about the dormitory girls up there: they ought to get married and get out.'

This was also, in reality, Collie's view. But she always opposed Greggie on principle and, moreover, in company she felt that a contradiction made conversation. 'Why should they get married? Let them enjoy themselves while they're young.'

'They need marriage to enjoy themselves properly,' Nicholas said, 'for sexual reasons.'

Joanna blushed. Nicholas added, 'Heaps of sex. Every night for a month, then every other night for two months, then three times a week for a year. After that, once a week.' He was adjusting the tape-recorder, and his words were like air.

'If you're trying to shock us, young man, we're unshock-able,' said Greggie, with a delighted glance round the four walls which were not accustomed to this type of talk, for, after all, it was the public recreation room.

'I'm shockable,' said Joanna. She was studying Nicholas with an apologetic look.

Collie did not know what attitude she should take up. Her fingers opened the clasp of her bag and snapped it shut again; then they played a silent tiptap on its worn bulging leather sides. Then she said, 'He isn't trying to shock us. He's very realistic. If one is growing in grace – I would go so far as to say when one *has* grown in grace – one can take realism, sex and so forth in one's stride.'

Nicholas beamed lovingly at this.

Collie gave a little half-cough, half-laugh, much encour-aged in the success of her frankness. She felt modern, and continued excitedly, 'It's a question of what you never have you never miss, of course.'

Greggie put on a puzzled air, as if she genuinely did not know what Collie was talking about. After thirty years' hostile fellowship with Collie, of course she did quite well understand that Collie had a habit of skipping several stages in the logical sequence of her thoughts, and would utter apparently disconnected statements, especially when confused by an unfamiliar subject or the presence of a man.

'Whatever do you mean?' said Greggie. '*What* is a question of what you never have you never miss?'

'Sex, of course,' Collie said, her voice unusually loud with the effort of the topic. 'We were discussing sex and getting married. I say, of course, there's a lot to be said for marriage, but if you never have it you never miss it.'

Joanna looked at the two excited women with meek compassion. To Nicholas she looked stronger than ever in her meekness, as she regarded Greggie and Collie at their rivalry to be uninhibited.

'What do you mean, Collie?' Greggie said. 'You're quite wrong there, Collie. One does miss sex. The body has a life of its own. We do miss what we haven't had, you and I. Biologically. Ask Sigmund Freud. It is revealed in dreams. The absent touch of the warm limbs at night, the absent –'

'Just a minute,' said Nicholas, holding up his hand for silence, in the pretence that he was tuning-in to his empty tape-machine. He could see that the two women would go to any lengths, now they had got started.

'Open the door, please.' From behind the door came the warden's voice and the rattle of the coffee tray. Before Nicholas could leap up to open it for her she had pushed into the room with some clever manoeuvring of hand and foot like a business-like parlourmaid.

'The Beatific Vision does not appear to *me* to be an adequate compensation for what we miss,' Greggie said conclusively, getting in a private thrust at Collie's religiosity.

While coffee was being served and the girls began to fill the room, Jane entered, fresh from her telephone conversation with Tilly, and, feeling somewhat absolved by it, she handed over to Nicholas her brain-work letter from Charles Morgan. While reading it, he was handed a cup of coffee. In the process of taking the cup he splashed some coffee on the letter.

'Oh, you've ruined it!' Jane said. 'I'll have to do it all over again.'

'It looks more authentic than ever,' Nicholas said. 'Naturally, if I've received a letter from Charles Morgan telling me I'm a genius, I am going to spend a lot of time reading it over and over, in the course of which the letter must begin to look a bit worn. Now, are you sure George will be impressed by Morgan's name?'

'Very,' said Jane.

'Do you mean you're very sure or that George will be very impressed?'

'I mean both.'

'It would put me off, if I were George.'

The recital of *The Wreck of the Deutschland* started presently. Joanna stood with her book ready.

'Not a hush from anybody,' said the warden, meaning, 'Not a sound.' – 'Not a hush,' she said, 'because this instrument of Mr Farringdon's apparently registers the drop of a pin.'

One of the dormitory girls, who sat mending a ladder in a stocking, carefully caused her needle to fall on the parquet floor, then bent and picked it up again. Another dormitory girl who had noticed the action snorted a suppressed laugh. Otherwise there was silence but for the quiet purr of the machine waiting for Joanna.

> Thou mastering me
> God! giver of breath and bread;
> World's strand, sway of the sea;
> Lord of living and dead;
> Thou hast bound bones and veins in me, fastened me flesh,
> And after it almost unmade . . .

CHAPTER 8

A SCREAM OF panic from the top floor penetrated the house as Jane returned to the club on Friday afternoon, the 27th of July. She had left the office early to meet Tilly at the club. She did not feel that the scream of panic meant anything special. Jane climbed the last flight of stairs. There was another more piercing scream, accompanied by excited voices. Screams of panic in the club might relate to a laddered stocking or a side-splitting joke.

When she reached the top landing, she saw that the commotion came from the wash-room. There, Anne and Selina, with two of the dormitory girls, were attempting to extricate from the little slit window another girl who had evidently been attempting to climb out and had got stuck. She was struggling and kicking without success, exhorted by various instructions from the other girls. Against their earnest advice, she screamed aloud from time to time. She had taken off her clothes for the attempt and her body was covered with a greasy substance; Jane immediately hoped it had not been taken from her own supply of cold cream which stood in a jar on her dressing-table.

'Who is it?' Jane said, with a close inspective look at the girl's unidentifiable kicking legs and wriggling bottom which were her only visible portions.

Selina brought a towel which she attempted to fasten round the girl's waist with a safety-pin. Anne kept imploring the girl not to scream, and one of the others went to the top of the stairs to look over the banister in the hope that nobody in authority was being unduly attracted upward.

'Who is it?' Jane said.

Anne said, 'I'm afraid it's Tilly.'

'Tilly!'

'She was waiting downstairs and we brought her up here for a lark. She said it was like being back at school, here at the club, so Selina showed her the window. She's just half an inch too large, though. Can't you get her to shut up?'

Jane spoke softly to Tilly. 'Every time you scream,' she said, 'it makes you swell up more. Keep quiet, and we'll work you out with wet soap.'

Tilly went quiet. They worked on her for ten minutes, but she remained stuck by the hips. Tilly was weeping. 'Get George,' she said at last, 'get him on the phone.'

Nobody wanted to fetch George. He would have to come upstairs. Doctors were the only males who climbed the stairs, and even then they were accompanied by one of the staff.

Jane said, 'Well, I'll get somebody.' She was thinking of Nicholas. He had access to the roof from the Intelligence Headquarters; a hefty push from the roof-side of the window might be successful in releasing Tilly. Nicholas had intended to come to the club after supper to hear the lecture and observe, in a jealous complex of curiosity, the wife of Selina's former lover. Felix himself was to be present.

Jane decided to telephone and beg Nicholas to come immediately and help with Tilly. He could then have supper at the club, his second supper, Jane reflected, that week. He might now be home from work, he usually returned to his room at about six o'clock.

'What's the time?' said Jane.

Tilly was weeping, with a sound that threatened a further outburst of screams.

'Just on six,' said Anne.

Selina looked at her watch to see if this was so, then walked towards her room.

'Don't leave her, I'm getting help,' Jane said. Selina opened the door of her room, but Anne stood gripping Tilly's ankles. As Jane reached the next landing she heard Selina's voice.

'Poise is perfect balance, an equanimity . . . '

Jane laughed foolishly to herself and descended to the telephone boxes as the clock in the hall struck six o'clock.

*

It struck six o'clock on that evening of July 27th. Nicholas had just returned to his room. When he heard of Tilly's predicament he promised eagerly to go straight to the Intelligence Headquarters, and on to the roof.

'It's no joke,' Jane said.

'I'm not saying it's a joke.'

'You sound cheerful about it. Hurry up. Tilly's crying her eyes out.'

'As well she might, seeing Labour have got in.'

'Oh, hurry up. We'll all be in trouble if –'

He had rung off.

At that hour Greggie came in from the garden to hang about the hall, awaiting the arrival of Mrs Dobell who was to speak after supper. Greggie would take her into the warden's sitting-room, there to drink dry sherry till the supper-bell went. Greggie hoped also to induce Mrs Dobell to be escorted round the garden before supper.

A distant anguished scream descended the staircase.

'Really,' Greggie said to Jane, who was emerging from the telephone box, 'this club has gone right down. What are visitors to think? Who's screaming up there on the top floor? It sounds exactly as it must have been when this house was in private hands. You girls behave exactly like servant girls in the old days when the master and mistress were absent. Romping and yelling.'

> Make me thy lyre, even as the forest is:
> What if my leaves are falling like its own!
> The tumult of thy mighty harmonies

'George, I want George,' Tilly wailed thinly from far above. Then someone on the top floor thoughtfully turned on the wireless to all-drowning pitch:

> There were angels dining at the Ritz
> And a nightingale sang in Berkeley Square.

And Tilly could be heard no more. Greggie looked out of the open front door and returned. She looked at her watch. 'Six-fifteen,' she said. 'She should be here at six-fifteen. Tell them to turn down the wireless up there. It looks so vulgar, so bad . . .'

'You mean it sounds so vulgar, so bad.' Jane was keeping an eye out for the taxi which she hoped would bring Nicholas, at any moment, to the functional hotel next door.

'Once again,' said Joanna's voice clearly from the third floor to her pupil. 'The last three stanzas again, please.'

> Drive my dead thoughts over the universe
> Like withered leaves to quicken a new birth!

Jane was suddenly overcome by a deep envy of Joanna, the source of which she could not locate exactly at that hour of her youth. The feeling was connected with an inner knowledge of Joanna's disinterestedness, her ability, a gift, to forget herself and her personality. Jane felt suddenly miserable, as one who has been cast out of Eden before realizing that it had in fact been Eden. She recalled two ideas about Joanna that she had gathered from various observations made by Nicholas: that Joanna's enthusiasm for poetry was limited to one kind, and that Joanna was the slightest bit melancholy on the religious side; these thoughts failed to comfort Jane.

Nicholas arrived in a taxi and disappeared in the hotel entrance. As Jane started to run upstairs another taxi drew up. Greggie said, 'Here's Mrs Dobell. It's twenty-two minutes past six.'

Jane bumped into several of the girls who were spilling in lively groups out of the dormitories. She thrust her way through their midst, anxious to reach Tilly and tell her that help was near.

'Jane-*ee!*' said a girl. 'Don't be so bloody rude, you nearly pushed me over the banister to my death.'

But Jane was thumping upward.

Now sleeps the crimson petal, now the white . . .

Jane arrived at the top floor to find Anne and Selina frantic-ally clothing Tilly's lower half to make her look decent. They had got as far as the stockings. Anne was holding a leg while Selina, long-fingered, smoothed the stocking over it.

'Nicholas has come. Is he out on the roof yet?'

Tilly moaned, 'Oh, I'm dying. I can't stand it any more. Fetch *George*, I want George.'

'Here's Nicholas,' said Selina, tall enough to see him emerging from the low doorway of the hotel attic, as he had lately done on the calm summer nights. He stumbled over a rug which had been bundled beside the door. It was one of the rugs they had brought out to lie on. He recovered his balance, started walking quickly over towards them, then fell flat on his face. A clock struck the half-hour. Jane heard herself say in a loud voice, 'It's half past six.' Suddenly, Tilly was sitting on the bathroom floor beside her. Anne, too, was on the floor crumpled with her arm over her eyes as if trying to hide her presence. Selina lay stunned against the door. She opened her mouth to scream, and probably did scream, but it was then that the rumbling began to assert itself from the garden below, mounting swiftly to a mighty crash. The house trembled again, and the girls who had tried to sit up were thrown flat. The floor was covered with bits of glass, and Jane's blood flowed from somewhere in a trickle, while some sort of time passed silently by. Sensations of voices, shouts, mounting footsteps and falling plaster brought the girls back to various degrees of responsiveness. Jane saw, in an unfocused way, the giant face of Nicholas peering through the open slit of the little window. He was exhorting them to get up quick.

'There's been an explosion in the garden.'

'Greggie's bomb,' Jane said, grinning at Tilly. 'Greggie was right,' she said. This was a hilarious statement, but Tilly did not laugh, she closed her eyes and lay back. Tilly was only half-dressed and looked very funny indeed. Jane then laughed loudly at Nicholas, but he too had no sense of humour.

*

Down in the street the main body of the club had congregated, having been in one of the public rooms on the ground floor at the time of the explosion, or else lingering in the dormitories. There, the explosion had been heard more than it was felt. Two ambulances had arrived and a third was approaching. Some of the more dazed among the people were being treated for shock in the hall of the neighbouring hotel.

Greggie was attempting to assure Mrs Felix Dobell that she had foreseen and forewarned the occurrence. Mrs Dobell, a handsome matron of noticeable height, stood out on the edge of the pavement, taking little notice of Greggie. She was looking at the building with a surveyor's eye, and was possessed of that calm which arises from a misunderstanding of the occasion's true nature, for although she was shaken by the explosion, Mrs Dobell assumed that belated bombs went off every day in Britain, and, content to find herself intact, and slightly pleased to have shared a war experience, was now curious as to what routine would be adopted in the emergency. She said, 'When do you calculate the dust will settle?'

Greggie said, yet once more, 'I knew that live bomb was in that garden. I knew it. I was always saying that bomb was there. The bomb-disposal squad missed it, they missed it.'

Some faces appeared at an upper bedroom. The window opened. A girl started to shout, but had to withdraw her head; she was choking with the dust that was still surrounding the house in clouds.

It was difficult to discern the smoke, when it began to show, amongst the dust. A gas-main had, in fact, been ruptured by the explosion and a fire started to crawl along the basement from the furnaces. It started to crawl and then it flared. A roomful of flame suddenly roared in the ground-floor offices, lapping against the large window-panes, feeling for the woodwork, while Greggie continued to shrill at Mrs Dobell above the clamour of the girls, the street-crowd, the ambulances, and the fire-engines. 'It was ten chances to one we might have been in the garden when the bomb went off. I was going to take you round the garden before supper. We would have been buried, dead, killed. It was ten to one, Mrs Dobell.'

Mrs Dobell said, as one newly enlightened, 'This is a terrible incident.' And being more shaken than she appeared to be, she added, 'This is a time that calls for the exercise of discretion, the woman's prerogative.' This saying was part of the lecture she had intended to give after supper. She looked round in the crowd for her husband. The warden, whose more acute shock-effects had preceded Mrs Dobell's by a week, was being carried off through the crowd on a stretcher.

'Felix!' yelled Mrs Dobell. He was coming out of the hotel adjoining the club, with his olive-greenish khaki uniform dusky with soot and streaked as with black oil. He had been investigating the back premises of the club. He said:

'The brick-work of the walls looks unsteady. The top half of the fire-escape has collapsed. There are some girls trapped up there. The firemen are directing them up to the top floor; they'll have to be brought through the skylight on to the roof.'

*

'Who?' said Lady Julia.

'Jane Wright speaking. I rang you last week to see if you could find out some more about –'

'Oh yes. Well, I'm afraid there's very little information from the FO. They never comment officially, you know. From what I can gather, the man was making a complete nuisance of himself, preaching against the local superstitions. He had several warnings and apparently he got what he asked for. How did you come to know him?'

'He was friendly with some of the girls at the May of Teck Club when he was a civilian, I mean before he joined this Order. He was there on the night of the tragedy, in fact, and –'

'It probably turned his brain. Something must have affected his brain, anyhow, because from what I gather unofficially he was a complete . . . '

*

The skylight, although it had been bricked up by someone's hysterical order, at that time in the past when a man had penetrated the attic-floor of the club to visit a girl, was not beyond being unbricked by the firemen. It was all a question of time.

Time was not a large or present fact to those girls of the May of Teck Club, thirteen of them, who, with Tilly Throvis-Mew, remained in the upper storeys of the building when, following the explosion in the garden, fire broke out in the house. A large portion of the perfectly safe fire-escape which had featured in so many safety-instruction regulations, so many times read out to the members at so many supper-times, now lay in zigzag fragments among the earthy mounds and upturned roots of the garden.

Time, which was an immediate onward-rushing enemy to the onlookers in the street and the firemen on the roof, was only a small far-forgotten event to the girls; for they were stunned not only by the force of the explosion, but, when they recovered and looked round, still more by the sudden dislocation of all familiar appearances. A chunk of the back wall of the house gaped to the sky. There, in 1945, they were as far removed from the small fact of time as weightless occupants of a space-rocket. Jane got up, ran to her room, and with animal instinct snatched and gobbled a block of chocolate which remained on her table. The sweet stuff assisted her recovery. She turned to the wash-rooms where Tilly, Anne, and Selina were slowly rising to their feet. There were shouts from the direction of the roof. An unrecognized face looked in the slit window, and a large hand wrenched the loose frame away from it.

But the fire had already started to spread up the main staircase, preceded by heraldic puffs of smoke, the flames sidling up the banisters.

The girls who had been in their rooms on the second and third floors at the time of the explosion had been less shaken than those at the top of the house, since there some serious defect in the masonry had been caused indirectly by a bombardment early in the war. The girls on the second and third floors were cut and bruised, but were stunned by the sound of the blast rather than the house-shaking effects of it.

Some of the second-floor dormitory girls had been quick and alert enough to slip down the staircase and out into the street, in the interval between the explosion of the bomb and the start of the fire. The remaining ten, when they variously attempted to escape by that route, met the fire and retreated upward.

Joanna and Nancy Riddle, having finished their elocution lessons, had been standing at the door of Joanna's room when the bomb went off, and so had escaped the glass from the window. Joanna's hand was cut, however, by the glass from a tiny travelling clock which she had been winding at the time. It was Joanna who, when the members shrieked at the sight of the fire, gave the last shriek, then shouted: 'The fire-escape!' Pauline Fox fled behind her, and the others followed along the second-floor corridors and up the narrow back staircase to the third-floor passage-way where the fire-escape window had always stood. This was now a platform open to the summer evening sky, for here the wall had fallen away and the fire-escape with it. Plaster tumbled from the bricks as the ten women crowded to the spot that had once been the fire-escape landing. They were still looking in a bewildered way for the fire-escape stairway. Voices of firemen shouted at them from the garden. Voices came from the direction of the flat roof above, and then one voice clearly through a megaphone ordered them back, lest the piece of floor they stood on should collapse.

The voice said, 'Proceed to the top floor.'

'Jack will wonder what's happened to me,' said Pauline Fox. She was first up the back stairs to the wash-rooms where Anne, Selina, Jane, and Tilly were now on their feet, having steadied themselves on learning of the fire. Selina was taking off her skirt.

Above their heads, set in a sloping ceiling, was the large square outline of the old, bricked-in skylight. Men's voices, the scrabble of ladders and loud thumps of bricks being tested, came down from this large square. The men were evidently trying to find a means of opening the skylight to release the girls, who meanwhile stared up at the square mark in the ceiling. Tilly said, 'Won't it open?' Nobody answered, because the girls of the club knew the answer. Everyone in the club had heard the legend of the man who had got in by the skylight and, some said, been found in bed with a girl.

Now Selina stood on the lavatory seat and jumped up to the slit window. She slid through it to the roof with an easy diagonal movement. There were now thirteen women in the wash-room. They stood in the alert, silent attitude of jungle-danger, listening for further instruction from the megaphone on the roof outside.

Anne Baberton followed Selina through the slit window, with difficulty, because she was flustered. But a man's two hands came up to the window to receive her. Tilly Throvis-Mew began to sob. Pauline Fox ripped off her dress and then her underclothes until she was altogether naked. She had an undernourished body; there would have been no difficulty for her in getting through the slit window fully clothed, but she went naked as a fish.

Only Tilly sobbed heavily, but the rest of the girls were trembling. The noises from the sloping roof ceased as the firemen jumped down from investigating the skylight on to the flat roof area; footsteps beat and shuffled there, beyond the slit window, where throughout the summer Selina had lain with Nicholas, wrapped in rugs, under the Plough, which constituted the only view in Greater London that remained altogether intact.

Within the wash-room the eleven remaining women heard a fireman's voice addressing them through the window, against the simultaneous blare of megaphone instructions to the firemen. The man at the window said, 'Stay where you are. Don't panic. We're sending for tools to uncover the brick-work over the skylight. We won't be long. It's a question of time. We are doing everything we can to get you out. Remain where you are. Don't panic. It's just a question of time.'

The question of time opened now as a large thing in the lives of the eleven listeners.

*

Twenty-eight minutes had passed since the bomb had exploded in the garden. Felix Dobell joined Nicholas Farringdon on the flat roof after the fire started. They assisted the three slim girls through the window. Anne and naked Pauline Fox had been huddled into the two blankets of variable purpose, and hustled through the roof-hatch of the neighbouring hotel, the back windows of which had been smashed by the blast. Nicholas was as fleetingly impressed as was possible in the emergency, by the fact that Selina allowed the other girls to take the blankets. She lingered, shivering a little, but with an appealing grace, like a wounded roe deer, in her white petticoat and bare feet. Nicholas thought she was lingering for his sake, since Felix had disappeared with the two other girls to help them down to the first-aid ambulances. He left Selina standing thoughtfully on the hotel side of the roof, and returned to the slit window of the club to see for himself if any of the remaining girls were slim enough to escape by that way. It had been said by the firemen that the building might collapse within the next twenty minutes.

As he approached the slit window Selina slipped past him and, clutching the sill, heaved herself up again.

'Come down, what are you doing?' Nicholas said. He tried to grasp her ankles, but she was quick and, crouching for a small second on the narrow sill, she dipped her head and sidled through the window into the wash-room.

Nicholas immediately supposed she had done this in an attempt to rescue one of the girls, or assist their escape through the window.

'Come back out here, Selina,' he shouted, heaving himself up to see through the slit. 'It's dangerous. You can't help anybody.'

Selina was pushing her way through the standing group. They moved to give way without resistance. They were silent, except for Tilly, who now sobbed convulsively without tears, her eyes, like the other eyes, wide and fixed on Nicholas with the importance of fear.

Nicholas said, 'The men are coming to open the skylight. They'll be here in a moment. Are there any others of you who would be able to get through the window here? I'll give them a hand. Hurry up, the sooner the better.'

Joanna held a tape-measure in her hand. At some time in the interval between the firemen's discovery that the skylight was firmly sealed and this moment, Joanna had rummaged in one of these top bedrooms to find this tape-measure, with which she had measured the hips of the other ten trapped with herself, even the most helpless, to see what were their possibilities of escape by the seven-inch window slit. It was known all through the club that thirty-six and a quarter inches was the maximum for hips that could squeeze themselves through it, but as the exit had to be effected sideways with a manoeuvring of shoulders, much depended on the size of the bones, and on the texture of the individual flesh and muscles, whether flexible enough to compress easily or whether too firm. The latter had been Tilly's case. But apart from her, none of the women now left on the top floor was slim in anything like the proportions of Selina, Anne, and Pauline Fox. Some were plump. Jane was fat. Dorothy Markham, who had previously been able to slither in and out of the window to sunbathe, was now two months pregnant; her stomach was taut with an immovable extra inch. Joanna's efforts to measure them had been like a scientific ritual in a hopeless case, it had been a something done, it provided a slightly calming distraction.

Nicholas said, 'They won't be long. The men are coming now.' He was hanging on to the ledge of the window with his toes dug into the brick-work of the wall. He was looking towards the edge of the flat roof where the fire ladders were set. A file of firemen were now mounting the ladders with pickaxes, and heavy drills were being hauled up.

Nicholas looked back into the wash-room.

'They're coming now. Where did Selina go?'

No one answered.

He said, 'That girl over there − can't she manage to come through the window?'

He meant Tilly. Jane said, 'She's tried once. She got stuck. The fire's crackling like mad down there. The house is going to collapse any minute.'

In the sloping roof above the girls' heads the picks started to clack furiously at the brick-work, not in regular rhythm as in normal workmanship, but with the desperate hack-work of impending danger. It would not be long, now, before the whistles would blow and the voice from the megaphone would order the firemen to abandon the building to its collapse.

Nicholas had let go his hold to observe the situation from the outside. Tilly appeared at the slit window, now, in a second attempt to get out. He recognized her face as that of the girl who had been stuck there at the moment before the explosion, and whom he had been summoned to release. He shouted at her to get back lest she should stick again, and jeopardize her more probable rescue through the skylight. But she was frantic with determination, she yelled to urge herself on. It was a successful performance after all. Nicholas pulled her clear, breaking one of her hip-bones in the process. She fainted on the flat roof after he had set her down.

He pulled himself up to the window once more. The girls huddled, trembling and silent, round Joanna. They were looking up at the skylight. Some large thing cracked slowly on a lower floor of the house and smoke now started to curl in the upper air of the wash-rooms. Nicholas then saw, through the door of the wash-room, Selina approaching along the smoky passage. She was carrying something fairly long and limp and evidently light in weight, enfolding it carefully in her arms. He thought it was a body. She pushed her way through the girls coughing delicately from the first waves of smoke that had reached her in the passage. The others stared, shivering only with their prolonged apprehension, for they had no curiosity about what she had been rescuing or what she was carrying. She climbed up on the lavatory seat and slid through the window, skilfully and quickly pulling her object behind her. Nicholas held up his hand to catch her. When she landed on the roof-top she said, 'Is it safe out here?' and at the same time was inspecting the condition of her salvaged item. Poise is perfect balance. It was the Schiaparelli dress. The coat-hanger dangled from the dress like a headless neck and shoulders.

'Is it safe out here?' said Selina.

'Nowhere's safe,' said Nicholas.

Later, reflecting on this lightning scene, he could not trust his memory as to whether he then involuntarily signed himself with the cross. It seemed to him, in recollection, that he did. At all events, Felix Dobell, who had appeared on the roof again, looked at him curiously at the time, and later said that Nicholas had crossed himself in superstitious relief that Selina was safe.

She ran to the hotel hatch. Felix Dobell had taken up Tilly in his arms, for although she had recovered consciousness she was too injured to walk. He bore her to the roof-hatch, following Selina with her dress; it was now turned inside-out for safe-keeping.

From the slit window came a new sound, faint, because of the continuous tumble of hose-water, the creak of smoulder- ing wood and plaster in the lower part of the house, and, above, the clamour and falling bricks of the rescue work on the skylight. This new sound rose and fell with a broken hum between the sounds of desperate choking cough. It was Joanna, mechanically reciting the evening psalter of Day 27, responses and answers.

The voice through the megaphone shouted, 'Tell them to stand clear of the skylight in there. We'll have it free any minute now. It might collapse inwards. Tell those girls to stand clear of the skylight.'

Nicholas climbed up to the window. They had heard the instructions and were already crowding into the lavatory by the slit window, ignoring the man's face that kept appearing in it. As if hypnotized, they surrounded Joanna, and she herself stood as one hypnotized into the strange utterances of Day 27 in the Anglican order, held to be applicable to all sorts and conditions of human life in the world at that particular moment, when in London homing workers plodded across the park, observing with curiosity the fire-engines in the distance, when Rudi Bittesch was sitting in his flat at St John's Wood trying, without success, to telephone to Jane at the club to speak to her privately, the Labour Government was new-born, and else-where on the face of the globe people slept, queued for liberation-rations, beat the tom-toms, took shelter from the bombers, or went for a ride on a dodgem at the fun-fair.

Nicholas shouted, 'Keep well away from the skylight. Come right in close to the window.'

The girls crowded into the lavatory space. Jane and Joanna, being the largest, stood up on the lavatory seat to make room for the others. Nicholas saw that every face was streaming with perspiration. Joanna's skin, now close to his eyes, seemed to him to have become suddenly covered with large freckles as if fear had acted on it like the sun; in fact it was true that the pale freckles on her face, which normally were almost invisible, stared out in bright gold spots by contrast with her skin, which was now bloodless with fear. The versicles and responses came from her lips and tongue through the din of demolition.

> Yea, the Lord hath done great things for us already: whereof, we rejoice.
> Turn our captivity, O Lord: as the rivers in the south.
> They that sow in tears: shall reap in joy.

Why, and with what intention, was she moved to indulge in this? She remembered the words, and she had the long habit of recitation. But why, in this predicament and as if to an audience? She wore a dark green wool jersey and a grey skirt. The other girls, automatically listening to Joanna's voice as they had always done, were possibly less frantic and trembled less, because of it, but they turned their ears more fearfully and attentively to the meaning of the skylight noises than they did to the actual meaning of her words for Day 27.

> Except the Lord build the house: their labour is but lost that build it.
> Except the Lord keep the city: the watchman waketh but in vain.
> It is but lost labour that ye haste to rise up early, and so late take rest, and eat the bread of carefulness: for so he giveth his beloved sleep.
> Lo, children . . .

Any Day's liturgy would have been equally mesmeric. But the words for the right day was Joanna's habit. The skylight thudded open with a shower of powdery plaster and some lop-sided bricks. While the white dust was still falling the firemen's ladder descended. First up was Dorothy Markham, the chattering débutante whose bright life, for the past forty-three minutes, had gone into a bewildering darkness like illuminations at a seaside town when the electricity system breaks down. She looked haggard and curiously like her aunt, Lady Julia, the chairman of the club's committee who was at that moment innocently tying up refugee parcels at Bath. Lady Julia's hair was white, and so now was the hair of her niece Dorothy, covered as it was by falling plaster-dust, as she clambered up the fire-ladder to the sloping tiles and was assisted to the safe flat roof-top. At her heels came Nancy Riddle, the daughter of the Low-Church Midlands clergyman, whose accents of speech had been in process of improvement by Joanna's lessons. Her elocution days were over now, she would always speak with a Midlands accent. Her hips looked more dangerously wide than they had ever noticeably been, as she swung up the ladder behind Dorothy. Three girls then attempted to follow at once; they had been occupants of a four-bed dormitory on the third floor, and were all newly released from the Forces; all three had the hefty, built-up appearance that five years in the Army was apt to give to a woman. While they were sorting themselves out, Jane grasped the ladder and got away. The three ex-warriors then followed.

Joanna had jumped down from the lavatory seat. She was now circling round, vaguely wobbling, like a top near the end of its spin. Her eyes shifted from the skylight to the window in a puzzled way. Her lips and tongue continued to recite compulsively the litany of the Day, but her voice had weakened and she stopped to cough. The air was still full of powdered plaster and smoke. There were three girls left beside herself. Joanna groped for the ladder and missed. She then stopped to pick up the tape-measure which was lying on the floor. She groped for it as if she were partially blind, still intoning:

> So that they who go by say not so much as, The Lord prosper you:
>   we wish you good luck in the Name of the Lord.
> Out of the deep have I called . . .

The other three took the ladder, one of them, a surprisingly slender girl called Pippa, whose non-apparent bones had evidently been too large to have allowed her escape through the window, shouted back, 'Hurry up, Joanna.'

'Joanna, the ladder!'

And Nicholas shouted from the window, 'Joanna, get up the ladder.'

She regained her senses and pressed behind the last two girls, a brown-skinned heavily-sinewed swimmer and a voluptuous Greek exile of noble birth, both of whom were crying with relief. Joanna promptly started to clamber after them, grasping in her hand a rung that the last girl's foot had just left. At that moment, the house trembled and the ladder and wash-room with it. The fire was extinguished, but the gutted house had been finally thrown by the violence of the work on the sky-light. A whistle sounded as Joanna was half-way up. A voice from the megaphone ordered the men to jump clear. The house went down as the last fireman waited at the skylight for Joanna to emerge. As the sloping roof began to cave in, he leapt clear, landing badly and painfully on the flat roof-top. The house sank into its centre, a high heap of rubble, and Joanna went with it.

CHAPTER 9

THE TAPE-RECORDING had been erased for economy reasons, so that the tape could be used again. That is how things were in 1945. Nicholas was angry in excess of the occasion. He had wanted to play back Joanna's voice to her father who had come up to London after her funeral to fill in forms as to the effects of the dead. Nicholas had written to him, partly with an urge to impart his last impressions of Joanna, partly from curiosity, partly, too, from a desire to stage a dramatic play-back of Joanna doing *The Wreck of the Deutschland*. He had mentioned the tape-recording in his letter.

But it was gone. It must have been wiped out by someone at his office.

> Thou hast bound bones and veins in me, fastened me flesh,
>   And after it almost unmade, what with dread,
>   Thy doing: and dost thou touch me afresh?

Nicholas said to the rector, 'It's infuriating. She was at her best in *The Wreck of the Deutschland*. I'm terribly sorry.'

Joanna's father sat, pink-faced and white-haired. He said, 'Oh, please don't worry.'

'I wish you could have heard it.'

As if to console Nicholas in his loss, the rector murmured with a nostalgic smile:

> It was the schooner *Hesperus*
>   That sailed the wintry sea . . .

'No, no, the *Deutschland*. *The Wreck of the Deutschland*.'

'Oh, the *Deutschland*.' With a gesture characteristic of the English aquiline nose, his seemed to smell the air for enlightenment.

Nicholas was moved by this to a last effort to regain the lost recording. It was a Sunday, but he managed to get one of his colleagues on the telephone at home.

'Do you happen to know if anyone removed a tape from that box I borrowed from the office? Like a fool I left it in my room at the office. Someone's removed an important tape. Something private.'

'No, I don't think ... just a minute ... yes, in fact, they've wiped out the stuff. It was poetry. Sorry, but the economy regulations, you know ... What do you think of the news? Takes your breath away, doesn't it?'

Nicholas said to Joanna's father, 'Yes, it really has been wiped out.'

'Never mind. I remember Joanna as she was in the rectory. Joanna was a great help in the parish. Her coming to London was a mistake, poor girl.'

Nicholas refilled the man's glass with whisky and started to add water. The clergyman signed irritably with his hand to convey the moment when the drink was to his taste. He had the mannerisms of a widower of long years, or of one unaccustomed to being in the company of critical women. Nicholas perceived that the man had never seen the reality of his daughter. Nicholas was consoled for the blighting of his show; the man might not have recognized Joanna in the *Deutschland*.

The frown of his face
Before me, the hurtle of hell
Behind, where, where was a, where was a place?

'I dislike London. I never come up unless I've got to,' the clergyman said, 'for convocation or something like that. If only Joanna could have settled down at the rectory ... She was restless, poor girl.' He gulped his whisky like a gargle, tossing back his head.

Nicholas said, 'She was reciting some sort of office just before she went down. The other girls were with her, they were listening in a way. Some psalms.'

'Really? No one else has mentioned it.' The old man looked embarrassed. He swirled his drink and swallowed it down, as if Nicholas might be going on to tell him that his daughter had gone over to Rome at the last, or somehow died in bad taste.

Nicholas said violently, 'Joanna had religious strength.'

'I know that, my boy,' said the father, surprisingly.

'She had a sense of Hell. She told a friend of hers that she was afraid of Hell.'

'Really? I didn't know that. I've never heard her speak morbidly. It must have been the influence of London. I never come here, myself, unless I've got to. I had a curacy once, in Balham, in my young days. But since then I've had country parishes. I prefer country parishes. One finds better, more devout, and indeed in some cases, quite holy souls in the country parishes.'

Nicholas was reminded of an American acquaintance of his, a psycho-analyst who had written to say he intended to practise in England after the war, 'away from all these neurotics and this hustling scene of anxiety'.

'Christianity is all in the country parishes these days,' said this shepherd of the best prime mutton. He put down his glass as if to seal his decision on the matter, his grief for the loss of Joanna turning back, at every sequence, on her departure from the rectory.

He said, 'I must go and see the spot where she died.'

Nicholas had already promised to take him to the demolished house in Kensington Road. The father had reminded Nicholas of this several times as if afraid he might inattentively leave London with this duty unfulfilled.

'I'll walk along with you.'

'Well, if it's not out of your way I'll be much obliged. What do you make of this new bomb? Do you think it's only propaganda stuff?'

'I don't know, sir,' said Nicholas.

'It leaves one breathless with horror. They'll have to make an armistice if it's true.' He looked around him as they walked towards Kensington. 'These bomb-sites look tragic. I never come up if I can help it, you know.'

Nicholas said, presently, 'Have you seen any of the girls who were trapped in the house with Joanna, or any of the other members of the club?'

The rector said, 'Yes, quite a few. Lady Julia was kind enough to have a few to tea to meet me yesterday afternoon. Of course, those poor girls have been through an ordeal, even the onlookers among them. Lady Julia suggested we didn't discuss the actual incident. You know, I think that was wise.'

'Yes. Do you recall the girls' names at all?'

'There was Lady Julia's niece, Dorothy, and a Miss Baberton who escaped, I believe, through a window. Several others.'

'A Miss Redwood? Selina Redwood?'

'Well, you know, I'm rather bad at names.'

'A very tall, very slender girl, very beautiful. I want to find her. Dark hair.'

'They were all charming, my dear boy. All young people are charming. Joanna was, to me, the most charming of all, but there I'm partial.'

'She was charming,' said Nicholas, and held his peace.

But the man had sensed his pursuit with the ease of the pastoral expert on home ground, and he inquired solicitously, 'Has this young girl disappeared?'

'Well, I haven't been able to trace her. I've been trying for the past nine days.'

'How odd. She couldn't have lost her memory, I suppose? Wandering the streets . . . ?'

'I think she would have been found in that case. She's very conspicuous.'

'What does her family report?'

'Her family are in Canada.'

'Perhaps she's gone away to forget. It would be understandable. Was she one of the girls who were trapped?'

'Yes. She got out through a window.'

'Well, I don't think she was at Lady Julia's from your description. You could telephone and ask.'

'I have telephoned, in fact. She hasn't heard anything of Selina and neither have any of the other girls. But I was hoping they might be mistaken. You know how it is.'

'Selina . . .' said the rector.

'Yes, that's her name.'

'Just a moment. There was a mention of a Selina. One of the girls, a fair girl, very young, was complaining that Selina had gone off with her only ball dress. Would that be the girl?'

'That's the girl.'

'Not very nice of her to pinch another girl's dress, especially when they've all lost their wardrobes in the fire.'

'It was a Schiaparelli dress.'

The rector did not intrude on this enigma. They came to the site of the May of Teck Club. It looked now like one of the familiar ruins of the neighbourhood, as if it had been shattered years ago by a bomb-attack, or months ago by a guided missile. The paving stones of the porch lay crookedly leading nowhere. The pillars lay like Roman remains. A side wall at the back of the house stood raggedly at half its former height. Greggie's garden was a heap of masonry with a few flowers and rare plants sprouting from it. The pink and white tiles of the hall lay in various aspects of long neglect, and from a lower part of the ragged side wall a piece of brown drawing-room wall-paper furled more raggedly.

Joanna's father stood holding his wide black hat.

At the top of the house the apples are laid in rows . . .

The rector said to Nicholas, 'There's really nothing to see.'
'Like my tape-recording,' said Nicholas.
'Yes, it's all gone, all elsewhere.'

Rudi Bittesch lifted and flicked through a pile of notebooks that lay on Nicholas's table. He said, 'Is this the manuscript of your book by the way?'

He would not have taken this liberty in the normal course, but Nicholas was under a present obligation to him. Rudi had discovered the whereabouts of Selina.

'You can have it,' said Nicholas, meaning the manuscript. He said, not foreseeing the death he was to die, 'You can keep it. It might be valuable one day when I'm famous.'

Rudi smiled. All the same, he tucked the books under his arm and said, 'Coming along?'

On the way to pick up Jane to go and see the fun at the Palace, Nicholas said, 'Anyway, I've decided not to publish the book. The typescripts are destroyed.'

'I have this bloody big lot of books to carry, and now you tell me this. What value to me if you don't publish?'

'Keep them, you never know.'

Rudi had a caution about these things. He kept *The Sabbath Notebooks*, eventually to reap his reward.

'Would you like a letter from Charles Morgan to me saying I'm a genius?' Nicholas said.

'You're bloody cheerful about something or other.'

'I know,' said Nicholas. 'Would you like to have the letter, though?'

'What letter?'

'Here it is.' Nicholas brought Jane's letter from his inside pocket, crumpled like a treasured photograph.

Rudi glanced at it. 'Jane's work,' he said, and handed it back. 'Why are you so cheerful? Did you see Selina?'

'Yes.'

'What did she say?'

'She screamed. She couldn't stop screaming. It's a nervous reaction.'

'The sight of you must have brought all back to her. I advised you to keep away.'

'She couldn't stop screaming.'

'You frightened her.'

'Yes.'

'I said keep away. She's no good, by the way, with a crooner in Clarges Street. You see him?'

'Yes, he's a perfectly nice chap. They're married.'

'So they say. You want to find a girl with character. Forget her.'

'Oh, well. Anyway, he was very apologetic about her screaming, and I was very apologetic, of course. It made her scream more. I think she'd have preferred to see a fight.'

'You don't love her that much, to fight a crooner.'

'He was quite a decent crooner.'

'You heard him croon?'

'No, of course, that's a point.'

Jane was restored to her normal state of unhappiness and hope, and was now established in a furnished room in Kensington Church Street. She was ready to join them.

Rudi said, 'You don't scream when you see Nicholas?'

'No,' she said, 'but if he goes on refusing to let George publish his book I will scream. George is putting the blame on me. I told him about the letter from Charles Morgan.'

'You should fear him,' Rudi said. 'He makes ladies scream by the way. Selina got a fright from him today.'

'I got a fright from her last time.'

'Have you found her then?' said Jane.

'Yes, but she's suffering from shock. I must have brought all the horrors back to her mind.'

'It was hell,' Jane said.

'I know.'

'Why is he in love with Selina by the way?' Rudi said. 'Why doesn't he find a woman of character or a French girl?'

*

'This is a toll call,' Jane said, rapidly.

'I know. Who's speaking?' said Nancy, the daughter of the Midlands clergyman, now married to another Midlands clergyman.

'It's Jane. Look, I've just got another question to ask you, quickly, about Nicholas Farringdon. Do you think his conversion had anything to do with the fire? I've got to finish this big article about him.'

'Well, I always like to think it was Joanna's example. Joanna was very High Church.'

'But he wasn't in love with Joanna, he was in love with Selina. After the fire he looked for her all over the place.'

'Well, he couldn't have been converted by Selina. Not converted.'

'He's got a note in his manuscript that a vision of evil may be as effective to conversion as a vision of good.'

'I don't understand these fanatics. There's the pips, Jane. I think he was in love with us all, poor fellow.'

*

The public swelled on VJ night of August as riotously as on the victory night of May. The little figures appeared duly on the balcony every half-hour, waved for a space and disappeared.

Jane, Nicholas and Rudi were suddenly in difficulties, being pressed by the crowd from all sides. 'Keep your elbows out if possible,' Jane and Nicholas said to each other, almost simultaneously; but this was useless advice. A seaman, pressing on Jane, kissed her passionately on the mouth; nothing whatsoever could be done about it. She was at the mercy of his wet beery mouth until the crowd gave way, and then the three pressed a path to a slightly healthier spot, with access to the park.

Here, another seaman, observed only by Nicholas, slid a knife silently between the ribs of a woman who was with him. The lights went up on the balcony, and a hush anticipated the Royal appearance. The stabbed woman did not scream, but sagged immediately. Someone else screamed through the hush, a woman, many yards away, some other victim. Or perhaps that screamer had only had her toes trodden upon. The crowd began to roar again. All their eyes were at this moment fixed on the Palace balcony, where the royal family had appeared in due order. Rudi and Jane were busy yelling their cheers.

Nicholas tried unsuccessfully to move his arm above the crowd to draw attention to the wounded woman. He had been shouting that a woman had been stabbed. The seaman was shouting accusations at his limp woman, who was still kept upright by the crowd. These private demonstrations faded in the general pandemonium. Nicholas was borne away in a surge that pressed from the Mall. When the balcony darkened, he was again able to make a small clearing through the crowd, followed by Jane and Rudi towards the open park. On the way, Nicholas was forced to a standstill and found himself close by the knifer. There was no sign of the wounded woman. Nicholas, waiting to move, took the Charles Morgan letter from his pocket and thrust it down the seaman's blouse, and then was borne onwards. He did this for no apparent reason and to no effect, except that it was a gesture. That is the way things were at that time.

They walked back through the clear air of the park, stepping round the couples who lay locked together in their path. The park was filled with singing. Nicholas and his companions sang too. They ran into a fight between British and American servicemen. Two men lay unconscious at the side of the path, being tended by their friends. The crowds cheered in the distance behind them. A formation of aircraft buzzed across the night sky. It was a glorious victory.

Jane mumbled, 'Well, I wouldn't have missed it, really.' She had halted to pin up her straggling hair, and had a hair-pin in her mouth as she said it. Nicholas marvelled at her stamina, recalling her in this image years later in the country of his death – how she stood, sturdy and bare-legged on the dark grass, occupied with her hair – as if this was an image of all the May of Teck establishment in its meek, unselfconscious attitudes of poverty, long ago in 1945.

THE DRIVER'S SEAT

CHAPTER 1

'AND THE MATERIAL doesn't stain,' the salesgirl says.

'Doesn't stain?'

'It's the new fabric,' the salesgirl says. 'Specially treated. Won't mark. If you spill like a bit of ice-cream or a drop of coffee, like, down the front of this dress it won't hold the stain.'

The customer, a young woman, is suddenly tearing at the fastener at the neck, pulling at the zip of the dress. She is saying, 'Get this thing off me. Off me, at once.'

The salesgirl shouts at the customer who, up to now, has been delighted with the bright coloured dress. It is patterned with green and purple squares on a white background, with blue spots within the green squares, cyclamen spots within the purple. This dress has not been a successful line; other dresses in the new stainless fabric have sold, but this, of which three others, identical but for sizes, hang in the back storeroom awaiting the drastic reductions of next week's sale, has been too vivid for most customers' taste. But the customer who now steps speedily out of it, throwing it on the floor with the utmost irritation, had almost smiled with satisfaction when she had tried it on. She had said, 'That's my dress.' The salesgirl had said it needed taking up at the hem. 'All right,' the customer had said, 'but I need it for tomorrow.' 'We can't do it before Friday, I'm sorry,' the salesgirl had said. 'Oh, I'll do it myself, then,' the customer had said, and turned round to admire it sideways in the long mirror. 'It's a good fit. Lovely colours,' she said.

'And it doesn't stain,' the salesgirl had said, with her eye wandering to another unstainable and equally unsaleable summer dress which evidently she hoped, now, to offer the satisfied customer.

'Doesn't stain?'

The customer has flung the dress aside.

The salesgirl shouts, as if to assist her explanation. 'Specially treated fabric . . . If you spill like a drop of sherry you just wipe it off. Look, Miss, you're tearing the neck.'

'Do you think I spill things on my clothes?' the customer shrieks. 'Do I look as if I don't eat properly?'

'Miss, I only remarked on the fabric, that when you tell me you're going abroad for your vacation, there is always the marks that you pick up on your journey. Don't treat our clothes like that if you please. Miss, I only said stain-resisting and then you carry on, after you liked it.'

'Who asked you for a stain-resisting dress?' the customer shouts, getting quickly, with absolute purpose, into her own blouse and skirt.

'You liked the colours, didn't you?' shouts the girl. 'What difference does it make, so it resists stains, if you liked the fabric before you knew?'

The customer picks up her bag and goes to the door almost at a run, while two other salesgirls and two other customers gasp and gape. At the door she turns to look back and says, with a look of satisfaction at her own dominance over the situation with an undoubtable excuse, 'I won't be insulted!'

She walks along the broad street, scanning the windows for the dress she needs, the necessary dress. Her lips are slightly parted; she, whose lips are usually pressed together with the daily disapprovals of the accountants' office where she has worked continually, except for the months of illness, since she was eighteen, that is to say, for sixteen years and some months. Her lips, when she does not speak or eat, are normally pressed together like the ruled line of a balance sheet, marked straight with her old-fashioned lipstick, a final and a judging mouth, a precision instrument, a detail-warden of a mouth; she has five girls under her and two men. Over her are two women and five men. Her immediate superior had given her the afternoon off, in kindness, Friday afternoon. 'You've got your packing to do, Lise. Go home, pack and rest.' She had resisted. 'I don't need a rest. I've got all this work to finish. Look – all this.' The superior, a fat small man, looked at her with frightened eyeglasses. Lise smiled and bent her head over her desk. 'It can wait till you get back,' said the man, and when she looked up at him he showed courage and defiance in his rimless spectacles. Then she had begun to laugh hysterically. She finished laughing and started crying all in a flood, while a flurry at the other desks, the jerky backward movements of her little fat superior, conveyed to her that she had done again what she had not done for five years. As she ran to the lavatory she shouted to the whole office who somehow or other were trying to follow or help her. 'Leave me alone! It doesn't matter. What does it matter?' Half an hour later they said, 'You need a good holiday, Lise. You need your vacation.' 'I'm going to have it,' she said, 'I'm going to have the time of my life,' and she had looked at the two men and five girls under her, and at her quivering superior, one by one, with her lips straight as a line which could cancel them all out completely.

Now, as she walks along the street after leaving the shop, her lips are slightly parted as if to receive a secret flavour. In fact her nostrils and eyes are a fragment more open than usual, imperceptibly but thoroughly they accompany her parted lips in one mission, the sensing of the dress that she must get.

She swerves in her course at the door of a department store and enters. Resort Department: she has seen the dress. A lemon-yellow top with a skirt patterned in bright V's of orange, mauve and blue. 'Is it made of that stain-resisting material?' she asks when she has put it on and is looking at herself in the mirror. 'Stain-resisting? I don't know, Madam. It's a washable cotton, but if I were you I'd have it dry-cleaned. It might

243

shrink.' Lise laughs, and the girl says, 'I'm afraid we haven't anything really stain-resisting. I've never heard of anything like that.' Lise makes her mouth into a straight line. Then she says, 'I'll have it.' Meanwhile she is pulling off a hanger a summer coat with narrow stripes, red and white, with a white collar; very quickly she tries it on over the new dress. 'Of course, the two don't go well together,' says the salesgirl. 'You'd have to see them on separate.'

Lise does not appear to listen. She studies herself. This way and that, in the mirror of the fitting-room. She lets the coat hang open over the dress. Her lips part, and her eyes narrow; she breathes for a moment as in a trance.

The salesgirl says, 'You can't really see the coat at its best, Madam, over that frock.'

Lise appears suddenly to hear her, opening her eyes and closing her lips. The girl is saying, 'You won't be able to wear them together, but it's a lovely coat, over a plain dress, white or navy, or for the evenings . . .'

'They go very well together,' Lise says, and taking off the coat she hands it carefully to the girl. 'I'll have it; also, the dress. I can take up the hem myself.' She reaches for her blouse and skirt and says to the girl, 'Those colours of the dress and the coat are absolutely right for me. Very natural colours.'

The girl, placating, says, 'Oh, it's how you feel in things yourself, Madam, isn't it? It's you's got to wear them.' Lise buttons her blouse disapprovingly. She follows the girl to the shop-floor, pays the bill, waits for the change and, when the girl hands her first the change then the large bag of heavy paper containing her new purchases, she opens the top of the bag enough to enable her to peep inside, to put in her hand and tear a corner of the tissue paper which enfolds each garment. She is obviously making sure she is being handed the right garments. The girl is about to speak, probably to say, 'Everything all right?' or 'Thank you, Madam, goodbye,' or even, 'Don't worry; everything's there all right.' But Lise speaks first;

she says, 'The colours go together perfectly. People here in the North are ignorant of colours. Conservative; old-fashioned. If only you knew! These colours are a natural blend for me. Absolutely natural.' She does not wait for a reply; she does not turn towards the lift, she turns, instead, towards the down escalator, purposefully making her way through a short lane of dresses that hang in their stands.

She stops abruptly at the top of the escalator and looks back, then smiles as if she sees and hears what she had expected. The salesgirl, thinking her customer is already on the escalator out of sight, out of hearing, has turned to another black-frocked salesgirl. 'All those colours together!' she is saying. 'Those incredible colours! She said they were perfectly natural. Natural! Here in the North, she said . . .' Her voice stops as she sees that Lise is looking and hearing. The girl affects to be fumbling with a dress on the rack and to be saying something else without changing her expression too noticeably. Lise laughs aloud and descends the escalator.

'Well, enjoy yourself Lise,' says the voice on the telephone. 'Send me a card.'

'Oh, of course,' Lise says, and when she has hung up she laughs heartily. She does not stop. She goes to the wash-basin and fills a glass of water, which she drinks, gurgling, then another, and still nearly choking she drinks another. She has stopped laughing, and now breathing heavily says to the mute telephone, 'Of course. Oh, of course.' Still heaving with exhaustion she pulls out the hard wall-seat which adapts to a bed and takes off her shoes, placing them beside the bed. She puts the large carrier-bag containing her new coat and dress in a cupboard beside her suitcase which is already packed. She places her hand-bag on the lamp-shelf beside the bed and lies down.

Her face is solemn as she lies, at first staring at the brown pinewood door as if to see beyond it. Presently her breathing becomes normal. The room is meticulously neat. It is a one-room flat in an apartment house. Since it was put up the designer has won prizes for his interiors, he has become known throughout the country and far beyond and is now no longer to be obtained by landlords of moderate price. The lines of the room are pure; space is used as a pattern in itself, circumscribed by the dexterous pinewood outlines that ensued from the designer's ingenuity and austere taste when he was young, unknown, studious and strict-principled. The company that owns the apartment house knows the worth of these pinewood interiors. Pinewood alone is now nearly as scarce as the architect himself, but the law, so far, prevents them from raising the rents very much. The tenants have long leases. Lise moved in when the house was new, ten years ago. She has added very little to the room; very little is needed, for the furniture is all fixed, adaptable to various uses, and stackable. Stacked into a panel are six folding chairs, should the tenant decide to entertain six for dinner. The writing desk extends to a dining table, and when the desk is not in use it, too, disappears into the pinewood wall, its bracket-lamp hingeing outward and upward to form a wall-lamp. The bed is by day a narrow seat with overhanging bookcases; by night it swivels out to accommodate the sleeper. Lise has put down a patterned rug from Greece. She has fitted a hopsack covering on the seat of the divan. Unlike the other tenants she has not put unnecessary curtains in the window; her flat is not closely overlooked and in summer she keeps the venetian blinds down over the windows and slightly opened to let in the light. A small pantry-kitchen adjoins this room. Here, too, everything is contrived to fold away into the dignity of unvarnished pinewood. And in the bathroom as well, nothing need be seen, nothing need be left lying about. The bed-supports, the door, the window-frame, the hanging cupboard, the storage space, the shelves, the desk that extends, the tables that stack – they are made of such pinewood as one may never see again in a modest bachelor apartment. Lise keeps her flat as clean-lined and clear to return to after her work as if it were uninhabited. The swaying tall pines among the litter of cones on the forest floor have been subdued into silence and into obedient bulks.

Lise breathes as if sleeping, deeply tired, but her eye-slits open from time to time. Her hand moves to her brown leather bag on the lamp-shelf and she raises herself, pulling the bag towards her. She leans on one elbow and empties the contents on the bed. She lifts them one by one, checking carefully, and puts them back; there is a folded envelope from the travel agency containing her air ticket, a powder compact, a lipstick, a comb. There is a bunch of keys. She smiles at them and her lips are parted. There are six keys on the steel ring, two Yale door-keys, a key that might belong to a functional cupboard or drawer, a small silver-metal key of the type commonly belonging to zip-fastened luggage, and two tarnished car-keys. Lise takes the car-keys off the ring and lays them aside; the rest go back in her bag. Her passport, in its transparent plastic envelope, goes back in her bag. With straightened lips she prepares for her departure the next day. She unpacks the new coat and dress and hangs them on hangers.

Next morning she puts them on. When she is ready to leave she dials a number on the telephone and looks at herself in the mirror which has not yet been concealed behind the pinewood panels which close upon it. The voice answers and Lise touches her pale brown hair as she speaks. 'Margot, I'm just off now,' Lise says. 'I'll put your car-keys in an envelope and I'll leave them downstairs with the door-keeper. All right?'

The voice says, 'Thanks. Have a good holiday. Have a good time. Send me a card.'

'Yes, of course, Margot.'

'Of course,' Lise says when she has replaced the receiver. She takes an envelope from a drawer, writes a name on it, puts the two car-keys in it and seals the envelope. Then she telephones for a taxi, lifts her suitcase out to the landing, fetches her hand-bag and the envelope, and leaves the flat.

When she reaches the street floor, she stops at the windows of the porter's wood-lined cabin. Lise rings the bell and waits. No one appears, but the taxi has pulled up outside. Lise shouts to the driver, 'I'm just coming!' and indicates her suitcase which the taxi-driver fetches. While he is stacking it in the front of the cab a woman with a brown overall comes up behind Lise. 'You want me, Miss?'

Lise turns quickly to face the woman. She has the envelope in her hand and is about to speak when the woman says, 'Well, well, my goodness, what colours!' She is looking at Lise's red and white striped coat, unbuttoned, and the vivid dress beneath, the purple, orange and blue V-patterns of the skirt and the yellow top. The woman laughs hugely as one who has nothing to gain by suppressing her amusement, she laughs and opens the pinewood door into the porter's office; there she slides open the window panel and laughs aloud in Lise's face. She says, 'Are you going to join a circus?' Then again she throws back her head, looking down through half-closed lids at Lise's clothes, and gives out the high, hacking cough-like ancestral laughter of the streets, holding her breasts in her hands to spare them the shake-up. Lise says, with quiet dignity, 'You are insolent.' But the woman laughs again, now no longer spontaneously but with spiteful and deliberate noise, forcing the evident point that Lise habitually is mean with her tips, or perhaps never tips the porter at all.

Lise walks quietly out to the cab, still holding in her hand the envelope which contains the car-keys. She looks at this envelope as she goes, but whether she has failed to leave it at the door-keeper's desk by intention, or whether through the distraction of the woman's laughter, one could not tell from her serene face with lips slightly parted. The woman comes to the street door emitting noise like a brown container of laughing-gas until the taxi is out of her scope.

CHAPTER 2

LISE IS THIN. Her height is about five-foot-six. Her hair is pale brown, probably tinted, a very light streaked lock sweeping from the middle of her hair-line to the top of her crown; her hair is cut short at the sides and back, and is styled high. She might be as young as twenty-nine or as old as thirty-six, but hardly younger, hardly older. She has arrived at the airport; she has paid the taxi-driver quickly and with an expression of abstract eagerness to be somewhere else. Likewise, with the porter, while he takes her bag and follows her to the desk to have it weighed-in. She seems not to see him.

There are two people in front of her. Lise's eyes are widely spaced, blue-grey and dull. Her lips are a straight line. She is neither good-looking nor bad-looking. Her nose is short and wider than it will look in the likeness constructed partly by the method of identikit, partly by actual photography, soon to be published in the newspapers of four languages.

Lise looks at the two people in front of her, first a woman and then a man, swaying to one side and the other as she does so, either to discern in the half-faces visible to her someone she might possibly know, or else to relieve, by these movements and looks, some impatience she might feel.

When it comes to her turn she heaves her luggage on to the scale and pushes her ticket to the clerk as quickly as possible. While he examines it she turns to look at a couple who are now waiting behind her. She glances at both faces, then looks back to the clerk, regardless of their returning her stares and their unanimous perception of her bright-coloured clothes.

'Any hand-luggage?' says the clerk, peering over the top of the counter.

Lise simpers, placing the tips of her upper teeth over her lower lip, and draws in a little breath.

'Any hand-luggage?' The busy young official looks at her as much as to say, 'What's the matter with *you*?' And Lise answers in a voice different from the voice in which she yesterday spoke to the shop assistant when buying her lurid outfit, and has used on the telephone, and in which early this morning she spoke to the woman at the porter's desk; she now speaks in a little-girl tone which presumably is taken by those within hearing to be her normal voice even if a nasty one. Lise says, 'I only have my hand-bag with me. I believe in travelling light because I travel a lot and I know how terrible it is for one's neighbours on the plane when you have great huge pieces of hand-luggage taking up everybody's foot-room.'

The clerk, all in one gesture, heaves a sigh, purses his lips, closes his eyes, places his chin in his hands and his elbow on the desk. Lise turns round to address the couple behind her. She says, 'When you travel as much as I do you have to travel light, and I tell you, I nearly didn't bring any luggage at all, because you can get everything you want at the other end, so the only reason I brought that suitcase there is that the customs get suspicious if you come in and out without luggage. They think you're smuggling dope and diamonds under your blouse, so I packed the usual things for a holiday, but it was all quite unnecessary, as you get to understand when you've travelled about as you might say with experience in four languages over the years, and you know what you're doing –'

'Look, Miss,' the clerk says, pulling himself straight and stamping her ticket, 'you're holding up the people behind you. We're busy.'

Lise turns away from the bewildered-looking couple to face the clerk as he pushes her ticket and boarding card towards her.

'Boarding card,' says the clerk. 'Your flight will be called in twenty-five minutes' time. Next please.'

Lise grabs the papers and moves away as if thinking only of the next formality of travel. She puts the ticket in her bag, takes out her passport, slips the boarding card inside it, and makes straight towards the passport boxes. And it is almost as if, satisfied that she has successfully registered the fact of her presence at the airport among the July thousands there, she has fulfilled a small item of a greater purpose. She goes to the emigration official and joins the queue and submits her passport. And now, having received her passport back in her hand, she is pushing through the gate into the departure lounge. She walks to the far end, then turns and walks back. She is neither good-looking nor bad-looking. Her lips are slightly parted. She stops to look at the departures chart, then walks on. The people around her are mostly too occupied with their purchases and their flight-numbers to notice her, but some of those who sit beside their hand-luggage and children on the leather seats waiting for their flights to be called look at her as she walks past, noting without comment the lurid colours of her coat, red and white stripes, hanging loose over her dress, yellow-topped, with its skirt of orange, purple and blue. They look, as she passes, as they look also at those girls whose skirts are specially short, or those men whose tight-fitting shirts are patterned with flowers or are transparent. Lise is conspicuous among them only in the particular mixture of her colours, contrasting with the fact that her hem-line has been for some years an old-fashioned length, reaching just below her knees, as do the mild dresses of many other, but dingy, women travellers who teem in the departure lounge. Lise puts her passport into her hand-bag, and holds her boarding card.

She stops at the bookstall, looks at her watch and starts looking at the paperback stands. A white-haired, tall woman who has been looking through the hardback books piled up on a table, turns from them and, pointing to the paperbacks, says to Lise in English, 'Is there anything there predominantly pink or green or beige?'

'Excuse me?' says Lise politely, in a foreignly accented English, 'what is that you're looking for?'

'Oh,' the woman says, 'I thought you were American.'

'No, but I can speak four languages enough to make myself understood.'

'I'm from Johannesburg,' says the woman, 'and I have this house in Jo'burg and another at Sea Point on the Cape. Then my son, he's a lawyer, he has a flat in Jo'burg. In all our places we have spare bedrooms, that makes two green, two pink, three beige, and I'm trying to pick up books to match. I don't see any with just those pastel tints.'

'You want English books,' Lise says. 'I think you find English books on the front of the shop over there.'

'Well, I looked there and I don't find my shades. Aren't these English books here?'

Lise says, 'No. In any case they're all very bright-coloured.' She smiles then, and with her lips apart starts to look swiftly through the paperbacks. She picks out one with bright green lettering on a white background with the author's name printed to look like blue lightning streaks. In the middle of the cover are depicted a brown boy and girl wearing only garlands of sunflowers. Lise pays for it, while the white-haired woman says, 'Those colours are too bright for me. I don't see anything.'

Lise is holding the book up against her coat, giggling merrily, and looking up to the woman as if to see if her purchase is admired.

'You going on holiday?' the woman says.

'Yes. My first after three years.'

'You travel much?'

'No. There is so little money. But I'm going to the South now. I went before, three years ago.'

'Well, I hope you have a good time. A very good time. You look very gay.'

The woman has large breasts, she is clothed in a pink summer coat and dress. She smiles and is amiable in this transient intimacy with Lise, and not even sensing in the least that very soon, after a day and a half of hesitancy, and after a long midnight call to her son, the lawyer in Johannesburg, who advises her against the action, she nevertheless will come forward and repeat all she remembers and all she does not remember, and all the details she imagines to be true and those that are true, in her conversation with Lise when she sees in the papers that the police are trying to trace who Lise is, and whom, if anyone, she met on her trip and what she had said. 'Very gay,' says this woman to Lise, indulgently, smiling all over Lise's vivid clothes.

'I look for a gay time,' Lise is saying.

'You got a young man?'

'Yes, I have my boy-friend!'

'He's not with you, then?'

'No. I'm going to find him. He's waiting for me. Maybe I should get him a gift at the duty-free shop.'

They are walking towards the departures chart. 'I'm going to Stockholm. I have three-quarters of an hour wait,' says the woman.

Lise looks at the chart as the amplified voice of the announcer hacks its way through the general din. Lise says, 'That's my flight. Boarding at Gate 14.' She moves off, her eyes in the distance as if the woman from Johannesburg had never been there. On her way to Gate 14 Lise stops to glance at a gift-stall. She looks at the dolls in folk-costume and at the corkscrews. Then she lifts up a paper-knife shaped like a scimitar, of brass-coloured metal with inset coloured stones. She removes it from its curved sheath and tests the blade and the point with deep interest. 'How much?' she asks the assistant who is at that moment serving someone else.

The girl says impatiently aside to Lise, 'The price is on the ticket.'

'Too much. I can get it cheaper at the other end,' Lise says, putting it down.

'They're all fixed prices at the duty-free,' the girl calls after Lise as she walks away towards Gate 14.

A small crowd has gathered waiting for embarkation. More and more people straggle or palpitate, according to temperament, towards the group. Lise surveys her fellow-passengers, one by one, very carefully but not in a manner to provoke their attention. She moves and mingles as if with dreamy feet and legs, but quite plainly, from her eyes, her mind is not dreamy as she absorbs each face, each dress, each suit of clothes, all blouses, blue jeans, each piece of hand-luggage, each voice which will accompany her on the flight now boarding at Gate 14.

CHAPTER 3

SHE WILL BE found tomorrow morning dead from multiple stab-wounds, her wrists bound with a silk scarf and her ankles bound with a man's necktie, in the grounds of an empty villa, in a park of the foreign city to which she is travelling on the flight now boarding at Gate 14.

Crossing the tarmac to the plane Lise follows, with her quite long stride, closely on the heels of the fellow-passenger whom she appears finally to have chosen to adhere to. This is a rosy-faced, sturdy young man of about thirty; he is dressed in a dark business suit and carries a black brief-case. She follows him purposefully, careful to block the path of any other traveller whose aimless hurry might intervene between Lise and this man. Meanwhile, closely behind Lise, almost at her side, walks a man who in turn seems anxious to be close to her. He tries unsuccessfully to catch her attention. He is bespectacled, half-smiling, young, dark, long-nosed and stooping. He wears a check shirt and beige corduroy trousers. A camera is slung over his shoulders and a coat over his arm.

Up the steps they go, the pink and shiny businessman, Lise at his heels, and at hers the hungrier-looking man. Up the steps and into the plane. The air-hostess says good morning at the door while a steward farther up the aisle of the economy class blocks the progress of the staggering file and helps a young woman with two young children to bundle their coats up on the rack. The way is clear at last. Lise's businessman finds a seat next to the right-hand window in a three-seat row. Lise takes the middle seat next to him, on his left, while the lean hawk swiftly throws his coat and places his camera up on the rack and sits down next to Lise in the end seat.

Lise begins to fumble for her seat-belt. First she reaches down the right-hand side of her seat which adjoins that of the dark-suited man. At the same time she takes the left-hand section. But the right-hand buckle she gets hold of is that of her neighbour. It does not fit in the left-hand buckle as she tries to make it do. The dark-suited neighbour, fumbling also for his seat-belt, frowns as he seems to realize that she has the wrong part, and makes an unintelligible sound. Lise says, 'I think I've got yours.'

He fishes up the buckle that properly belongs to Lise's seat-belt. She says, 'Oh yes. I'm so sorry.' She giggles and he formally smiles and brings his smile to an end, now fastening his seat-belt intently and then looking out of the window at the wing of the plane, silvery with its rectangular patches.

Lise's left-hand neighbour smiles. The loudspeaker tells the passengers to fasten their seat-belts and refrain from smoking. Her admirer's brown eyes are warm, his smile, as wide as his forehead, seems to take up most of his lean face. Lise says, audibly above the other voices on the plane, 'You look like Red Riding-Hood's grandmother. Do you want to eat me up?'

The engines rev up. Her ardent neighbour's widened lips give out deep, satisfied laughter, while he slaps her knee in applause. Suddenly her other neighbour looks at Lise in alarm. He stares, as if recognizing her, with his brief-case on his lap, and his hand in the position of pulling out a batch of papers. Something about Lise, about her exchange with the man on her left, has caused a kind of paralysis in his act of fetching out some papers from his brief-case. He opens his mouth, gasping and startled, staring at her as if she is someone he has known and forgotten and now sees again. She smiles at him; it is a smile of relief and delight. His hand moves again, hurriedly putting back the papers that he had half-drawn out of his brief-case. He trembles as he unfastens his seat-belt and makes as if to leave his seat, grabbing his brief-case.

On the evening of the following day he will tell the police, quite truthfully, 'The first time I saw her was at the airport. Then on the plane. She sat beside me.'

'You never saw her before at any time? You didn't know her?'

'No, never.'

'What was your conversation on the plane?'

'Nothing. I moved my seat. I was afraid.'

'Afraid?'

'Yes, frightened. I moved to another seat, away from her.'

'What frightened you?'

'I don't know.'

'Why did you move your seat at that time?'

'I don't know. I must have sensed something.'

'What did she say to you?'

'Nothing much. She got her seat-belt mixed with mine. Then she was carrying on a bit with the man at the end seat.'

Now, as the plane taxis along the runway, he gets up. Lise and the man in the aisle seat look up at him, taken by surprise at the abruptness of his movements. Their seat-belts fasten them to their seats and they are unable immediately to make way for him, as he indicates that he wants to pass. Lise looks, for an instant, slightly senile, as if she felt, in addition to bewilderment, a sense of defeat or physical incapacity. She might be about to cry or protest against a pitiless frustration of her will. But an air-hostess, seeing the standing man, has left her post by the exit-door and briskly comes up the aisle to their seat. She says, 'The aircraft is taking off. Will you kindly remain seated and fasten your seat-belt?'

The man says, in a foreign accent, 'Excuse me, please. I wish to change.' He starts to squeeze past Lise and her companion.

The air-hostess, evidently thinking that the man has an urgent need to go to the lavatory, asks the two if they would mind getting up to let him pass and return to their seats as quickly as possible. They unfasten their belts, stand aside in the aisle, and he hurries up the plane with the air-hostess leading the way. But he does not get as far as the toilet cubicles. He stops at an empty middle seat upon which the people on either side, a white-haired fat man and a young girl, have dumped hand-luggage and magazines. He pushes himself past the woman who is seated on the outside seat and asks her to remove the luggage. He himself lifts it, shakily, his solid strength all gone. The air-hostess turns to remonstrate, but the two people have obediently made the seat vacant for him. He sits, fastens his seat-belt, ignoring the air-hostess, her reproving, questioning protests, and heaves a deep breath as if he had escaped from death by a small margin.

Lise and her companion have watched the performance. Lise smiles bitterly.

The dark man by her side says, 'What's wrong with him?'

'He didn't like us,' Lise says.

'What did we do to him?'

'Nothing. Nothing at all. He must be crazy. He must be nutty.'

The plane now comes to its brief halt before revving up for the take-off run. The engines roar and the plane is off, is rising and away. Lise says to her neighbour, 'I wonder who he is?'

'Some kind of a nut,' says the man. 'But it's all the better for us, we can get acquainted.' His stringy hand takes hers; he holds it tightly. 'I'm Bill,' he says. 'What's your name?'

'Lise.' She lets him grip her hand as if she hardly knows that he is holding it. She stretches her neck to see above the heads of the people in front, and says, 'He's sitting there reading the paper as if nothing had happened.'

The stewardess is handing out copies of newspapers. A steward who has followed her up the aisle stops at the seat where the dark-suited man has settled and is now tranquilly scanning the front page of his newspaper. The steward inquires if he is all right now, sir?

The man looks up with an embarrassed smile and shyly apologizes.

'Yes, fine. I'm sorry...'

'Was there anything the matter, sir?'

'No, really. Please. I'm fine here, thanks. Sorry... it was nothing, nothing.'

The steward goes away with his eyebrows mildly raised in resignation at the chance eccentricity of a passenger. The plane purrs forward. The no-smoking lights go out and the loud-speaker confirms that the passengers may now unfasten their seat-belts and smoke.

Lise unfastens hers and moves to the vacated window seat.

'I knew,' she says. 'In a way I knew there was something wrong with him.'

Bill moves to sit next to her in the middle seat and says, 'Nothing wrong with him at all. Just a fit of puritanism. He was unconsciously jealous when he saw we'd hit it off together, and he made out he was outraged as if we'd been doing something indecent. Forget him; he's probably a clerk in an insurance brokers' from the looks of him. Nasty little bureaucrat. Limited. He wasn't your type.'

'How do you know?' Lise says immediately as if responding only to Bill's use of the past tense, and, as if defying it by a counter-demonstration to the effect that the man continues to exist in the present, she half-stands to catch sight of the stranger's head, eight rows forward in a middle seat, at the other side of the aisle, now bent quietly over his reading.

'Sit down,' Bill says. 'You don't want anything to do with that type. He was frightened of your psychedelic clothes. Terrified.'

'Do you think so?'

'Yes. But I'm not.'

259

The stewardesses advance up the aisle bearing trays of food which they start to place before the passengers. Lise and Bill pull down the table in front of their seats to receive their portions. It is a mid-morning compromise snack composed of salami on lettuce, two green olives, a rolled-up piece of boiled ham containing a filling of potato salad and a small pickled something, all laid upon a slice of bread. There is also a round cake, swirled with white and chocolate cream, and a corner of silver-wrapped processed cheese with biscuits wrapped in cellophane. An empty plastic coffee cup stands by on each of their trays.

Lise takes from her tray the transparent plastic envelope which contains the sterilized knife, fork and spoon necessary for the meal. She feels the blade of the knife. She presses two of her fingers against the prongs of her fork. 'Not very sharp,' she says.

'Who needs them, anyway?' says Bill. 'This is awful food.'

'Oh, it looks all right. I'm hungry. I only had a cup of coffee for my breakfast. There wasn't time.'

'You can eat mine too,' says Bill. 'I stick as far as possible to a very sensible diet. This stuff is poison, full of toxics and chemicals. It's far too Yin.'

'I know,' said Lise. 'But considering it's a snack on a plane –'

'You know what Yin is?' he says.

She says, 'Well, sort of . . .' in a vaguely embarrassed way, 'but it's only a snack, isn't it?'

'You understand what Yin is?'

'Well, something sort of like this – all bitty.'

'No, Lise,' he says.

'Well it's a kind of slang, isn't it? You say a thing's a bit too yin . . .'; plainly she is groping.

'Yin,' says Bill, 'is the opposite of Yang.'

She giggles and, half-rising, starts searching with her eyes for the man who is still on her mind.

'This is serious,' Bill says, pulling her roughly back into her seat. She laughs and begins to eat.

'Yin and Yang are philosophies,' he says. 'Yin represents space. Its colour is purple. Its element is water. It is external. That salami is Yin and those olives are Yin. They are full of toxics. Have you ever heard of macrobiotic food?'

'No, what is it?' she says cutting into the open salami sandwich.

'You've got a lot to learn. Rice, unpolished rice is the basis of macrobiotics. I'm going to start a centre in Naples next week. It is a cleansing diet. Physically, mentally and spiritually.'

'I hate rice,' she says.

'No, you only think you do. He who hath ears let him hear.' He smiles widely towards her, he breathes into her face and touches her knee. She eats on with composure. 'I'm an Enlightenment Leader in the movement,' he says.

The stewardess comes with two long metal pots. 'Tea or coffee?' 'Coffee,' says Lise, holding out her plastic cup, her arm stretched in front of Bill. When this is done, 'For you, sir?' says the stewardess.

Bill places his hand over his cup and benignly shakes his head.

'Don't you want anything to eat, sir?' says the stewardess, regarding Bill's untouched tray.

'No, thank you,' says Bill.

Lise says, 'I'll eat it. Or at least, some of it.'

The stewardess passes on to the next row, unconcerned.

'Coffee is Yin,' says Bill.

Lise looks towards his tray. 'Are you sure you don't want that open sandwich? It's delicious. I'll eat it if you don't want it. After all, it's paid for, isn't it?'

'Help yourself,' he says. 'You'll soon change your eating habits, though, now that we've got to know each other.'

'Whatever do you eat when you travel abroad?' Lise says, exchanging his tray for hers, retaining only her coffee.

'I carry my diet with me. I never eat in restaurants and hotels unless I have to. And if I do, I choose very carefully. I go where I can get a little fish, maybe, and rice, and perhaps a bit of goat's cheese. Which are Yang. Cream cheese – in fact butter, milk, anything that comes from the cow – is too Yin. You become what you eat. Eat cow and you become cow.'

A hand, fluttering a sheet of white paper, intervenes from behind them.

They turn to see what is being offered. Bill grasps the paper. It is the log of the plane's flight, informing the passengers as to the altitude, speed and present geographical position, and requesting them to read it and pass it on.

Lise continues to look back, having caught sight of the face behind her. In the window seat, next to a comfortably plump woman and a young girl in her teens, is a sick-looking man, his eyes yellow-brown and watery, deep-set in their sockets, his face pale green. It was he who had handed forward the chart. Lise stares, her lips parted slightly, and she frowns as if speculating on the man's identity. He looks away, first out of the window, then down towards the floor, embarrassed. The woman does not change her expression, but the young girl, understanding Lise to be questioning by her stare the man behind, says, 'It's only the flight chart.' But Lise stares on. The sick-looking man looks at his companions and then down at his knees, and Lise's stare does not appear to be helping his sickness.

A nudge from Bill composes her so far that she turns and faces forward again. He says, 'It's only the flight chart. Do you want to see it?' And since she does not reply he thrusts it forward to bother it about the ears of the people in front until they receive it from his hand.

Lise starts to eat her second snack. 'You know, Bill,' she says, 'I think you were right about that crazy man who moved his seat. He wasn't my type at all and I wasn't his type. Just as a matter of interest, I mean, because I didn't take the slightest notice of him and I'm not looking to pick up strangers. But you mentioned that he wasn't my type and, of course, let me tell you, if he thought I was going to make up to him he made a mistake.'

'I'm your type,' Bill says.

She sips her coffee and looks round, glimpsing through the partition of the seats the man behind her. He stares ahead with glazed and quite unbalanced eyes, those eyes far too wide open to signify anything but some sort of mental distance from reality; he does not see Lise now, as she peers at him, or, if so, he appears to have taken a quick turn beyond caring and beyond embarrassment.

Bill says, 'Look at me, not at him.'

She turns back to Bill with an agreeable and indulgent smile. The stewardesses come efficiently collecting the trays, cluttering one upon the other. Bill, when their trays are collected, puts up first Lise's table and then his own. He puts his arm through hers.

'I'm your type,' he says, 'and you're mine. Are you planning to stay with friends?'

'No, but I have to meet somebody.'

'No chance of us meeting some time? How long are you planning to stay in the city?'

'I have no definite plans,' she says. 'But I could meet you for a drink tonight. Just a short drink.'

'I'm staying at the Metropole,' he says. 'Where will you be staying?'

'Oh, just a small place. Hotel Tomson.'

'I don't think I know Hotel Tomson.'

'It's quite small. It's cheap but clean.'

'Well, at the Metropole,' Bill says, 'they don't ask any questions.'

'As far as I'm concerned,' Lise says, 'they can ask any questions they like. I'm an idealist.'

'That's exactly what I am,' Bill says. 'An idealist. You're not offended, are you? I only meant that if we get acquainted, I think, somehow, I'm your type and you're my type.'

'I don't like crank diets,' Lise says. 'I don't need diets. I'm in good form.'

'Now, I can't let that pass, Lise,' Bill says. 'You don't know what you're talking about. The macrobiotic system is not just a diet, it's a way of life.'

She says, 'I have somebody to meet some time this after-noon or this evening.'

'What for?' he says. 'Is it a boy-friend?'

'Mind your own business,' she says. 'Stick to your yin and your yang.'

'Yin and Yang,' he says, 'is something that you've got to understand. If we could have a little time together, a little peaceful time, in a room, just talking, I could give you some idea of how it works. It's an idealist's way of life. I'm hoping to get the young people of Naples interested in it. I should think there would be many young people of Naples interested. We're opening a macrobiotic restaurant there, you know.'

Lise peers behind her again at the staring, sickly man. 'A strange type,' she says.

'With a room behind the public dining-hall, a room for strict observers who are on Regime Seven. Regime Seven is cereals only, very little liquid. You take such a very little liquid that you can pee only three times a day if you're a man, two if you're a woman. Regime Seven is a very elevated regime in macrobiotics. You become like a tree. People become what they eat.'

'Do you become a goat when you eat goat's cheese?'

'Yes, you become lean and stringy like a goat. Look at me, I haven't a spare piece of fat on my body. I'm not an Enlighten-ment Leader for nothing.'

'You must have been eating goat's cheese,' she says. 'This man back here is like a tree, have you seen him?'

'Behind the private room for observers of Regime Seven,' Bill says, 'there will be another little room for tranquillity and quiet. It should do well in Naples once we get the youth movement started. It's to be called the Yin-Yang Young. It does well in Denmark. But middle-aged people take the diet too. In the States many senior citizens are on macrobiotics.'

'The men in Naples are sexy.'

'On this diet the Regional Master for Northern Europe recommends one orgasm a day. At least. In the Mediterranean countries we are still researching that aspect.'

'He's afraid of me,' Lise whispers, indicating with a jerk of her head the man behind her. 'Why is everybody afraid of me?'

'What do you mean? I'm not afraid of you.' Bill looks round, impatiently, and as if only to oblige her. He looks away again. 'Don't bother with him,' he says. 'He's a mess.'

Lise gets up. 'Excuse me,' she says, 'I have to go and wash.'

'See you come back,' he says.

She passes across him to the aisle, holding in her hand both her hand-bag and the paperback book she bought at the airport, and as she does so she takes the opportunity to look carefully at the three people in the row behind, the ill-looking man, the plump woman and the young girl, who sit without conversing, as it seems unconnected with each other. Lise stands for a moment in the aisle, raising the arm on which the hand-bag is slung from the wrist, so that the paperback, now held between finger and thumb, is visible. She seems to display it deliberately, as if she is one of those spies one reads about who effect recognition by pre-arranged signals and who verify their contact with another agent by holding a certain paper in a special way.

Bill looks up at her and says, 'What's the matter?'

She starts moving forward, at the same time answering Bill: 'The matter?'

'You won't need that book,' Bill says.

She looks at the book in her hand as if wondering where it came from and with a little laugh hesitates by his side long enough to toss it on to her seat before she goes up the plane towards the toilets.

Two people are waiting in line ahead of her. She takes her place abstractedly, standing in fact almost even with the row where her first neighbour, the businessman, is sitting. But she does not seem to be aware of him or to care in the slightest that he glances up at her twice, three times, at first apprehensively and then, as she continues to ignore him, less so. He turns a page of his newspaper and folds it conveniently for reading, and reads it without looking at her again, settling further into his seat with the slight sigh of one whose visitor has left and who is at last alone.

It has turned out that the sick-looking man is after all connected with the plump woman and the young girl who sat beside him on the plane. He is coming out of the airport building, now, not infirmly but with an air of serious exhaustion, accompanied by the woman and the girl.

Lise stands a few yards away. By her side is Bill; their luggage is on the pavement beside them. She says, 'Oh there he is!' and leaves Bill's side, running up to the sick-eyed man. 'Excuse me!' she says.

He hesitates, and makes an awkward withdrawal: two steps backward, and with the steps he seems to withdraw even more his chest, shoulders, legs and face. The plump woman looks at Lise inquiringly while the girl just stands and looks.

Lise addresses the man in English. She says, 'Excuse me, but I wondered if you wanted to share a limousine to the centre. It works out cheaper than a taxi, if the passengers agree to share, and it's quicker than the bus, of course.'

The man looks at the pavement as if inwardly going through a ghastly experience. The plump woman says, 'No, thank you. We're being met.' And touching the man on the arm, moves on. He follows, as if bound for the scaffold while the girl stares blankly at Lise before walking round and past her. But Lise quickly moves with the group, and once again confronts the man. 'I'm sure we've met somewhere before,' she says. The man rolls his head slightly as if he has toothache or a headache. 'I would be so grateful,' Lise says, 'for a lift.'

'I'm afraid –' says the woman. And just then a man in a chauffeur's uniform comes up. 'Good morning, m' lord,' he says. 'We're parked over there. Did you have a good trip?'

The man has opened his mouth wide but without making a sound; now he closes his lips tight.

'Come along,' says the plump woman, while the girl turns in an unconcerned way. The plump woman says sweetly to Lise, while brushing past her, 'I'm sorry, we can't stop at the moment. The car's waiting and we have no extra room.'

Lise shouts, 'But your luggage – you've forgotten your luggage.'

The chauffeur turns cheerily and says over his shoulder, 'No luggage, Miss, they don't bring luggage. Got all they need at the villa.' He winks and breezes about his business.

The three follow him across the street to the rows of waiting cars and are followed by other travellers who stream out of the airport building.

Lise runs back to Bill. He says, 'What are you up to?'

'I thought I knew him,' Lise says. She is crying, her tears fall heavily. She says, 'I was sure he was the right one. I've got to meet someone.'

Bill says, 'Don't cry, don't cry, people are looking. What's the matter? I don't get it.' At the same time he grins with his wide mouth as if to affirm that the incomprehensible needs must be a joke. 'I don't get it,' he says, pulling out of his pocket two men's-size paper handkerchiefs, and, selecting one, handing it to Lise. 'Who did you think he was?'

Lise wipes her eyes and blows her nose. She clutches the paper handkerchief in her fist. She says, 'It's a disappointing start to my holidays. I was sure.'

'You've got me for the next few days if you like,' Bill says. 'Don't you want to see me again? Come on, we'll get a taxi, you'll feel better in a taxi. You can't go on the bus, crying like that. I don't get it. I can give you what you want, wait and see.'

On the pavement, further up, among a cluster of people waiting for a taxi is the sturdy young man in his business suit, holding his brief-case. Lise looks listlessly at Bill, then beyond Bill, and just as listlessly takes in the man whose rosy face is turned towards her. He lifts his suitcase immediately he catches sight of her and crosses the road amongst the traffic, moving quickly away and away. But Lise is not watching him any more, she does not even seem to have remembered him.

In the taxi she laughs harshly when Bill tries to kiss her. Then she lets him kiss her, emerging from the contact with raised eyebrows as who should say, 'What next?' 'I'm your type,' Bill says.

The taxi stops at the grey stone downtown Hotel Tomson. She says, 'What's all that on the floor?' and points to a scatter of small seeds. Bill looks at them closely and then at his zipper-bag which has come unzipped by a small fraction.

'Rice,' he says. 'One of my sample packs must have burst and this bag isn't closed properly.' He zips up the bag and says, 'Never mind.'

He takes her to the narrow swing doors and hands her suitcase to the porter. 'I'll look for you at seven in the hall of the Metropole,' he says. He kisses her on the cheek and again she raises her eyebrows. She pushes the swing door and goes with it, not looking back.

CHAPTER 4

AT THE HOTEL desk she seems rather confused as if she is not quite sure where she is. She gives her name and when the concierge asks for her passport she evidently does not immediately understand, for she asks him what he wants first in Danish, then French. She tries Italian, lastly English. He smiles and responds to Italian and English, again requesting her passport in both languages.

'It is confusing,' she says in English, handing over her passport.

'Yes, you left part of yourself at home,' the concierge says. 'That other part, he is still en route to our country but he will catch up with you in a few hours' time. It's often the way with travel by air, the passenger arrives ahead of himself. Can I send you to your room a drink or a coffee?'

'No, thank you.' She turns to follow the waiting page-boy, then turns back. 'When will you be finished with my passport?'

'Any time, any time, Madam. When you come down again. When you go out. Any time.' He looks at her dress and coat, then turns to some other people who have just arrived. While the boy waits, dangling a room-key, to take her up, Lise pauses for a moment to have a good look at them. They are a family: mother, father, two sons and a small daughter all speaking German together volubly. Lise is meanwhile gazed back at by the two sons. She turns away, impatiently gesturing the page-boy towards the lift, and follows him.

In her room she gets rid of the boy quickly, and without even taking her coat off lies down on the bed, staring at the ceiling. She breathes deeply and deliberately, in and out, for a few minutes. Then she gets up, takes off her coat, and examines what there is of the room.

It is a bed with a green cotton cover, a bedside table, a rug, a dressing-table, two chairs, a small chest of drawers; there is a wide tall window which indicates that it had once formed part of a much larger room, now partitioned into two or three rooms in the interests of hotel economy; there is a small bathroom with a bidet, a lavatory, a wash-basin and a shower. The walls and a built-in cupboard have been a yellowish cream but are now dirty with dark marks giving evidence of past pieces of furniture now removed or rearranged. Her suitcase lies on a rack-table. The bedside light is a curved chromium stand with a parchment shade. Lise switches it on. She switches on the central light which is encased in a mottled glass globe; the light flicks on, then immediately flickers out as if, having served a long succession of clients without complaint, Lise is suddenly too much for it.

She tramps heavily into the bathroom and first, without hesitation, peers into the drinking-glass as if fully expecting to find what she does indeed find: two Alka-Seltzers, quite dry, having presumably been put there by the previous occupant who no doubt had wanted to sober up but who had finally lacked the power or memory to fill the glass with water and drink the salutary result.

By the side of the bed is a small oblong box bearing three pictures without words to convey to clients of all languages which bell-push will bring which room attendant. Lise examines this with a frown, as it were deciphering with the effort necessary to those more accustomed to word-reading the three pictures which represent first a frilly maid with a long-handled duster over her shoulder, next a waiter carrying a tray and lastly a man in buttoned uniform bearing a folded garment over his arm. Lise presses the maid. A light goes on in the box illuminating the picture. Lise sits on the bed and waits. Then she takes off her shoes and, watching the door for a few seconds more, presses the buttoned valet who likewise does not come. Nor does room-service after many more minutes. Lise lifts the telephone, demands the concierge and complains in a torrent that the bell-pushes bring no answer, the room is dirty, the tooth-glass has not been changed since the last guest left, the central light needs a new bulb, and that the bed, contrary to the advance specifications of her travel agency, has a too-soft mattress. The concierge advises her to press the bell for the maid.

Lise has started reciting her list over again from the beginning, when the maid does appear with a question-mark on her face. Lise puts down the receiver rather loudly and points to the light which the maid tries for herself, then, nodding her understanding of the case, makes to leave. 'Wait!' says Lise, first in English then in French, to neither of which the maid responds. Lise produces the glass with its Alka-Seltzers nestled at the bottom. 'Filthy!' Lise says in English. The maid obligingly fills the glass from the tap and hands it to Lise. 'Dirty!' Lise shouts in French. The maid understands, laughs at the happening, and this time makes a quick getaway with the glass in her hand.

Lise slides open the cupboard, pulls down a wooden hanger and throws it across the room with a clatter, then lies down on the bed. Presently she looks at her watch. It is five past one. She opens her suitcase and carefully extracts a short dressing-gown. She takes out a dress, hangs it in the cupboard, takes it off the hanger again, folds it neatly and puts it back. She takes out her sponge-bag and bedroom slippers, undresses, puts on her dressing-gown and goes into the bathroom, shutting the door. She has reached the point of taking a shower when she hears voices from her room, a scraping sound, a man's and a girl's. Putting forth her head from the bathroom door, she sees a man in light brown overalls with a pair of steps and an electric light bulb, accompanied by the maid. Lise comes

271

out in her dressing-gown without having properly dried herself in the evident interest of protecting her hand-bag which
lies on the bed. Her dressing-gown clings damply to her.
'Where is the tooth-glass?' Lise demands. 'I must have a glass
for water.' The maid touches her head to denote forgetfulness
and departs with a swish of her skirt, never to return within
Lise's cognizance. However, Lise soon makes known her need
for a drinking-glass on the telephone to the concierge,
threatening to leave the hotel immediately if she doesn't get
her water-glass right away.

While waiting for the threat to take effect Lise again
considers the contents of her suitcase. This seems to present
her with a problem, for she takes out a pink cotton dress, hangs
it in the cupboard, then after hesitating for a few seconds she
takes it off the hanger again, folds it carefully and lays it back in
her case. It may be that she is indeed contemplating an immediate departure from the hotel. But when another maid arrives
with two drinking-glasses, apologies in Italian and the explanation that the former maid had gone off duty, Lise continues to
look through her belongings in a puzzled way, taking nothing
further out of her suitcase.

This maid, seeing laid out on the bed the bright-coloured
dress and coat in which Lise had arrived, inquires amiably if
Madam is going to the beach.

'No,' says Lise.

'You American?' says the maid.

'No,' Lise says.

'English?'

'No.' Lise turns her back to continue her careful examination of her clothes in the suitcase, and the maid goes out with
an unwanted air, saying, 'Good day.'

Lise is lifting the corners of her carefully packed things, as if
in absent-minded accompaniment to some thought, who
knows what? Then, with some access of decision, she takes
off her dressing-gown and slippers and starts putting on again

the same clothes that she wore on her journey. When she is dressed she folds the dressing-gown, puts the slippers back in their plastic bag, and replaces them in her suitcase. She also puts back everything that she has taken out of her sponge-bag, and packs this away.

Now she takes from an inside pocket of her suitcase a brochure with an inset map which she spreads out on the bed. She studies it closely, finding first the spot where the Hotel Tomson is situated and from there traces with her finger various routes leading into and away from the centre of the town. Lise stands, bending over it. The room is dark although it is not yet two in the afternoon. Lise switches on the central light and pores over her map.

It is marked here and there with tiny pictures which denote historic buildings, museums and monuments. Eventually Lise takes a ball-point pen from her bag and marks a spot in a large patch of green, the main parkland of the city. She puts a little cross beside one of the small pictures which is described on the map as 'The Pavilion'. She then folds up the map and replaces it in the pamphlet which she then edges in her hand-bag. The pen lies, apparently forgotten, on the bed. She looks at herself in the glass, touches her hair, then locks her suitcase. She finds the car-keys that she had failed to leave behind this morning and attaches them once more to her key-ring. She puts the bunch of keys in her hand-bag, picks up her paperback book and goes out, locking the door behind her. Who knows her thoughts? Who can tell?

She is downstairs at the desk where, behind the busy clerks, numbered pigeon-holes irregularly contain letters, packages, the room-keys, or nothing, and above them the clock shows twelve minutes past two. Lise puts her room-key on the counter and asks for her passport in a loud voice causing the clerk whom she addresses, another clerk who sits working an adding machine, and several other people who are standing and sitting in the hotel lobby, to take notice of her.

The women stare at her clothes. They, too, are dressed brightly for a southern summer, but even here in this holiday environment Lise looks brighter. It is possibly the combination of colours – the red in her coat and the purple in her dress – rather than the colours themselves which drags attention to her, as she takes her passport in its plastic envelope from the clerk, he looking meanwhile as if he bears the whole of the eccentricities of humankind upon his slender shoulders.

Two girls, long-legged, in the very brief skirts of the times, stare at Lise. Two women who might be their mothers stare too. And possibly the fact that Lise's outfit comes so far and unfashionably below her knees gives an extra shockingness to her appearance that was not even apparent in the less up-to-date Northern city from which she set off that morning. Skirts are worn shorter here in the South. Just as, in former times, when prostitutes could be discerned by the brevity of their skirts compared with the normal standard, so Lise in her knee-covering clothes at this moment looks curiously of the street-prostitute class beside the mini-skirted girls and their mothers whose knees at least can be seen.

So she lays the trail, presently to be followed by Interpol and elaborated upon with due art by the journalists of Europe for the few days it takes for her identity to be established.

'I want a taxi,' Lise says loudly to the uniformed boy who stands by the swing door. He goes out to the street and whistles. Lise follows and stands on the pavement. An elderly woman, small, neat and agile in a yellow cotton dress, whose extremely wrinkled face is the only indication of her advanced age, follows Lise to the pavement. She, too, wants a taxi, she says in a gentle voice, and she suggests to Lise that they might share. Which way is Lise going? This woman seems to see nothing strange about Lise, so confidently does she approach her. And in fact, although this is not immediately apparent, the woman's eyesight is sufficiently dim, her hearing faint enough, to eliminate, for her, the garish effect of Lise on normal perceptions.

'Oh,' says Lise, 'I'm only going to the Centre. I've no definite plans. It's foolish to have plans.' She laughs very loudly.

'Thank you, the Centre is fine for me,' says the woman, taking Lise's laugh for acquiescence in the sharing of the taxi.

And, indeed, they do both load into the taxi and are off.

'Are you staying here long?' says the woman.

'This will keep it safe,' says Lise, stuffing her passport down the back of the seat, stuffing it down till it is out of sight.

The old lady turns her spry nose towards this operation. She looks puzzled for an instant, but soon complies with the action, moving forward to allow Lise more scope in shoving the little booklet out of sight.

'That's that,' says Lise, leaning back, breathing deeply, and looking out of the window. 'What a lovely day!'

The old lady leans back too, as if leaning on the trusting confidence that Lise has inspired. She says, 'I left my passport in the hotel, with the Desk.'

'It's according to your taste,' Lise says opening the window to the slight breeze. Her lips part blissfully as she breathes in the air of the wide street on the city's outskirts.

Soon they run into traffic. The driver inquires the precise point at which they wish to be dropped.

'The Post Office,' Lise says. Her companion nods.

Lise turns to her. 'I'm going shopping. It's the first thing I do on my holidays. I go and buy the little presents for the family first, then that's off my mind.'

'Oh, but in *these* days,' says the old lady. She folds her gloves, pats them on her lap, smiles at them.

'There's a big department store near the Post Office,' Lise says. 'You can get everything you want there.'

'My nephew is arriving this evening.'

'The traffic!' says Lise.

They pass the Metropole Hotel. Lise says, 'There's a man in that hotel I'm trying to avoid.'

'Everything is different,' says the old lady.

'A girl isn't made of cement,' Lise says, 'but everything is different now, it's all changed, believe me.'

At the Post Office they pay the fare, each meticulously contributing the unfamiliar coins to the impatient, mottled and hillocky palm of the driver's hand, adding coins little by little, until the total is reached and the amount of the tip equally agreed between them and deposited; then they stand on the pavement in the centre of the foreign city, in need of coffee and a sandwich, accustoming themselves to the lay-out, the traffic crossings, the busy residents, the ambling tourists and the worried tourists, and such of the unencumbered youth who swing and thread through the crowds like antelopes whose heads, invisibly antlered, are airborne high to sniff the prevailing winds, and who so appear to own the terrain beneath their feet that they never look at it. Lise looks down at her clothes as if wondering if she is ostentatious enough.

Then, taking the old lady by the arm, she says, 'Come and have a coffee. We'll cross by the lights.'

All perky for the adventure, the old lady lets Lise guide her to the street-crossing where they wait for the lights to change and where, while waiting, the old lady gives a little gasp and a jerk of shock; she says, 'You left your passport in the taxi!'

'Well, I left it there for safety. Don't worry,' Lise says. 'It's taken care of.'

'Oh, I see.' The old lady relaxes, and she crosses the road with Lise and the waiting herd. 'I am Mrs Fiedke,' she says. 'Mr Fiedke passed away fourteen years ago.'

In the bar they sit at a small round table, place their bags, Lise's book and their elbows on it and order each a coffee and a ham-and-tomato sandwich. Lise props up her paperback book against her bag, as it were so that its bright cover is addressed to whom it may concern. 'Our home is in Nova Scotia,' says Mrs Fiedke, 'where is yours?'

'Nowhere special,' says Lise waving aside the triviality. 'It's written on the passport. My name's Lise.' She takes her arms out of the sleeves of her striped cotton coat and lets it fall behind her over the back of the chair. 'Mr Fiedke left everything to me and nothing to his sister,' says the old lady, 'but my nephew gets everything when I'm gone. I would have liked to be a fly on the wall when she heard.'

The waiter comes with their coffee and sandwiches, moving the book while he sets them down. Lise props it up again when he has gone. She looks around at the other tables and at the people standing up at the bar, sipping coffee or fruit-juice. She says, 'I have to meet a friend, but he doesn't seem to be here.'

'My dear, I don't want to detain you or take you out of your way.'

'Not at all. Don't think of it.'

'It was very kind of you to come along with me,' says Mrs Fiedke, 'as it's so confusing in a strange place. Very kind indeed.'

'Why shouldn't I be kind?' Lise says, smiling at her with a sudden gentleness.

'Well, I'll be all right just here after we've finished our snack. I'll just take a look round and do a bit of shopping. I won't keep you, my dear.'

'You can come shopping with me,' Lise says, very genially. 'Mrs Fiedke, it's a pleasure.'

'How very kind you are!'

'One should always be kind,' Lise says, 'in case it might be the last chance. One might be killed crossing the street, or even on the pavement, any time, you never know. So we should always be kind.' She cuts her sandwich daintily and puts a piece in her mouth.

Mrs Fiedke said, 'That's a very, very beautiful thought. But you mustn't think of accidents. I can assure you, I'm terrified of traffic.'

'So am I. Terrified.'

'Do you drive an automobile?' says the old lady.

'I do, but I'm afraid of traffic. You never know what crackpot's going to be at the wheel of another car.'

'These days,' says Mrs Fiedke.

'There's a department store not far from here,' Lise says. 'Want to come?'

They eat their sandwich and drink their coffee. Lise then orders a rainbow ice while Mrs Fiedke considers one way or another whether she really wants anything more, and eventually declines.

'Strange voices,' says the old lady looking round. 'Look at the noise.'

'Well, if you know the language.'

'Can you speak the language?'

'A bit. I can speak four.'

Mrs Fiedke marvels benevolently while Lise bashfully plays with crumbs on the tablecloth. The waiter brings the rainbow ice and while Lise lifts the spoon to start Mrs Fiedke says, 'It matches with your outfit.'

Lise laughs at this, longer than Mrs Fiedke had evidently expected. 'Beautiful colours,' Mrs Fiedke offers, as one might offer a cough-sweet. Lise sits before the brightly streaked ice-cream with her spoon in her hand and laughs on. Mrs Fiedke looks frightened, and more frightened as the voices of the bar stop to watch the laughing one; Mrs Fiedke shrinks into her old age, her face dry and wrinkled, her eyes gone into a far retreat, not knowing what to do. Lise stops suddenly and says, 'That was funny.'

The man behind the bar, having started coming over to their table to investigate a potential disorder, stops and turns back, muttering something. A few young men round the bar start up a mimic laugh-laugh-laugh but are stopped by the barman.

'When I went to buy this dress,' Lise says to Mrs Fiedke, 'do you know what they offered me first? – A stainless dress. Can you believe it? A dress that won't hold the stain if you drop coffee or ice-cream on it. Some new synthetic fabric. As if I would want a dress that doesn't show the stains!'

Mrs Fiedke, whose eager spirit is slowly returning from wherever it had been to take cover from Lise's laughter, looks at Lise's dress and says, 'Doesn't hold the stains? Very useful for travelling.'

'Not this dress,' Lise says, working her way through the rainbow ice; 'it was another dress. I didn't buy it, though. Very poor taste, I thought.' She has finished her ice. Again the two women fumble in their purses and at the same time Lise gives an expert's glance at the two small tickets, marked with the price, that have been left on the table. Lise edges one of them aside. 'That one's for the ice,' she says, 'and we share the other.'

'The torment of it,' Lise says. 'Not knowing exactly where and when he's going to turn up.'

She moves ahead of Mrs Fiedke up the escalator to the third floor of a department store. It is ten minutes past four by the big clock, and they have had to wait more than half an hour for it to open, both of them having forgotten about the southern shopping hours, and in this interval have walked round the block looking so earnestly for Lise's friend that Mrs Fiedke has at some point lost the signs of her initial bewilderment when this friend has been mentioned, and now shows only the traces of enthusiastic co-operation in the search. As they were waiting for the store to open, having passed the large iron-grated shutters again and again in their ambles round the block, Mrs Fiedke started to scan the passers-by.

'Would that be him, do you think? He looks very gaily dressed like yourself.'

'No, that's not him.'

'It's quite a problem, with all this choice. What about this one? No this one, I mean, crossing in front of that car? Would he be too fat?'

'No, it isn't him.'

'It's very difficult, my dear, if you don't know the cast of person.'

'He could be driving a car,' Lise had said when they at last found themselves outside the shop at the moment the gates were being opened.

They go up, now, to the third floor where the toilets are, skimming up with the escalator from which they can look down to see the expanse of each floor as the stairs depart from it. 'Not a great many gentlemen,' Mrs Fiedke remarks. 'I doubt if you'll find your friend here.'

'I doubt it too,' says Lise. 'Although there are quite a few men employed here, aren't there?'

'Oh, would he be a shop assistant?' Mrs Fiedke says.

'It depends,' says Lise.

'These days,' says Mrs Fiedke.

Lise stands in the ladies' room combing her hair while she waits for Mrs Fiedke. She stands at the basin where she has washed her hands, and, watching herself with tight lips in the glass, back-combs the white streak, and with great absorption places it across the darker locks on the crown of her head. At the basins on either side of her two other absorbed young women are touching up their hair and faces. Lise wets the tip of a finger and smooths her eyebrows. The women on either side collect their belongings and leave. Another woman, matronly with her shopping, bustles in and swings into one of the lavatory cubicles. Mrs Fiedke's cubicle still remains shut. Lise has finished tidying herself up; she waits. Eventually she knocks on Mrs Fiedke's door. 'Are you all right?'

She says again, 'Are you all right?' And again she knocks. 'Mrs Fiedke, are you all right?'

The latest comer now bursts out of her cubicle and makes for the wash-basin. Lise says to her, while rattling the handle of Mrs Fiedke's door, 'There's an old lady locked in here and I can't hear a sound. Something must have happened.' And she calls again, 'Are you all right, Mrs Fiedke?'

'Who is she?' says the other woman.

'I don't know.'

'But you're with her, aren't you?' The matron takes a good look at Lise.

'I'll go and get someone,' Lise says, and she shakes the handle one more time. 'Mrs Fiedke! Mrs Fiedke!' She presses her ear to the door. 'No sound,' she says, 'none at all.' Then she grabs her bag and her book from the wash-stand and dashes out of the ladies' room leaving the other woman listening and rattling at the door of Mrs Fiedke's cubicle.

Outside, the first department is laid out with sports equipment. Lise walks straight through, stopping only to touch one of a pair of skis, feeling and stroking the wood. A salesman approaches, but Lise has walked on, picking her way among the more populated area of School Clothing. Here she hovers over a pair of small, red fur-lined gloves laid out on the counter. The girl behind the counter stands ready to serve. Lise looks up at her. 'For my niece,' she says. 'But I can't remember the size. I think I won't risk it, thank you.' She moves across the department floor to Toys, where she spends some time examining a nylon dog which, at the flick of a switch attached to its lead, barks, trots, wags its tail and sits. Through Linen, to the down escalator goes Lise, scanning each approaching floor in her descent, but not hovering on any landing until she reaches the ground floor. Here she buys a silk scarf patterned in black and white. At a gadgets counter a salesman is demonstrating a cheap electric food-blender. Lise buys one of these, staring at the salesman when he attempts to include personal charm in his side of the bargain. He is a thin, pale man of early middle age, eager-eyed. 'Are you on holiday?' he says. 'American? Swedish?' Lise says, 'I'm in a hurry.' Resigned to his mistake, the salesman wraps her parcel, takes her money, rings up the till and gives her the change. Lise then takes the wide staircase leading to the basement. Here she buys a plastic zipper-bag in which she places her packages. She stops at the Records and Record-Players department and loiters with the small group that has gathered to hear a new pop-group disc. She holds her paperback well in evidence, her hand-bag and the new zipper-bag slung over her left arm just above the wrist, and her hands holding up the book in front of her chest like an identification notice carried by a displaced person.

> Come on over to my place
> For a sandwich, both of you,
> Any time . . .

The disc comes to an end. A girl with long brown pigtails is hopping about in front of Lise, continuing the rhythm with her elbows, her blue jeans, and apparently her mind, as a newly beheaded chicken continues for a brief time, now squawklessly, its panic career. Mrs Fiedke comes up behind Lise and touches her arm. Lise says, turning to smile at her, 'Look at this idiot girl. She can't stop dancing.'

'I think I fell asleep for a moment,' Mrs Fiedke says. 'It wasn't a bad turn. I just dropped off. Such kind people. They wanted to put me in a taxi. But why should I go back to the hotel? My poor nephew won't be there till 9 o'clock tonight or maybe later; he must have missed the earlier plane. The porter was so kind, ringing up to find out the time of the next plane. All that.'

'Look at her,' Lise says in a murmur. 'Just look at her. No, wait! – She'll start again when the man puts on the next record.'

The record starts, and the girl swings. Lise says, 'Do you believe in macrobiotics?'

'I'm a Jehovah's Witness,' says Mrs Fiedke. 'But that was after Mr Fiedke passed on. I have no problems any more. Mr Fiedke cut out his sister you know, because she had no religion. She questioned. There are some things which you can't. But I know this, if Mr Fiedke was alive today he would be a Witness too. In fact he was one in many ways without knowing it.'

'Macrobiotics is a way of life,' Lise says. 'That man at the Metropole, I met him on the plane. He's an Enlightenment Leader of the macrobiotics. He's on Regime Seven.'

'How delightful!' says Mrs Fiedke.

'But he isn't my type,' Lise says.

The girl with the pigtails is dancing on by herself in front of them, and as she suddenly steps back Mrs Fiedke has to retreat out of her way. 'Is she what they call a hippy?' she says.

'There were two others on the plane. I thought they were my type, but they weren't. I was disappointed.'

'But you are to meet your gentleman soon, won't you? Didn't you say?'

'Oh, *he's* my type,' Lise says.

'I must get a pair of slippers for my nephew. Size nine. He missed the plane.'

'This one's a hippy,' says Lise, indicating with her head a slouching bearded youth dressed in tight blue jeans, no longer blue, his shoulders draped with an assortment of cardigans and fringed leather garments, heavy for the time of year.

Mrs Fiedke looks with interest and whispers to Lise, 'They are hermaphrodites. It isn't their fault.' The young man turns as he is touched on the shoulder by a large blue-suited agent of the store. The bearded youth starts to argue and gesticulate, but this brings another, slighter, man to his other shoulder. They lead him protesting away towards the emergency exit stairway. A slight disturbance then occurs amongst the record-hearing crowd, some of whom take the young man's part, some of whom do not. 'He wasn't doing any harm!' 'He smelt awful!' 'Who do *you* think you are?'

Lise walks off towards Televisions, followed anxiously by Mrs Fiedke. Behind them the pigtailed girl is addressing her adjacent crowd: 'They think they're in America where if they don't like a man's face they take him out and shoot him.' A man's voice barks back: 'You couldn't see his face for the hair. Go back where you came from, little whore! In this country, we . . .'

The quarrel melts behind them as they come to the television sets where the few people who have been taking an interest in the salesman appear now to be torn between his calm rivulet of words and the incipient political uprising over at Records and Record-Players. Two television screens, one vast and one small, display the same programme, a wild-life documentary film which is now coming to an end; a charging herd of buffalo, large on one screen and small on the other, cross the two patches of vision while music of an unmistakably finale nature sends them on their way with equal volume from both machines. The salesman turns down the noise from the larger set, and continues to address his customers, who have now dwindled to two, meanwhile keeping an interested eye on Lise and Mrs Fiedke who hover behind.

'Would that be your gentleman?' Mrs Fiedke says, while the screens give a list of names responsible for the film, then another and another list of names. Lise says, 'I was just wondering myself. He looks a respectable type.'

'It's up to you,' says Mrs Fiedke. 'You're young and you have your life in front of you.'

A well-groomed female announcer comes on both televisions, small and large, to give out the early evening headlines, first stating that the time is 17.00 hours, then that a military coup has newly taken place in a middle-eastern country details of which are yet unknown. The salesman, abandoning his potential clients to their private deliberations, inclines his head towards Mrs Fiedke and inquires if he can help her.

'No thank you,' Lise replies in the tongue of the country. Whereupon the salesman comes close up and pursues Mrs Fiedke in English. 'We have big reductions, Madam, this week.' He looks winningly at Lise, eventually approaching to squeeze her arm. Lise turns to Mrs Fiedke. 'No good,' she says. 'Come on, it's getting late,' and she guides the old lady away to Gifts and Curios at the far end of the floor. 'Not my man at all. He tried to get familiar with me,' Lise says. 'The one I'm looking for will recognize me right away for the woman I am, have no fear of that.'

'Can you credit it?' says Mrs Fiedke looking back indignantly in the direction of Televisions. 'Perhaps we should report him. Where is the Office?'

'What's the use?' Lise says. 'We have no proof.'

'Perhaps we should go elsewhere for my nephew's slippers.'

'Do you really want to buy slippers for your nephew?' Lise says.

'I thought of slippers as a welcome present. My poor nephew – the hotel porter was so nice. The poor boy was to have arrived on this morning's flight from Copenhagen. I waited and I waited. He must have missed the plane. The porter looked up the time-table and there's another arriving tonight. I must remember not to go to bed. The plane gets in at ten-twenty but it may be eleven-thirty, twelve, before he gets to the hotel, you know.'

Lise is looking at the leather notecases, embossed with the city's crest. 'These look good,' Lise says. 'Get him one of these. He would remember all his life that you gave it to him.'

'I think slippers,' says Mrs Fiedke. 'Somehow I feel slippers. My poor nephew has been unwell, we had to send him to a clinic. It was either that or the other, they gave us no choice. He's so much better now, quite well again. But he needs rest. Rest, rest and more rest is what the doctor wrote. He takes size nine.'

Lise is playing with a corkscrew, then with a ceramic-handled cork. 'Slippers might make him feel like an invalid,' she says. 'Why don't you buy him a record or a book? How old is he?'

'Only twenty-four. It comes from the mother's side. Perhaps we should go to another shop.'

Lise leans over the counter to inquire which department is men's slippers. Patiently she translates the answer to Mrs Fiedke. 'Footwear on the third floor. We'll have to go back up. The other stores are much too expensive, they charge you what they like. The travel-folder recommends this place as they've got fixed prices.'

Up they go, once more, surveying the receding departments as they rise; they buy the slippers; they descend to the ground floor. There, near the street door, they find another gift department with a miscellany of temptations. Lise buys another scarf, bright orange. She buys a striped man's necktie, dark blue and yellow. Then, glimpsing through the crowd a rack from which dangles a larger assortment of men's ties, each neatly enfolded in transparent plastic, she changes her mind about the coloured tie she has just bought. The girl at the counter is not pleased by the difficulties involved in the refund of money, and accompanies Lise over to the rack to see if an exchange can be effected.

Lise selects two ties, one plain black knitted cotton, the other green. Then, changing her mind once more, she says, 'That green is too bright, I think.' The girl conveys exasperation, and in a manner of vexed resignation Lise says, 'All right, give me two black ties, they're always useful. Please remove the prices.' She returns to the counter where she had left Mrs Fiedke, pays the difference and takes her package. Mrs Fiedke appears from the doorway where she has been examining, by daylight, two leather notecases.

A shopman, who has been hovering by, in case she should be one of those who make a dash for it, goods in hand, follows her back to the counter. He says, 'They're both very good leather.'

Mrs Fiedke says, 'I think he has one already.' She chooses a paper-knife in a sheath. Lise stands watching. She says, 'I nearly bought one of those for my boy-friend at the airport before I left. It was almost the same but not quite.' The paper-knife is made of brassy metal, curved like a scimitar. The sheath is embossed but not, like the one Lise had considered earlier in the day, jewelled. 'The slippers are enough,' Lise says.

Mrs Fiedke says, 'You're quite right. One doesn't want to spoil them.' She looks at a key-case, then buys the paper-knife.

'If he uses a paper-knife,' Lise says, 'obviously he isn't a hippy. If he were a hippy he would open his letters with his fingers.'

'Would it be too much trouble,' she says to Lise, 'to put this in your bag? And the slippers – oh, where are the slippers?'

Her package of slippers is lost, is gone. She claims to have left it on the counter while she had been to the door to compare the two leather notecases. The package has been lifted, has been taken away by somebody. Everyone looks around for it and sympathizes, and points out that it was her own fault.

'Maybe he has plenty of slippers, anyway,' Lise says. 'Is he my type of man, do you think?'

'We ought to see the sights,' says Mrs Fiedke. 'We shouldn't let this golden opportunity go by without seeing the ruins.'

'If he's my type I want to meet him,' Lise says.

'Very much your type,' says Mrs Fiedke, 'at his best.'

'What a pity he's coming so late,' Lise says. 'Because I have a previous engagement with my boy-friend. However, if he doesn't turn up before your nephew arrives I want to meet your nephew. What's his name did you say?'

'Richard. We never called him Dick. Only his mother, but not us. I hope he gets the plane all right. Oh – where's the paper-knife?'

'You put it in here,' says Lise, pointing to her zipper-bag. 'Don't worry, it's safe. Let's get out of here.'

As they drift with the outgoing shoppers into the sunny street, Mrs Fiedke says, 'I hope he's on that plane. There was some talk that he would go to Barcelona first to meet his mother, then on here to meet up with me. But I wouldn't play. I just said No! No flying from Barcelona, I said. I'm a strict believer, in fact, a Witness, but I never trust the airlines from those countries where the pilots believe in the after-life. You are safer when they don't. I've been told the Scandinavian airlines are fairly reliable in that respect.'

Lise looks up and down the street and sighs. 'It can't be long now. My friend's going to turn up soon. He knows I've come all this way to see him. He knows it, all right. He's just waiting around somewhere. Apart from that I have no plans.'

'Dressed for the carnival!' says a woman, looking grossly at Lise as she passes, and laughing as she goes her way, laughing without possibility of restraint, like a stream bound to descend whatever slope lies before it.

CHAPTER 5

'IT IS IN my mind,' says Mrs Fiedke; 'it is in my mind and I can't think of anything else but that you and my nephew are meant for each other. As sure as anything, my dear, you are the person for my nephew. Somebody has got to take him on, anyhow, that's plain.'

'He's only twenty-four,' considers Lise. 'Much too young.'

They are descending a steep path leading from the ruins. Steps have been roughly cut out of the earthy track, outlined only by slats of wood which are laid at the edge of each step. Lise holds Mrs Fiedke's arm and helps her down one by one.

'How do you know his age?' says Mrs Fiedke.

'Well, didn't you tell me, twenty-four?' Lise says.

'Yes, but I haven't seen him for quite a time you know. He's been away.'

'Maybe he's even younger. Take care, go slowly.'

'Or it could be the other way. People age when they've had unpleasant experiences over the years. It just came to me while we were looking at those very interesting pavements in that ancient temple up there, that poor Richard may be the very man that you're looking for.'

'Well, it's your idea,' says Lise, 'not mine. I wouldn't know till I'd seen him. Myself, I think he's around the corner some-where, now, any time.'

'Which corner?' The old lady looks up and down the street which runs below them at the bottom of the steps.

'Any corner. Any old corner.'

'Will you feel a presence? Is that how you'll know?'

'Not really a presence,' Lise says. 'The lack of an absence, that's what it is. I know I'll find it. I keep on making mistakes, though.' She starts to cry, very slightly sniffing, weeping, and they stop on the steps while Mrs Fiedke produces a trembling pink face-tissue from her bag for Lise to dab her eyes with and blow her nose on. Sniffing, Lise throws the shredded little snitch of paper away and again takes Mrs Fiedke's arm to resume their descent. 'Too much self-control, which arises from fear and timidity, that's what's wrong with them. They're cowards, most of them.'

'Oh, I always believe *that*,' says Mrs Fiedke. 'No doubt about it. The male sex.'

They have reached the road where the traffic thunders past in the declining sunlight.

'Where do we cross?' Lise says, looking to right and left of the overwhelming street.

'They are demanding equal rights with us,' says Mrs Fiedke. 'That's why I never vote with the Liberals. Perfume, jewellery, hair down to their shoulders, and I'm not talking about the ones who were born like that. I mean, the ones that can't help it should be put on an island. It's the others I'm talking about. There was a time when they would stand up and open the door for you. They would take their hat off. But they want their equality today. All I say is that if God had intended them to be as good as us he wouldn't have made them different from us to the naked eye. They don't want to be all dressed alike any more. Which is only a move against us. You couldn't run an army like that, let alone the male sex. With all due respects to Mr Fiedke, may he rest in peace, the male sex is getting out of hand. Of course, Mr Fiedke knew his place as a man, give him his due.'

'We'll have to walk up to the intersection,' Lise says, guiding Mrs Fiedke in the direction of a distant policeman surrounded by a whirlpool of traffic. 'We'll never get a taxi here.'

'Fur coats and flowered poplin shirts on their backs,' says Mrs Fiedke as she winds along, conducted by Lise this way and that to avoid the oncoming people in the street. 'If we don't look lively,' she says, 'they will be taking over the homes and the children, and sitting about having chats while we go and fight to defend them and work to keep them. They won't be content with equal rights only. Next thing they'll want the upper hand, mark my words. Diamond ear-rings, I've read in the paper.'

'It's getting late,' says Lise. Her lips are slightly parted and her nostrils and eyes, too, are a fragment more open than usual; she is a stag scenting the breeze, moving step by step, inhibiting her stride to accommodate Mrs Fiedke's pace, she seems at the same time to search for a certain air-current, a glimpse and an intimation.

'I clean mine with toothpaste when I'm travelling,' confides Mrs Fiedke. 'The better stuff's in the bank back home, of course. The insurance is too high, isn't it? But you have to bring a few bits and pieces. I clean them with my toothbrush and ordinary toothpaste, then I rub them with the hand-towel. They come up very nicely. You can't trust the jewellers. They can always take them out and replace them with a fake.'

'It's getting late,' says Lise. 'There are so many faces. Where did all the faces come from?'

'I ought to take a nap,' says Mrs Fiedke, 'so that I won't feel too tired when my nephew arrives. Poor thing. We have to leave for Capri tomorrow morning. All the cousins, you know. They've taken such a charming villa and the past will never be mentioned. My brother made that clear to them. I made it clear to my brother.'

They have reached the circular intersection and turn into a side-street where a few yards ahead at the next corner there is a taxi-rank occupied by one taxi. This one taxi is taken by someone else just as they approach it.

'I smell burning,' says Mrs Fiedke as they stand at the corner waiting for another taxi to come along. Lise sniffs, her lips parted and her eyes moving widely from face to face among the passers-by. Then she sneezes. Something has happened to the people in the street, they are looking round, they are sniffing too. Somewhere nearby a great deal of shouting is going on.

Suddenly round the corner comes a stampede. Lise and Mrs Fiedke are swept apart and jostled in all directions by a large crowd composed mainly of young men, with a few smaller, older and grimmer men, and here and there a young girl, all yelling together and making rapidly for somewhere else. 'Tear-gas!' someone shouts and then a lot of people are calling out, 'Tear-gas!' A shutter on a shop-front near Lise comes down with a hasty clatter, then the other shops start closing for the day. Lise falls and is hauled to her feet by a tough man who leaves her and runs on.

Just before it reaches the end of the street which joins the circular intersection the crowd stops. A band of grey-clad policemen come running towards them, in formation, bearing tear-gas satchels and with their gas-masks at the ready. The traffic on the circular intersection has stopped. Lise swerves with her crowd into a garage where some mechanics in their overalls crouch behind the cars and others take refuge underneath a car which is raised on a cradle in the process of repair.

Lise fights her way to a dark corner at the back of the garage where a small red Mini-Morris, greatly dented, is parked behind a larger car. She wrenches at the door, forcefully, as if she expects it to be locked. It opens so easily as to throw her backwards, and as soon as she regains her balance she gets inside, locks herself in and puts her head down between her knees, breathing heavily, drawing in the smell of petrol blended faintly with a whiff of tear-gas. The demonstrators form up in the garage and are presently discovered and routed out by the police. Their exit is fairly orderly bar the shouting.

Lise emerges from the car with her zipper-bag and her hand-bag, looking to see what damage has been done to her clothes. The garage men are vociferously commenting on the affair. One is clutching his stomach proclaiming himself poisoned and vowing to sue the police for the permanent damage caused him by tear-gas. Another, with his hand to his throat, gasps that he is suffocating. The others are cursing the students whose gestures of solidarity, they declare in the colourful derisive obscenities of their mother-tongue, they can live without. They stop when Lise limps into view. There are six of them in all, including a young apprentice and a large burly man of middle age, without overalls, wearing only a white shirt and trousers and the definite air of the proprietor. Apparently seeing in Lise a tangible remnant of the troubles lately visited upon his garage, this big fellow turns on her to vent his fury with unmastered hysteria. He advises her to go home to the brothel where she came from, he reminds her that her grandfather was ten times cuckolded, that she was conceived in some ditch and born in another; after adorning the main idea with further illustrations he finally tells her she is a student.

Lise stands somewhat entranced; by her expression she seems almost consoled by this outbreak, whether because it relieves her own tensions after the panic or whether for some other reason. However, she puts a hand up to her eyes, covering them, and in the language of the country she says, 'Oh please, please. I'm only a tourist, a teacher from Iowa, New Jersey. I've hurt my foot.' She drops her hand and looks at her coat which is stained with a long black oily mark. 'Look at my clothes,' Lise says. 'My new clothes. It's best never to be born. I wish my mother and father had practised birth-control. I wish that pill had been invented at the time. I feel sick, I feel terrible.'

The men are impressed by this, one and all. Some are visibly cheered up. The proprietor turns one way and another with arms outstretched to call the whole assembly to witness his dilemma. 'Sorry, lady, sorry. How was I to know? Pardon me, but I thought you were one of the students. We have a lot of trouble from the students. Many apologies, lady. Was there something we can do for you? I'll call the First Aid. Come and sit down, lady, over here, inside my office, take a seat. You see the traffic outside, how can I call the ambulance through the traffic? Sit down, lady.' And, having ushered her into a tiny windowed cubicle, he sits Lise in its only chair beside a small sloping ledger-desk and thunders at the men to get to work.

Lise says, 'Oh please don't call anyone. I'll be all right if I can get a taxi to take me back to my hotel.'

'A taxi! Look at the traffic!'

Outside the archway that forms the entrance to the garage, there is a dense block of standing traffic.

The proprietor keeps going to look up and down the street and returning to Lise. He calls for benzine and a rag to clean Lise's coat. No rag clean enough for the purpose can be found and so he uses a big white handkerchief taken from the breast pocket of his coat which hangs behind the door of the little office. Lise takes off her black-stained coat and while he applies his benzine-drenched handkerchief to the stain, making it into a messy blur, Lise takes off her shoes and rubs her feet. She puts one foot up on the slanting desk and rubs. 'It's only a bruise,' she says, 'not a sprain. I was lucky. Are you married?'

The big man says, 'Yes, lady, I'm married,' and pauses in his energetic task to look at her with new, appraising and cautious eyes. 'Three children – two boys, one girl,' he says. He looks through the office at his men who are occupied with various jobs and who, although one or two of them cast a swift glance at Lise with her foot up on the desk, do not give any sign of noticing any telepathic distress signals their employer might be giving out.

The big man says to Lise, 'And yourself? Married?'

'I'm a widow,' Lise says, 'and an intellectual. I come from a family of intellectuals. My late husband was an intellectual. We had no children. He was killed in a motor accident. He was a bad driver, anyway. He was a hypochondriac, which means that he imagined that he had every illness under the sun.'

'This stain,' said the man, 'won't come out until you send the coat to the dry-cleaner.' He holds out the coat with great care, ready for her to put on; and at the same time as he holds it as if he means her, temptress in the old-fashioned style that she is, to get out of his shop, his eyes are shifting around in an undecided way.

Lise takes her foot off the desk, stands, slips into her shoes, shakes the skirt of her dress and asks him, 'Do you like the colours?'

'Marvellous,' he says, his confidence plainly diminishing in confrontation with this foreign distressed gentlewoman of intellectual family and conflicting appearance.

'The traffic's moving. I must get a taxi or a bus. It's late,' Lise says, getting into her coat in a business-like manner.

'Where are you staying, lady?'

'The Hilton,' she says.

He looks round his garage with an air of helpless, anticipatory guilt. 'I'd better take her in the car,' he mutters to the mechanic nearest him. The man does not reply but makes a slight movement of the hand to signify that it isn't for him to give permission.

Still the owner hesitates, while Lise, as if she had not overheard his remarks, gathers up her belongings, holds out her hand and says, 'Good-bye. Thank you very much for helping me.' And to the rest of the men she calls, 'Good-bye, good-bye, many thanks!'

The big man takes her hand and holds on to it tightly as if his grasp itself was a mental resolution not to let go this unforeseen, exotic, intellectual, yet clearly available treasure.

He holds on to her hand as if he was no fool, after all. 'Lady, I'm taking you to your hotel in the car. I couldn't let you go out into all this confusion. You'll never get a bus, not for hours. A taxi, never. The students, we have the students only to thank.' And he calls sharply to the apprentice to bring out his car. The boy goes over to a brown Volkswagen. 'The Fiat!' bellows his employer, whereupon the apprentice moves to a dusty cream-coloured Fiat 125, passes a duster over the outside of the windscreen, gets into it and starts to manoeuvre it forward to the main ramp.

Lise pulls away her hand and protests. 'Look, I've got a date. I'm late for it already. I'm sorry, but I can't accept your kind offer.' She looks out at the mass of slowly-moving traffic, the queues waiting at the bus stops, and says, 'I'll have to walk. I know my way.'

'Lady,' he says, 'no argument. It's my pleasure.' And he draws her to the car where the apprentice is now waiting with the door open for her.

'I really don't know you,' Lise says.

'I'm Carlo,' says the man, urging her inside and shutting the door. He gives the grinning apprentice a push that might mean anything, goes round to the other door, and drives slowly towards the street, slowly and carefully finding a gap in the line of traffic, working his way into the gap, blocking the oncoming vehicles for a while until finally he joins the stream.

It is also getting dark, as big Carlo's car alternately edges and spurts along the traffic, Carlo meanwhile denouncing the students and the police for causing the chaos. When they come at last to a clear stretch Carlo says, 'My wife I think is no good. I heard her on the telephone and she didn't think I was in the house. I heard.'

'You must understand,' Lise says, 'that anything at all that is overheard when the speaker doesn't know you're listening takes on a serious note. It always sounds far worse than their actual intentions are.'

'This was bad,' mutters Carlo. 'It's a man. A second cousin of hers. I made a big trouble for her that night, I can tell you. But she denied it. How could she deny it? I heard it.'

'If you imagine,' Lise says, 'that you are justifying any anticipations you may have with regards to me, you're mistaken. You can drop me off here, if you like. Otherwise, you can come and buy me a drink at the Hilton Hotel, and then it's good night. A soft drink. I don't take alcohol. I've got a date that I'm late for already.'

'We go out of town a little way,' says Carlo. 'I know a place. I brought the Fiat, did you see? The front seats fold back. Make you comfortable.'

'Stop at once,' Lise says. 'Or I put my head out of the window and yell for help. I don't want sex with you. I'm not interested in sex. I've got other interests and as a matter of fact I've got something on my mind that's got to be done. I'm telling you to stop.' She grabs the wheel and tries to guide it in to the kerb.

'All right, all right,' he says, regaining control of the car which has swerved a little with Lise's interference. 'All right. I'm taking you to the Hilton.'

'It doesn't look like the Hilton road to me,' Lise says. The traffic lights ahead are red but as there is very little traffic about on this dark, wide residential boulevard, he chances it and skims across. Lise puts her head out of the window and yells for help.

He pulls up at last in a side lane where, back from the road, there are the lights of two small villas; beyond that the road is a mass of stony crevices. He embraces her and kisses her mightily while she kicks him and tries to push him off, gurgling her protests. When he stops for breath he says, 'Now we put back the seats and do it properly.' But already she has jumped out of the car and has started running towards the gate of one of the houses, wiping her mouth and screaming, 'Police! Call the police!' Big Carlo overtakes her at the gate.

'Quiet!' he says. 'Be quiet, and get into the car. Please. I'll take you back, I promise. Sorry, lady, I haven't done any harm at all to you, have I? Only a kiss, what's a kiss.'

She runs and makes a grab for the door of the driver's seat, and as he calls after her, 'The other door!' she gets in, starts up, and backs speedily out of the lane. She leans over and locks the other door just in time to prevent him from opening it. 'You're not my type in any case,' she screams. Then she starts off, too quickly for him to be able to open the back door he is now grabbing at. Still he is running to catch up, and she yells back at him, 'If you report this to the police I'll tell them the truth and make a scandal in your family.' And then she is away, well clear of him.

She spins along in expert style, stopping duly at the traffic lights. She starts to sing softly as she waits:

> Inky-pinky-winky-wong
> How do you like your potatoes done?
> A little gravy in the pan
> For the King of the Cannibal Islands.

Her zipper-bag is on the floor of the car. While waiting for the lights to change she lifts it on to the seat, unzips it and looks with a kind of satisfaction at the wrapped-up objects of different shape, as it might be they represent a good day's work. She comes to a crossroad where some traffic accumulates. Here, a policeman is on duty and as she passes at his bidding she pulls up and asks him the way to the Hilton.

He is a young policeman. He bends to give her the required direction.

'Do you carry a revolver?' Lise says. He looks puzzled and fails to answer before Lise adds, 'Because, if you did, you could shoot me.'

The policeman is still finding words when she drives off, and in the mirror she can see him looking at the retreating car, probably noting the number. Which in fact he is doing, so that, on the afternoon of the following day, when he has been shown her body, he says, 'Yes, that's her. I recognize the face. She said, "If you had a revolver you could shoot me."' Which is to lead to many complications in Carlo's private life when the car is traced back to him, he being released by the police only after six hours of interrogation. A photograph of Carlo and also a picture of his young apprentice who holds a lively press conference of his own, moreover will appear in every newspaper in the country.

But now, at the Hilton Hotel her car is held up just as it enters the gates in the driveway. There is a line of cars ahead, and beyond them a group of policemen. Two police cars are visible in the parking area on the other side of the entrance. The rest of the driveway is occupied by a line of four very large limousines each with a uniformed driver standing by.

The police collect on either side of the hotel doorway, their faces picked out by the bright lights, while there emerge down the steps from the hotel two women who seem to be identical twins, wearing black dresses and high-styled black hair, followed by an important-looking Arabian figure, sheikh-like in his head-dress and robes, with a lined face and glittering eyes, who descends the steps with a floating motion as if his feet are clearing the ground by an inch or two; he is flanked by two smaller bespectacled, brown-faced men in business-like suits. The two black-dressed women stand back with a respectful housekeeperly bearing while the robed figure approaches the first limousine; and the two men draw back too, as he enters the recesses of the car. Two black-robed women with the lower parts of their faces veiled and their heads shrouded in drapery then make their descent, and behind them another pair appear, menservants with arms raised, bearing aloft numerous plastic-enveloped garments on coat-hangers. Still in pairs, further components of the retinue appear, each two moving in such unison that they seem to share a single soul or else two well-rehearsed parts in the chorus of an opera by Verdi. Two men wearing western clothes but for their red fezes are duly admitted to one of the waiting limousines and, as Lise gets out of her car to join the watchers, two ramshackle young Arabs with rumpled grey trousers and whitish shirts end the procession, bearing two large baskets, each one packed with oranges and a jumbo-sized vacuum-flask which stands slightly askew among the fruit, like champagne in an ice-bucket.

A group of people who are standing near Lise on the driveway, having themselves got out of their held-up taxis and cars, are discussing the event: 'He was here on vacation. I saw it on the television. There's been a coup in his country and he's going back.' – 'Why should he go back?' – 'No, he won't go back, believe me. Never.' – 'What country is it? I hope it doesn't affect us. The last time there was a coup my shares regressed so I nearly had a breakdown. Even the mutual funds . . . '

The police have gone back to their cars, and escorted by them the caravan goes its stately way.

Lise jumps back into Carlo's car and conducts it as quickly as possible to the car park. She leaves it there, taking the keys. Then she leaps into the hotel, eyed indignantly by the doorman who presumably resents her haste, her clothes, the blurred stain on her coat, the rumpled aspect that she has acquired in the course of the evening and whose built-in computer system rates her low on the spending scale.

Lise makes straight for the ladies' toilets and while there, besides putting her appearance to rights as best she can, she takes a comfortable chair in the soft-lit rest-room and considers, one by one, the contents of her zipper-bag which she lays on a small table beside her. She feels the outside of the box containing the food-blender and replaces it in her bag. She also leaves unopened a soft package containing the neckties, but, having rummaged in her hand-bag for something which apparently is not there, she brings forth her lipstick and with it she writes on the outside of the soft package, 'Papa'. There is an unsealed paper bag which she peers into; it is the orange scarf. She puts it back into place and takes out another bag containing the black and white scarf. She folds this back and with her lipstick she traces on the outside of the bag in large capitals, 'Olga'. Another package seems to puzzle her. She feels round it with half-closed eyes for a moment, then opens it up. It contains the pair of men's slippers which Mrs Fiedke had mislaid in the shop having apparently in fact put them in Lise's bag. Lise wraps them up again and replaces them. Finally she takes out her paperback book and an oblong package which she opens. This is a gift-box containing the gilded paper-opener in its sheath, also Mrs Fiedke's property.

Lise slowly returns the lipstick to her hand-bag, places the book and the box containing the paper-knife on the table beside her, places the zipper-bag on the floor, then proceeds to examine the contents of her hand-bag. Money, the tourist folder with its inset map of the city, the bunch of six keys that she had brought with her that morning, the keys of Carlo's car, the lipstick, the comb, the powder compact, the air ticket. Her lips are parted and she leans back in a relaxed attitude but that her eyes are too wide open for restfulness. She looks again at the contents of her hand-bag. A notecase with paper money, a purse with loose change. She gathers herself together in such an abrupt manner that the toilet attendant who has been sitting vacantly in a corner by the wash-basins starts to her feet. Lise packs up her belongings. She puts the paper-knife box back in the zipper-bag, carefully tucking it down the side, and zips the bag up. Her hand-bag is also packed tidily again, except for the bunch of six keys that she had brought on her travels. She holds the book in her hand, and, placing the bunch of six keys with a clatter on the plate left out for the coins, the attendant's reward, she says to the woman, 'I won't be needing these now.' Then, with her zipper-bag, her book, her hand-bag, her hair combed and her face cleaned up, she swings out of the door and into the hotel lounge. The clock above the reception desk says nine thirty-five. Lise makes for the bar, where she looks round. Most of the tables are occupied by chattering groups. She sits at a vacant but rather out-of-the-way table, orders a whisky, and bids the tentative waiter hurry. 'I've got a train to catch.' She is served with the drink together with a jug of water and a bowl of peanuts. She drenches the whisky with water, sips a small part of it and eats all the peanuts. She takes another small sip from her glass, and, leaving it nearly full, stands up and motions the waiter to bring her bill. She pays for this high-priced repast with a note taken from her bag and tells the waiter to keep the change, which amounts to a very high tip. He accepts it with incredulous grace and watches her as she leaves the bar. He, too, will give his small piece of evidence to the police on the following day, as will also the toilet attendant, trembling at the event which has touched upon her life without the asking.

Lise stops short in the hotel lounge and smiles. Then without further hesitation she goes over to a group of armchairs, only one of which is occupied. In it sits a sickly-looking man. Bending over him deferentially to listen to something the man is saying is a uniformed chauffeur who presently turns to go, waved away by the seated man, just as Lise approaches.

'There you are!' says Lise. 'I've been looking for you all day. Where did you get to?'

The man shifts to look at her. 'Jenner's gone to have a bite. Then we're off back to the villa. Damn nuisance, coming back in to town all this way. Tell Jenner he's got half-an-hour. We must be off.'

'He'll be back in a minute,' Lise says. 'Don't you remember we met on the plane?'

'The Sheikh. Damn rotters in his country have taken over behind his back. Now he's lost his throne or whatever

302

it is he sits on. I was at school with him. Why did he ring me up? He rang me up. On the telephone. He brings me back to town all this way and when we get here he says he can't come to the villa after all, there's been a coup.'

'I'll take you back to the villa,' Lise says. 'Come on, get in the car with me. I've got a car outside.'

The man says, 'Last time I saw the Sheikh it was '38. He came on safari with me. Rotten shot if you know anything about big game. You've got to wait for the drag. They call it the drag, you see. It kills its prey and drags it into the bush then you follow the drag and when you know where it's left its prey you're all right. The poor bloody beast comes out the next day to eat its prey, they like it high. And you only have a few seconds. You're here and there's another fellow there and a third over here. You can't shoot from here, you see, because there's another hunter there and you don't want to shoot him. You have to shoot from over here or over there. And the Sheikh, I've known him for years, we were at school together, the bloody fool shot and missed it by five feet from a fifteen-foot range.'

His eyes look straight ahead and his lips quiver.

'You're not my type after all,' Lise says. 'I thought you were, but I was away out.'

'What? Want a drink? Where's Jenner?'

She gathers up the handles of her bags, picks up her book and looks at him and through him as if he were already a distant memory and leaves without a good-bye, indeed as if she had said good-bye to him long ago.

She brushes past a few people at the vestibule who look at her with the same casual curiosity with which others throughout the day have looked at her. They are mainly tourists; one exceptional sight among so many others does not deflect their attention for very long. Outside, she goes to the car park where she has left Carlo's car, and does not find it.

303

She goes up to the doorman. 'I've lost my car. A Fiat 125. Have you seen anyone drive off with a Fiat?'

'Lady, there are twenty Fiats an hour come in and out of here.'

'But I parked it over there less than an hour ago. A cream Fiat, a bit dirty, I've been travelling.'

The doorman sends a page-boy to find the parking attendant who presently comes along in a vexed mood since he has been called from conversation with a more profitable client. He owns to having seen a cream-coloured Fiat being driven away by a large fat man whom he had presumed to be the owner.

'He must have had extra keys,' says Lise.

'Didn't you see the lady drive in with it?' the doorman says.

'No, I didn't. The royalty and the police were taking up all my time, you know that. Besides, the lady didn't say anything to me, to look after her car.'

Lise says, opening her bag, 'Well, I meant to give you a tip later. But I'll give you one now.' And she holds out to him the keys of Carlo's car.

The doorman says, 'Look, lady, we can't take responsibility for your car. If you want to see the porter at the desk he can ring the police. Are you staying at the hotel?'

'No,' says Lise. 'Get me a taxi.'

'Have you got your licence?' says the parking attendant.

'Go away,' Lise says. 'You're not my type.' He looks explosive. Another of tomorrow's witnesses.

The porter is meanwhile busy helping some newcomers out of a taxi. Lise calls out to the taxi-driver, who nods his agreement to take her on.

As soon as the passengers are out, Lise leaps into the taxi.

The parking attendant shouts, 'Are you sure it was your own car, lady?'

She throws Carlo's keys out of the window on to the gravel and directs the taxi to the Hotel Metropole with tears falling over her cheeks.

'Anything the matter, lady?' says the driver.

'It's getting late,' she says, weeping. 'It's getting terribly late.'

'Lady, I can't go faster. See the traffic.'

'I can't find my boy-friend. I don't know where he's gone.'

'You think you'll find him at the Metropole?'

'There's always a chance,' she says. 'I make a lot of mistakes.'

CHAPTER 6

THE CHANDELIERS OF the Metropole, dispensing a vivid glow upon the just and unjust alike, disclose Bill the macrobiotic seated gloomily by a table near the entrance. He jumps up when Lise enters and falls upon her with a delight that impresses the whole lobby, and in such haste that a plastic bag that he is clutching, insufficiently sealed, emits a small trail of wild rice in his progress towards her.

She follows him back to his seat and takes a chair beside him. 'Look at my coat,' she says. 'I got mixed up in a student demonstration and I'm still crying from the effect of tear-gas. I had a date at the Hilton for dinner with a very important Sheikh but I was too late, as I went to buy him a pair of slippers for a present. He'd gone on safari. So he wasn't my type, anyway. Shooting animals.'

'I'd just about given you up,' says Bill. 'You were to be here at seven. I've been getting desperate.' He takes her hand, smiling with glad flashes of teeth and eyes. 'You wouldn't have been so unkind as to have dinner with someone else, would you? I'm hungry.'

'And my car got stolen,' she says.

'What car?'

'Oh, just a car.'

'I didn't know you had a car. Was it a hired car?'

'You know nothing whatsoever about me,' she says.

'Well I've got a car,' he said. 'A friend has lent me it. I'm taking it to Naples as soon as possible to get started on the Yin-Yang Young Culture Centre. I'm opening with a lecture called "The World – Where is it Going?" That will be a general

306

introduction to the macrobiotic way of life. It'll bring in the kids, all right.'

'It's getting late,' she says.

'I was nearly giving you up,' he says, squeezing her hand. 'I was just about to go out and look for another girl. I'm queer for girls. It has to be a girl.'

'I'll have a drink,' she says. 'I need one.'

'Oh no, you won't. Oh no, you won't. Alcohol is off the diet. You're coming to supper with me at a house I know.'

'What kind of a house?' she says.

'A macrobiotic family I know,' he says. 'They'll give us a good supper. Three sons, four daughters, the mother and father, all on macrobiotics. We'll have rice with carrots followed by rice biscuits and goat's cheese and a cooked apple. No sugar allowed. The family eat at six o'clock, which is the orthodox system, but the variation that I follow lets you eat late. That way, we'll get through to the young. So we'll go there and heat up a meal. Come on!'

She says, 'That tear-gas is still affecting me.' Tears brim in her eyes. She gets up with him and lets him, trailing rice, lead her past every eye of the Metropole lobby into the street, up the road, and into a small black utility model which is parked there.

'It's wonderful,' says Bill as he starts up the car, 'to think we're together again at last.'

'I must tell you,' says Lise, sniffing, 'that you're not my type. I'm sure of it.'

'Oh, you don't know me! You don't know me at all.'

'But I know my type.'

'You need love,' he says with a hand on her knee.

She starts away from him. 'Take care while you're driving. Where do your friends live?'

'The other side of the park. I must say, I feel hungry.'

'Then hurry up,' she says.

'Don't you feel hungry?'

'No, I feel lonely.'

'You won't be lonely with me.'

They have turned into the park.

'Turn right at the end of this road,' she says. 'There should be a road to the right, according to the map. I want to look at something.'

'There are better places farther on.'

'Turn right, I say.'

'Don't be nervy,' he says. 'You need to relax. The reason why you're so tense, you've been eating all the wrong things and drinking too much. You shouldn't have more than three glasses of liquid a day. You should pass water not more than twice a day. Twice for a woman, three times for a man. If you need to go more than that it means you're taking in too much fluid.'

'Here's the road. Turn right.'

Bill turns right, going slowly and looking about him. He says, 'I don't know where this leads to. But there's a very convenient spot farther up the main road.'

'What spot?' she says. 'What spot are you talking about?'

'I haven't had my daily orgasm. It's an essential part of this particular variation of the diet, didn't I tell you? Many other macrobiotic variations have it as an essential part. This is one of the main things the young Neapolitans must learn.'

'If you think you're going to have sex with me,' she says, 'you're very much mistaken. I have no time for sex.'

'Lise!' says Bill.

'I mean it,' she says. 'Sex is no use to me, I assure you.' She gives out her deep laughter.

The road is dimly lit by lamps posted at far intervals. Bill is peering to right and left.

'There's a building over there,' she says. 'That must be the Pavilion. And the old villa behind – they say in the brochure that it's to be restored and turned into a museum. But it's the famous Pavilion that I want.'

At the site of the Pavilion several cars and motor bicycles are parked. Another road converges, and a band of teenaged boys and girls are languidly leaning against trees, cars and anything else that can prop them up, looking at each other.

'There's nothing doing here,' says Bill.

'Stop, I want to get out and look around.'

'Too many people. What are you thinking of?'

'I want to see the Pavilion, that's all.'

'Why? You can come by daylight. Much better.'

Some iron tables are scattered on the ground in front of the Pavilion, a graceful three-storey building with a quaint gilded frieze above the first level of the façade.

Bill parks the car near the others, some of which are occupied by amorous couples. Lise jumps out as soon as the car stops. She takes with her the hand-bag leaving the zipper-bag and her book in the car. He runs after her, putting an arm round her shoulders, and says, 'Come on, it's getting late. What do you want to see?'

She says, 'Will your rice be safe in the car? Have you locked it?'

He says, 'Who's going to steal a bag of rice?'

'I don't know,' says Lise, making her way along the path which leads to the Pavilion. 'Maybe those young people might feel very intensely about rice.'

'The movement hasn't got started yet, Lise,' says Bill. 'And red beans are also allowed. And sesame-flour. But you can't expect people to know about it till you tell them.'

The ground floor of the Pavilion is largely glass-fronted. She goes up to it and peers in. There are bare café tables and chairs piled high in the classic fashion of restaurants closed for the night. There is a long counter and a coffee machine at the far end, with an empty glass sandwich-bar. There is nothing else except an expanse of floor, which in the darkness can only be half-seen, patterned in black-and-white chequered pavements. Lise cranes and twists to see the ceiling which obscurely seems to be painted with some classical scene; the hind-leg of a horse and one side of a cupid are all that is visible.

Still she peers through the glass. Bill tries to draw her away, but again she starts to cry. 'Oh,' she says, 'the inconceivable sorrow of it, those chairs piled up at night when you're sitting in a café, the last one left.'

'You're getting morbid, dear,' says Bill. 'Darling, it's all a matter of chemistry. You've been eating toxic foods and neglecting the fact that there are two forces in the world, centrifugal which is Yin and centripetal which is Yang. Orgasms are Yang.'

'It makes me sad,' she says. 'I want to go home, I think. I want to go back home and feel all that lonely grief again. I miss it so much already.'

He jerks her away and she calls out, 'Stop it! Don't do that!' A man and two women who are passing a few yards away turn to look, but the young group pays no attention.

Bill gives a deep sigh. 'It's getting late,' he says, pinching her elbow.

'Let me go, I want to look round the back. I've got to see how things are round here, it's important.'

'You'd think it was a bank,' Bill says, 'that you were going to do a stick-up in tomorrow. Who do you think you are? Who do you think I am?' He follows her as she starts off round the side of the building, examining the track. 'What do you think you're doing?'

She traverses the side of the building and turns round to the back where five large dust-bins stand waiting for tomorrow's garbage-men, who will also find Lise, not far off, stabbed to death. At this moment, a disturbed cat leaves off its foraging at one of the half-closed dust-bins and flows into an adjacent blackness.

Lise surveys the ground earnestly.

'Look,' says Bill, 'Lise, darling, over by the hedge. We're all right.'

He pulls her towards a hedge separating the back yard of the Pavilion from a foot-path which can be seen through a partly-open iron gate. A band of very tall fair young men all speaking together in a Scandinavian-sounding language passes by and stops to watch and comment buoyantly on the tussle that ensues between Bill and Lise, she proclaiming that she doesn't like sex and he explaining that if he misses his daily orgasm he has to fit in two the next day. 'And it gives me indigestion,' he says, getting her down on the gravel behind the hedge and out of sight, 'two in one day. And it's got to be a girl.'

Lise now shrieks for help in four languages, English, French, Italian and Danish. She throws her hand-bag into the hedge; then, 'He's taken my purse!' she cries in four languages. 'He's gone off with my hand-bag!' One of the onlookers tries to creak open the stiff iron gate, but meantime another has started to climb it, and gets over.

'What's going on?' he says to Lise in his own language. 'We're Swedes. What's wrong?'

Bill who has been kneeling to hold her down gets up and says, 'Go away. Clear off. What do you think's going on?'

But Lise has jumped to her feet and shouts in English that she never saw him before in her life, and that he is trying to rob her, and rape her. 'I just got out of my car to look at the Pavilion, and he jumped on me and dragged me here,' she screams, over and over again in four languages. 'Get the police!'

The other men have come into the yard. Two of them take hold of Bill who grins, trying hard to convince them that this turmoil is Lise's joke. One of them says he is going to find a policeman. Lise says, 'Where's my bag? He's got rid of it somewhere. What has he done with it?' Then, in a burst of

MURIEL SPARK

spontaneous composure she says, quietly, 'I'm going to find a policeman, too,' and walks off to the car. Most of the other parked cars have gone, as have also the young loiterers. One of the Swedes runs after her, advising her to wait till his friend brings a policeman.

'No, I'm going to the police station right away,' she says in a calm voice as she gets in and shuts the door. She has already made off, already thrown the bag of wild rice out of the window, when the police arrive on the scene. They hear the Swedes' account, they listen to Bill's protests, they search for Lise's bag, and find it. Then they ask Bill what the girl's name was since she was, as he claims, a friend of his. 'Lise,' he says. 'I don't know her other name. We met on the plane.'

They take Bill into custody anyway, mercifully for him as it turns out, since in the hours logically possible for the murder of Lise on that spot Bill is safely in a police cell, equally beyond suspicion and the exercise of his diet.

CHAPTER 7

IT IS LONG past midnight when she arrives at the Hotel Tomson which stands like the only living thing in the shuttered street. Lise parks the little black car in a spot near the entrance, takes her book and her zipper-bag and enters the hall.

At the desk the night-porter is on duty, the top three buttons of his uniform unfastened to reveal his throat and the top of his under-vest, a sign that the deep night has fallen and the tourists have gone to bed. The porter is talking on the desk telephone which links with the bedrooms. Meanwhile the only other person in the hall, a youngish man in a dark suit, stands before the desk with a brief-case and a tartan hold-all by his side.

'Please don't wake her. It isn't at all necessary at this late hour. Just show me my room —'

'She's on her way down. She says to tell you to wait, she's on her way.'

'I could have seen her in the morning. It wasn't necessary. It's so late.' The man's tone is authoritative and vexed.

'She's wide awake, sir,' says the porter. 'She was very definite that we were to let her know as soon as you arrived.'

'Excuse me,' Lise says to the porter, brushing against the dark-suited man as she comes up to the desk beside him. 'Would you like a book to read?' She holds out her paperback. 'I don't need it any more.'

'Oh, thanks, Miss,' says the porter, good-naturedly taking the book and holding it at arm's length before his eyes the better to see what the book is all about. Meanwhile the new arrival, having been jostled by Lise, turns to look at her. He starts, and bends to pick up his bags.

Lise touches him on the arm. 'You're coming with me,' she says.

'No,' he says, trembling. His round face is pink and white, his eyes are wide open with fear. He looks neat in his business suit and white shirt, as he did this morning when Lise first followed and then sat next to him on the plane.

'Leave everything,' says Lise. 'Come on, it's getting late.'

She starts propelling him to the door.

'Sir!' calls the porter. 'Your aunt's on her way —'

Lise, still holding her man, turns at the door and calls back, 'You can keep his luggage. You can have the book as well; it's a whydunnit in q-sharp major and it has a message: never talk to the sort of girls that you wouldn't leave lying about in your drawing-room for the servants to pick up.' She leads her man towards the door.

There, he puts up some resistance: 'No, I don't want to come. I want to stay. I came here this morning, and when I saw you here I got away. I want to get away.' He pulls back from her.

'I've got a car outside,' says Lise, and pushes open the narrow swing-door. He goes with her as if he is under arrest. She takes him to the car, lets go of his arm, gets into the driver's seat and waits while he walks round the front of the car and gets in beside her. Then she drives off with him at her side.

He says, 'I don't know who you are. I never saw you before in my life.'

'That's not the point,' she says. 'I've been looking for you all day. You've wasted my time. What a day! And I was right first time. As soon as I saw you this morning I knew that you were the one. You're my type.'

He is trembling. She says, 'You were in a clinic. You're Richard. I know your name because your aunt told me.'

He says, 'I've had six years' treatment. I want to start afresh. My family's waiting to see me.'

'Were the walls of the clinic pale green in all the rooms? Was there a great big tough man in the dormitory at night, patrolling up and down every so often, just in case?'

'Yes,' he says.

'Stop trembling,' she says. 'It's the madhouse tremble. It will soon be over. Before you went to the clinic how long did they keep you in prison?'

'Two years,' he said.

'Did you strangle or stab?'

'I stabbed her, but she didn't die. I never killed a woman.'

'No, but you'd like to. I knew it this morning.'

'You never saw me before in your life.'

'That's not the point,' Lise says. 'That's by the way. You're a sex maniac.'

'No, no,' he says. 'That's all over and past. Not any more.'

'Well you won't have sex with me,' Lise says. She is driving through the park and turns right towards the Pavilion. Nobody is in sight. The wandering groups are null and void, the cars have gone away.

'Sex is normal,' he says. 'I'm cured. Sex is all right.'

'It's all right at the time and it's all right before,' says Lise, 'but the problem is afterwards. That is, if you aren't just an animal. Most of the time, afterwards is pretty sad.'

'You're afraid of sex,' he says, almost joyfully, as if sensing an opportunity to gain control.

'Only of afterwards,' she says. 'But that doesn't matter any more.'

She pulls up at the Pavilion and looks at him. 'Why are you shaking?' she says. 'It will soon be over.' She reaches for her zipper-bag and opens it. 'Now,' she says, 'let's be lucid about this. Here's a present from your aunt, a pair of slippers. You can pick them up later.' She throws them on the back seat and pulls out a paper bag. She peers into it. 'This is Olga's scarf,' she says, putting it back in the bag.

'A lot of women get killed in the park,' he says, leaning back; he is calmer now.

'Yes, of course. It's because they want to be.' She is searching in the bag.

'Don't go too far,' he says quietly.

'I'll leave that to you,' she says and brings out another paper bag. She peers in and takes out the orange scarf. 'This is mine,' she says. 'A lovely colour by daylight.' She drapes the scarf round her neck.

'I'm getting out,' he says, opening the door on his side. 'Come on.'

'Wait a minute,' she says. 'Just wait a minute.'

'A lot of women get killed,' he says.

'Yes, I know, they look for it.' She brings out the oblong package, tears off the wrapping and opens the box that contains the curved paper-knife in its sheath. 'Another present for you,' she says. 'Your aunt bought it for you.' She takes the knife from the box which she throws out of the window.

He says, 'No, they don't want to be killed. They struggle. I know that. But I've never killed a woman. Never.'

Lise opens the door and gets out with the paper-knife in her hand. 'Come on, it's getting late,' she says. 'I know the spot.'

The morning will dawn, and by the evening the police will place in front of him the map marked with an X at the point where the famous Pavilion is located, the little picture.

'You made this mark.'

'No I didn't. She must have made it herself. She knew the way. She took me straight there.'

They will reveal, bit by bit, that they know his record. They will bark, and exchange places at the desk. They will come and go in the little office, already beset by inquietude and fear, even before her identity is traced back to where she came from. They will try soft speaking, they will reason with him in their secret dismay that the evidence already coming in seems to confirm his story.

'The last time you lost control of yourself didn't you take the woman for a drive in the country?'

'But this one took me. She made me go. She was driving. I didn't want to go. It was only by chance that I met her.'

'You never saw her before?'

'The first time was at the airport. She sat beside me on the plane. I moved my seat. I was afraid.'

'Afraid of what? What frightened you?'

Round and round again will go the interrogators, moving slowly forward, always bearing the same questions like the whorling shell of a snail.

Lise walks up to the great windows of the Pavilion and presses close to look inside, while he follows her. Then she walks round the back and over to the hedge.

She says, 'I'm going to lie down here. Then you tie my hands with my scarf; I'll put one wrist over the other, it's the proper way. Then you'll tie my ankles together with your necktie. Then you strike.' She points first to her throat. 'First here,' she says. Then, pointing to a place beneath each breast, she says, 'Then here and here. Then anywhere you like.'

'I don't want to do it,' he says, staring at her. 'I didn't mean this to happen. I planned everything to be different. Let me go.'

She takes the paper-knife from its sheath, feels the edge and the point, and says that it isn't very sharp but it will do. 'Don't forget,' she says, 'that it's curved.' She looks at the engraved sheath in her hand and lets it fall carelessly from her fingers. 'After you've stabbed,' she says, 'be sure to twist it upwards or it may not penetrate far enough.' She demonstrates the move-ment with her wrist. 'You'll get caught, but at least you'll have the illusion of a chance to get away in the car. So afterwards, don't waste too much time staring at what you have done, at what you have done.' Then she lies down on the gravel and he grabs at the knife.

'Tie my hands first,' she says, crossing her wrists. 'Tie them with the scarf.'

He ties her hands, and she tells him in a sharp, quick voice to take off his necktie and bind her ankles.

'No,' he says, kneeling over her, 'not your ankles.'

'I don't want any sex,' she shouts. 'You can have it afterwards. Tie my feet and kill, that's all. They will come and sweep it up in the morning.'

All the same, he plunges into her, with the knife poised high.

'Kill me,' she says, and repeats it in four languages.

As the knife descends to her throat she screams, evidently perceiving how final is finality. She screams and then her throat gurgles while he stabs with a turn of his wrist exactly as she instructed. Then he stabs wherever he likes and stands up, staring at what he has done. He stands staring for a while and then, having started to turn away, he hesitates as if he had forgotten something of her bidding. Suddenly he wrenches off his necktie and bends to tie her ankles together with it.

He runs to the car, taking his chance and knowing that he will at last be taken, and seeing already as he drives away from the Pavilion and away, the sad little office where the police clank in and out and the typewriter ticks out his unnerving statement: 'She told me to kill her and I killed her. She spoke in many languages but she was telling me to kill her all the time. She told me precisely what to do. I was hoping to start a new life.' He sees already the gleaming buttons of the policemen's uniforms, hears the cold and the confiding, the hot and the barking voices, sees already the holsters and epaulets and all those trappings devised to protect them from the indecent exposure of fear and pity, pity and fear.

THE ONLY PROBLEM

Surely I would speak to the Almighty,
and I desire to reason with God.

Book of Job, 13,3

PART 1

CHAPTER 1

HE WAS DRIVING along the road in France from St Dié to Nancy in the district of Meurthe; it was straight and almost white, through thick woods of fir and birch. He came to the grass track on the right that he was looking for. It wasn't what he had expected. Nothing ever is, he thought. Not that Edward Jansen could now recall exactly what he had expected; he tried, but the image he had formed faded before the reality like a dream on waking. He pulled off at the track, forked left and stopped. He would have found it interesting to remember exactly how he had imagined the little house before he saw it, but that, too, had gone.

He sat in the car and looked for a while at an old green garden fence and a closed gate, leading to a piece of overgrown garden. There was no longer a visible path to the stone house, which was something like a lodgekeeper's cottage with loose tiles and dark, neglected windows. Two shacks of crumbling wood stood apart from the house. A wider path, on Edward's side of the gate, presumably led to the château where he had no present interest. But he noticed that the car-tracks on the path were overgrown, very infrequently used, and yet the grass that spread over that path was greener than on the ground before him, inside the gate. If his wife had been there he would have pointed this out to her as a feature of Harvey Gotham, the man he had come to see; for he had a theory, too unsubstantiated to be formulated in public, but which he could share with Ruth, that people have an effect on the natural greenery around them regardless of whether they lay hands on it or not; some people, he would remark, induce fertility in their environment

323

and some the desert, simply by psychic force. Ruth would agree with him at least in this case, for she didn't seem to like Harvey, try as she might. It had already got to the point that everything Harvey did and said, if it was only good night, to her mind made him worse and worse. It was true there are ways and ways of saying good night. Yet Edward wondered if there wasn't something of demonology in those confidences he shared with Ruth about Harvey; Ruth didn't know him as well as Edward did. They had certainly built up a case against Harvey between themselves which they wouldn't have aired openly. It was for this reason that Edward had thought it fair that he should come alone, although at first he expected Ruth to come with him. She had said she couldn't face it. Perhaps, Edward had thought, I might be more fair to Harvey.

And yet, here he was, sitting in the car before his house, noting how the grass everywhere else was greener than that immediately surrounding the cottage. Edward got out and slammed the door with a bang, hoping to provoke the dark front door of the house or at least one of the windows into action. He went to the gate. It was closed with a rusty wire loop which he loosened. He creaked open the gate and walked up the path to the door and knocked. It was ten past three, and Harvey was expecting him; it had all been arranged. But he knocked and there was silence. This, too, was typical. He walked round the back of the house, looking for a car or a motor-cycle, which he supposed Harvey had. He found there a wide path, a sort of drive which led away from the back door, through the woods; this path had been hidden from the main road. There was no motor-cycle, but a newish small Renault, light brown, under a rush-covered shelter. Harvey, then, was probably at home. The back door was his front door, so Edward banged on that. Harvey opened it immediately and stood with that look of his, to the effect that he had done his utmost.

'You haven't cut your hair,' he said.

Edward had the answer ready, heated-up from the pre-cooking, so many times had he told Harvey much the same thing. 'It's my hair, not your hair. It's my beard, not your beard.' Edward stepped into the house as he said this, so that Harvey had to make way for him.

Harvey was predictable only up to a point. 'What are you trying to prove, Edward,' he said, 'wearing that poncho at your age?' In the living-room he pushed some chairs out of the way. 'And your hair hanging down your back,' he said.

Edward's hair was in fact shoulder-length. 'I'm growing it for a part in a film,' he said, then wished he hadn't given any excuse at all since anyway it was his hair, not Harvey's hair. Red hair.

'You've got a part?'

'Yes.'

'What are you doing here, then? Why aren't you rehearsing?'

'Rehearsals start on Monday.'

'Where?'

'Elstree.'

'Elstree.' Harvey said it as if there was a third party listening – as if to draw the attention of this third party to that definite word, Elstree, and whatever connotations it might breed.

Edward wished himself back in time by twenty minutes, driving along the country road from St Dié to Nancy, feeling the spring weather. The spring weather, the cherry trees in flower, and all the budding green on the road from St Dié had supported him, while here inside Harvey's room there was no outward support. He almost said, 'What am I doing here?' but refrained because that would be mere rhetoric. He had come about his sister-in-law Effie, Harvey's wife.

'Your wire was too long,' said Harvey. 'You could have saved five words.'

'I can see you're busy,' said Edward.

*

Effie was very far from Edward's heart of hearts, but Ruth worried about her. Long ago he'd had an affair with beautiful Effie, but that was a thing of the past. He had come here for Ruth's sake. He reminded himself carefully that he would do almost anything for Ruth.

'What's the act?' said Harvey. 'You are somehow not yourself, Edward.'

It seemed to Edward that Harvey always suspected him of putting on an act.

'Maybe I can speak for actors in general; that, I don't know,' Edward said. 'But I suppose that the nature of my profession is mirrored in my own experience; at least, for certain, I can speak for myself. That, I can most certainly do. In fact I know when I'm playing a part and when I'm not. It isn't every actor who knows the difference. The majority act better off stage than on.'

Edward went into the little sitting-room that Harvey had put together, the minimum of stuff to keep him going while he did the job he had set himself. Indeed, the shabby, green plush chairs with the stuffing coming out of them and the quite small work-table with the papers and writing materials piled on it (he wrote by hand) seemed out of all proportion to the project. Harvey was only studying a subject, preparing an essay, a thesis. Why all this spectacular neglect of material things? God knows, thought Edward, from where he has collected his furniture. There was a kitchen visible beyond the room, with a loaf of bread and a coffee mug on the table. It looked like a nineteenth-century narrative painting. Edward supposed there were habitable rooms upstairs. He sat down when Harvey told him to. From where he sat he could see through a window a washing-line with baby clothes on it. There was no sign of a baby in the house, so Edward presumed this washing had nothing to do with Harvey; maybe it belonged to a daily help who brought along her child's clothes to wash.

Harvey said, 'I'm awfully busy.'

'I've come about Effie,' Edward said.

Harvey took a long time to respond. This, thought Edward, is a habit of his when he wants an effect of weightiness.

Then, 'Oh, Effie,' said Harvey, looking suddenly relieved; he actually began to smile as if to say he had feared to be confronted with some problem that really counted.

Harvey had written Effie off that time on the Italian *autostrada* about a year ago, when they were driving from Bologna to Florence – Ruth, Edward, Effie, Harvey and Nathan, a young student-friend of Ruth's. They stopped for a refill of petrol; Effie and Ruth went off to the Ladies', then they came back to the car where it was still waiting in line. It was a cool, late afternoon in April, rather cloudy, not one of those hot Italian days where you feel you must have a cold drink or an ice every time you stop. It was sheer consumerism that made Harvey – or maybe it was Nathan – suggest that they should go and get something from the snack-bar; this was a big catering monopoly with huge windows in which were arranged straw baskets and pottery from Hong Kong and fantastically shaped bottles of Italian liqueurs. It was, 'What shall we have from the bar?' – 'A sandwich, a coffee?' – 'No, I don't want any more of those lousy sandwiches.' Effie went off to see what there was to buy, and came back with some chocolate. – 'Yes, that's what I'd like.' – She had two large bars. The tank was now full. Edward paid the man at the pump. Effie got in the front with him. They were all in the car and Edward drove off. Effie started dividing the chocolate and handing it round. Nathan, Ruth and Harvey at the back, all took a piece. Edward took a piece and Effie started eating her piece.

With her mouth full of chocolate she turned and said to Harvey at the back, 'It's good, isn't it? I stole it. Have another piece.'

'You what?' said Harvey. Ruth said something, too, to the same effect. Edward said he didn't believe it.

Effie said, 'Why shouldn't we help ourselves? These multinationals and monopolies are capitalizing on us, and two-thirds of the world is suffering.'

She tore open the second slab, crammed more chocolate angrily into her mouth, and, with her mouth gluttonously full of stolen chocolate, went on raving about how two-thirds of the world was starving.

'You make it worse for them and worse for all of us if you steal,' Edward said.

'That's right,' said Ruth, 'it really does make it worse for everyone. Besides, it's dishonest.'

'Well, I don't know,' Nathan said.

But Harvey didn't wait to hear more. 'Pull in at the side,' he said. They were going at a hundred kilometres an hour, but he had his hand on the back door on the dangerous side of the road. Edward pulled in. He forgot, now, how it was that they reasoned Harvey out of leaving the car there on the *autostrada*; however, he sat in silence while Effie ate her chocolate inveighing, meanwhile, against the capitalist system. None of the others would accept any more of the chocolate. Just before the next exit Harvey said, 'Pull in here, I want to pee.' They waited for him while he went to the men's lavatory. Edward was suspicious all along that he wouldn't come back and when the minutes went by he got out of the car to have a look, and was just in time to see Harvey get up into a truck beside the driver; away he went.

They lost the truck at some point along the road, after they reached Florence. Harvey's disappearance ruined Effie's holiday. She was furious, and went on against him so much that Ruth made that always infuriating point: 'If he's so bad, why are you angry with him for leaving you?' The rest of them were upset and uneasy for a day or two but after that they let it go. After all, they were on holiday. Edward refused to discuss the subject for the next two weeks; they were travelling along the Tuscan coast stopping here and there. It would have been a glorious trip but for Effie's fury and unhappiness.

Up to the time Edward went to see Harvey in France on her behalf, she still hadn't seen any more of him. They had no children and he had simply left her life, with all his possessions and the electricity bills and other clutter of married living on her hands. All over a bit of chocolate. And yet, no.

Ruth thought, and Edward agreed with her, that a lot must have led up to that final parting of Harvey from Effie.

Edward deeply envied Harvey, he didn't know exactly what for. Or rather, perhaps he had better not probe deeply enough into the possibility that if Ruth wasn't Ruth and, if they weren't always so much in agreement, he would have liked to walk off, just like that. When Harvey talked of his marriage it was always as if he were thinking of something else, and he never talked about it unless someone else did first. And then, it was as if the other person had mentioned something quite irrelevant to his life, provoking from him a puzzled look, then a frown, an effort of concentration, it seemed, then an impatient dismissal of the apparently alien subject. It seemed, it seemed, Edward thought; because one can only judge by appearances. How could Edward know Harvey wasn't putting on an act, as he so often implied that Edward did? To some extent we all put on acts.

Harvey began to be more sociable, for he had somehow dismissed the subject of Effie. He must have known Edward would bring up Effie later, that in fact all he had come for was to talk about her. Well, perhaps not all. Edward was an old friend. Harvey poured him a drink, and, for the moment Edward gave up trying to get on to the subject of Effie.

'Tell me,' said Harvey, 'about the new film. What's it called? What sort of part are you playing?'

'It's called *The Love-Hate Relationship*. That's only provisional as a title. I don't think it'll sell as a film on that title. But it's based on a novel called *The Love-Hate Relationship*. And that's what the film is about. There's a married couple and another man, a brother, in the middle. I'm playing the other man, the brother.' (Was Harvey listening? He was looking round into the other room.)

'If there's anything I can't stand it's a love-hate relationship,' Harvey said, turning back to Edward at last. 'The element of love in such a relation simply isn't worthy of the name. It boils down to hatred pure and simple in the end. Love comprises among other things a desire for the well-being and spiritual freedom of the one who is loved. There's an objective quality about love. Love-hate is obsessive, it is possessive. It can be evil in effect.'

'Oh well,' Edward said, 'love-hate is a frequent human problem. It's a very important problem, you can't deny it.'

'It's part of the greater problem,' said Harvey after a while. Edward knew what Harvey was coming round to and was pleased, now that he was sitting here with his drink and his old friend. It was the problem of suffering as it is dealt with in the biblical *Book of Job*. It was for this, in the first place, that Harvey had come to study here in the French countryside away from the environment of his family business and his friends.

Harvey was a rich man; he was in his mid-thirties. He had started writing a monograph about the *Book of Job* and the problem it deals with. For he could not face that a benevolent Creator, one whose charming and delicious light descended and spread over the world, and being powerful everywhere, could condone the unspeakable sufferings of the world; that God did permit all suffering and was therefore by logic of his omnipotence, the actual author of it, he was at a loss how to square with the existence of God, given the premise that God is good.

'It is the only problem,' Harvey had always said. Now, Harvey believed in God, and this was what tormented him. 'It's the only problem, in fact, worth discussing.'

It was just under a year after Harvey had disappeared that Effie traced him to St Dié. She hadn't been to see him herself, but she had written several times through his lawyer asking him what was the matter. She described to him the process by which she had tracked him down; when she read Edward the letter before she posted it he felt she could have left that part out, for she had traced him quite simply, but by trickery, of which Harvey would not see the charm; furthermore, her revelation of the trick compromised an innocent, if foolish, person, and this fact would not be lost on Harvey. His moral sense was always intensified where Effie was concerned.

'Don't tell him, Effie,' Edward said, 'how you got his address. He'll think you unprincipled.'

'He thinks that already,' she said.

'Well, this might be the finishing touch. There's no need to tell.'

'I don't want him back.'

'You only want his money,' Edward said.

'Oh, God, Edward, if you only knew what he was like to live with.'

Edward could guess. But he said, 'What people are like to live with . . . It isn't a good test to generalize on.'

'He's rich,' said Effie. 'He's spoilt.' Effie had a lover, Ernie Howe, an electronics expert. Effie was very good-looking and it was hardly to be expected that she would resist, year after year, the opportunities for love affairs that came her way all the time; she was really beautiful. Ernie Howe was a nice-looking man, too, but he lacked the sort of money Harvey had and Effie was used to. Ernie had his job, and quite a good one; Edward supposed that Effie, who herself had a job with an advertising firm, might have been content with the simpler life with him, if she was in love with Ernie. It was only that now she was expecting a baby she felt she might persuade Harvey to divorce her with a large settlement. Edward didn't see why this should not be.

Harvey had never replied to any of Effie's letters. She continued to write, care of his lawyer. She told him of her love affair and mentioned a divorce.

Finally she managed to find his actual whereabouts in St Dié, in a quite unpremeditated way. She had in fact visited the lawyer to try to persuade him to reveal the address. He answered that he could only forward a letter. Effie went home and wrote a letter, calling with it at the lawyer's office the next day to save the extra time it would have taken in the post. She gave it to the receptionist and asked that it be forwarded. There were two or three letters on the girl's desk, in a neat pile, already stamped. Acting on a brain-wave Effie said, casually, 'If you like, as I'm passing the post box, I'll pop them all in.'

'Oh, thanks,' said the foolish girl, 'I have to go beyond the bus stop to post letters.' So she hastily filled in Harvey's address and handed the letters to Effie with a smile. And although Edward said to Effie, 'You shouldn't tell Harvey how you got his address. It'll put him right off. Counter-productive. And rather unfair on the poor girl at the lawyer's office,' she went ahead and wrote to Harvey direct, telling him of her little trick. 'He'll realize all the more how urgent it is,' she said.

But still Harvey didn't reply.

That was how Edward came to be on this errand to Harvey on her behalf. Incidentally, Edward also hoped for a loan. He was short of money till he got paid under his contract with the film people.

Edward used to confide in Harvey, and he in Edward, during their student life together. Harvey had never, to Edward's knowledge, broken any of these confidences in the sense of revealing them to other people; but he had a way of playing them back to Edward at inopportune moments; it was disconcerting, it made Edward uncomfortable, especially as Harvey chose to remind him of things he had said which he would rather have forgotten. Harvey seemed especially to choose the negative remarks he made all those years ago, ten, twelve, years ago, such as when he had said something unfavourable about Ruth, something that sounded witty, perhaps, at the time, but which he probably didn't mean. Scarcely ever did Harvey remind him of the praise he devoted in sincere abundance to others, Ruth included. So many sweet things seemed to have spilled out of his ears as soon as they entered them; so many of the sour and the sharp, the unripe and frivolously carping observations he made, Harvey had saved up in his memory-bank at compound interest; it seemed to Edward that he capitalized on these past confidences at a time when they were likely to have the most deflating effect on him; he called this a breach of confidence in a very special sense. Harvey would deny this, of course; he would claim that he had a clear memory, that his reminders were salutary, that Edward was inclined to fool himself, and that the uncomfortable truths of the past were always happier in their outcome than convenient illusions.

And undoubtedly Harvey was often right. That he had a cold side was no doubt a personal matter. In Edward's view it wasn't incompatible with Harvey's extremely good mind and his occasional flashes of generosity. And indeed his moral judgement. Perhaps a bit too much moral judgement.

Edward always spoke a lot about himself and Harvey as they were in their young days, even to people who didn't know them. But few people listen carefully to the reminiscences of someone who has achieved nothing much in life; the end-product of a personal record has somehow to justify the telling. What did come across to Edward's friends was that he had Harvey more or less on his mind. Edward wished something to happen in his own life to make him forget Harvey, get his influence out of his system. Only some big change in my life could do that, Edward thought. Divorce from Ruth, which was unthinkable (then how did I come to think it?). Or great success as an actor; something I haven't got.

Eventually Edward said, as he sat in Harvey's cottage in France, 'I've come about Effie, mainly. Ruth's anxious about her, very anxious. I've come here for Ruth's sake.'

'I recall,' Harvey said, 'how you told me once, when you first married Ruth, "Ruth is a curate's wife and always will be."'

Edward was disconcerted. 'Oh, I was only putting on an act. You know how it was in those days.'

In those days Edward had been a curate, doing so well with church theatricals that he was in demand from other parishes up and down the country. It wasn't so very long before he realized he was an actor, not a curate, not a vicar in bud. Only his sermons interested him and that was because he had his own little stage up there in the pulpit, and an audience. The congregation loved his voice and his delivery. When he resigned, what they said mostly in their letters was 'You were always so genuine in your sermons,' and 'One knew you felt every word.' Well, in fact Edward was and did. But in fact he was more involved in the delivery of his sermons than in the substance. He said good-bye to the fund-raising performances of *The Admirable Crichton* and *The Silver Box*, not to mention *A Midsummer Night's Dream* on the one chilly midsummer night when he was a curate.

He had played parts in repertory theatre, then that principal part (in *The Curate's Egg*) in the West End, and was well launched in his film career, spasmodic and limited though it was, by the time he sat talking to Harvey on Effie's behalf, largely for Ruth's sake. To himself, Edward now described his acting career as 'limited' in the sense that too often he had been cast as a clergyman, an unfrocked priest or a welfare worker. But, at present, in the film provisionally entitled *The Love-Hate Relationship*, he had been cast in a different role, to his great pleasure; he was playing a sardonic scholar, a philosopher. Thinking himself into the part had made him feel extraordinarily equal to his discussion with Harvey; and he returned, with the confidence of the part, to the subject of Effie.

'She wants a divorce,' he said, and waited the inevitable few seconds for Harvey's reply.

'Nothing to stop her.'

'She wants to get married, she's expecting a baby by Ernie Howe. And you know very well she's written to you about it.'

'What she wrote to me about was money. She wants money to get married with. I'm a busy man with things to do. Money; not enough money, but a lot. That's what Effie boils down to.'

'Oh, not entirely. I should have thought you wanted her to be happy. After all, you left her. You left Effie abruptly.'

Harvey waited a while. Time was not of an essence, here. 'Well, she soon found consolation. But she can get a divorce quite easily. Ernie Howe has a job.'

Edward said, 'I don't know if you realize how hateful you can be, Harvey. If it wasn't for your money you wouldn't speak like that.' For it struck him that, since Harvey had recently come into a vast share of a Canadian uncle's fortune, he ought not to carry on as if he were the moderately well-off Harvey of old. This treatment of Effie was brutal.

'I don't know what you mean,' said Harvey, in his time. 'I really don't care what you mean, what you say. I'll give you a letter to Stewart Cowper, my lawyer in London, with suitable instructions.' Harvey got up and reached on a bookshelf for a block of writing paper and one envelope. He said, 'I'll write it now. Then you can go away.'

He wrote without much reflection, almost as if he had come to an earlier decision about the paying off of Effie, and by how much, and had just been waiting for the moment

Edward arrived to make a settlement. He addressed the envelope, put in the folded letter, then sealed it down. He handed it
to Edward. 'You can take it straight to him yourself. Quicker
than posting it.'

Edward was astonished that Harvey had sealed the letter
since he was to be the bearer. Bloody indelicate. He wondered
why Harvey was trying to diminish him.

'Harvey,' he said, 'are you putting on an act? Are you
playing the part of a man who's a swine merely because he
can afford to be?'

Harvey took a lot of thought. Then, 'Yes,' he said.

'Well, it doesn't suit you. One meets that sort of character
amongst the older generation of the motion picture and theatre
world. I remember hearing a producer say to a script writer,
"It's the man who writes the cheque who has the final say in
the script. And I'm the man who writes the cheque." One still
hears that sort of thing. He had yellow eye-balls.'

Harvey sat with folded arms staring at his loaded work-table.

'I suppose you're playing this part to relieve your feelings?'
Edward said.

'I imagine you are relieving yours, Edward.'

'I suppose you're fairly disgusted with things,' Edward said.
'With Effie and so on. I know you left her that day in disgust
when she was eating her stolen chocolate and talking about the
sufferings of the hungry. All that. But Effie has some good
points, you know. Some very good points.'

'If you want a loan why don't you ask for it?' Harvey said,
staring at his papers as if nostalgic for their lonely company.

Anxiety, suffering, were recorded in his face; that was certain.
Edward wasn't sure that this was not self-induced. Harvey had
once said, 'There can be only one answer to the question of
why people suffer, irrespective of whether they are innocent or
guilty; to the question of why suffering has no relation to the
moral quality of the individual, of the tribe or of the nation,

one way or another. If you believe that there is a Creator, a God, and that he is good, the only logical answer to the problem of suffering is that the individual soul has made a pact with God before he is born, that he will suffer during his lifetime. We are born forgetful of this pact, of course; but we have made it. Sufferers would, in this hypothesis, be pre-conscious volunteers. The same might apply to tribes or nations, especially in the past.'

Edward had been very impressed by this, by then the latest, idea of Harvey's. (How many ideas about *Job* they had formu-lated in the past!) But he had said he still couldn't see the need for suffering.

'Oh, development involves suffering,' Harvey had said.

'I wonder if I made that agreement with God before I was born,' said Edward at that time, 'for I've suffered.'

'We have all suffered,' said Harvey, 'but I'm talking about the great multitudes who are starving to death every year, for instance. The glaze-eyed infants.'

'Could your theory be borne out by science?'

'I think possibly there might be a genetic interpretation of it. But I'm talking theologically.'

When, now, Edward looked at his friend's face and saw stress on it, rich and authoritative as Harvey was, swine as he could be, he envied him for the detachment with which he was able to set himself to working on the problem through the *Book of Job*. It was possible for a man like Harvey to be detached and involved at the same time. As an actor, Edward envied him. He also envied the ease with which he could write to his lawyer about his divorce from Effie without a thought for the money involved. As for Edward's loan, Harvey had already written a cheque without a word, knowing, of course, that Edward would pay it back in time. And then, although Harvey wasn't consistently generous, and had ignored Effie's letters, Edward remembered how only a few months ago he had arranged bail through his ever-ready lawyer for Effie and

337

Ruth's student, Nathan, when they were arrested during a demonstration, and been had up for riot and affray. Effie didn't need the bail money, for her lover came to the rescue first, but Nathan did. They were both bound over to keep the peace. Harvey's money was so casual. Edward envied him that, and felt guilty, glimpsing again, for that sharp unthinkable instant, the possibility that he might like to part from Ruth as abruptly and as easily. Edward closed the subject in his mind quickly, very quickly. It had been established that Ruth and Edward always thought alike. Edward didn't want to dwell on that thought, either.

As a theological student Edward had spent many an hour lying with Harvey Gotham on the grass in the great green university square if the weather was fine in the early summer, while the croquet mallets clicked on another part of the green, and the croquet players' voices made slight exclamations, and together he and Harvey discussed the *Book of Job*, which they believed was not only as important, as amazing, a poem as it was generally considered to be, but also the pivotal book of the Bible.

Edward had always maintained that the link – or should he say fetter? – that first bound him to Harvey was their deep old love of marvellous Job, their studies, their analyses, their theories. Harvey used to lie on his back on the grass, one leg stretched out, the other bent at the knee, while Edward sat by his side sunning his face and contemplating the old castle, while he listened with another part of his mind to Harvey's talk. 'It is the only problem. The problem of suffering is the only problem. It all boils down to that.'

'Did you know,' Edward remembered saying, 'that when Job was finally restored to prosperity and family abundance, one of his daughters was called Box of Eye-Paint? Can we really imagine our tormented hero enjoying his actual reward?'

'No,' said Harvey. 'He continued to suffer.'

'Not according to the Bible.'

'Still, I'm convinced he suffered on. Perhaps more.'

'It seems odd, doesn't it,' Edward had said, 'after he sat on a dung-heap and suffered from skin-sores and put up with his friends' gloating, and lost his family and his cattle, that he should have to go on suffering.'

'It became a habit,' Harvey said, 'for he not only argued the problem of suffering, he suffered the problem of argument. And that is incurable.'

'But he wanted to argue with God.'

'Yes, but God as a character comes out badly, very badly. Thunder and bluster and I'm Me, who are you? Putting on an act. Behold now Leviathan. Behold now Behemoth. Ha, ha among the trumpets. Where wast thou when I laid the foundations of the earth? And Job, insincerely and wrongly, says, "I am vile." And God says, All right, that being understood, I give you back double your goods, you can have fourteen thousand sheep and six thousand camels and a thousand yoke of oxen, and a thousand she-asses. And seven sons and three daughters. The third daughter was Keren-happuch – that was Eye-Paint.'

Towards evening, on the day when Edward visited Harvey at his place near St Dié, Harvey went out and brought in the baby clothes. He didn't fold them; he just dumped them on a chair in the little scullery at the back of the kitchen. He seemed to forget that he was impatient for Edward to leave. He brought out some wine, some glasses, cheese and bread. In fact, Edward could see that Harvey didn't want him to leave, lest he should feel lonely afterwards. Edward had been feeling rather guilty at interrupting what was probably a fairly contented solitude. Now, it was not that he regretted imposing his presence, but that by doing so he must impose the absence to follow. For Harvey more and more seemed to want him to remain. Edward said something about catching a night ferry. He thought, Surely Harvey's involved with the mother of the baby whose clothes he's just brought in off the line.

They must be the clothes of an infant not more than a year old. Where are the mother and child?

There was no sign of any mother or child apart from the clothes Harvey had dumped on a chair. Edward was envious, too. He was envious of Harvey's woman and his child. He wanted, at that moment, to be free like Harvey and to have a girl somewhere, but not visible, with a baby.

Harvey said, 'It's fairly lonely here.' By which Edward knew for certain that Harvey was suddenly very lonely indeed at the thought of his leaving. The mother and child were probably away for the night.

'Stay the night,' said Harvey. 'There's plenty of room.'

Edward wanted to know where Harvey had been and what he'd been doing since he disappeared on the *autostrada*. But they did not talk of that. Harvey told him that Effie was writing a thesis on child-labourers in the Western democracies, basing much of it on Kingsley's *The Water Babies*. She hadn't told Edward this. Harvey seemed pleased that he had a bit more news of her than Edward had. But then they had a laugh over Effie and her zeal in the sociological industry.

Harvey made up a bed for him in a sort of cupboard-room upstairs. It was nearly four in the morning when he pulled the extra rough covers over a mattress and piled two cushions for a pillow. From the doorway into Harvey's bedroom Edward could see that the bed was narrow, the furniture quite spare in a cheap new way. He said, 'Where's the baby?'

'What baby?' Harvey said.

'The baby whose washing was out on the line.'

'Oh that,' said Harvey; 'that's only my safeguard. I put baby clothes out on the line every day and bring them in at night. I change the clothes every other day, naturally.'

Edward wondered if Harvey had really gone mad.

'Well, I don't understand,' Edward said, turning away as if it didn't matter.

'You see,' said Harvey, 'the police don't break in and shoot if there's likely to be a baby inside. Otherwise they might just break in and shoot.'

'Go to hell,' Edward said.

'Well, if I told you the truth you wouldn't understand.'

'Thanks,' he said.

'You wouldn't believe,' said Harvey.

'All right, I don't want to know.'

'When I settled here I strung up the clothes-line. I have a sure system of keeping away the well-meaning women who always come round a lone man, wanting to cook and launder and mend socks and do the shopping; they love a bachelor; even in cities – no trouble at all getting domestic help for a single man. In my wanderings since I left Effie I've always found that a line of baby clothes, varying from day to day, keeps these solicitous women away; they imagine without thinking more of it, that there's already a woman around.'

But Edward knew him too well; it was surely one of those demonstrative acts by which Harvey attempted to communicate with a world whose intelligence he felt was away behind his own. Harvey was always in a state of exasperation, and, it was true, always ten thoughts ahead of everybody around him. Always likely to be outrageous. The baby clothes probably belonged to his girl.

Edward left three hours later before Harvey was up. He still felt envious of Harvey for his invisible and probably non-existent girl and her baby.

CHAPTER 2

NATHAN FOX WAS sitting up with Ruth when Edward got back to London. It was a Sunday, a Pimlico Sunday with vacant parking spaces and lights in some of the windows.

Nathan had graduated in English literature, at the university where Ruth was now teaching, over a year before. He couldn't get a job. Ruth looked after him most of the time. Edward always said he himself would do almost anything for Ruth; they saw eye to eye. So Nathan was quite welcome. But just that night on his return from France, very tired, and needing to get to bed for an early rise the next morning – he was due at the studio at seven – just that night Edward wished Nathan Fox wasn't there. Edward was not at all sure how they would manage without Nathan. Nathan wasn't ashamed of calling himself an intellectual, which, for people like themselves, made life so much easier; not that he was, in fact, an intellectual, really; he was only educated. But they could talk to Nathan about anything; and at the same time he made himself useful in the house. Indeed, he was a very fair cook. To a working couple like Ruth and Edward he was an invaluable friend.

It was just that night, and on a few previous occasions, Edward wished he wasn't there. Edward wanted to talk to Ruth, to get to bed early. Nathan sat there in his tight jeans and his T-shirt with 'Poetry Is Emotion Recollected In Tranquillity' printed on it. He was a good-looking boy, tall, with an oval face, very smooth and rather silvery-green in colour – really olive. His eyebrows were smooth, black and arched, his hair heavy and sleek, quite black. But he wasn't vain at all. He got up in the morning, took a shower, shaved and dressed, all in less than seven minutes. It seemed to Edward that the alarm in their room had only just gone off when he could smell the coffee brewing in the kitchen, and hear Nathan already setting the places for breakfast. Ruth, too, wondered how he managed it. His morning smile was delightful; he had a mouth like a Michelangelo angel and teeth so good, clear, strong and shapely it seemed to Edward, secretly, that they were the sexiest thing about him.

The only problem with Nathan was how to explain what he saw in them. They paid him and fed him as well as they could, but it was supposed to be only a fill-in job. They were together as on a North Sea oil platform. It wasn't that Nathan wouldn't leave them, it now seemed he couldn't. Edward thought, He is hankering after Effie, and we are the nearest he can get to her. Edward often wondered whether Effie would really marry Ernie Howe when she got her divorce from Harvey.

When Edward got back from France they had supper; he told Nathan and Ruth what had happened at Harvey's cottage, almost from start to finish. Ruth wanted actually to see with her eyes the sealed letter to the lawyer; so that Edward got up from the table and fished it out of his duffel bag.

She turned it over and over in her hand; she examined it closely; she almost smelt it. She said, 'How rude to seal down a letter you were to carry by hand.'

'Why?' said Nathan.

'Because one doesn't,' Ruth piped primly, 'seal letters that other people are to carry.'

'What about the postman?'

'Oh, I mean one's friends.'

'Well, open it,' said Nathan.

Edward had been rather hoping he would suggest this, and he knew Ruth had the same idea in mind. If they'd been alone, neither of them would have suggested it out loud, although it would certainly have occurred to them, so eager were they to know what Harvey had settled on Effie in this letter to his solicitors. They would have left the letter and their secret desires unopened. They were still somewhat of the curate and his wife, Ruth and himself.

But Nathan seemed to serve them like a gentleman who takes a high hand in matters of form, or an unselfconscious angel. In a way, that is what he was there for, if he had to be there. He often said things out of his inexperience and cheerful ignorance that they themselves wanted to say but did not dare.

'Open it?' said Ruth.

'Oh, we can't do that,' said Edward.

'You can steam it open,' suggested Nathan, as if they didn't know. 'You only need a kettle.'

'Really?' said Ruth.

Nathan proceeded, very know-all: 'It won't be noticed. You can seal it up again. My mother steamed open my aunt's letters. Only wanted to know what was in them, that's all. Then later my aunt would tell a lot of lies about what was in the letters, but my mother knew the truth, of course. That was after my father died, and my mother and my auntie were living together.'

'I don't know that we have the right,' said Ruth.

'It's your duty,' Nathan pronounced. He turned to Edward, appealing: 'In my mother's case it wasn't a duty, although she said it was. But in your case it's definitely a duty to steam open that letter. It might be dynamite you've been carrying.'

Edward said, 'He should have left it open. It might be really offensive or something. It was ill-mannered of Harvey. I noticed it at the time, in fact.'

'You should have objected,' Nathan said. Edward was now delighted that Nathan was there with them that evening.

'It's difficult to object,' Ruth said. 'But I think we have a right to know what's in it. At least you do, Edward, since you're the bearer.'

They steamed open the letter in the kitchen and stood reading it together.

Dear Stewart,

This letter is being brought to you by Edward Jansen, an old friend of mine from university days. I don't know if you've met him. He's a sort of actor but that is by the way. My wife Effie is his sister-in-law. He came to see me about Effie's divorce. As you know I'm not contesting it. She wants a settlement. Let her go on wanting, let her sue.

The object of this letter is to tell you that I agree the date of *Job* is post-exile, that is, about 500 BC, but it could be the middle of the 5th century. It could easily be contemporaneous with the *Prometheus Bound* of Aeschylus. (The *Philoctetes* of Sophocles, another *Job*-style work, is dated I think about 409.)

Yours,
Harvey

'I won't deliver it,' Edward said.

'Oh, you must,' said Nathan. 'You mustn't let him think you've opened it.'

'There's something fishy about it,' Edward said. He was greatly annoyed.

'Calling you a sort of actor,' Ruth said, in a soothing voice that made him nearly choleric.

'It's Effie's fault,' said Ruth. 'She's brought out this quality in Harvey.'

'Well, I'm too busy tomorrow to go in person to Gray's Inn,' Edward said.

'I'll deliver it,' said Nathan.

CHAPTER 3

IT WAS OCTOBER. Harvey sat at his writing-table, set against the wall of the main room in his little house.

'*Job* 37, 5,' he wrote, 'God thundereth marvellously with his voice . . .'

'I think we'll have to send to England for some more cretonne fabric,' said Ruth, looking over his shoulder.

It was at the end of August that Ruth had moved in, bringing with her Effie's baby, a girl. The baby was now asleep for a merciful moment, upstairs.

Harvey looked up from his work. 'I try to exude goodwill,' he said.

'You positively try to sweat it,' Ruth said, kindly. And she wondered how it was that she had disliked and resented Harvey for so many years. It still amazed her to find herself here with him. That he was perfectly complacent about the arrangement, even cheerful and happy, did not surprise her so much; everything around him, she knew – all the comings and goings – were really peripheral to his preoccupation with the *Book of Job*. But her being there, with Effie's baby, astonished her sometimes to the point of vertigo. This was not at all what she had planned when she decided to turn up at the cottage with Effie's baby daughter.

Once, after she had settled in, she said to Harvey, 'I didn't plan this.'

'It wasn't a plan,' said Harvey, 'it was a plot.'

'I suppose it looks like that from the outside,' Ruth said. To her, what she had wanted was justice. Given Effie's character, it was not to be expected that she would continue to live with

346

Ernie Howe on his pay in a small house. Ruth had offered to take the baby when Effie decided she wasn't in love with Ernie any more. Harvey's money would perhaps not have made much difference to Effie's decision. At any rate, Ruth had known that, somehow, in the end, she would have to take on Effie's baby. It rather pleased her.

Effie was trying to sue Harvey for alimony, so far without success. 'The lawyers are always on the side of the money,' she said. Harvey continued to ignore her letters.

The baby, named Clara, had been born toward the end of June. Effie went back to her job in advertising for a short while after she had left Ernie Howe. Then she took a job with an international welfare organization in Rome. Ernie wasn't at all happy, at first, with Ruth's plan to take the baby Clara to visit Harvey. They sat in the flat in Pimlico where Ernie often came, now, for consolation, as much as to see his daughter.

'He doesn't sound the sort of man to have any *sent-y-ments*,' Ernie said.

Edward wanted very much to give Ernie some elocution lessons to restore his voice to the plain tones of his origins. 'He hasn't any sentimentality, but of course he has sentiments,' said Edward.

'Especially about his wife's baby by a, well, a lover.'

'As to that,' said Edward, 'he won't care who the father is. He just won't have any sentimental feelings, full stop.'

'It's a matter of justice,' Ruth said.

'How do you work that out?' said Nathan.

'Well, if it hadn't been for Harvey leaving Effie she would never have had a baby by Ernie,' Ruth said. 'Harvey should have given her a child. So Harvey's responsible for Clara; it's a question of justice, and with all his riches it would be the best thing if he could take responsibility, pay Effie her alimony. He might even take Effie back.'

'Effie doesn't want to go back to Harvey Gotham,' said Ernie.

'Harvey won't take her back,' Edward said. 'He believes that Effie boils down to money.'

'Alas, he's right,' said Ernie.

'Why can't Clara go on living with us?' said Nathan, who already knew how to prepare the feeds and bath the baby.

'I'm only taking her for a visit,' Ruth said. 'What's wrong with that? You went to see Harvey, Edward. Now I'll have a try.'

'Be sure to bring her back, Ree-uth,' said Ernie. 'The legal position –'

'Do you still want to marry Effie?' Edward asked him.

'No, quite frankly, I don't.'

'Effie's so beautiful,' Nathan said. He got up to replenish the drinks. 'What a beautiful girl she is!'

'A matter of justice. A balancing of accounts.' This was how Ruth put it to Harvey. 'I'm passionate about justice,' she said.

'People who want justice,' Harvey said, 'generally want so little when it comes to the actuality. There is more to be had from the world than a balancing of accounts.'

She supposed he was thinking of his character Job, as in fact he was. She was used to men answering her with one part of their mind on religion. That was one of the reasons why Edward had become so unsatisfactory after he had ceased to be a curate and become an actor.

Ruth and Effie grew up in a country rectory that today is converted into four commodious flats. The shabbiness of the war still hung over it in the late fifties, but they were only aware of the general decay by the testimony of their elders as to how things were 'in the old days', and the evidence of pre-war photographs of garden parties where servants and trees stood

348

about, well-tended, and the drawing-room chintzes were well-fitted and new. Otherwise, they simply accepted that life was a muddle of broken barrows, tin buckets in the garden sheds, overgrown gardens, neglected trees. They had an oak of immense girth; a mulberry tree older than the house, to judge from early sketches of the place. The graveyard had a yew the circumference and shape of their oval dining-table; the tree was hollow inside and the bark had formed itself into the shape of organ pipes. Yews were planted in graveyards, origin-ally, because they poisoned cattle, and as they were needed for long-bows they were planted in a place where cattle didn't go. All this Ruth picked up from God knows where; the air she breathed informed her. House-martins nested under the eaves outside Ruth's room and used to make a dark-and-white flash almost up to the open window as they came and fled in the morning.

There was a worn carpet on the staircase up to the first landing. After that, bare wood. Most of the rooms were simply shut for ever. They had been civil servants' bedrooms in war-time before Ruth was born, and she never knew what it was like to see the houseful of people that the rectory was made for.

For most of Ruth's life, up to the time Edward became an actor, religion was her bread and butter. Her father was what Edward at one time called a career-Christian; she assumed he was a believer too, as was her mother; but she never got the impression that either had time to think about it.

Effie was three years younger than Ruth. The sisters were very close to each other all their schooldays and in their early twenties. Ruth often wondered when exactly they had separ-ated in their attitude to life. It was probably after Ruth's return from Paris where she had spent a year with a family. Shortly afterwards Effie, too, went off to be an *au pair* in France.

If you are the child of a doctor or a butcher you don't have to believe in your father's occupation. But, in their childhood, they had to believe in their father's job as a clergyman in a special way. Matins and Sunday services and Evensong were part of the job; the family was officially poor, which was to say they were not the poor in the streets and cottages, but poor by the standards of a country rector. Ruth's mother was a free-lance typist and always had some work in hand. She could do seventy words a minute on her old pre-war typewriter. Before her marriage she had done a hundred and thirty words a minute at Pitman's shorthand. Ruth used to go to sleep on a summer night hearing the tap-tapping of the typewriter below, and wake to the almost identical sound of the wood-pecker in the tree outside her window. Ruth supposed this was Effie's experience too, but when she reminded her sister of it many years later Effie couldn't recall any sound effects.

Effie went to a university on her return from France and left after her first year about the time that Ruth graduated and married Edward. Ruth worked with and for Edward and the parish, organizing a live crib at Christmas with a real baby, a real cow and a real virgin; she wrote special prayers to the Holy Spirit and the Trinity for the parish magazine (which she described as Prayers to the HS etc.) and she arranged bring-and-pay garden lunches. She lectured and made bedspreads, and she taught child-welfare and jam preserving. Ruth was very much in the business. Effie, meanwhile, went off the rails, and when this was pointed out to her in so many words, she said, 'What rails? Whose rails?' It was Effie who first called Edward an actor more than a man of God, and she probably put the idea in his mind.

Effie was doing social work when Ruth got married. The sisters looked very much alike in their separate features; it was one of those cases where the sum total of each came out with a difference, to the effect that Effie was extremely beautiful and Ruth was nothing remarkable; perhaps it was a question of colouring and complexion. Whatever the reason, everyone looked at Effie in a special way. Both sisters were fair with the fair-lashed look and faint eyebrows of some Dutch portraits.

It was Edward who introduced Effie to Harvey Gotham. Effie was in the habit of despising the rich, but she married him. They had a small house in Chelsea and at first they travelled everywhere together.

When Edward became an actor Ruth got a job in a university, teaching twentieth-century history. Edward had a television part which came to an end about the time Ruth discerned that Effie and Harvey were not getting on. Effie's young men-friends from her days of welfare-work were always in her house, discussing their social conscience. Harvey was often away.

'You're sleeping around,' Ruth said to Effie.

'What do you mean?' she said.

'I know,' Ruth said.

'What do you know?'

Ruth said, 'I know all about it.' What she meant was that she knew Effie.

'You must be guessing,' said Effie, very shaken.

'I know,' Ruth said, 'that you're having affairs. Not one only. Plural.'

Edward was still out of a job. They hadn't any prospect of a holiday that year, but Effie and Harvey had planned a motoring trip in Italy.

Ruth said, 'Why don't you get Harvey to invite us to join you on your holiday in Italy?'

'He wouldn't like that,' she said. 'Four in the car.'

'It's a big car.'

'You couldn't afford your share,' said Effie, 'could you?'

'No, not all of it.'

'What all this has to do with my love affairs, real or imagined,' said Effie, 'I really do not know.'

'Don't you?' said Ruth.

'Ruth,' she said, 'you're a blackmailer, aren't you?'

'Only in your eyes. In my eyes it is simply that we're going to come to Italy with you. Harvey won't mind the money.'

'Oh, God,' she said, 'I'd rather you went ahead and told him all you know. Think of all the suffering in the world, the starving multitudes. Can't you sacrifice a pleasure? Go ahead and tell Harvey what you know. Your sordid self-interest, your –'

'You shock me,' Ruth said. 'Stick to the point. Is it likely that I would go to your husband and say . . . ?'

They went on holiday with Effie and Harvey, and they took Ruth's student, Nathan, as well. Effie stole two bars of chocolate from the supermarket on the *autostrada* and Harvey left them abruptly. It was the end of their marriage. Fortunately Effie had enough money on her to pay for the rest of the trip. It was a holiday of great beauty. Effie tried to appreciate the pictures in the art galleries, the fountains in the squares, the ancient monuments and the Mediterranean abundance, but even basking on the beach she was uneasy.

Harvey saw Effie's features in Ruth; it struck him frequently that she was what Effie should have been. It had been that situation where the visitor who came to stay remained to live. (Harvey had heard of an author who had reluctantly granted an interview to a young critic, who then remained with him for life.) The arrangement was not as uncomfortable as it might have been, for Ruth had claimed and cleared one of the shacks outside the house, where she spent most of the day-time with the baby. She was careful to make the changes unobtrusively. Delivery vans drove up with rugs or with an extra stove, but it was all done in a morning. Harvey paid for the things. When the baby cried it upset him, but that was seldom, for Ruth drove off frequently with the child, no doubt to let it cry elsewhere. She took it with her when she went shopping.

It was three weeks after she had arrived that Ruth said, 'I'm going to write to Edward.'

'I have written,' said Harvey.

'I know,' she said, and he wondered how she knew, since he had posted the letter himself. 'But I'll write myself. I couldn't be the wife of an actor again.'

'If he was a famous actor?'

'Well, he isn't a famous actor. A part here, a part there, and sometimes a film. So full of himself when he has a part. It was a much better life for me when he was a curate.'

But she had no nostalgia even for those days of church fêtes, evening lectures and sewing classes. She already had a grip of her new life, dominated as it was by the *Book of Job*.

'You feel safer when you're living with someone who's in the God-business,' Harvey said. 'More at home.'

'Perhaps that's it,' she said.

'And a steadier income.'

'Such as it is,' she said, for she asked little for herself. 'But,' she said, 'I was bored. He always agreed with me, and you don't.'

'That's because you're one of my comforters,' Harvey said. 'Job had his comforters to contend with; why shouldn't I?'

'Do you think of yourself as Job?'

'Not exactly, but one can't help sympathizing with the man.'

'I don't know about that,' said Ruth. 'Job was a very rich man. He lost all his goods, and all his sons and daughters, and took it all very philosophically. He said, "The Lord gave, the Lord taketh away, blessed be the name of the Lord." Then he gets covered with boils; and it's only then that his nerve gives way, he's touched personally. He starts his complaint against God at that point only. No question of why his sons should have lost their lives, no inquiries of God about the cause of their fate. It's his skin disease that sets him off.'

'Maybe it was shingles,' Harvey said. 'A nervous disease. Anyway, it got on his nerves.'

Ruth said, 'He had to be touched himself before he would react. Touched in his own body. Utterly selfish. He doesn't seem to have suffered much or he wouldn't have been able to go into all that long argument. He couldn't have had a temperature.'

'I don't agree. I think he had a high temperature all through the argument,' Harvey said. 'Because it's high poetry. Or else, maybe you're right; maybe it was the author who had the temperature. Job himself just sat there with a long face arguing against the theories of his friends.'

'Make a note of that,' Ruth commanded.

'I'll make a note.' He did so.

'Someone must have fed him,' said Ruth. 'Someone must have brought him meals to eat as he sat on the dung-hill outside the town.'

'I'm not sure he sat on a dung-hill outside the town. That is an assumption based on an unverified Greek version of the text. He is merely said to have sat in the ashes on the ground. Presumably at his own hearth. And his good wife, no doubt, brought him his meals.'

Ruth had proved to be an excellent cook, cramped in the kitchen with that weird three-tiered kerosene stove of hers.

'What do you mean, "his good wife"?' Ruth said. 'She told him, "Curse God and die."'

'That was a way of expressing her exasperation. She was tired of his griping and she merely wanted him to get it off his chest quickly, and finish.'

'I suppose the wife suffered,' said Ruth. 'But whoever wrote the book made nothing of her. Job deserved all he got.'

'That was the point that his three friends tried to get across to him,' Harvey said. 'But Job made the point that he didn't deserve it. Suffering isn't in proportion to what the sufferer deserves.'

Ruth wrote in September:

Dear Edward,

I suppose you have gathered by now that I've changed my mind about Harvey. I don't know what he's written to you.

He really is a most interesting man. I believe I can help Harvey.

I can't return to face the life we had together, ever again. My dear, I don't know how I could have thought I would. My plan was, as you know, entirely different. I feel Harvey needs me. I am playing a role in his life. He is serious. Don't imagine I'm living in luxury. He never mentions his wealth. But of course I am aware that if there is anything I require for myself or Clara, I can have it.

You may have heard from Ernie Howe that he is coming to visit Clara. She's well and pretty, and full of life.

I'm sure you have heard from Harvey how things are between him and me. It's too soon to talk of the future.

This has been a difficult letter to write. I know that you'll agree with what I say. You always do.

Ruth

She gave Harvey the letter to read, watching him while he read it. He looked younger than Edward, probably because of Edward's beard, although he was a little older. Harvey was lean and dark, tall, stringy.

'It's a bit dry,' Harvey said.

'It's all I can do. Edward knows what I'm like.'

'I suppose,' said Harvey, 'he'll be hurt.'

'He doesn't love me,' Ruth said.

'How do you know?'

'How does one know?'

'Still, he won't want to lose his property.'

'That's something else.'

Now, in October, Ruth was talking about sending to England for cretonne fabric. 'One can't get exactly what I want in France,' she said.

Harvey wrote:

Dear Edward,

Thanks for yours.

The infant is cutting a tooth and makes a din at night. Ruth has very disturbed nights. So do I. It's been raining steadily for three days. Ernie Howe came. We had a chat. He seems to feel fraternal towards me because we both had to do with Effie. He wants to talk about Effie. I don't. Afterwards, in the place next door that Ruth has fixed up for herself and Clara, Ernie asked her if she would go home and live with him and bring the baby. Ruth said no. I think he's after Ruth because she reminds him of Effie. He said he wouldn't take the child away from Ruth if she doesn't want to part with it, which she doesn't.

I'm sorry to hear that you don't miss Ruth. You ought to.

Cheque enclosed. I know you're not 'selling your wife'. Why should I think you are? You took money before I was sleeping with Ruth, so where's the difference?

I don't agree the comforters just came to gloat. They relieved Job's suffering by arguing with him, keeping him talking. In different ways they keep insinuating that Job 'deserved' his misfortunes; he must have done something wrong. While Job insists that he hasn't, that the massed calamities that came on him haven't any relation to his own actions. He upsets all their theology. Those three friends of his are very patient and considerate, given their historical position. But Job is having a nervous crisis. He can't sleep. See 7, 13–16.

> When I say, My bed shall
> comfort me, my couch shall ease
> my complaint;
> Then thou scarest me with
> dreams, and terrifiest me through
> visions:
> So that my soul chooseth
> strangling, and death rather than
> my life.

356

> I loathe it; I would not
> live alway: let me alone . . .

So I say, at least the three comforters kept him company. And they took turns as analyst. Job was like the patient on the couch.

Ruth doesn't sympathize with Job. She sees the male pig in him. That's a point of view.

The baby has started to squawk. I don't know what I'm going to do about the noise.

Yours,
Harvey

Ruth came in, jogging in her arms the baby Clara who had a whole fist in her mouth and who made noises of half-laughing, half-crying. Soon, she would start to bawl. Ruth's hair fell over her face, no longer like that of a curate's wife.

'Did you know that they want to sell the château?' she said.

The château was half a mile up the grassy pathway which led away from the cottage. Harvey knew the owner and had seen the house; that was when he first rented the cottage. He knew it was up for sale, and had been for some years.

'It's falling to bits,' he said to Ruth.

'What a pity to neglect it like that!' Ruth said. 'It's a charming house. It reminds me of something from my childhood, I don't know quite what. Perhaps somewhere we visited. I think something could be done to it.'

She brought the fretful child close to Harvey so that he could make an ugly face. He showed his teeth and growled, whereupon Clara temporarily forgot her woes. She smelt of sour milk.

CHAPTER 4

UP AT THE château where the neglected lawns were greener than the patch round Harvey's house, and where the shrubberies were thick and very dark evergreen, the workmen were putting in the daylight hours of the last few days before the Christmas holidays. She had already reclaimed one wing for habitation. The roof had been secured in that part, but most of the rooms were cold. Ruth had arranged one sitting-room, however, with a fire, and two bedrooms with oil stoves. A good start.

What a business it had been to persuade Harvey to buy the château! And now he was enchanted. Once he agreed to buy – and that was the uphill work – it was simple. Harvey sent for his London lawyer, Stewart Cowper, and for his French lawyer, Martin Deschamps, to meet in Nancy and discuss the deal with the family who owned the château. Ruth had gone with Harvey to this meeting, in October, with Clara in her folding pram. When the hotel room got too boring for the baby, Ruth hushed her, put her in her pram and took her for a walk in Place Stanislas. It was not long before Ruth saw through the splendid gilt gates the whole business group, with Harvey, trooping out to take the sun and continue the deal in the glittering square. Harvey, his two lawyers, and the three members of the de Remiremont family, which comprised a middle-aged man, his daughter and his nephew, came and joined Ruth. The daughter put her hand on the handle of the pram. They all ambled round in a very unprofessional way, talking of notaries and tax and the laws governing foreigners' property in France. You could see that this was only a preliminary.

Harvey said, 'We have to leave you. I'm writing a book on the *Book of Job*.'

It was difficult to get across to them what the *Book of Job* was. Harvey's French wasn't at fault, it was their knowledge of the Bible of which, like most good Catholics, they had scant knowledge. They stood around, the father in his old tweed coat and trousers, the daughter and nephew in their woollen jumpers and blue jeans, puzzling out what was *Job*. Finally, the father remembered. It all came back to him. 'You shouldn't be in a hurry, then,' he said. 'Job had patience, isn't that right? One says, "the patience of Job".'

'In fact,' said Harvey, 'Job was the most impatient of men.'

'Well, it's good to know what it is you're writing in that wretched little cottage,' said the elder man. 'I often wondered.'

'I hope we'll soon have the house,' said Ruth.

'So do we,' said the owner. 'We'll be glad to get rid of it.' The young man and the girl laughed. The lawyers looked a little worried about the frankness and the freedom, suspecting, no doubt, some façade covering a cunning intention.

Ruth and Harvey left them then. It was all settled within a month except for the final bureaucracy, which might drag on for years. Anyhow, Harvey had paid, and Ruth was free to order her workmen to move in.

'Instead of disabusing myself of worldly goods in order to enter the spirit of *Job* I seem to acquire more, ever more and more,' was all that Harvey said.

Ruth wrote to Effie with her letter-pad on her knee, beside the only fireplace, while the workmen hammered away, a few days before Christmas.

Dear Effie,

I really am in love with Harvey and you have no reason to say I am not. The lovely way he bought the house – so casual – we just walked round the *Place* with Clara and the family who used to own the château – and Harvey shook hands and that was all. The lawyers are working it out, but the house is ours.

I can't make out your letter. You don't want Clara, at least not the bother of her. You despise Harvey. What do you mean, that I have stolen your husband and your child? Be civilized.

Ruth stopped, read what she had written, and tore it up. Why should I reply to Effie? What do I owe her? She stole a bit of chocolate, on principle. I stole her husband, not on principle. As for her child, I haven't stolen her, she has abandoned her baby. All right, Effie is young and beautiful, and now has to work for her living. Possibly she's broke.

Dear Effie,
    What attracted me most about the château was the woodpecker in the tree outside the bedroom window. Why don't you come and visit Clara?
                        Love,
                        Ruth

She sealed it up and put it on the big plate in the hall to be posted, for all the world as if the château was already a going concern. The big plate on a table by the door was all there was in the huge dusty hall, but it was a beginning.

Now she took sleeping Clara in her carry-cot and set her beside the driver's seat in the car. She put a basket in the back containing bread, pâté, a roast bantam hen and a bottle of Côte du Rhône, and she set off down the drive to Harvey's house for lunch. The tired patch of withered shrubbery round Harvey's cottage was still noticeably different from the rest of the château's foliage, although Ruth had dug around a few bushes to improve them, and planted some bulbs. As soon as she pushed open the door she saw he had a visitor. She dumped the food basket and went back for the baby, having glimpsed the outline of a student, a young man, any student, with those blue jeans of such a tight fit, they were reminiscent of Elizabethan women's breasts, in that you wondered, looking at their portraits, where they put their natural flesh. The student followed her out to the car. It was Nathan. 'Nathan! It's you, – you here. I didn't recognize . . .' He woke Clara with his big kiss, and the child wailed. He picked her up and pranced up and down with the wakened child. Harvey's studious cottage was a carnival. Harvey said to Ruth, 'I've told Nathan there will be room for him up at the house.'

Nathan had brought some food, too. He had been skilful as ever in finding the glasses, the plates; everything was set for lunch. Ruth got Clara back to sleep again, but precariously, clutching a ragged crust.

Harvey said very little. He had closed the notebook he was working on, and unnaturally tidied his papers; his pens were arranged neatly, and everything on his writing-table looked put-away. He sat looking at the floor between his feet.

Nathan announced, 'I just had to come. I had nothing else to do. It's a long time since I had a holiday.'

'And Edward, how's Edward?' Ruth said.

'Don't you hear from Edward?'

'Yes of course,' said Ruth, and Harvey said the same.

Nathan opened his big travel pack and brought out yet more food purchases that he had picked up on the way: cheese, wine, pâté and a bottle of Framboise. He left the pack open while he took them to the table. Inside was a muddle of clothes and spare shoes, but Harvey noticed the edges of Christmas-wrapped parcels sticking up from the bottom of the pack. My God, he has come for Christmas. Harvey looked at Ruth: did she invite him? Ruth fluttered about with her thanks and her chatter.

'Are you off to Paris for Christmas?' Harvey inquired. This was his first meeting with Nathan since the holiday in Italy when Harvey had abandoned his party on the *autostrada*; he felt he could be distant and impersonal without offence.

'I've come mainly to visit Clara for Christmas,' said Nathan. He was lifting the baby out of the carry-cot.

'Let her sleep,' Harvey said.

'Oh, Nathan must stay over Christmas,' Ruth said. 'Paris will be crowded. And dreadfully expensive.' She added, 'Nathan is a marvellous cook.'

'So I have heard.'

Ruth didn't notice, or affected not to notice, a look of empty desperation on Harvey's face; a pallor, a cornered look; his lips were parted, his eyes were focusing only on some anguished thought. And he was, in fact, suddenly aghast: What am I doing with these people around me? Who asked this fool to come and join us for Christmas? What do I need with Christmas, and Ruth, and a baby and a bloody little youth who needs a holiday? Why did I buy that château if not for Ruth and the baby to get out of my way? He looked at his writing-table, and panicked.

'I'm going out, I'll just fetch my coat,' he said, thumping upstairs two at a time.

'Harvey, what's the matter?' said Ruth when he appeared again with his sheepskin jacket, his woollen hat. Rain had started to splash down with foul eagerness.

'Don't you want lunch?' she said.

'Excuse me. I'm studious,' said Harvey, as he left the cottage. The car door slammed. The starter wouldn't work at first try. The sound of Harvey working and working at the starter became ever more furious until finally he was off.

When he came back in the evening the little house was deserted, all cleaned up. He poured himself a whisky, sat down and started to think of Effie. She was different from Ruth, almost a race apart. Ruth was kind, or comparatively so. Effie wasn't comparatively anything, certainly not kind.

She was absolutely fascinating. Harvey remembered Effie at parties, her beauty, part of which was a quick-witted merriment. How could two sisters be so physically alike and yet so totally different? At any moment Ruth might come in and reproach him for not having the Christmas spirit. Effie would never do that. Ruth was thoroughly bourgeois by nature; Effie, anarchistic, aristocratic. I miss Effie, I miss her a lot, Harvey told himself. The sound of Ruth's little car coming down the drive, slowly in the mist, chimed with his thought as would the stroke of eight if there was a clock in the room. He looked at his watch; eight o'clock precisely. She had come to fetch him for dinner; three dinner-places set out on the table of the elegant room in the château, and the baby swinging in a hammock set up in a corner.

Ruth came in. 'You know, Harvey,' she said, 'I think you might be nicer to Nathan. After all, it's Christmas time. He's come all this way, and one should have the Christmas spirit.'

Nathan was there, at the château, settled in for Christmas. Harvey thought: I should have told him to go. I should have said I wanted Ruth and the baby to myself for Christmas. Why didn't I? – Because I don't want them to myself. I don't want them enough; not basically.

Ruth looked happy, having said her say. No need to say any more. I can't hold these women, Harvey thought. Neither Effie nor Ruth. My mind isn't on them enough, and they resent it, just as I resent it when they put something else before me, a person, an idea. Yes, it's understandable.

He swallowed down a drink and put on his coat.

'Nathan thinks it was marvellous of you to buy the château just to make me comfortable with Clara,' said Ruth.

'I bought it for myself, too, you know. I always thought I might acquire it.'

'Nathan has been reading the *Book of Job*, he has some ideas.'

'He did his homework, you mean. He must think I'm some sort of monster. In return for hospitality he thinks he has to discuss my subject.'

'He's polite. Besides, it's my subject too, now,' said Ruth.

'Why?' said Harvey. 'Because I've put you in the château?'

He thought, on the way through the misty trees that lined the long drive, They think I'm such a bore that I have to bribe them to come and play the part of comforters.

He made himself cheerful at the château; he poured drinks. In his anxiety to avoid the subject of *Job*, to be normal, to make general conversation, Harvey blurted out the other thing he had on his mind: 'Any news of Effie?'

God, I've said the wrong thing. Both Nathan and Ruth looked, for a moment, startled, uncomfortable; both, discernibly, for different reasons. Nathan, Harvey supposed, had been told to avoid the subject of Effie. Ruth didn't want to bring Effie into focus; it was enough that she was still Harvey's wife, out there vaguely somewhere else, out of sight.

'Effie?' said Ruth.

'I heard from her,' said Nathan. 'Only a postcard, after she got out.'

'Out from where?'

'From prison in Trieste. Didn't you hear about it?'

'Harvey never discusses Effie,' said Ruth. 'I've only just heard about it. She wrote to me last week from London, but she didn't mention prison.'

'What happened?' said Harvey.

'She was caught shop-lifting in a supermarket in Trieste. She said she did it to obtain an opportunity to study a women's prison at first hand. She got out after three days. There was a small paragraph about it in the *Telegraph*, nothing in the other papers; it was about a month ago,' Ruth said. 'Nathan just told me.'

'All she said on the card was that she was going to Munich,' said Nathan.

'I wish her well of Munich,' said Harvey.

'I thought it was a beautiful town,' Ruth said.

'You thought strangely. There is a carillon clock with dancers coming out of the clock-tower twice a day. That's all there is in Munich.'

'She has friends there,' Nathan said. 'She said on the card she was joining friends in Munich. She seems to be getting around.'

'Well, I'm glad, for Effie, there is something else in Munich besides the carillon clock. Who made this soup?'

'Nathan did,' said Ruth.

'It's great.' He wondered why Stewart Cowper hadn't told him about Effie being arrested. He felt over-protected. How can you deal with the problem of suffering if everybody conspires to estrange you from suffering? He felt like the rich man in the parable: it is easier for a camel to go through the eye of a needle than for him to enter the Kingdom of Heaven.

'One must approach these things with balanced thought,' Ruth was saying, alarmingly. Harvey bent his mind to take in what they were discussing. It emerged that they were talking about the huge price Nathan had paid for the taxi from the airport to the château.

'There's a train service,' Harvey said.

'I've just been telling him that,' said Ruth. 'Spending all that money, as much as the air fare. He could have phoned me from the airport.'

'I don't have the number,' said Nathan.

'Oh, yes, I forgot,' said Ruth. 'No one gets the number. Harvey has to be protected; in his position everyone wants him for something. He's here to study an important subject, write a thesis, get away from it all. You have to realize that, Nathan.'

Nathan turned to Harvey. 'Maybe I shouldn't have told you about Effie.'

'Oh, that's all right. I asked you about her, after all.'

'Yes, you did,' said Ruth. She had served veal, delicately cooked in white wine. 'You did bring up the subject, Harvey.'

'A beautiful girl, Effie,' said Nathan. 'What a lovely girl she is!'

Harvey wondered how much he knew about how beautiful Effie was. He looked at Nathan and thought, He has barged into my peace, he's taking his place for Christmas, he's discussing my wife as if she was everybody's girl (which she is), and he's going to get together again with Ruth; they will conspire how to protect me. Finally, he will ask me for a loan.

'Will you be all right up here alone in the château tonight?' Harvey said with determination. 'Ruth and I always shack down in my cottage; Ruth brings the baby back here immediately after early breakfast so that I can start on my work at about seven-thirty.'

'If you'll leave Clara with me I won't feel lonely,' said Nathan.

'Not at all,' said Harvey. 'We have a place for her. She's teething.'

'Nathan's used to Clara,' said Ruth. 'He's known her and looked after her since she was born.'

'I don't think we need ask our guests to baby-sit for us.' Don't think, Harvey said within himself, that you are one of the family here; you are one of 'our guests' in this house.

'Well, as she's teething,' said Ruth, 'I'd better take her with me. I really do think so, Nathan.'

'We'll move up here to the château for Christmas,' Harvey said, now that Ruth was winding up the feast with a cheese *soufflé* as light as could be. He fetched the brandy glasses.

CHAPTER 5

DEAR EDWARD,

Happy New Year. Thanks for yours.

The day before Christmas Eve he turned up. After dinner he sat up late discussing his ideas on *Job* – he'd done some reading (for my benefit, which I suppose is a compliment). I don't agree with you that he seems 'positively calculating', I don't agree at all. I think he wanted to spend Christmas with Ruth and the baby. He would have preferred to spend Christmas with Effie. He didn't want to spend Christmas alone with you; that's why you're sour. You should get a lot of friends and some of your colleagues, pretty young actresses, have parties. Nathan would like that.

We went to Midnight Mass at the local church. Nathan carried Clara in a sling on his back and she slept throughout. There was a great crowd.

He hasn't left yet. He shows no sign of leaving.

I agree that Job endlessly discusses morals but there is nothing moral about the *Book of Job*. In fact it is shockingly amoral.

God has a wager with Satan that Job will not lose faith, however much he is afflicted. Job never knows about this wager, neither do his friends. But the reader knows. Satan finally makes the explicit challenge (2,5):

> But put forth thy hand
> now, and touch his bone and
> his flesh, and he will
> curse thee to thy face.

And God says, Go ahead ('Behold, he is in thine hand; but save his life.')

Consequently Job, having lost his sons and his goods, is now covered with sores. He is visited by his bureaucratic friends who tell him he must have deserved it. The result is that Job has a sort of nervous breakdown. He demands an explanation and he never gets it.

Do you know that verse of Kipling's?

> The toad beneath the harrow knows
> Exactly where each tooth-point goes;
> The butterfly upon the road
> Preaches contentment to that toad.

I think this expresses Job's plight. The boils are personal, they loosen his tongue, they set him off. He doesn't reproach God in so many words, but he does by implication.

I must tell you that early in the New Year we started to be bothered by people hanging around the house. Some 'tourists' (at this time of year!) went to the château and asked if they could see round the house – a couple of young men. Nathan got rid of them. Ruth says she heard there were 'strangers' in the village shop asking questions about me the other day. A suspicious-looking workman came to my cottage, saying he'd been sent to test the electricity (not to read the meter, but to test). He showed me his card, it looked all right. But the electricity department hadn't heard of him. We suspect that Effie is putting in some private detectives. I've written to Stewart Cowper. Where would she get the money?

Why didn't you tell me that Effie had been arrested for shoplifting in Trieste?

I hope you get that part in the play you write about in your letter. You must know by now.

Yours,
Harvey

Please check the crocodiles for me at the London Zoo. Their eyelids are vertical, are they not? Leviathan in *Job* is generally supposed to be the crocodile. It is written of Leviathan, 'his eyes are like the eyelids of the morning'. None of the commentaries is as yet satisfactory on this. You may remember they never were.

PART 2

CHAPTER 6

THE VILLAGE SHOP, about two kilometres from Harvey's cottage, was normally busy when, about nine in the morning, Harvey stopped to buy a newspaper and cigarettes. He remembered this clearly later, when the day had developed and in the later profusion of events he set about to decipher them, starting from this, the beginning of his day.

The shop was divided into two parts, one leading into the other. The owner, a large man in his forties, wearing a dark grey working apron the colour of his hair, looked after the part which sold groceries, detergents, ham, pâté, sausage, cheese, fruit, vegetables, all well laid-out; and also a large stock of very good Vosges wines stacked in rows and arranged according to types and prices. The other part of the shop was presided over by the wife, plump, ruddy-cheeked, with short black curly hair, in her mid-thirties. She looked after the coffee machine, the liquor bar, the pre-wrapped buns and sweets, the newspapers and cigarettes, some stationery and other conveniently saleable goods.

That morning Harvey took an espresso coffee, his packet of cigarettes and the Vosges local paper which he scarcely glanced at. He looked around as he drank his coffee; the suspect people were not there today; it was not to be expected that they would always be at the bar, it would have been too obvious had they been hanging around all day and every day: two young Belgians, touring forests and caves, students, campers, the shopkeepers had said. It seemed unlikely; they were too old for students. There had been another man and woman, older still, in their forties; they looked like a couple of *concierges* from

Paris. Harvey was convinced these were Effie's detectives, getting enough evidence for Effie's huge alimonial scoop. The owners of the shop had seemed to take them for granted as they walked up and down in the road. The so-called Belgians had a dormobile with a Lyons registration number – that meant nothing, they had probably hired it. The middle-aged couple, both of them large and solid, came and went in a sad green Citroën Dyane 6. Harvey, having got such a brisk reply to his casual enquiries about the Belgians, had not ventured to enquire about the second couple. Maybe the shopkeepers were in their pay.

This morning, the strangers were not in sight. Only two local youths were at the bar; some countrywomen queued up at the counter on the grocery side. Harvey drank his coffee, paid, took up his paper and cigarettes and left. As he went out he heard behind him the chatter of the women, just a little more excited and scandalized than usual. '*Les supermarchés, les supermarchés . . .*' was the phrase he took in most, and assumed there was a discussion in progress about prices and food.

He put down the paper beside him and as he drove off his eye caught a picture on the front page. It was a group of three identikits, wanted people, two men and a girl. The outlines of the girl's face struck him as being rather like Ruth's. He must remember to let her see it. He turned at the end of the road towards Epinal, the town he was bound for.

After about two kilometres he ran into a road-block; two police motor-cycles, three police cars, quite a lot. It was probably to do with the identikits. Harvey produced his papers and sat patiently while the policeman studied them, gave a glance at the car, and waved him on. While waiting, Harvey looked again at the newspaper on the seat by his side. The feature with the identikits was headed 'Armed Robberies in the Vosges'. Undoubtedly the police were looking for the gang. At Epinal he noticed a lot of police actively outside the commissariat on the banks of the Moselle, and, above that, at the grand prefecture. There, among the fountains and flags, he could see in the distance flashes of blue and white uniforms, blue, red and white police cars, a considerable display. He noticed, and yet took no notice. He had come to look once more, as he had often done before, at the sublime painting, *Job Visited by His Wife* at the *Musée* of Epinal. He parked his car and went in.

He was well known to the receptionist who gave him a sunny greeting as he passed the desk.

'No schoolchildren today,' she said. Sometimes when there were school-groups or art-college students in the gallery Harvey would turn away, not even attempting to see the picture. But very often there were only one or two visitors. Sometimes, he had the museum to himself; he was already half-way up the stairs when the receptionist told him so; she watched him approvingly, even admiringly, as he ran up the staircase, as if even his long legs, when they reached the first turning of the stairs, had brought a touch of pleasure into her morning. The dark-blue custodian with his hands behind his back as he made his stately round, nodded familiarly as Harvey reached the second floor; as usual the man went to sit patiently on a chair at the other end of the room as Harvey took his usual place on a small bench in front of the picture.

The painting was made in the first part of the seventeenth century by Georges de La Tour, a native of Lorraine. It bears a resemblance to the Dutch candle-light pictures of the time. Its colours and organization are superb. It is extremely simple, and like so much great art of the past, surprisingly modern.

Job visité par sa femme: to Harvey's mind there was much more in the painting to illuminate the subject of Job than in many of the lengthy commentaries that he knew so well. It was eloquent of a new idea, and yet, where had the painter found justification for his treatment of the subject?

Job's wife, tall, sweet-faced, with the intimation of a beautiful body inside the large tent-like case of her firm clothes, bending, long-necked, solicitous over Job. In her hand is a lighted candle. It is night, it is winter; Job's wife wears a glorious red tunic over her dress. Job sits on a plain cube-shaped block. He might be in front of a fire, for the light of the candle alone cannot explain the amount of light that is cast on the two figures. Job is naked except for a loin-cloth. He clasps his hands above his knees. His body seems to shrink, but it is the shrunkenness of pathos rather than want. Beside him is the piece of broken pottery that he has taken to scrape his wounds. His beard is thick. He is not an old man. Both are in their early prime, a couple in their thirties. (Indeed, their recently-dead children were not yet married.) His face looks up at his wife, sensitive, imploring some favour, urging some cause. What is his wife trying to tell him as she bends her sweet face towards him? What does he beg, this stricken man, so serene in his faith, so accomplished in argument?

The scene here seemed to Harvey so altogether different from that suggested by the text of *Job*, and yet so deliberately and intelligently contemplated that it was impossible not to wonder what the artist actually meant. Harvey stared at the picture and recalled the verses that followed the account of Job's affliction with boils:

And he took him a potsherd to scrape himself withal; and he sat down among the ashes.
Then said his wife unto him, Dost thou still retain thine integrity? curse God, and die.
But he said unto her, Thou speakest as one of the foolish women speaketh. What? shall we receive good at the hand of God, and shall we not receive evil? In all this did not Job sin with his lips.

But what is she saying to him, Job's wife, in the serious, simple and tender portrait of Georges de La Tour? The text of the poem is full of impatience, anger; it is as if she is possessed by Satan. 'Dost thou still retain thine integrity?' She seems to gloat, 'Curse God and die.' Harvey recalled that one of the standard commentators has suggested a special interpretation, something to the effect, 'Are you still going to be so righteous? If you're going to die, curse God and get it off your chest first. It will do you good.' But even this, perhaps homely, advice doesn't fit in with the painting. Of course, the painter was idealizing some notion of his own; in his dream, Job and his wife are deeply in love.

Some people had just arrived in the museum; Harvey could hear voices downstairs and footsteps mounting. He continued to regard the picture, developing his thoughts: Here, she is by no means the carrier of Satan's message. She comes to comfort Job, reduced as he is to a mental and physical wreck. 'You speak,' he tells her, 'as one of the foolish women'; that is to say, he doesn't call her a foolish woman, he rather implies that she isn't speaking as her normal self. And he puts it to her, 'Shall we receive good at the hand of God, and shall we not receive evil?' That domestic 'we' is worth noticing, thought Harvey; he doesn't mean to abandon his wife, he has none of the hostility towards her that he has, later, for his friends. In order to have a better look at Job's wife's face, Harvey put his head to one side. Right from the first he had been struck by her resemblance to Effie in profile. She was like Ruth, too, but more like Effie, especially about the upper part of her face. Oh, Effie, Effie, Effie.

There were people behind Harvey. He glanced round and was amazed to see four men facing towards him, not looking at the other pictures as he had expected. Nor were they looking at the painting of Job. They were looking at him, approaching him. At the top of the staircase two other men in police uniform appeared. The keeper looked embarrassed, bewildered. Harvey got up to face them. He realized that, unconsciously, he had been hearing police sirens for some time. With the picture of Job still in his mind's eye, Harvey had time only to form an abrupt impression before they moved

375

in on him, frisked him, and invited him to descend to the waiting police cars.

Harvey had time to go over again all the details of the morning, later, in between interrogations. He found it difficult to get the rest of his life into focus; everything seemed to turn on the morning: the time he had stopped at the village shop; the drive to Epinal; the thoughts that had gone through his mind in front of the painting, *Job visité par sa femme*, at the museum; the moment he was taken to the police car, and driven over the bridge to the commissariat for questioning.

He answered the questions with lucidity so long as they lasted. On and off, he was interrogated for the rest of the day and half the night.

'No, I've never heard of the FLE.'

'*Fronte de la Libération de l'Europe*. You haven't heard of it?'

'No, I haven't heard of it.'

'You know that your wife belongs to this organization?'

'I don't know anything about it.'

'There was an armed robbery in a supermarket outside Epinal this morning. You were waiting here to join your wife.'

'I'm separated from my wife. I haven't seen her for nearly two years.'

'It was a coincidence that you were in Epinal this morning visiting a museum while your estranged wife was also in Epinal engaged in an armed robbery?'

'If my wife was in Epinal, yes, it was a coincidence.'

'Is that your English sense of humour?'

'I'm a Canadian.'

'Is it a coincidence that other supermarkets and a jeweller's shop in the Vosges have been robbed by this gang in the last two weeks? Gérardmer, La Bresse, Baccarat; this morning, Epinal.'

'I don't read the papers.'

'You bought one this morning.'

'I give no weight to local crimes.' If Effie's involved, thought Harvey, plainly she's in this district to embarrass me. It was essential that he shouldn't suggest this, for at the same time it would point to Effie's having directive authority over the gang.

'I still can't believe that my wife's involved,' said Harvey. He partly meant it.

'Three of them, perhaps four. Where are they?'

'I don't know. You'd better look.'

'You recently bought the château. Why?'

'I thought I might as well. It was convenient.'

'You've been a year at the cottage?'

'About a year and a half.'

'How did you find it?'

'I've already explained –'

'Explain again.'

'I found the cottage,' recited Harvey, 'because I was in the Vosges at that time. I had come here to Epinal expressly to look at the painting *Job Visited by His Wife* by Georges de La Tour. I had heard through some friends that the château was for sale. I went to look it over. I said I'd think about it, but I was struck by the suitability of the cottage to my needs, and took that on in the meantime. The owner, Claude de Remiremont, let me have it.'

'How much rent do you pay?'

'I have no idea,' Harvey said. 'Very little. My lawyer attends to that.'

(The rich!)

This interrogator was a man of about Harvey's age, not more than forty, black hair, blue eyes, a good strong face, tall. A chief-inspector, special branch; no fool. His tone of voice varied. Sometimes he put his questions with the frank lilt of a query at the end; at other times he simply made a statement as if enunciating a proved fact. At the end of the table where they sat facing each other, was a hefty policeman in uniform, older, with sandy hair growing thin and faded. The door of the room opened occasionally, and other men in uniform and ordinary clothes came and went.

'Where did you learn French?'

'I have always spoken French.'

'You have taken part in the French-Canadian liberation movement.'

'No.'

'You don't believe in it?'

'I don't know anything about it,' said Harvey. 'I haven't lived in Canada since I was eighteen.'

'You say that your wife's sister has been living with you since last October.'

'That's right.'

'With a baby.'

'Yes. My wife's baby daughter.'

'But there was a woman with a baby in your house for a year before that.'

'Not at all. The baby was only born at the end of June last year.'

'There was another infant in your house. We have evidence, M. Gotham, that there was a small child's washing on the line outside your house at least from April of last year.'

'That is so. But there wasn't any baby, there wasn't any woman.'

'Look, M. Gotham, it is a simple trick for terrorists to take the precaution, in the case of discovery, to keep a woman and a child in the house in order to avoid a shoot-out. Rather a low and dangerous trick, using a baby as a cover, but people of that nature –'

'There was no baby at all in my house, nobody but myself,' Harvey explained patiently. 'It was a joke – for the benefit of my brother-in-law who came to visit me. I brought some baby clothes and put them out on the line. He obviously thought

I had a girl living with me. I only put them out a few times after that. I told my brother-in-law that I did it to keep women from bothering me with offers of domestic care. As they do. They would assume, you see, that there was a woman. I suppose I'm an eccentric. It was a gesture.'

'A gesture.'

'Well, you might say,' said Harvey, thinking fast how to say it, 'that it was a surrealistic gesture.'

The inspector looked at Harvey for rather a long time. Then he left the room and came back with a photograph in his hand. Effie, in half-profile, three years ago, with her hair blowing around.

'Is that your wife?'

'Yes,' said Harvey. 'Where did you get this photograph?'

'And the woman you are living with, Ruth, is her sister?'

'Mme Jansen is her sister. Where did you get this photograph of my wife? Have you been ransacking through my papers?'

The inspector took up the photograph and looked at it. 'She resembles her sister,' he said.

'Did you have a search warrant?' said Harvey.

'You will be free to contact a lawyer as soon as you have answered our questions. I presume you have a lawyer in Paris? He will explain the law to you.'

'I have, of course, a French lawyer,' Harvey said. 'But I don't need him at the moment. Waste of money.'

Just then a thought struck him: Oh, God, will they shoot Ruth in mistake for Effie?

'My sister-in-law, Ruth Jansen, is, as you say, very like her sister. She's caring for the baby of nine months. Be very careful not to confuse them should you come to a confrontation. She has the baby there in the château.'

'We have the baby.'

'What?'

'We are taking care of the baby.'

'Where is she?'

The sandy-faced policeman spoke up. He had a perfectly human smile: 'I believe she is taking the air in the courtyard. Come and see out of the window.'

Down in the courtyard among the police cars and motor bicycles, a large policeman in uniform, but without his hat, whom Harvey recognized as one of those who had escorted him from the museum, was holding Clara in his arms, wrapped up in her woollies; he was jogging her up and down while a young policewoman was talking to her. Another, younger policeman, in civilian clothes, was also attempting to curry favour with her. Clara had her chubby arms round the large man's neck, enjoying the attention, fraternizing with the police all round.

'Is she getting her feeds?' said Harvey. 'I believe she has some special regular feeds that have to be –'

'Mme Jansen is seeing to all that, don't worry. Let's proceed.'

'I want to know where Ruth Jansen is,' said Harvey.

'She's downstairs, answering some questions. The sooner we proceed with the job the sooner you will be able to join her. Why did you explain your baby clothes to your brother-in-law Edward Jansen in the words, "The police won't shoot if there's a baby in the house"?'

'Did I say that?' said Harvey.

'Mme Jansen has admitted it,' said the inspector.

Admitted it. What had Edward told Ruth, what was Ruth telling them downstairs? But 'admitted' was not the same as 'volunteered' the information.

'You probably suggested the phrase to her,' said Harvey. The old police trick: Is it true that he said 'The police won't shoot...'?

'Did you or did you not say those words last April when M. Jansen came to see you?'

'If I did it was a joke.'

'Surrealism?'

'Yes, call it that.'

'You are a man of means?'

'Oh, yes.'

'Somebody is financing the FLE,' said the inspector.

'But I am not financing it.'

'Why do you live in that shack?'

'It doesn't matter to me where I work. I've told you. All I want is peace of mind. I'm studious.'

'Scholarly,' said the inspector dreamily.

'No, studious. I can afford to study and speculate without achieving results.'

The inspector raised his shoulders and exchanged a glance with the sandy-haired policeman. Then he said, 'Studious, scholarly . . . Why did you buy the château?'

'It was convenient for me to do so. Mme Jansen thought it desirable for her to have a home for herself and the baby.'

'It isn't your child.'

It was Harvey's turn to shrug. 'It's my wife's child. It makes no difference to me who the father is.'

'The resemblance between your wife and her sister might be very convenient,' said the inspector.

'I find them quite distinct. The resemblance is superficial. What do you mean – "convenient"?' Harvey, not quite knowing what the man was getting at, assumed he was implying that an exchange of lovers would be easy for him, the two sisters being, as it were, interchangeable. 'They are very different,' said Harvey.

'It would be convenient,' said the inspector, 'for two women who resemble each other to be involved in the same criminal organization. I am just hypothesizing, you understand. A question of one being able to provide an alibi for the other; it's not unknown . . . '

'My papers are in order,' Harvey said now, for no reason that was apparent, even to himself.

The inspector was very polite. 'You maintain your wife financially, of course.'

'I've given her no money since I left her. But if I had, that wouldn't signify that I was financing a terrorist organization.'

'Then you know that your wife is an active member of the FLE, and consequently have refused to supply money.'

'I never knew of the existence of the FLE until now. I don't at all know that my wife is a member of the group.'

'And you give your wife no money,' the policeman said.

'No money.'

'You knew that she was arrested in Trieste.'

'I didn't know until the other day. Nobody told me.'

'Nobody told you,' stated the inspector.

'That's right. Nobody told me. I'm studious, you see. I have arranged for people not to bother me, and they don't; rather to excess. I think someone should have told me. Not that it would have made any difference.'

'Your wife knows where you live?'

'Yes.'

'You have written to her?'

'No. I left her two years ago. Eventually she found out where I lived.'

'How did she find out?'

'I suppose she got it out of someone. She's an intelligent woman. I doubt very much she's mixed up with a terrorist group.'

'You must have had some reason to abandon her. Why are you so eager to protect her?'

'Look, I just want to be fair, to answer your questions.'

'We know she's an activist in the FLE.'

'Well, what exactly have they done?'

'Armed robbery and insurrection in various places. Of recent weeks they've been operating in the Vosges. Where are their headquarters?'

'Not in my house. And if my wife is involved in these incidents — which I don't admit she is — isn't it possible she has been kidnapped and forced to join this FLE? It's happened before. The Hearst case in the United States . . .'

'Do you have reason to believe she has been kidnapped?'

'I don't know. I have no idea. Has anyone been killed, injured, by this group?'

'Injured? But they are armed. They've collected a good deal of money, wounded twelve, damaged many millions of francs' worth of property. They are dangerous. Three men and a girl. The girl is your wife. Who are the others?'

'How should I know? I've never heard of the —'

'Nobody told you.'

'Correct.'

'It's time for lunch,' said the inspector, looking at his watch; and, as he got up, he said, 'Can you explain why Nathan Fox disappeared from the château last night?'

'Nathan Fox. Disappeared?'

'Nobody told you.'

'No. I left my cottage at nine this morning.'

'Where is Nathan Fox?' said the inspector, still standing.

'I have no idea. He's free to come and go . . . I don't really know.'

'Well, think it over.' The inspector left the room.

Harvey's cottage was in darkness when he drove back at four in the morning. He was tempted to go in and see what had happened to his papers, his work; had they been careful or had they turned everything upside down? Later, he found everything more or less intact with hardly a sign of a search; he had suspected that at least half the time he was kept for questioning had been for the purpose of giving the police leisure to continue their search at the cottage and the château; much good it had done them.

He didn't stop at the cottage that early morning, but drove up to the château. A police car was parked at a bend in the drive. Harvey tooted twice, softly and quickly, as he passed it. Friendly gesture. The light was on in the porch. He let himself in. Ruth came out of the living-room in her dressing-gown; she had been sleeping on a sofa, waiting for him. 'They brought us back at half-past six,' she said. She came to hug him, to kiss him. 'Are you all right?' they both said at the same time. Clara was sleeping in her carry-cot.

The first thing that struck him was the colour in the room. There was nothing new, but after the grey and neutral offices, hour after hour, at the police headquarters, the blue of Ruth's dressing-gown, the flower-patterned yellow sofa, green foliage arranged in a vase, the bright red tartan rug folded over Clara's cot, made a special impact on his senses. He smiled, almost laughed.

'Do you want to go to bed? Aren't you tired?' Ruth said.

'No. I'm wide awake.'

'Me, too.'

They poured whiskies and sodas. 'I simply told them the truth,' Ruth said. She decided she couldn't face her whisky and took orange juice.

'Me, too. What else could one say?'

'Oh, I know you told them everything,' Ruth said, 'I could guess by the questions.'

Harvey quoted, ' "The police won't shoot if there's a baby in the house." '

'Yes, why did you bring that up?' said Ruth. 'Was it necessary? They're suspicious enough –'

'I didn't suggest it to them.'

'Well, neither did I,' said Ruth. 'The inspector asked me if it was true you'd made that remark. I said I believed so. Edward told me, of course –'

'They're quite clever,' Harvey said. 'How did they treat you?'

'Very polite. They were patient about my *au pair* French.'

'How many?'

'Two plain-clothes men and a glamorous policewoman. Did you see the policewoman?' said Ruth.

'I saw one, from the window, playing with Clara.'

'They were very decent about Clara.'

Harvey's interrogators had been three, one after the other, then starting in the late afternoon with the first again.

Ruth and Harvey described and identified their respective policemen, and in a euphoric way compared a great many of their experiences of the day, questions and answers. Finally Ruth said, 'Do you really think Effie's in it?'

'Up to the neck,' said Harvey.

'Can you blame them for suspecting us?'

'No. I think, in fact, that Effie has chosen this district specifically to embarrass me.'

'So do I.'

He sat on the sofa beside her, relaxed, with his arm round her. She said, 'You know, I'm more afraid of Effie than the police.'

'Did you tell them that?'

'No.'

'Did they come and look round the château while you were at the headquarters?'

'I don't think so, because when they brought me back they asked if they might have a look round. I said, of course. They went all over, attics, cellars, and both towers. Actually, I was quite relieved that they didn't find anything, or rather anyone. It would be easy to hide in this house, you know.'

'Did you tell them you were relieved?'

'No.'

'Now tell me about Nathan.'

'It's a long story,' said Ruth. 'He's in love with Effie. He'd do anything she asked him.' Her voice had changed to a mumble.

Harvey said, 'But when did you know –' Then he stopped. 'My God,' he said, 'I'm becoming another interrogator. I expect you've had enough.'

'Quite enough.'

It was he who had the idea to go and make breakfast, which he brought in on a tray. 'I had a lousy pizza for supper,' he said.

She said, 'Nathan must have left last night. He didn't sleep here. He wasn't here when I came up from the cottage this morning. His bed wasn't slept in.'

'Did Anne-Marie see him?' Anne-Marie was a local woman who had been coming daily to help in the house for the past two weeks.

'No, he wasn't here when she arrived at eight. He'd taken nothing special that I could see. But he had a phone call yesterday. He said it was from London. I was annoyed at the time, because I'd told him not to give anyone your number.'

The telephone at the château operated through an exchange for long distance. 'One could easily find out if it came from London,' Harvey said.

'The police say there was no call from London,' Ruth said.

'Then it might have been a national call. He could have been in touch with Effie.'

'Exactly,' she said.

'How much did you tell them about Nathan?'

'Everything I know.'

'Quite right.'

'And another thing,' Ruth said, 'I told them –'

'Let's forget it and go to bed.'

Clara woke up just then. They shoved a piece of toast into her hand, which seemed to please her mightily.

It was nine-fifteen when the telephone rang. This time it was from London. At the same time the doorbell rang. Harvey had been dreaming that his interrogator was one of those electric typewriters where the typeface can be changed by easy manipulation; the voice of the interrogator changed like the type, and in fact was one and the same, now roman, now élite, now italics. In the end, bells on the typewriter rang to wake him up to the phone and the doorbell.

He looked out of the window while Ruth went to answer the phone. Reporters, at least eight, some with cameras, some with open umbrellas or raincoats over their heads to shield them from the pouring rain. Up the drive came a television van. Behind him, through the door of the room, Ruth called to him, 'Harvey, it's urgent for you, from London.'

'Get dressed,' Harvey said. 'Don't open the door. Those are reporters out there. Keep them in the rain for a while, at least.'

Clara began to wail. The doorbell pealed on. From round the side of the château someone was banging at another door.

On the phone was Stewart Cowper from London.

'What's going on there?' said Stewart.

Harvey thought he meant the noise.

'There's been a bit of trouble. Reporters are at the doors of the house and the baby's crying.'

'There are headlines in all the English papers. Are you coming back to England?'

'Not at the moment,' Harvey said. 'I don't know about Ruth and the child; but we haven't discussed it. What are the headlines?'

'Headlines and paras, Harvey. Hold on, I'll read you a bit:

Millionaire's religious sect possibly involved in French terrorist activities. Wife of English actor involved...

And here's another:

Playboy Harvey Gotham, 35, with his arsenal of money from Gotham's Canadian Salmon, whose uncles made a fortune in the years before and during the second world war, has been questioned by the *gendarmes d'enquêtes* of the Vosges, France, in connection with hold-ups and bombings of supermarkets and post offices in that area. It is believed that his wife, Mrs Effie Gotham, 25, is a leading member of FLE, an extreme leftist terrorist movement. Mr Gotham, who has recently acquired a base in that area, denies having in any way financed the group or having been in touch with his estranged wife. He claims to be occupied with religious studies. Among his circle are his sister-in-law, Ruth, 28, sister of the suspected terrorist, and Nathan Fox, 25, who disappeared from the Gotham château on the eve of the latest armed robbery at Epinal, capital of the Vosges.

There's a lot more,' said Stewart. 'If you're not coming back to England I'd better come there. Have you got hold of Martin Deschamps?'

'Who the hell is he?'

'Your Paris lawyer.'

'Oh, him. No. I don't need lawyers. I'm not a criminal. Look, I've got to get rid of these reporters. By the way,' Harvey continued, partly for the benefit of the police who had undoubtedly tapped the phone, and partly because he meant it, 'I must tell you that the more I look at La Tour's "Job" the more I'm impressed by the simplicity, the lack of sentimentality above all. It's a magnificent –'

'Don't get on the wrong side of the press,' shouted Stewart.

'Oh, I don't intend to see them. Ruth and I have had very little sleep.'

'Make an appointment for a press conference, late afternoon, say five o'clock,' said Stewart. 'I'll send you Deschamps.'

'No need,' said Harvey, and hung up.

None the less, he managed to mollify the soaking pressmen outside his house, speaking to them from an upstairs window, by making an appointment with them for five o'clock that afternoon. They didn't all go away, but they stopped battering at the doors.

Then, to Ruth's amazement their newly-engaged, brisk domestic help, Anne-Marie, arrived, with a bag of provisions. It was her second week on the job. She managed to throw off the reporters who crowded round her with questions, by upbraiding them for disturbing the baby, and by pushing her way through. Inside the front door, Harvey stood ready to open it quickly, admitting her and nobody else.

'The police,' Anne-Marie said, 'were at my house yesterday for hours. Questions, questions.' But she seemed remarkably cheerful about the questions.

CHAPTER 7

A LONG RING at the front doorbell. Outside in the pouring rain a police car waited. From the upper window Harvey saw the interrogator he had left less than twelve hours ago in the headquarters at Epinal.

'Ah,' said Harvey from the window. 'I've been missing you dreadfully.'

'Look,' said the man, 'I'm not enjoying this, am I? Just one or two small questions to clarify –'

'I'll let you in.'

The policeman glanced through the open door at the living-room as he passed. Harvey conducted him to a small room at the back of this part of the château. The room had a desk and a few chairs; it hadn't been furnished or repainted; it was less smart and new than the police station at Epinal, but it was the next best thing.

'You have no clue, absolutely no idea where your wife is?'

'No. Where do you yourselves think she is?'

'Hiding out in the woods. Or gone across into Germany. Or hiding in Paris. These people have an organization,' said the inspector.

'If she's in the woods she would be wet,' said Harvey, glaring at the sheet rain outside the window.

'Is she a strong woman? Any health complications?'

'Well, she's slim, rather fragile. Her health's all right so far as I know,' Harvey said.

'If she contacts you, it would be obliging if you would invite her to the house. The same applies to Nathan Fox.'

'But I don't want my wife in the house. I don't want to oblige her. I don't need Nathan Fox,' Harvey said.

'When things quieten down she might try to contact you. You might oblige us by offering her a refuge.'

'I should have thought you had the house surrounded.'

'We do. We mean to keep it surrounded. You know, these people are heavily armed, they have sophisticated weapons. It might occur to them to take you hostages, you and the baby. Of course, they would be caught before they could get near you. But you might help us by issuing an invitation.'

'It's all a supposition,' Harvey said. 'I'm not convinced that this woman-terrorist is my wife, nor that my wife is a terrorist. As for Nathan Fox, he's a mystery to me, but I wouldn't have thought he'd draw attention to himself by going off and joining an armed band at the very moment when they were active.'

'If your wife is a fascinating woman –'

'I hope,' said Harvey, 'that you're taking special precautions to protect the baby.'

'You admit that the baby might be in danger?'

'With an armed gang around, any baby might be in danger.'

'But you admit that your wife's baby might be an object of special interest to your wife.'

'She has taken no interest in the child.'

'Then why are you suggesting that we specially protect this child?'

'I hope you have made arrangements to do so,' said Harvey.

'We have your house and grounds surrounded.'

'The baby,' said Harvey, 'must be sent back to England. My sister-in-law will take her.'

'A good idea. We can arrange for them to leave, quietly, with every protection. But it would be advisable for you to keep the move as secret as possible. I mean the press. We don't want this gang to know every move. I warn you to be careful what you say to the press. The examining magistrate –'

'The press! They've already –'

The man spread his hands helplessly. 'This wasn't my fault. These things leak out. After all, it's a matter of national concern. But not a word about your plans to send the child away.'

'The maid will know. They talk –'

'Anne-Marie is one of our people,' said the inspector.

'You don't say! We rather liked her.'

'She'd better stay on with you, then. And hang out baby clothes on the line, as you always want to do. I might look in again soon.'

'Don't stand on ceremony.'

'How is it possible,' Ruth said, 'that the police think the gang might turn up here, now that this story's all over the papers, on the radio, the television? It's the last place they would come to. Clara's safer here than anywhere. How can they think –'

'The police don't think so, they only say they think so.'

'Why?'

'How do I know? They suspect me strongly. They want the baby out of France. Maybe it's got something to do with their public image.'

'I don't want to go,' said Ruth.

'I don't want you to go,' said Harvey, 'but I think you should. It's only for a while. I think you must.'

'Are you free to come, too? Harvey, let's both get away.'

'On paper, I'm free to go. In fact, they might detain me. The truth is, I don't want to leave just at this moment. Just bloody-mindedness on my part.'

'I can be stubborn, too,' said Ruth; but she spoke with a fluidity that implied she was giving way. 'But, after all,' she went on, 'I suppose you didn't ask me to come here in the first place.'

Harvey thought, I don't love her, I'm not in the least in love with her. Much of the time I don't even like her very much.

Anne-Marie had put some soup on the table. Harvey and Ruth were silent before her, now that she wasn't a maid but a police auxiliary. When she had left, Ruth said, 'I don't know if I'll be able to keep this down. I'm pregnant.'

'How did that happen?' Harvey said.

'The same as it always happens.'

'How long have you known?'

'Three weeks.'

'Nobody tells me anything,' Harvey said.

'You don't want to know anything.'

Had Ruth stopped taking the pill? Was it his child or Nathan's? She didn't guess his first thought, but she did his second. 'I never slept with Nathan, ever,' she said. 'His mind's on Effie – that's one thing I didn't mention to the police.'

'Take some bread with your soup. You'll keep it down better.'

'You know, I'd rather not go back to England. Now that Edward's having this amazing success –'

'What success?'

'He's having an astonishing success in the West End. That play –'

'Well, how long have you known about this?'

'Three weeks. It's been in the papers, and he wrote –'

'Nobody tells me anything.'

'I think it funny Edward hasn't rung us up today. He must have seen the papers,' Ruth said. 'Maybe it scared him. A scandal.'

'Where would you like to go?' Harvey said.

'Have you got anyone in Canada I could take Clara to?'

'I have an aunt and I have an uncle in Toronto. They're married but they live in separate houses. You could go to either. I'll ring up.'

'I'll go to the uncle,' said Ruth. She started to smile happily, but she was crying at the same time.

'There's nothing to worry about,' Harvey said.

'Yes there is. There's Effie. There's Edward.'

'What about Edward?'

'He's a shit. He might have wanted to know if I was all right. He's been writing all the time I've been here, and phoning every day since we got the telephone put in. Up to now.'

Anne-Marie came in with a splendid salad, a tray of cheeses. 'Shall I help Madame to pack after lunch?' she said.

'How did she know I was leaving?' Ruth said when the maid had gone out.

'Somebody told her. Everyone knows everything,' said Harvey, 'except me.'

Ruth was in the bedroom, packing, and Harvey was pushing the furniture here and there to make a distance between the place where he intended to sit to receive the reporters, and the part of the room reserved for them. Ruth, Harvey thought as he did so, has been crying a lot over the past few weeks, crying and laughing. I noticed, but I didn't notice. I wonder if she cried under the interrogation, and laughed? Anyway, it isn't this quite unlooked-for event that's caused her to cry and laugh, it started earlier. Did she tell the police she was pregnant? Probably. Maybe that's why they want to get rid of her. Is she really pregnant? Harvey plumped up a few cushions. Yellow chintzes, lots of yellow; at least, the chintzes had a basis of yellow, so that you saw yellow when you came into the room. New chintzes: all right, order new chintzes. Curtains and cushions and cosiness: all right, order them; have them mail my lawyer the bill. You say you need a château: all right, have the château, my lawyers will fix it. Harvey kicked an armchair. It moved smoothly on its castors into place. Ruth, he thought, is fond of the baby. She adores Clara. Who wouldn't? But Clara belongs to me, that is, to my wife, Effie. No, Clara belongs to Ruth and depends on Ruth. It's good-bye, good-bye, to Clara. He looked at his watch. Time to telephone

Toronto, it's about ten in the morning there. The story of playboy Harvey Gotham and his terrorist connections are certainly featured in the Canadian press, on the radio, the television.

Anne-Marie had come in, shiny black short hair, shiny black eyes, clear face. She had a small waist, stout hips. She carried a transistor radio playing rock music softly enough not to justify complaint.

'Do you know how to get a number on the telephone, long-distance to Toronto?' Harvey said.

'Of course,' said the policewoman.

He thought, as he gave her the number, She doesn't look like a police official, she looks like a maid. Bedworthy and married. She's somebody's wife. Every woman I have to do with is somebody's wife. Ruth, Job's wife, and Effie who is still my wife, and who is shooting up the supermarkets. Twelve people hurt and millions of francs' theft and damage. If the police don't soon get the gang there will be deaths; house-wives, policemen, children murdered. Am I responsible for my wife's debts? Her wounded, her dead?

Anne-Marie had left the transistor while she went to telephone; the music had been interrupted and the low murmur of an announcement drew Harvey's attention; he caught the phrases: terrorist organization . . . errors of just-ice . . . ; he turned the volume up. It was a bulletin from FLE issued to a Paris news agency, vindicating its latest activities. The gang was going to liberate Europe from its errors. 'Errors of society, errors of the system.' Most of all, liberation from the diabolical institution of the *gendarmerie* and the brutality of the *Brigade Criminelle*. It was much the same as every other terrorist announcement Harvey had ever read. 'The multinationals and the forces of the reactionary imperialist powers . . . ' It was like an alarm clock that ceases to wake the sleeper who, having heard it morning after morning, simply puts out a hand and switches it off without even opening his eyes.

The bulletin was followed by an announcement that fifty inspectors of the *Brigade Criminelle* were now investigating FLE's activities in the Vosges where the terrorists were still believed to be hiding out. End of announcement: on with the music.

'Your call to Toronto,' said Anne-Marie.

Ruth was to go to Paris and leave next morning, with Clara, for Canada. A Volvo pulled up at the door. When he had finished his call, Harvey saw two suitcases already packed in the hall. Those people work fast. 'Not so fast,' Harvey said to Anne-Marie. 'The child's father might not agree to her going to Canada. We must get his permission.'

'We have his permission. Mr Howe will call you tonight. He has agreed with Scotland Yard.'

'The press will be here any minute,' said Harvey. 'They'll see Madame and the baby driving off.'

'No, the police have the road cordoned off. Madame and the child will leave by a back door, anyway.' She went out and gave instructions to the driver of the Volvo, who took off, round to the back of the house. Anne-Marie lifted one of the suitcases and gestured to Harvey to take the other. He followed her, unfamiliar with all the passages of his château, through a maze of grey kitchens, dairies and wash-houses as yet unrestored. By a door leading to a vast and sad old plantation which must have once been a kitchen garden, Ruth stood, huddled in her sheepskin coat, crying, cuddling the baby.

'Is it to be Toronto?' she said.

'Oh, yes, you'll be met. Do you have the money with you?' Harvey had given her charge of a quantity of cash long before the trouble started.

'I've taken most of it.'

'You'll be all right once you're at my Uncle Joe's.'

'Who did you say I was?' she said.

'My sister-in-law.'

'And Clara?'

'Your niece. Ernie Howe has given his permission –'

'Oh, I know. I spoke to him myself,' she said.

'Nobody tells me anything,' Harvey said.

'Will I like your Uncle Joe?'

'I hope so. If not, you can go to my Auntie Pet.'

'What is "Pet" short for?' said Ruth.

'I really don't know.' He could see she wanted to delay the parting. 'Ring me tonight from Paris,' he said. He kissed Ruth and he kissed Clara, and practically pushed them towards Anne-Marie who had already seen the suitcases into the car, and was waiting for Ruth, almost taking her under arrest. With a hand under Ruth's arm she led her along the little path towards the wider path where the car waited. They were off, Ruth and Clara in the front seat beside the driver. They were like an affluent married couple and child. Anne-Marie came back to the house, closed and locked the back door. Harvey said, 'You lead the way back. I'll follow you. I don't know my way about this place.' She laughed.

Twenty minutes later the press were let in. 'Quiet!' said Anne-Marie. 'We have a baby in the house. You mustn't wake her.'

Harvey, freshly and acutely aware of Clara's innocent departure, was startled for an instant, then remembered quickly that Ruth and Clara were gone in secret.

'Madame is resting, too,' announced Anne-Marie, 'please, gentlemen, ladies, no noise.'

There were eighteen men, five women; the rest were at the road-block outside the house arguing vainly with the police. This, Harvey learned from the reporters themselves, who crowded into the living-room. There was a predominance of French, British and Americans among them. Harvey scrutinized them, as best he could trying to guess which one of them was a police agent. A wiry woman of about fifty with a red

397

face, broken-veined, and thin grey hair fluffed out and falling
all over her face as if to make the most of it, seemed to him a
possible *flic*, if only for the reason that unlike the others she
seemed to have no one to talk to.

'Mr Gotham, when did you last see –'

'I will answer no questions,' Harvey said, 'until you stop
these flash-photographs.' He sat back in his chair with folded
arms. 'Stop,' he said, 'just stop. I'll answer questions first,
if they're reasonable. Then you can take some photos. But
not all at once. Kindly keep your voices down; as you've
heard, there's a baby sleeping upstairs and a lady who needs a
lot of rest.' One of the reporters, slouching by the door, a large
fair middle-aged man, was already taking notes. What of? The
man's face seemed familiar to Harvey but he couldn't place it.

The French journalists were the most vociferous. 'Do you
know where your wife is?' – 'How long has she been a
member – ?' – 'Your wife Effie's terrorist activities, do you
ascribe them to a reaction against her wealthy matrimonial
experience, with all the luxury and boredom that capitalism
produces?' – 'What exactly are the creed and aims of your
religious group, Mr Gotham?'

Harvey said, 'One at a time, please.'

'With all your prospects and holdings, you still believe
in God, is that right?' – 'Are you asking us to believe that
you have come to this château to study the Bible?' – 'Isn't it
so that you originally lived in that little lodge at the end of
the drive?'

'Yes,' said Harvey, 'I went to work down there.'

'Where does your wife get the money for her terrorist
activities?'

'I don't know that my wife is engaged in terrorist activities.'

'But the police have identified her. Look, Mr Gotham,
those people of the FLE get their money from someplace.'
This came from a fat young American who spoke like a
machine-gun.

'Would you mind speaking French so that we all know where we are?' said Harvey. A Frenchman swiftly came to his American colleague's aid, and repeated the question in French.

'Apparently they bomb supermarkets and rob the cash. Haven't you read the papers?' Harvey said.

'If your wife came in here with a sub-machine-gun right now – ?'

'That is a hypothetical question,' Harvey said. The question was asked by a timid young Asiatic type with fine features and a sad pallor, who had evidently been let in to the conference on a quota system. He looked puzzled. 'Your question is all theory,' Harvey said, to help him. The young man nodded wisely and made some notes. What notes? – God knows.

'Didn't you hear a registration in the police station of your wife's voice on a loudspeaker warning the people to leave the supermarket before the bombing? – Surely you recognized your wife's voice?' said an American.

'I heard no registration. But if my wife should happen to give a warning to anyone in danger at any time, that would be very right of her, I think,' Harvey said.

Most of the reporters were younger than Harvey. One, a bearded Swede, was old, paunchy. He alone seemed to know what the *Book of Job* was. He asked Harvey, 'Would you say that you yourself are in the position of Job, in so far as you are a suspicious character in the eyes of the world, yet feel yourself to be perfectly innocent?'

Harvey saw his chance and took it: 'I am hardly in the position of Job. He was covered with boils, for one thing, which I am not. And his friends, merely on the basis of his suffering, accused him of having sinned in some way. What Job underwent was tantamount to an interrogation by the Elders of his community. I intend no personal analogy. But I am delighted to get down at last to the subject of this conference: what was the answer to Job's question? Job's question was, why does God cause me to suffer when I've done nothing to deserve it? Now, Job was in no doubt whatsoever that his sufferings came from God and from no other source. The very rapidity with which one calamity followed upon another, shattering Job's world, leaving him destitute, bereft and sick all in a short space of time, gave dramatic evidence that the cause was not natural, but supernatural. The supernatural, with power to act so strongly and disastrously, could only, in Job's mind, be God. And we know he was right in the context of the book, because in the Prologue you read specifically that it was God who brought up the subject of Job to Satan; it was God, in fact, who tempted Satan to torment Job, not Satan who tempted God. I'm afraid my French version of the scriptures isn't to hand, it's down in my study in the cottage, or I'd quote you the precise passage. But —'

'Mr Gotham,' said a young Englishwoman dressed entirely in dark grey leather, 'I'm sorry to interrupt but I have to file my story at six. Is it true that Nathan Fox is your wife's lover?'

'Please stick to French if you can. Anyway, I am addressing this gentleman,' said Harvey, indicating the elderly Swede, 'on a very important subject and —'

'Oh, no, Mr Gotham. Oh, no.' This was a tough pressman, indeterminately British or American, who spoke with a loud, fierce voice. 'Oh, no, Mr Gotham. You're here to answer our questions.'

'Keep your voice down, please. The fact is that I am here because it is my home. You are here to listen to me. The subject is the *Book of Job* to which I have dedicated many years of my life. This gentleman,' said Harvey, nodding to the grave and rather flattered Swede, 'has asked me an interesting question on the subject. I have answered his question and I am elaborating on it. Your chance, and that of your colleagues, to put further questions will come in due course. As I was about to remark, Job's problem was partly a lack of knowledge. He was without access to any system of study which would point to the reason for his afflictions. He said specifically, "I desire to reason with God," and expected God to come out like a man and state his case.'

'Mr Gotham –'

'Mr Gotham, can you state if you would side with your wife in any sense if she came up for trial? Do you yourself feel politically that the FLE have something to offer the young generation?' – This was from a lanky French journalist with bright eyes and a wide smile. He was rather a sympathetic type, Harvey thought, probably new to his trade.

'I'm really sorry to disappoint you,' said Harvey with some charm, 'but I'm giving you a seminar on *Job* without pay.'

A hubbub had now started to break out. Protests and questions came battering in on Harvey from every side.

'Quiet!' bawled Harvey. 'Either you listen to me in silence or you all go. Job's problem, as I was saying, was partly a lack of knowledge. Everybody talked but nobody told him anything about the reason for his sufferings. Not even God when he appeared. Our limitations of knowledge make us puzzle over the cause of suffering, maybe it is the cause of suffering itself. Quiet, over there! The baby's asleep. And I said, no photographs at present. As I say, we are plonked here in the world and nobody but our own kind can tell us anything. It isn't enough. As for the rest, God doesn't tell. No, I've already told you that I don't know where my wife is. How the *Book of Job* got into the holy scriptures I really do not know. That's the greatest mystery of all. For it doesn't –'

'Mr Gotham,' said the tough pressman, 'the FLE have held up supermarkets, jewellers and banks at Gérardmer, La Bresse, Rambervillers, Mirecourt and Baccarat. Your wife is –'

'You've left out Epinal,' said Harvey. Cameras flashed. 'Will you allow me to continue to answer the question put to me, or will you go?'

'Your wife –' ... 'Your background, Mr Gotham –' ... 'Your wife's sister –'

'Conference over,' said Harvey.

'Oh, no.' – 'No, Mr Gotham.' – 'Wait a minute.'

Some were swearing and cursing; some were laughing.

But Harvey got up and made for the door. Most of the reporters were on their feet, very rowdy. The wiry red-faced woman, the possible police agent, sat holding her tape-recorder modestly on her lap. The large fair man at the door had grabbed a belt as if from nowhere and was fastening it rapidly round his waist. Harvey saw that it was packed neatly with cartridges and that a revolver hung from a holster, with the man's hand on it. He recognized him now as the sandy-haired policeman who, in uniform, had sat at the table throughout his interrogation at Epinal.

Harvey said, 'I must tell you that there is a policeman in the room.'

'What police? *La Brigade antigang*?'

'I have no idea what variety. Kindly leave quietly and in order, and don't wake the baby.'

They left without order or quietness.

'Why don't you get out while you can? Get back to Canada,' said a girl. – 'We'll be seeing you in the courtroom,' said another. Some joked as they left, some overturned chairs as they went. From everywhere came the last-minute flashes of the cameras recording the policeman, the overturned chairs, and recording Harvey standing in the middle of it, an image to be reproduced in one of next morning's papers under the title, 'Don't Wake the Baby'. But at last they had gone. The wiry red-faced woman said sadly to Harvey as she passed him, 'I'm afraid you'll get a very bad press.'

The policeman followed them out and chivied them down the drive from his car. Before he shut the door Harvey noticed something new in the light cast from the hall: a washing-line had been slung well in evidence of the front portico. Anne-Marie had just finished taking baby clothes from it, had evidently been photographed doing so. She came towards him.

'Not very convincing,' Harvey said. 'Nobody hangs washing within sight of the approach to a château.'

'Nobody used to,' Anne-Marie said. 'They do now. We, for example, are doing it. Nobody will find it in the least suspect.'

'Didn't she tell you the hotel where she was going to in Paris?' Harvey said.

'Not me,' said Anne-Marie. 'I think she'll ring you if she said she would. In any case, the inspector is sure to know where she's staying.'

It was nine-thirty, and Anne-Marie was leaving for the night, anxious about being extraordinarily late in returning home; she lived several miles away. A car driven by a plain-clothes policeman was waiting at the door. She hurried away, banged the car door, and was off.

Stewart Cowper had arrived about an hour before, full of travel-exasperation and police-harassment; he had been frisked and questioned at the entrance to the house; he had been travelling most of the day and he was cold. At present he was having a shower.

Harvey and Anne-Marie had together put the living-room to rights. Ruth had not yet rung him from Paris as she had promised. Where was she? Harvey then noticed something new in the room, a large bowl of early spring flowers, profes-sionally arranged, beautiful. Irises, jonquils, lilies, daffodils; all too advanced to be local products; they must have come from an expensive shop in Nancy. Anne-Marie must have put them there at some time between the clearing up of the mess and her leaving, but Harvey hadn't noticed them. They stood on a low round table, practically covering it as the outward leaves of the arrangement bent gracefully over the edge of the bowl. Harvey hadn't noticed them, either, while he was sitting having a drink with Stewart, trying to calm him down, nor while Anne-Marie, anxious about the time, laid out a cold supper that was still sitting on the small dining-table, waiting for Stewart to wash and change. Where did those flowers come from? Who brought them, who sent them? Anne-Marie hadn't left the house. And why should she order flowers?

Stewart came in and went to get himself another drink. He was a man of medium height, in his mid-forties with a schoolboy's round face and round blue eyes; but this immature look was counteracted by a deep and expressive quality in his voice, so that as soon as he spoke the total effect was of a certain maturity and intelligence, cancelling that silly round-eyed look.

'Did you bring these flowers?' said Harvey.

'Did I bring what?'

'These flowers – I don't know where they've come from. The maid – and by the way she's a policewoman – must have put them there some time this evening. But why?'

Stewart brought his drink to the sofa and sat sipping it.

Harvey's mind was working fast, and faster. 'I think I know why they're there. Have you ever heard of a vase of flowers being bugged?'

'Rather an obvious way to plant a bug if the flowers weren't there already,' said Stewart.

But Harvey was already pulling the flower-arrangement to bits. He shook each lily, each daffodil; he tore at the petals of the irises. Stewart drank his drink and told Harvey to calm down; he watched Harvey with his big blue eyes and then took another sip. Harvey splashed the water from the bowl all over the table and the floor. 'I don't see anything,' he said.

'From what I understand the police have had every opportunity to plant bugs elsewhere in the house; they need not introduce a bunch of flowers for the purpose,' Stewart said. 'What a mess you've made of a lovely bunch of flowers.'

'I'd take you out to dinner,' said Harvey. He sat on the sofa with his dejected head in his hands. He looked up. 'I'd take you out to eat but I've got to wait in for a call from Ruth. She's in Paris but I don't know where. I've got to let my uncle in Toronto know the time of her arrival and her flight number. Did I tell you that she's taking the baby to my Uncle Joe's?'

'No,' said Stewart.

'Well, she is. I've got to arrange for her to be met, and get through to Toronto and give them reasonable notice. And I've got to have a call from Ernie Howe, I think. At least he said he'd ring.'

'How many other things have you got to do?'

'I don't know.'

'Why don't you relax? You're in a hell of a state.'

'I know. What are you supposed to be doing here?'

'Giving you some advice,' Stewart said. 'Of course, I can't act for you here in France.'

'I don't need anyone. I've got what's-his-name in Paris if necessary.'

'Martin Deschamps? – I've been in touch with him. He can't act for you in a case like this. No one in his firm can, either. That means they won't. Terrorism is too unladylike for those fancy lawyers. I'm hungry.'

'Let's sit down, then,' said Harvey; they sat at the table to eat the cold supper. Harvey's hand shook as he started to pour the wine. He stopped and looked at his hand. 'I'm shaking,' he said. 'I wonder why Ruth hasn't rung?'

Stewart took the bottle from him and poured out the wine. 'Your nerves,' he said.

'She must have had her dinner and put the baby to bed by now,' Harvey said. 'I'll give it another hour, then I'm going to ring the police and find out where she is. Ernie Howe should have rung, too.'

'Maybe she didn't stop over in Paris. Perhaps she went straight to the airport.'

'She should have rung. She could have been taken ill. She's pregnant.'

'Is she?'

'So she says.'

The telephone rang. An inspector of police. 'M. Gotham? – I want to let you know that Mme Ruth Jansen has arrived in London.'

'In London? I thought she was going to stop overnight in Paris. I've arranged for her to go to Canada to my –'

'She changed her mind.'

'Where is she in London?'

'I can't tell you. Good night.'

'If she didn't ring you as promised,' said Stewart the next morning, 'and Ernie Howe didn't ring you as promised, and if, in addition, it transpires she went to London, I should have thought you would suspect that the two were together.'

'You think she has gone to Ernie Howe? Why should she go to him? She is pregnant by me.'

'She has Ernie Howe's baby in her arms. It would be natural to take her to the father. You can't possess everything, Harvey.'

'Do you know more than you say?' said Harvey.

'No, it's only a supposition.'

'I'll ring Ernie Howe's flat as soon as my call to Canada has come through. It's hard on my uncle, mucking him about like this. He's not so young. I've just put through a call.'

'It's the middle of the night in Toronto,' said Stewart.

'I don't care.'

Anne-Marie arrived in her thick coat, scarves and boots. 'Good morning,' she said, and then gave a pained wail. Her eyes were on the flowers that she had left in such a formal display the night before, now all pulled to pieces, even the petals torn to bits.

'I was looking for an electronic bug,' Harvey said.

'I think you are not human,' said Anne-Marie. She was now in tears, aimlessly lifting a daffodil, putting it down, then a blue, torn iris.

'Who ordered them, who sent them?' said Harvey.

Stewart said, 'I'll help to clear the mess. Leave it to me.'

'I had them sent myself,' said Anne-Marie. 'To give you some joy after your ordeal with the press and your loss of the baby. My sister-in-law has a flower shop and I made a special-messenger arrangement with her for the most beautiful flowers; a personal present. I thought that with the loss of Madame and Clara you would enjoy those lovely spring flowers.'

Stewart had his arm round the police agent's shoulders. 'His nerves gave way,' said Stewart. 'That's all.'

The telephone rang; Harvey's call to Canada. It was a sleepy manservant who answered, as Harvey had counted on. He was able to explain, without having to actually talk to his uncle, that Ruth and the baby were probably not coming after all, and that any references to him in the newspapers and on the television were probably false.

He put down the receiver. The telephone rang: 'Hallo, Harvey!' The telephone rang off. Again it rang: 'Harvey, it's Ruth.' She was speaking in a funny way. She was calling herself Ree-uth, although definitely the voice was hers. It must be the London influence, Harvey registered all in a moment. But she was going on. 'I changed my mind, Harvey. I had to bring Clara (pronounced Clah-rah) to her father (pronounced fahthar).'

'What are you saying?' said Harvey. 'You mean you're not going to my Uncle Joe in Toronto. You've decided to shack down with Ernie Howe, is that it?'

'That's it,' said Ruth.

'Then I think you might have had enough considera-tion for my Uncle Joe – he's seventy-eight – to let me know.'

'Oh, I was busy with Clah-rah.'

'Pass me Ernie,' said Harvey.

'Ernie, do you mind?' said Ruth's voice, apart.

'Hallo,' said the other voice.

'Ernie Howe?'

'That's me.'

'What are you doing with Ruth?'

'We've just had a tunah-fish salad. We fed Clahrah.'

Harvey then remembered Ernie's voice (that's where Ruth got the Clah-rah).

'I make a good fah-thah,' said Ernie; 'and I don't like your tone of superiority.'

After a great many more hot words, Harvey began to recollect, at the back of his mind, that he really had no rights in the matter; not much to complain of at all. He said good night, hung up, and returned to the sitting-room hoping for some consolation from his friend.

His friend was sitting on the sofa holding hands with Anne-Marie. Harvey was in time to hear him say, 'May I fall in love with you?'

'She's married,' said Harvey in English.

'Not at all,' said Anne-Marie in her most matter-of-fact voice. 'I live with my married brother.'

'Well, I thought you were married,' said Harvey.

'That's when you thought I was a maid.'

'If you're not a maid then what are you doing here?' said Harvey.

'He's exasperated,' said Stewart. 'Don't mind him.'

Anne-Marie took a long glance at the disorderly table of ruined flowers and said, 'I have to remain here on duty. I'm going to make the coffee.'

When she had left, Harvey said, 'You're behaving like an undergraduate who's just put foot on the Continent for the first time, meeting his first Frenchwoman.'

'What was the news from England?'

'Ruth is with Ernie Howe.'

'What do the newspapers say?'
'I don't know. Find out; it's your job.'
'Is it?' said Stewart.
'If it isn't, what are you doing here?'
'I suppose I'm just a comforter,' Stewart said.
'I suppose you are.'

CHAPTER 8

'IS IT POSSIBLE,' said Harvey, 'for anyone to do something perfectly innocent but altogether unusual, without giving rise to suspicion?'

Stewart said, 'Not if his wife is a terrorist.'

'Assume that she is not.'

'All right, I assume. But here you were in a small hamlet in France, a rich man living in primitive conditions. Well, nobody bothered you until the police began to suspect a link between you and the FLE a certain time ago, and even then they only had you under surveillance, from a distance; they didn't haul you in immediately or harass you so that your life was uncomfortable. You weren't even aware of their presence till lately. And now you've been questioned, grilled; it's only natural. It might have been worse. Much worse. You don't know the police.'

'My papers have been scrutinized, all my work, my private things –'

'I can't sympathize too much, Harvey. I can't say you've really suffered. These police obviously are going carefully with you. They're protecting you from the mob, the phone calls. They probably believe you; they know by now, I should think, that you have no contact with Effie. I think they're right to watch out in case she has any contact with you.'

'You are wrong,' said Harvey, 'to say that I haven't suffered. Did you hear the press round-up on the radio this morning? – My name's worse than Effie's in the eyes of the press.'

The local newspaper, the only one so far to arrive in his hands, was on the coffee-table in front of them, with the front page uppermost. The headline, 'The Guru of the Vosges' stretched above a picture of Harvey, distraught, in his sitting-room of final disorder at the press conference. Under the picture was the title-paragraph of the subsequent article:

Harvey Gotham, the American 'prophet', inveighing against God, who he claims has unjustly condemned the world to suffering. *God is a Shit* was one of the blasphemies preached at an international press conference held yesterday in his 40-roomed château recently acquired by this multi-millionaire husband of the gangster-terrorist Effie Gotham, leading activist of FLE.

In the article, the writer of it reflected on the influence of Harvey on a girl like Effie 'from the poorer classes of London', and on her sister and an infant, Clara, still under his control at the château.

Harvey said to Stewart, 'I never once said "*Dieu est merde*."'

'Maybe you implied it.'

'Perhaps I did. But I did not speak as a prophet; I discussed some aspects of *Job* in an academic sense.'

'For a man of your intelligence, you are remarkably stupid,' said Stewart. 'It's Effie they wanted news of. Failing that, they made the best of what they got. You should have let Effie divorce you with a huge settlement a long time ago. She can get a divorce any time; it's the money she wanted.'

'To finance FLE?'

'You asked me to assume she isn't involved.'

'I don't want to divorce Effie. I don't want a divorce.'

'Are you still in love with Effie?'

'Yes.'

'Then you're an unhappy man. Why did you leave her?'

'I couldn't stand her sociological clap-trap. If she wanted to do some good in the world she had plenty of opportunity. There was nothing to stop her taking up charities and causes; she could have had money for them, and she always had plenty of time. But she has to rob supermarkets and banks and sleep with people like *that*.' He pointed to a row of photographs in the paper. Three young men and Effie. The photograph of Effie was that which the police had found among his papers. Harvey told Stewart this, and said, 'They don't seem to have any other picture of Effie. I wonder how they got photos of her friends.'

'In the same way that they got Effie's, I expect. Through rummaging in the homes of their families, their girl-friends.'

'What can she see in them?' Harvey said. Stewart turned the paper round to see it better. One of the men was dressed in a very padded-shouldered coat, a spotted bow tie and hair falling down past the point where the picture ended, which was just above his elbow; the second man was a blond, blank-faced boy with thick lips; the third seemed to be positively posing as the criminal he was alleged to be, being sneery, narrow-eyed and double-chinned, and bearing a two-day stubble beard. There was Effie amongst them, looking like Effie. The men were identified by French names, Effie by the name of Effie Gotham, wife of the millionaire guru.

'What does she see in them?' demanded Harvey. 'It's not so much that I'm jealous as that I'm intellectually insulted by the whole thing. I always have been by Effie's attitude to life. I thought she'd grow out of it.'

'I am to assume that Effie is not involved,' said Stewart.

'Well, there's her picture along with the others. It's difficult for me to keep up the fiction,' Harvey said.

'Do you mean that the photograph convinces you?' Stewart said. 'You know where the police got the photograph. Out of a drawer in your desk.'

'It wasn't exactly out of a drawer in a desk,' Harvey said. 'It was out of a box. I keep things in boxes down there in my working cottage. I'll take you to see it. I haven't been back to the cottage since I was arrested in Epinal three days ago.'

'Were you really arrested?'

'Perhaps not technically. I was definitely invited to come along to the commissariat. I went.'

'I wonder,' said Stewart, 'why there's been so little in the press about Nathan Fox. I only heard on the radio that he'd disappeared suddenly from your house. And they don't include him in the gang. Maybe they couldn't find a photograph of him. A photo makes a gangster real.'

'There was an identikit of Effie in the papers the day I was hauled in,' said Harvey.

'Did it look like Effie?'

'I'm afraid so. In fact it looked like Ruth. But it would pass for Effie. It looked like Job's wife, too. You know, it was a most remarkable thing, Stewart, I was sitting in the museum at Epinal reflecting on that extraordinary painting of Job and his wife by Georges de La Tour, when suddenly the police –'

'You told me that last night,' said Stewart.

'I know. I want to talk about it.'

'Don't you think,' said Stewart, 'that it would be odd if Effie wanted alimony from you simply to finance the FLE, when she could have sold her jewellery?'

'Hasn't she done that?'

'No, it's still in the safety-box at the bank. I hold the second key. There's still enough money in her bank to meet the standing orders for insurances and charities. Nothing's changed.'

'Well, why did she want to fleece me?'

'I don't see why she shouldn't have tried to get maintenance of some sort from you. It's true that her child by Ernie Howe damaged her case. But you walked out on her. She behaved like a normal woman married to a man in your position.'

'Effie is not a normal woman,' said Harvey.

'Oh, if you're talking in a basic sense, what woman is?'

'Women who don't get arrested in Trieste for shop-lifting are normal,' said Harvey. 'Especially women with her kind of jewellery in the bank. Whose side are you on, anyway, mine or Effie's?'

'In a divorce case, that is the usual question that the client puts, sooner or later. It's inevitable,' said the lawyer.

'But this is something different from a divorce case. Don't you realize what's happened?'

'I'm afraid I do,' said Stewart.

Next day was a Saturday. They sat in Harvey's cottage, huddling over the stove because the windows had been opened to air the place. There had been a feeling of spring in the early March morning, but this had gone by eleven o'clock; it was now winter again, bleak, with a slanting rain. As Harvey unlocked the door of his little house Stewart said, 'Lousy soil you've got here. Nothing much growing.'

'I haven't bothered to cultivate it.'

'It's better up at the château.'

'Oh, yes, it's had more attention.'

This was Harvey's first visit to the cottage since the police had pounced. He looked round carefully, opening the windows upstairs and downstairs, while Stewart lit the stove. 'They haven't changed the décor,' Harvey said. 'But a few bundles of papers are not in the places I left them in. Shifted, a matter of inches – but I know, I know.'

'Have they taken any of your papers, letters, business documents?'

'What letters and business papers? You have the letters and the business papers. All I have are my notes, and the manuscript of my little book, so far as it goes – it's to be a monograph, you know. I don't know if they've subtracted the few files, but they could have photographed them; much good might it do them. Files of notes on the *Book of Job*.

They did take the photograph of Effie; that, they did take. I want it back.'

'You're entitled to ask for it,' said Stewart.

From the window, a grey family Citroën could be seen parked round a bend in the path, out of sight of the road; in it were two men in civilian clothes occupying the front seats. The rain plopped lazily on to the roof of the car and splashed the windscreen. 'Poor bastards,' Harvey said. 'They do it in three- or four-hour shifts.'

'Well, it's a protection for you, anyway. From the press if not from the terrorists.'

'I wish I was without the need for protection, and I wish you were in your office in London.'

'I don't go to the office on Saturday,' Stewart said.

'What do you do at the week-ends?'

'Fuck,' said Stewart.

'Do you mean, fuck the question or that on Saturdays and Sundays you fuck?'

'Both.'

'Don't you ever go to a concert or a film on Sundays? Never go to church?'

'Sometimes I go to a concert. I go away for the week-ends, often. I do the usual things.'

'Well, you're wasting your time here,' Harvey said.

'No, because first you're my most valuable client. That's from a practical point of view. And secondly, I'm interested in your *Book of Job*; it just beats me how a man of your scope should choose to hide himself away in this hole. And thirdly, of course, I'm a friend; I want to see you out of this mess. I strongly advise you to come back to London here and now. Do you have your passport?'

'Yes, they gave me back my passport.'

'Oh, they took it away?'

'Yes, they took the stuff out of my pockets,' Harvey said. 'They gave it all back. I'm not leaving.'

'Why?'

'Well, all my books and things are here. I don't see why I should run away. I intend to go on as usual. Besides, I'm anxious about Effie.'

'Maybe Effie would move to another field of action if you weren't in the Vosges,' said Stewart. 'You see, I don't want you to become an unwilling accomplice.'

'Effie follows the gang,' said Harvey.

'Doesn't she lead it?'

'Oh, I don't know. I don't even know for certain that she's in it. It's all mere allegation on the part of the police.'

Stewart walked about the little room, with his scarf wound round his neck. 'It's chilly,' he said. He was looking at the books. 'Does Anne-Marie cook for you?' he said.

'Yes, indifferently. She's a police agent by profession.'

'Oh, that doesn't mean much,' said Stewart, 'when you know that she is.'

'I used to love mealtimes with Effie,' said Harvey. 'I enjoyed the mealtimes more than the meals.'

'Let's go out somewhere for lunch,' said Stewart.

'We can go in to Nancy. Undoubtedly we'd be followed.'

'That doesn't mean much if you know you are being followed,' said Stewart.

Harvey stood in the middle of the room watching with an irritated air while Stewart fingered his books.

'There's nothing of interest,' said Harvey, 'unless you're interested in the subject.'

'Well, you know I am. I still don't see why you can't write your essay elsewhere.'

'I've got used to it here.'

'Would you like to have Ruth back?' said Stewart.

'Not particularly. I would like to have Clara back.'

'With Effie?'

'No, Effie isn't a motherly type.'

'Ruth is a mother?'

416

'She is a born children's nurse.'

'But you would like to have Effie back?' Stewart said, and he made light of this, as of all his questions, by putting them simultaneously with a flicking-through of the pages of Harvey's books.

'Yes, I would; in theory,' said Harvey. 'That is the *New English Bible*. The translation is godforsaken.'

'Then you'd be willing to take Ruth back if she brought Clara. But you'd prefer to have Effie to make love to?'

'That is the unattainable ideal. The *New English Bible*'s version of *Job* makes no distinction between Behemoth and Leviathan. They translate the two as "the crocodile", which has of course some possibility as a theory, but it simply doesn't hold in the context.'

'I thought Behemoth was the hippopotamus,' said Stewart.

'Well, that's the general view, not necessarily correct. However, the author of *Job* turns God into a poet at that point, proclaiming wonderful hymns to his own creation, the buffalo, the ostrich, the wild ass, the horse, the eagle; then there's the sparrow-hawk. And God says, Consider this, look at that, reflect on their ways, how they live and survive; I did it all; where were you when I did it? Finally come Behemoth and Leviathan. Well, if you are going to translate both Behemoth and Leviathan as the crocodile, it makes far too long a passage, it gives far more weight to the crocodile as one of God's marvels than is obviously intended. As for the features of Behemoth, they fit in with the hippopotamus or some large and similar creature equally as well as with the crocodile. Why should God be so proud of his crocodile that he devotes thirty-eight verses to it, and to the horse only seven?'

'There must be some good arguments in favour of Behemoth and Leviathan both being the crocodile, though,' Stewart said.

'Of course there are arguments. The scholars try to ration-alize *Job* by rearranging the verses where there is obviously no sense in them. Sometimes, of course, the textual evidence irresistibly calls for a passage to be moved from the traditional place to another. But moving passages about for no other reason than that they are more logical is no good for the *Book of Job*. It doesn't make it come clear. The *Book of Job* will never come clear. It doesn't matter; it's a poem. As for Leviathan and Behemoth, Lévêque who is the best modern scholar on *Job* distinguishes between the two.' Harvey was apparently back in his element. He seemed to have forgotten about the police outside his house, and that Effie was a criminal at large.

Stewart said, 'You amaze me.'

'Why?'

'Don't you want to know the facts about Effie?'

'Oh, Effie.'

Harvey had in his hands one of Lévêque's volumes. 'He accepts Leviathan as the crocodile and Behemoth as the hippo-potamus. He takes Behemoth to be a hippopotamus or at least a large beast.'

'What about these other new Bibles?' said Stewart, pointing to a couple of new translations. He wondered if perhaps Harvey was not so guileless as he seemed. Stewart thought perhaps Harvey might really be involved with Effie and her liberation movement. There was something not very con-vincing about Harvey's cool-headedness.

'Messy,' said Harvey. 'They all try to reach everybody and end by saying nothing to anybody. There are no good new Bibles. The 1945 *Knox* wasn't bad but still obscure – it's a Vulgate translation, of course; the *Jerusalem Bible* and this *Good News Bible* are not much improvement on the old *Moffat*.'

'You stick to the *Authorized* then?'

'For my purpose, it's the best English basis. One can get to know the obvious mistakes and annotate accordingly.'

Harvey poured drinks and handed one to Stewart.

'I think I can see,' said Stewart, 'that you're happy here. I didn't realize how much this work meant to you. It has puzzled me slightly; I knew you were dedicated to the subject but didn't understand how much, until I came here. You shouldn't think of marriage.'

'I don't. I think of Effie.'

'Only when you're not thinking of *Job*?'

'Yes. What can I do for her by thinking?'

'Your work here would make a good cover if you were in with Effie,' said the lawyer.

'A very bad cover. The police aren't really convinced by my story. Why should you be?'

'Oh, Harvey, I didn't mean –'

Anne-Marie arrived with a grind of brakes in the little Renault. She left the car with a bang of the door and began to proclaim an urgency before she had opened the cottage gate.

'Mr Gotham, a phone call from Canada.'

Harvey went to open the door to her. 'What is it from Canada?' he said.

'Your aunt on the telephone. She'll ring you back in ten minutes.'

'I'll come up to the house right away.'

To Stewart, he said, 'Wait for me. I'll be back shortly and we'll go out to lunch. You know, there could have been an influence of *Prometheus* on *Job*; the dates could quite possibly coincide. But I find vast differences. Prometheus wasn't inno- cent, for one thing. He stole fire from Heaven. Job was innocent.'

'Out to lunch!' said Anne-Marie. 'I'm preparing lunch at the château.'

'We'll have it cold for dinner,' thundered Harvey as he got into the car. Anne-Marie followed him; looking back at Stewart who gave her a long smile full of what looked like meaning, but decidedly so unspecific as to mean nothing.

As they whizzed up the drive to the château Anne-Marie said, 'You think because you are rich you can do anything with people. I planned a lunch.'

'You should first have inquired whether we would be in for lunch,' said Harvey.

'Oh, no,' she said, with some point. 'It was for you to say you would be out.'

'I apologize.'

'The apologies of the rich. They are cheap.'

Half an hour went by before the telephone rang again. The police were vetting the calls, turning away half the world's reporters and others who wanted to speak to the terrorist's guru husband. Harvey therefore made no complaint. He sat in patience reading all about himself once more in the local morning newspaper, until the telephone rang.

'Oh, it's you, Auntie Pet. It must be the middle of the night with you; how are you?'

'How are *you*?'

'All right.'

'I saw you on the television and it's all in the paper. How could you blaspheme in that terrible way, saying those things about your Creator?'

'Auntie Pet, you've got to understand that I said nothing whatsoever about God, I mean our Creator. What I was talking about was a fictional character in the *Book of Job*, called God. I don't know what you've seen or read, but it's not yet proved finally that Effie, my wife, is a terrorist.'

'Oh, Effie isn't involved, it goes without saying. I never said Effie was a terrorist, I know she isn't, in fact. What I'm calling about is this far more serious thing, it's a disgrace to the family. I mean, this is to blaspheme when you say that God is what you said he was.'

'I never said what they said I said he was,' said Harvey. 'How are you, Auntie Pet? How is Uncle Joe?'

'Uncle Joe, I never hear from. But I get to know.'

'And yourself? I haven't heard from you for ages.'

'Well, I don't write much. The prohibitive price of stamps. My health is everything that can be expected by a woman who does right and fears the Lord. Your Uncle Joe just lives on there with old Collier who is very much to blame, too. Neither of them has darkened the door of the church for as long as I can remember. They are unbelievers like you.'

'On the contrary, I have abounding faith.'

'You shouldn't question the Bible. Job was a good man. There is a Christian message in the *Book of Job*.'

'But Job didn't know that.'

'How do you know? We have a lovely Bible, there. Why do you want to change it? You should look after your wife and have a family, and be a good husband, with all your advantages, and the business doing so well. Your Uncle Joe refused the merger.'

'Well, Auntie Pet, it's been a pleasure to talk to you. I have to go out with my lawyer for lunch, now. I'm glad you managed to get my number so you could put your mind at rest.'

'I got your number with the utmost difficulty.'

'Yes, I was wondering how you got it, Auntie Pet.'

'Money,' said Auntie Pet.

'Ah,' said Harvey.

'I'll be in touch again.'

'Keep well. Don't take the slightest notice of what the newspapers and the television say.'

'What about the radio?'

'Also, the radio.'

'Are you starting a new religion, Harvey?'

'No.'

Stewart and Harvey crossed the Place Stanislas at Nancy. The rain had stopped and a silvery light touched the gilded gates at the corners of the square, it glittered on the lamp posts with their golden garlands and crown-topped heads, and on the bright and lacy iron-work of all the balconies of the *hôtel de ville*.

'The square always looks lovely out of season,' said Stewart.

'It's supposed to have crowds,' Harvey said. 'That's what it was evidently made for.'

Two police cars turned into the square and followed them at a crawl.

'The bistro I had in mind is down a narrow street,' said Harvey. 'Let them follow us there. The police have to eat, too.'

But they had a snack-lunch in the police station at Nancy, two policemen having got out of their car and invited Harvey and Stewart to join them.

'What's the matter, now?' Harvey had said when the police approached them.

Stewart said, 'I require an explanation.'

The explanation was not forthcoming until they were taken later in the afternoon to the police headquarters in Epinal.

'A policeman has been killed in Paris.'

CHAPTER 9

STEWART COWPER, HAVING invoked the British Consul, was allowed to leave the police headquarters the same afternoon that he was detained with Harvey. He refused to answer any questions at all, and his parting advice to Harvey was to do likewise. They were alone in a corridor.

'The least I can do,' said Harvey, 'is to defend Effie.'

'Understandable,' said Stewart, and left to collect his luggage from the château and get a hired car to Paris, and a plane to London.

Harvey got home later that night, having failed to elicit, from the questions he was asked by an officer who had come to Epinal for the purpose – the same old questions – what had exactly happened in Paris that morning, and where Effie was supposed to fit into the murder of the policeman.

'Did you hear about the killing on the radio, M. Gotham?'

'No. I've only just learned of it from you. I wasn't in the château this morning. I was in the cottage with my English lawyer, Stewart Cowper.'

'What did you discuss with your lawyer?'

'The different versions of the *Book of Job* in various recent English translations of the Bible.'

Harvey's interrogator looked at him with real rage. 'One of our policemen has been killed,' he said.

'I'm sorry to hear it,' said Harvey.

They escorted him to pick up his car at Nancy, and followed him home.

Next day the Sunday papers had the same photograph of Effie. There was also a photograph of the policeman, lying in the street beside a police car, covered by a sheet, with some police standing by. Effie had been recognized by eye-witnesses at the scene of the killing, in the eighteenth *arrondissement*. A blonde, long-haired girl with a gun. She was the killer. Her hair was drawn back in a pony-tail at the time of the commando-raid; she was wearing blue jeans and a grey pull-over. The Paris security police and the *gendarmerie* were now operating jointly in the search for FLE and its supporters, and especially for the Montmartre killers.

That was the whole of the news, though it filled several pages of the newspapers. The volume of printed words was to be explained by the length of the many paragraphs ending with a question mark, by numerous interpolations about Harvey and his Bible-sect, his wealth, his château, and by details of the unfortunate policeman's family life.

It was not till after lunch on Monday that he was invited to the commissariat at Epinal once more. Two security men from Paris had arrived to interrogate him. Two tall men, one of them in his late forties, robust, with silvering sideburns, the other fair and skinny, not much over thirty, with gilt-rimmed glasses, an intellectual. Harvey thought, if he had seen them together in a restaurant, he would have taken the older man for a businessman, the younger for a priest.

Later, when he chewed over their questions, he was to find it difficult to distinguish between this second interrogation and the first one of a few days ago. This was partly because the older man, who introduced himself by the name of Chatelain, spent a lot of time going over Harvey's previous deposition.

'My house is surrounded by your men,' said Harvey. 'You have your young woman auxiliary in my house. What are you accusing me of?' (Stewart Cowper had advised him: If they question you again, ask them what they have against you, demand to know what is the charge.)

'We are not accusing, Mr Gotham, we are questioning.'

'Questions can sound like accusations.'

'A policeman has been shot dead.'

And their continual probe into why he had settled in France: Harvey recalled later.

'I liked the house,' said Harvey, 'I got my permit to stay in France. I'm regular with the police.'

'Your wife has been in trouble before.'

'I know,' said Harvey.

'Do you love your wife?'

'That's rather a personal question.'

'It was a personal question for the policeman who was killed.'

'I wonder,' said Harvey, conversationally. He was suddenly indignant and determined to be himself, thoughtfully in charge of his reasoning mind, not any sort of victim. 'I wonder . . . I'm not sure that death is personal in the sense of being in love. So far as we know, we don't feel death. We know the fear of death, we know the process of dying. From the outside it looks the most personal of phenomena. But isn't death the very negation of the personal, therefore strictly speaking impersonal? A dead body is the most impersonal thing I can think of. Unless one believes in the continuity of personality in its terrestrially recognizable form, as opposed to life-after-death which is something else. Many disbelieve in life after death, of course, but –'

'*Pardon?* Are you trying to tell me that the death of one of our men is trivial?'

'No. I was reflecting on a remark of yours. Philosophizing, I'm afraid. I meant –'

'Kindly don't philosophize,' said Chatelain. 'This is not the place. I want to know where your wife is. Where is Effie?'

'I don't know where Mme Gotham is.'

And again:

'A policeman has been killed by the FLE gang. Two men and a girl, all armed. In the eighteenth *arrondissement* in Paris.'

'I'm sorry that a policeman has been shot,' said Harvey. 'Why in the eighteenth *arrondissement*?'

'That's what we're asking you,' said Chatelain.

'I have no idea. I thought these terrorists acted mainly in popular suburbs.'

'Was your wife ever before in the eighteenth *arrondissement*, do you know?'

'Of course,' said Harvey. 'Who hasn't been in the eighteenth? It's Montmartre.'

'Have you and your wife any friends there?'

'I have friends there and I suppose my wife has, too.'

'Who are your friends?'

'You should know. Your colleagues here went through my address book last week and checked all my friends.'

In the middle of the afternoon Chatelain became more confidential. He began to melt, but only in resemblance to a refrigerator which thaws when the current is turned off. True warmth, thought Harvey at the time, doesn't drip, drip, drip. And later, in his cottage, when he reconstituted the scene he thought: And I ask myself, why was he a refrigerator in the first place?

'Don't think I don't sympathize with you, Mr Gotham,' said Chatelain, on the defreeze. 'Not to know where one's wife is cannot be a pleasant experience.'

'Don't think I don't sympathize with you,' said Harvey. 'I know you've lost one of your men. That's serious. And I sympathize, as everyone should, with his family. But you offer no proof that my wife, Effie, is involved. You offer only a photograph that you confiscated from a box on my table.'

'We confiscated . . . ?' The man consulted Harvey's thick file which lay on the desk. 'Ah, yes. You are right. The Vosges police obtained that photograph from your house. Witnesses have identified that photograph as the girl in the gang. And look – the identikit, constructed with the help of eye-witnesses to a bank robbery and supermarket bombings, some days prior to our obtaining the photograph. Look at it – isn't that your wife?'

Harvey looked at the drawing.

'When I first saw it in the paper I thought it resembled my wife's sister, Ruth, rather than my wife,' he said. 'Since it couldn't possibly refer to Ruth it seems to me even more unlikely that it refers to Effie.'

'Mme Gotham was arrested in Trieste.'

Harvey was still looking at the identikit. It reminded him, now, of Job's wife in La Tour's painting even though the drawing was full-face and the painting showed a profile.

'She was arrested for shop-lifting,' said Harvey.

'Why did she do that?'

Harvey put down the identikit and gave Chatelain his attention. 'I don't know that she did it. If she did, it does not follow that she bombs supermarkets and kills policemen.'

'If I was in your place,' said Chatelain, 'I would probably speak as you do. But if you were in my place, you would press for some indication, any indication, any guess, as to where she is. I don't blame you for trying to protect your wife. You see,' he said, leaning back in his chair and looking away from Harvey, towards the window, 'a policeman has been shot dead. His wife is in a shop on the outskirts of Paris where they live, a popular quarter, with her twelve-year-old daughter who has a transistor radio. The lady is waiting her turn at the cash-desk. The child draws her mother's attention to a flash item of news that has interrupted the music. A policeman has been shot and killed in the eighteenth *arrondissement*; the name is being withheld until the family can be informed. The assassins, two men and a girl, have escaped. The terrorist gang FLE have immediately telephoned the press to claim the crime. The main points of the news flash are repeated: a policeman killed, leaving a wife and two daughters aged fourteen and twelve respectively.

Now this lady, the policeman's wife, is always worried when she hears of the death or wounding of a policeman. In this case the description is alarmingly close. The eighteenth *arrondisse-ment* where her husband is on duty; the ages of their daughters. She hurries home and finds a police car outside her block of flats. It is indeed her husband who has been killed. Did she deserve this?'

'No,' said Harvey. 'Neither did the policeman. We do not get what we merit. The one thing has nothing to do with the other. Your only course is to prevent it happening again.'

'Depend on us,' said the policeman.

'If I may say so,' said Harvey, 'you are wasting efforts on me which might profitably be directed to that end.'

'Any clue, any suggestion . . .' said Chatelain, with great patience. He almost pleaded. 'Are there any houses in Paris that you know of, where they might be found?'

'None,' said Harvey.

'No friends?'

'The few people I know with establishments in Paris are occupied with business affairs in rather a large, multinational way. I don't believe they would like the FLE.'

'Nathan Fox is a good housekeeper?'

'I believe he can be useful in a domestic way.'

'He could be keeping a safe house for the gang in Paris.'

'I don't see him as the gangster type. Honestly, you know, I don't think he's in it.'

'But your wife . . . She is different?'

'I didn't say so.'

'And yourself?'

'What about myself? What are you asking?' Harvey said.

'You have a connection with the gang?'

'No.'

'Why did you hang baby clothes on the line outside your cottage as early as last spring?' said Chatelain next.

Harvey was given a break at about seven in the evening. He was accompanied to a café for a meal by the tall young Parisian inspector with metal-rimmed glasses, Louis Pomfret by name.

Pomfret spoke what could be described as 'perfect English', that awful type of perfect English that comes over Radio Moscow. He said something apologetic, in semi-disparagement of the police. Harvey couldn't now remember the exact words. But he recalled Pomfret remarking, too, on the way to the café, 'You must understand that one of their men has been killed.' ('Their' men, not 'our' men, Harvey noted.)

At the café table the policeman told Harvey, 'A Canadian lady arrived in Paris who attempted to reach you on the telephone, and we intercepted her. She's your aunt. We've escorted her safely to the château where she desired to go.'

'God, it's my Aunt Pet. Don't give her any trouble.'

'But, no.'

If you think you'll make me grateful for all this courtesy, thought Harvey, you are mistaken. He said, 'I should hope not.'

The policeman said, 'I'm afraid the food here is ghastly.'

'They make a good omelette. I've eaten here before,' said Harvey.

Ham omelettes and wine from the Vosges.

'It's unfortunate for you, Gotham,' said Pomfret, 'but you appreciate, I hope, our position.'

'You want to capture these members of the FLE before they do more damage.'

'Yes, we do. And of course, we will. Now that a member of the police has been killed... You appreciate, his wife was shopping in a supermarket with her son of twelve, who had a transistor radio. She was taking no interest in the programme. At one point the boy said –'

'Are you sure it was a boy?' Harvey said.

429

'It was a girl. How do you know?'

'The scene has been described to me by your colleague.'

'You're very observant,' Pomfret smiled, quite nicely.

'Well, of course I'm observant in a case like this,' said Harvey. 'I'm hanging on your lips.'

'Why?'

'To hear if you have any evidence that my wife is involved with a terrorist gang.'

'We have a warrant for her arrest,' said Pomfret.

'That's not evidence.'

'I know. But we don't put out warrants without reason. Your wife was arrested in Trieste. She was definitely lodging there with a group which has since been identified as members of the FLE gang. When the police photograph from the incident at Trieste noticeably resembled the photograph we obtained from you, and also resembled the identikit made up from eye-witnesses of the bombings and incursions here in France, we call that sufficient evidence to regard your wife as a suspect.'

'I would like to see the photograph from Trieste,' said Harvey. 'Why haven't I been shown it?'

'You are not investigating the case. We are.'

'But I'm interested in her whereabouts,' Harvey said. 'What does this photograph from the police at Trieste look like?'

'It's an ordinary routine photograph that's taken of all people under arrest. Plain and flat, like a passport photograph. It looks like your wife. It's of no account to you.'

'Why wasn't I shown it, told about it?'

'I think you can see it if you want.'

'Your people at the commissariat evidently don't believe me when I say I don't know where Effie is.'

'Well, I suppose that's why you've been questioned. You've never been officially convoked.'

'The English word is summoned.'

'Summoned; I apologize.'

'Lousy wine,' said Harvey.

'It's what you get in a cheap café,' said Pomfret.

'They had better when I ate here before,' said Harvey. 'Look, all you've got to go on is an identikit made in France which resembles two photographs of my wife.'

'And the address she was residing at in Trieste. That's most important of all.'

'She is inclined to take up with unconventional people,' said Harvey.

'Evidently, since she married yourself.'

'Do you know,' said Harvey, 'I'm very conventional, believe it or not.'

'I don't believe it, of course.'

'Why?'

'Your mode of life in France. For an affluent man to establish himself in a cottage and study the *Book of Job* is not conventional.'

'Job was an affluent man. He sat among the ashes. Some say, on a dung-heap outside the city. He was very conventional. So much so that God was bored with him.'

'Is that in the scriptures?' said the policeman.

'No, it's in my mind.'

'You've actually written it down. They took photocopies of some of your pages.'

'I object to that. They had no right.'

'It's possible they had no right. Why have you never brought in a lawyer?'

'What for?'

'Exactly. But it would be the conventional thing to do.'

'I hope you're impressed,' said Harvey. 'You see, if I were writing a film-script or a pornographic novel, you wouldn't find it so strange that I came to an out-of-the-way place to work. It's the subject of *Job* you can't understand my giving my time to.'

'More or less. I think, perhaps, you've been trying to put yourself in the conditions of Job. Is that right?'

'One can't write an essay on *Job* sitting round a swimming pool in a ten-acre park, with all that goes with it. But I could just as well study the subject in a quiet apartment in some city. I came to these parts because I happened to find the cottage. There is a painting of Job and his wife here in Epinal which attracts me. You should see it.'

'I should,' said Pomfret. 'I shall.'

'Job's wife looks remarkably like my wife. It was painted about the middle of the seventeenth century so it can't be Effie, if that's what you're thinking.'

'We were discussing Job, not Mme Effie.'

'Then what am I doing here,' said Harvey, 'being interrogated by you?'

Pomfret remained good-natured. He said something about their having a supper and a talk, not an interrogation. 'I am genuinely interested,' said Pomfret, 'speaking for myself. You are isolated like Job. But you haven't lost your goods and fortune. Any possibility of that?'

'No, but I'm as good as without them here. More so before I took the château.'

'Oh, I was forgetting the château. I've only seen your cottage, from the outside. It looks impoverished enough.'

'It was the boils that worried Job.'

'*Pardon?* The boils?'

'Boils. Skin-sores. He was covered with them.'

'Ah, yes, that is correct. Don't you, like Job, feel the need of friends to talk to in your present troubles?'

'One thing that the *Book of Job* teaches us,' Harvey said, 'is the futility of friendship in times of trouble. That is perhaps not a reflection on friends but on friendship. Friends mean well, or make as if they do. But friendship itself is made for happiness, not trouble.'

'Is your aunt a friend?'

'My Aunt Pet, who you tell me has arrived at the château? – I suppose she thinks of herself as a friend. She's a bore, coming at this moment. At any moment. – You don't suppose this is anything but an interrogation, do you? Any more questions?'

'Would you like some cheese?'

Harvey couldn't help liking the young man, within his reservation that the police had, no doubt, sent him precisely to be liked. Soften me up as much as you please, Harvey thought, but it doesn't help you; it only serves to release my own love, my nostalgia, for Effie. And he opened his mouth and spoke in praise of Effie, almost to his own surprise describing how she was merry at parties, explaining that she danced well and was fun to talk to. 'She's an interesting woman, Effie.'

'Intellectual?'

'We are all more intellectual than we know. She doesn't think of herself as an intellectual type. But under a certain stimulus, she is.'

They were walking back to the commissariat. Harvey had half a mind to go home and let them come for him with an official summons, if they wanted. But it was only half a mind; the other half, mesmerized and now worked up about Effie, propelled him on to the police station with his companion.

'She tried some drugs, I suppose,' said Pomfret.

'You shouldn't suppose so,' said Harvey. 'Effie is entirely anti-drug. It would be extraordinary if she's taken to drugs in the last two years.'

'You must recognize,' said Pomfret, 'that she is lively and vital enough to be a member of a terrorist gang.'

'Lively and vital,' said Harvey, 'lively and vital – one of those words is redundant.'

Pomfret laughed.

'However,' said Harvey, 'it's out of the question that she could be a terrorist.' He had a suspicion that Pomfret was now genuinely fascinated by the images of Effie that Harvey was able to produce, Effie at a party, Effie an interesting talker, a rich man's wife; his imagination was involved, beyond his investigator's role, in the rich man's mechanism, his free intellectual will, his casual purchase of the château; Pomfret was fascinated by both Effie and Harvey.

'A terrorist,' said Pomfret. 'She obviously has an idealistic motive. Why did you leave her?'

The thought that Effie was a member of a terrorist band now excited Harvey sexually.

'Terrorist is out of the question,' he said. 'I left her because she seemed to want to go her own way. The marriage broke up, that's all. Marriages do.'

'But on a hypothesis, how would you feel if you knew she was a terrorist?'

Harvey thought, I would feel I had failed her in action. Which I have. He said, 'I can't imagine.'

At the police station Pomfret left him in a waiting-room. Patiently sitting there was a lean-faced man with a dark skin gone to a muddy grey, bright small eyes and fine features. He seemed to be a Balkan. What was he doing there? It was after nine in the evening. Surely it was in the morning that he would come about his papers. Perhaps he had been picked up without papers? What sort of work was he doing in Epinal? He wore a black suit, shiny with wear; a very white shirt open at the neck; brown, very pointed shoes; and he had with him a brown cardboard brief-case with tinny locks, materials such as Harvey had only seen before in the form of a suitcase on a train in a remote part of Sicily. The object in Sicily had been old and battered, but his present companion's brief-case had a new-bought look. It was not the first time Harvey had noticed that poor people from Eastern Europe resembled, not only in their possessions and clothes, but in their build and expression, the poor of Western Europe years ago. Who he was, where he came from and why, Harvey was never to know, for he was just about to say something when the door opened and a policeman in uniform beckoned the man away. He followed with nervous alacrity and the door closed again on Harvey. Patience, pallor and deep anxiety: there goes suffering, Harvey reflected. And I found him interesting. Is it only by recognizing how flat would be the world without the sufferings of others that we know how desperately becalmed our own lives would be without suffering? Do I suffer on Effie's account? Yes, and perhaps I can live by that experience. We all need something to suffer about. But *Job*, my work on *Job*, all interrupted and neglected, probed into and interfered with: that is experience, too; real experience, not vicarious, as is often assumed. To study, to think, is to live and suffer painfully.

Did Effie really kill or help to kill the policeman in Paris whose wife was shopping in the suburbs at the time? Since he had left the police station on Saturday night he had recurrently put himself to imagine the scene. An irruption at a department store. The police arrive. Shots fired. Effie and her men friends fighting their way back to their waiting car (with Nathan at the wheel?). Effie, lithe and long-legged, a most desirable girl, and quick-witted, unmoved, aiming her gun with a good aim. She pulls the trigger and is away all in one moment. Yes, he could imagine Effie in the scene; she was capable of that, capable of anything.

'Will you come this way, please, Mr Gotham?'

There was a stack of files on Chatelain's desk.

The rest of that night Harvey remembered as a sort of roll-call of his visitors over the past months; it seemed to him like the effect of an old-fashioned village policeman going his rounds, shining his torch on name-plates and door-knobs; one by one, each name surrounded by a nimbus of agitated suspicion as his friends' simple actions, their ordinary comings and goings came up for questioning. It was strange how guilty everything looked under the policeman's torch, how it sounded here in the police headquarters. Chatelain asked Harvey if he would object to the conversation being tape-recorded.

'No, it's a good thing. I was going to suggest it. Then you won't have to waste time asking me the same questions over and over again.'

Chatelain smiled sadly. 'We have to check.' Then he selected one of the files and placed it before him.

'Edward Jansen,' he said, 'came to visit you.'

'Yes, he's the husband of my wife's sister, Ruth, now separated. He came to see me last April.'

Chatelain gave a weak smile and said, 'Your neighbours seem to remember a suspicious-looking character who visited you last spring.'

'Yes, I daresay that was Edward Jansen. He has red hair down to his shoulders. Or had. He's an actor and he's now famous. He is my brother-in-law through his marriage to my wife's sister, but he's now separated from his wife. A lot can happen in less than a year.'

'He asked you why there were baby clothes on the line?'

'I don't remember if he actually asked, but he made some remark about them because I answered, as you know, "The police won't shoot if there's a baby in the house."'

'Why did you say that?'

'I can't answer precisely. I didn't foresee any involvement with the police, or I wouldn't have said it.'

'It was a joke?'

'That sort of thing.'

'Do you still hear from Edward Jansen?' Chatelain opened one of the files.

'I haven't heard for some time.'

Chatelain flicked through the file.

'There's a letter from him waiting for you at your house.'

'Thanks. I expect you can tell me the contents.'

'No, we can't.'

'That could be taken in two senses,' Harvey said.

'Well, you can take it in one sense: we haven't opened it. The name and address of the sender is on the outside of the envelope. As it happens, we know quite a lot about Mr Jansen, and he doesn't interest us at the moment. He's also been questioned.' Chatelain closed the file, evidently Edward's dossier; it was rather thin compared with some of the others. Chatelain took up another and opened it, as if starting on a new subject. Then, 'What did you discuss with Edward Jansen last April?'

'I can't recall. I know his wife, Ruth, was anxious for me to make a settlement on her sister and facilitate a divorce. I am sure we didn't discuss that very much, for I had no intention of co-operating with my wife to that end. I know we discussed the *Book of Job*.'

'And about Ruth Jansen. Did you invite her to stay?'

'No, she came unexpectedly with her sister's baby, about the end of August.'

'Why did she do that?'

'August is a very boring month for everybody.'

'You really must be serious, Mr Gotham.'

'It's as good a reason as any. I can't analyse the motives of a woman who probably can't analyse them herself.'

Chatelain tapped the file. 'She says here that she brought the baby, hoping to win you over to her view that the child would benefit if you made over a substantial sum of money to its mother, that is, to your wife Effie.'

'If that's what Ruth says, I suppose it is so.'

'She greatly resembles your wife.'

'Yes, feature by feature. But of course, to anyone who knows them they are very different. Effie is more beautiful, really. Less practical than Ruth.'

Pomfret came in and sat down. He was less free of manner in the presence of the other officer. He peered at the tape-recording machine as if to make sure everything was all right with it.

'So you had a relation with Mrs Jansen.'

'Yes.'

'Your sister-in-law and wife of your friend.'

'Yes, I grew fond of Ruth. I was particularly taken by the baby. Of course, by this time Ruth and Edward had parted.'

'Things happen fast in your set.'

'Well, I suppose the parting had been working up for a long time. Is there any point in all these questions?'

'Not much. We want to check, you see, against the statements made in England by the people concerned. Did Ruth seem surprised when she heard that Effie was involved in the terrorist attacks?'

What were these statements of Ruth, of Edward, of others? Harvey said firmly, even as he felt his way, 'She was very much afraid of the police, coming into our lives as they did. It was quite unforeseen. She could no more blame her sister for it than she could blame her for an earthquake. I feel the same, myself.'

'She did not defend her sister?'

'She had no need to defend Effie to me. It isn't I who accuse Effie of being a terrorist. I say there is a mistake.'

'Now, Nathan Fox,' said the officer, reaching for a new file. 'What do you know about him?'

'Not very much. He made himself useful to Ruth and Edward when they were living in London. He's a graduate but can't find a job. He came to my house, here, to visit Ruth and the baby for Christmas.'

'He is a friend of your wife?'

'Well, he knows her, of course.'

'He is a weak character?'

'No, in fact I think it shows a certain strength of character in him to have turned his hand to domestic work since he can't find anything else to do. He graduated at an English university, I have no idea which one.'

'What about his friends? Girls or boys?'

'I know nothing about that.'

'Why did he disappear from your house?'

'I don't know. He just left. Young people do.'

'He had a telephone call and left overnight without saying good-bye.'

'I believe so,' said Harvey.

'He said the telephone call was from London. It wasn't.'

'So I understand. I was working in my cottage that night. You must understand I'm very occupied, and all these questions of yours, and all these files, have nothing whatever to do with me. I've agreed to come here simply to help you to eliminate a suspect, my wife.'

'But you have no idea why he should say he got a phone call from London, when he didn't. It must have been an internal call.'

'Perhaps some girl of his turned up in France; maybe in Paris, and called him. And he skipped.'

'Some girl or some boy?'

'Your question is beyond me. If I hear from him I'll ask him to get in touch with you. Perhaps he's come down with influenza.'

Pomfret now spoke: 'Why do you suggest that?' He was decidedly less friendly in French.

'Because people do come down with 'flu. They stay in bed. This time of year is rather the time for colds. Perhaps he's gone back to England to start a window-cleaning business. I believe I heard him speculating on the idea. There's always a need for window-cleaners.'

'Anything else?' said Chatelain.

'The possibilities of Nathan Fox's whereabouts are such that I could go on all night and still not exhaust them.'

'Would he go to join your wife if she asked him?'

Harvey considered. 'That's also a possibility; one among millions.'

'What are his political views?'

'I don't know. He never spoke of politics to me.'

'Did he ask you for money?'

'After Christmas he asked me for his pay. I told him that Ruth had the housekeeping money, and kept the accounts.'

'Then Mrs Jansen did give him money?'

'I only suppose,' said Harvey, 'that she paid him for his help. I really don't know.'

'Do you think Ruth Jansen is a calculating woman? She left her husband, came to join you with the baby, induced you to buy the château –'

'She wanted the château because of a tree outside the house with a certain bird – how do you say "woodpecker"?' – Harvey put the word to Pomfret in English.

Pomfret didn't recognize the word.

'It makes a sound like a typewriter. It pecks at the wood of the tree.'

'*Pic*,' said Pomfret.

'Well, she liked the sound of it,' said Harvey.

'Are you saying that is why you bought the château?'

'I'd already thought of buying it. And now, with Ruth and the baby, it was convenient to me.'

'Ernest L. Howe,' said Chatelain. 'He came to see you, didn't he?'

'Yes, some time last autumn. He came to see his baby daughter. He wanted Ruth to go back to London with the baby and live with him. Which, in fact, she has now done. You see, he doesn't think of what's best for the child; he thinks of what's most pleasant for himself. To console his hurt pride that Effie walked out on him – and I don't blame her – he's persuaded her sister to go and live with him, using the child as an excuse. It's contemptible.'

Harvey was aware that the two men were conscious of a change in his tone, that he was loosening up. Harvey didn't care. He had nothing, Effie had nothing, to lose by his expressing himself freely on the subject of Ernie Howe. He was tired of being what was so often called civilized about his wife's lover. He was tired of the questioning. He was tired, anyway, and wanted a night's sleep. He deliberately gave himself and his questioners the luxury of his true opinion of Ernie.

'Would you care for a drink?' said Pomfret.

'A double scotch,' said Harvey, 'with a glass of water on the side. I like to put in the water myself.'

Chatelain said he would have the same. Pomfret disappeared to place the orders. Chatelain put a new tape in the recording machine while Harvey talked on about Ernie.

'He sounds like a shit,' said Chatelain. 'Let me tell you in confidence that even from his statement which I have in front of me here, he sounds like a shit. He stated categorically that he wasn't at all surprised that Effie was a terrorist, and further, he says that you know it.'

'He's furious that Effie left him,' Harvey said. 'He thought she would get a huge alimony from me to keep him in comfort for the rest of his life. I'm sure she came to realize what he was up to, and that's why she left him.'

Pomfret returned, followed by a policeman with a tray of drinks. It was quite a party. Harvey felt easier.

'I'm convinced of it,' he said, and for the benefit of Pomfret repeated his last remarks.

'It's altogether in keeping with the character of the man, but he was useful,' said Chatelain. He said to Pomfret, 'I have revealed to M. Gotham what Ernest Howe stated about Effie Gotham.'

And what Chatelain claimed Ernie had said was evidently true, for Pomfret quite spontaneously confirmed it: 'Yes, I'm afraid he was hardly gallant about her. He is convinced she's a terrorist and that you know it.'

'When did you get these statements?' said Harvey.

'Recently. Ernest Howe's came through from Scotland Yard on Sunday.'

'You've got Scotland Yard to help you?'

'To a certain degree,' said Chatelain, waving his right hand lightly, palm-upward.

Was he softening up these men, Harvey wondered, or they him?

'It would interest me,' said Harvey, 'to see the photograph of my wife that was taken of her by the police in Trieste, when she was arrested for shop-lifting.'

'You may see it, of course. But it isn't being handed out to the newspapers. It has been useful for close identification purposes by eye-witnesses. You will see it looks too rigid – like all police photos – to be shown to the public as the girl we are actually looking for. She is quite different in terrorist action, as they all are.' He turned to Pomfret. 'Can you find the Trieste photograph?'

Pomfret found it. The girl in the photo was looking straight ahead of her, head uplifted, eyes staring, against a plain light background. Her hair was darker than Effie's in real life, but that might be an effect of the flash-photography. It looked like Effie, under strain, rather frightened.

'It looks like a young shop-lifter who's been hauled in by the police,' said Harvey.

'Do you mean to say it isn't your wife?' said Pomfret. 'She gave her name as Signora Effie Gotham. Isn't it her?'

'I think it is my wife. I don't think it looks like the picture of a hardened killer.'

'A lot can happen in a few months,' said Chatelain. 'A lot has happened to that young woman. Her battle-name isn't Effie Gotham, naturally. It is Marion.'

In the meantime Pomfret had extracted from his papers the photograph of Effie that the police had found in Harvey's cottage. 'You should have this back,' said Pomfret. 'It is yours.'

'Thank you. You've made copies. I see this photo in every newspaper I open.'

'It is the girl we are looking for. There is movement and life in that photograph.'

'I think you should publish the police-photo from Trieste,' said Harvey. 'To be perfectly fair. They are both Effie. The public might not then be prejudiced.'

'Oh, the public is not so subtle as to make these nice distinctions.'

'Then why don't you publish the Trieste photograph?'

'It is the property of the Italian police. For them, the girl in their photograph is a kleptomaniac, and in need of treatment. They had put the treatment in hand, but she skipped off, as they all do.'

'I thought she went to prison.'

'She had a two weeks' sentence. That is a different thing from imprisonment. It was not her first offence, but she was no more than three days in prison. She agreed to treatment. She was supposed to register with the police every day, but of course −'

'Look,' said Harvey. 'My wife is suffering from an illness, kleptomania. She needs treatment. You are hounding her down as a terrorist, which she isn't. Effie couldn't kill anyone.'

'Why did you leave her on the motorway in Italy?' said Pomfret. 'Was it because she stole a bar of chocolate? If so, why didn't you stand by her and see that she had treatment?'

'She has probably told Ernie Howe that story, and he has told you.'

'Correct,' said Chatelain.

'Well, if I'd given weight to a bar of chocolate, I would have stood by her. I didn't leave her over a bar of chocolate. To be precise, it was two bars.'

'Why did you leave her?'

'Private reasons. Incompatibility, mounting up. A bar of chocolate isn't a dead policeman.'

'We know,' said Chatelain. 'We know that only too well. We are not such fools as to confuse a shop-lifter with a dangerous assassin.'

'But why,' said Pomfret, 'did you leave her? We think we know the answer. She isn't a kleptomaniac at all. Not at all. She stole, made the easy gesture, on ideological grounds. They call it proletarian reappropriation. You must already have perceived the incipient terrorist in your wife; and on this silly occasion, suddenly, you couldn't take it. Things often happen that way.'

'Let me tell you something,' said Harvey. 'If I'd thought she was a terrorist in the making, I would not have left her. I would have tried to reason her out of it. I know Effie well. She isn't a terrorist. She's a simple shop-lifter. Many rich girls are.'

'Is she rich?'

'She was when she was with me.'

'But afterwards?'

'Look, if she needed money, she could have sold her jewellery. But she hasn't. It's still in the bank. My lawyer told me.'

'Didn't you say – I think you said –' said Pomfret, 'that you only discussed the recent English translations of the Bible with your lawyer?'

'I said that was what we were discussing on Saturday morning, instead of listening to the news on the radio. I haven't said that I discussed nothing else with him. You see, I, too, am anxious to trace the whereabouts of my wife. She isn't your killer in Paris. She's somewhere else.'

'Now, let us consider,' said Chatelain, 'her relations with Ernest Howe. He has stated that he knows her character. She is the very person, according to him, who would take up with a terrorist group. The Irish terrorists had her sympathy. She was writing a treatise on child-labour in England in the nineteenth century. She often –'

'Oh, I know all that,' Harvey said. 'The only difficulty is that none of her sympathies makes her a terrorist. She shares these sympathies with thousands of people, especially young people. The young are very generous. Effie is generous in spirit, I can say that.'

'But she has been trying to get money out of you, a divorce settlement.'

'That's understandable. I'm rich. But quite honestly, I hoped she'd come back. That's why I refused the money. She could have got it through the courts, but I thought she'd get tired of fighting for it.'

'What do you mean, "come back"?' said Pomfret. 'It was you who left her.'

'In cases of desertion in marriage, it is always difficult to say who is the deserter. There is a kind of constructional desertion, you know. Technically, yes, I left her. She also had left me. These things have to be understood.'

'I understand,' said Chatelain. 'Yes, I understand your point.'

Pomfret said, 'But where is she getting the money from?'

'I suppose that the girl who calls herself Marion has funds from the terrorist supporters,' said Harvey. 'They are never short of funds. It has nothing whatsoever to do with my wife, Effie.'

'Well, let us get back to your visitors, M. Gotham,' said Chatelain. 'Has there been anyone else besides those we have mentioned?'

'The police, and Anne-Marie.'

'No one else?'

'Clara,' said Harvey. 'Don't you want to hear about Clara?'

'Clara?'

'Clara is the niece of my wife's sister.'

Chatelain was getting tired. He took a long moment to work out Harvey's representation, and was still puzzling while Pomfret was smiling. 'The niece?' said Chatelain. 'Whose daughter is she?'

'My wife's.'

'You mean the infant?'

'That's right. Don't you have a dossier on Clara?' Harvey asked the security men.

'M. Gotham, this is serious. A man has been fatally shot. More deaths may follow. We are looking for a political fanatic, not a bar of chocolate. Can you not give us an idea, a single clue, as to where your wife can be hiding? It might help us to eliminate her from the enquiry.'

'I wish I could find her, myself.'

CHAPTER 10

'I BROUGHT YOU some English mustard,' said Auntie Pet. 'They say English mustard in France is a prohibitive price even compared to Canadian prices.'

Harvey had slept badly after his late return from the session with the security police at Epinal. He hadn't shaved.

'You got home late,' said Auntie Pet. Already, the château was her domain.

'I was with the police,' said Harvey.

'What were you doing with them?' she said.

'Oh, talking and drinking.'

'I shouldn't hob-nob too close with them,' she said, 'if I were you. Keep them in their place. I must say those plain-clothes officers who escorted me here were very polite. They were useful with the suitcases, too. But I kept them in their place.'

'I should imagine you would,' Harvey said.

They were having breakfast in the living-room which the presence of Auntie Pet somehow caused to look very shabby. She was large-built, with a masculine, military face; grey eyes which generally conveyed a warning; heavy, black brows and a head of strong, wavy, grey hair. She was sewing a piece of stuff; some kind of embroidery.

'When I arrived,' she said, 'there was a crowd of reporters and photographers on the road outside the house. But the police soon got rid of them with their cars and motor-cycles. No problem.' Her eyes rose from her sewing. 'Harvey, you have let your house go into a state of dilapidation.'

447

'I haven't had time to put it straight yet. Only moved in a few months ago. It takes time.'

'I think it absurd that your maid brings her baby's washing to do in your house every day. Hasn't she got a house of her own? Why are you taking a glass of scotch with your breakfast?'

'I need it after spending half the night with the police.'

'They were all right to me. I was glad of the ride. The prohibitive price of fares,' said his aunt, as one multimillionaire to another.

'I can well believe they were civil to you. I should hope they would be. Why shouldn't they be?' He looked at her solid, irreproachable shape, her admonishing face; she appeared to be quite sane; he wondered if indeed the police had been half-afraid of her. Anne-Marie was already tip-toeing around in a decidedly subdued way. Harvey added, 'You haven't committed any offence.'

'Have you?' she said.

'No.'

'Well, I should have said you have. It's certainly an offence if you're going to attack the Bible in a foreign country.'

'The French police don't care a damn about the Bible. It's Effie. One of their policemen has been shot, killed, and they think she's involved.'

'Oh, no, not Effie,' said Auntie Pet. 'Effie is your wife. She is a Gotham as of now, unfortunately, whatever she was before. No Gotham would stoop to harm a policeman. The police have always respected and looked up to us. And you're letting yourself go, Harvey. Just because your wife is not at home, there isn't any reason to neglect to shave.'

Harvey escaped to go and shave, leaving Auntie Pet to quarrel with Anne-Marie, and walk about the grounds giving orders to the plain-clothes police, whom she took for gardeners and woodsmen, for the better upkeep of shrubs and flower-beds, for the cultivation of vegetables and the felling of over-shady trees. From his bathroom window Harvey saw her finding cigarette-ends on the gravel path, and chiding the men in full spate of Canadian French. Prompted by Anne-Marie, they took it fairly well; and it did actually seem to Harvey, as he found it did to Anne-Marie, that they were genuinely frightened of her, armed though they were to the full capacity of their leather jackets.

When Harvey came down he found in the living-room a batch of press-cuttings which he at first presumed to be about himself and Effie; Stewart Cowper had left them behind. But a glance at the top of the bundle showed him Edward's face, now beardless. The cuttings were, in reality, all reviews of the play Edward had made such an amazing success in; they were apparently full of lavish praise of the new star, but Harvey put them aside for a more serene moment. Amongst some new mail, a letter from Edward was lying on the table. Edward's name and address was written on the back of the envelope. Maybe the police hadn't read it; maybe they had. Harvey left this aside, too, as Auntie Pet came back into the room.

'I have something to tell you,' she said. 'I have come all the way from Toronto to say it. I know it is going to hurt you considerably. After all, you are a Gotham, and must feel things of a personal nature, a question of your honour. But say it I had to. Not on the telephone. Not through the mail. But face to face. Your wife, Effie, is consorting with a young man in a commune, as they call it, in the mountains of California, east of Santa Barbara if I recall rightly. I saw her myself on the television in a documentary news-supplement about communes. They live by Nature and they have a sort of religion. They sleep in bags. They –'

'When did you see this?'

'Last week.'

'Was it an old film – was it live?'

'I guess it was live. As I say, it was a news item, about a drug-investigation by the police, and they had taken this commune by surprise at dawn. The young people were all scrambling out of their bags and into their clothes. And I am truly sorry to tell you this, Harvey, but I hope you'll take it like a man: Effie was sleeping in a double bag, a double sleeping-bag, do you understand; there was a young man right in there with her, and they got out of that bag sheer, stark naked.'

'Are you sure it was Effie? Are you sure?'

'I remember her well from the time she came when you were engaged, and then from the wedding, and I have the wedding-photo of you both on my piano, right there in the sitting-room where I go every day. I ought to recognize Effie when I see her. She was naked, with her hair hanging down her shoulders, and laughing, and then pulling her consort after her out of the extra-marital bag, without shame; I am truly sorry, Harvey, to be the bearer of this news. To a Gotham. Better she killed a policeman. It's a question of honour. Mind you, I always suspected she was unvirtuous.'

'You always suspected?'

'Yes, I did. All along I feared the worst.'

'Are you sure,' said Harvey, very carefully, 'that perhaps your suspicions have not disposed you to imagine that the girl you saw on the television was Effie, when in fact it was someone who resembled her?'

'Effie is not like anybody else,' said Auntie Pet.

'She resembles her sister,' said Harvey.

'How could it be Ruth? Ruth is not missing, is she?'

'No. I don't say it could have been Ruth. I only say that there is one case where Effie looks like somebody else. I know of another.'

'Who is that?'

'Job's wife, in a painting.'

450

'Job's wife it could not be. She was a foolish woman but she never committed adultery in a sack. You should read your Bible, Harvey, before you presume to criticize it.'

Harvey poured himself a drink.

'Don't get over-excited,' said Auntie Pet. 'I know this is a blow.'

'Look, Auntie Pet, I must know the details, every detail. I have to know if you're absolutely sure, if you're right. Would you mind describing the man to me?'

'I hope you're not going to cite him as co-respondent, Harvey. You would have to replay that news item in court. It would bring ridicule on our heads. You've had enough publicity.'

'Just describe the young man she was with, please.'

'Well, this seems like an interrogation. The young man looked like a Latin-Mediterranean type, maybe Spanish, young, thin. I didn't look closely, I was looking at Effie. She had nothing on.'

Auntie Pet had not improved with the years. Harvey had never known her so awful. He thought, She is mistaken but at least, sincere. He said, 'I must tell the police.'

'Why?' said Auntie Pet.

'For many reasons. Not the least of which is that, if Effie and her friend are in California and decide to leave, – they might come here, for instance, here to France, or here to see me; if they do that, they could be shot at sight.'

'That's out of the question. Effie wouldn't dare come to your house, now. But if you tell the police how I saw them, the story will go round the world. And the television picture, too. Think of your name.'

Harvey got through to the commissariat. 'My wife has been seen in California within the last few days.'

'Who saw her?'

'My aunt.'

'Ah, the aunt,' said the police inspector.

'She says she saw her in a youth-documentary on the television.'

'We had better come and talk to your aunt.'

'It isn't necessary.'

'Do you believe your aunt?'

'She's truthful. But she might be mistaken. That's all I have to say.'

'I would like to have a word with her.'

'All right,' said Harvey. 'You'll find her alone because I'm going down to my cottage to work.'

He then rang Stewart Cowper in London but found he was out of the office. 'Tell him,' said Harvey to the secretary, 'that I might want him to go to the United States for me.'

He had been in his cottage half an hour when he saw the police car going up the drive, with the two security men from Paris. He wished them well of Auntie Pet.

Harvey had brought his mail with him, including Edward's letter.

In his old environment, almost smiling to himself with relief at being alone again, he sat for a while sorting out his thoughts.

Effie and Nathan in a commune in California: it was quite likely. Effie and Nathan in Paris, part of a band of killers: not unlikely.

He began to feel uneasy about Auntie Pet, up there at the house, being questioned by the security men. He was just getting ready to go and join them, and give his aunt a show of support, when the police car with the two men inside returned, passed his cottage, and made off. Either they had made short work of Auntie Pet or she of them. Harvey suspected the latter. Auntie Pet had been separated from Uncle Joe for as long as Harvey could remember. They lived in separate houses. There was no question of a divorce, no third parties, no lovers and mistresses. 'I had to make a separate arrangement,' Uncle Joe had once confided to Harvey. 'She would have made short work of me if I'd stayed.'

Harvey himself had never felt in danger of being made short work of by his aunt. Probably there was something in his nature, a self-sufficiency, that matched her own.

He wondered how much to believe of what she had told him. He began to wonder such things as why a news supplement from California should be shown on a main network in Toronto. Auntie Pet wasn't likely to tune in to anything but a main network. He wondered why she had felt it necessary to come to France to give him these details; and at the same time he knew that it was quite reasonable that she should do so. It would certainly be, for her, a frightful tale to tell a husband and a Gotham.

And to his own amazement, Harvey found himself half-hoping she was wrong. Only half-hoping; but still, the thought was there: he would rather think of Effie as a terrorist than laughing with Nathan, naked, in a mountain commune in California. But really, thought Harvey, I don't wish it so. In fact, I wish she wasn't a terrorist; and in fact, I think she is. Pomfret was right; I saw the terrorist in Effie long ago. Even if she isn't the killer they're looking for, but the girl in California, I won't live with her again.

He decided to get hold of Stewart Cowper later in the day, when he was expected back at his office. Stewart would go to California and arrange to see a replay of the programme Auntie Pet had seen. Stewart would find out if Effie was there. Or he would go himself; that would be the decent thing to do. But he knew he wouldn't go himself. He was waiting here for news of Effie. He was writing his monograph on the *Book of Job* as he had set himself to do. ('Live? – Our servants can do it for us.') He wouldn't even fight with Ernie Howe himself; if necessary, Stewart would do it for him.

He opened Edward's letter.

Dear Harvey,

The crocs at the zoo have rather lack-lustre eyes, as can be expected. Perhaps in their native habitat their eyes are 'like the eyelids of the dawn' as we find in *Job*, especially when they're gleefully devouring their prey. Yes, their eyes are vertical. Perhaps Leviathan is not the crocodile. The zoo bores me to a degree.

I wish you could come over and see the play before it closes. My life has changed, of course. I don't feel that my acting in this play, which has brought me so much success, is really any different from my previous performances in films, plays, tv. I think the psychic forces, the influences around me have changed. Ruth wasn't good for me. She made me into a sort of desert. And now I'm fertile. (We are the best of friends, still. I saw her the other day. I don't think she's happy with Ernie Howe. She's only sticking to him because of Clara, and as you know she's pregnant herself at long last. She claims, and of course I believe her, that she's preg by you. – Congratulations!) Looking back – and it seems a long time to look back although it's not even a year – I feel my past life had a drabness that I wasn't fully aware of at the time. It lies like a shabby old pair of trousers that I've let fall on the bedroom floor: I'll never want to wear *those* again. It isn't only the success and the money, although I don't overlook that aspect of things – I don't want to crow about them, esp to you. It's simply a new sense of possibility. One thing I do know is when I'm playing a part and when I'm not. I used to 'play a part' most of the time. Now I only do it when I'm onstage. You should come over and see the play. But I suspect that possibly you can't. The police quizzed me and I made a statement. What could I say? Very little. Fortunately the public is sympathetic towards my position – brother-in-law, virtually *ex*-brother-in-law of a terrorist. (Our divorce is going through.) It isn't a close tie.

I've almost rung you up on several occasions. But then I supposed your phone was bugged, and felt it better not to get involved. Reading the papers – of course you can't trust them – it seems you're standing by Effie, denying that she's the wanted girl, and so on. Now, comes this ghastly murder of the policeman. I admire your stance, but do you feel it morally necessary to protect her? I must say, I find it odd that having left her as you did, you now refuse to see (or

THE ONLY PROBLEM

admit?) how she developed. To me (and Ruth agrees with me) she
has always had this criminal streak in her. I know she is a beautiful
girl, but there are plenty of lovely girls like Effie. You can't have
been so desperately in love with her. Quite honestly, when you
were together, I never thought you were really crazy about her.
I don't like giving advice, but you should realize that something
tragic has happened to Effie. She is a fanatic – she always had
that violent, reckless streak. There is nothing, Harvey, nothing
at all that anyone can do for her. You shouldn't try. Conclude
your work on *Job*, then get away and start a new life. If your new
château is as romantic and grand as Ruth says it is, I'd love to see
it. I'll come, if you're still there, when the play closes. It'll be good
to see you.

Affectionately,
Edward

Harvey's reply:

Dear Edward,
    That was good of you to go to the zoo for me. You say the zoo
bores you to a degree. What degree?
    I congratulate you on your success. It was always in you, so I'm
not surprised. No, I can't leave here at present. Ruth would be here
still if it were not that the place is bristling with the police – no place
for Clara whom I miss terribly.
    As to your advice, do you remember how Prometheus says, 'It's
easy for the one who keeps his foot on the outside of suffering to
counsel and preach to the one who's inside'? I will just say that I'm
not taking up Effie's defence. I hold that there's no proof that the girl
whom the police are looking for is Effie. A few people have 'identified' her from a photograph.
    Auntie Pet has arrived from Toronto wearing those remarkable
clothes that so curiously bely her puritanical principles. This morning
she was wearing what appeared to be the wallpaper. Incidentally, she
recognized Effie in a recent television documentary about a police-
raid on a mountain commune in California. She was with a man
whose description could fit Nathan Fox.

455

I've been interrogated several times. What they can't make out is why I'm here in France, isolated, studying *Job*. The last time it went something like this:

Interrogator – You say you're interested in the problem of suffering?

Myself – Yes.

Interrogator – Are you interested in violence?

Myself – Yes, oh, yes. A fascinating subject.

Interrogator – *Fascinating?*

Almost anything you answer is suspect. At the same time, supermarkets have been bombed, banks robbed, people terrorized and a policeman killed. They are naturally on edge.

There is a warrant of arrest out for my wife. The girl in the gang, whoever she is, could be killed.

But 'no-one pities men who cling wilfully to their sufferings' (*Philoctetes* – speech of Neoptolemus). I'm not even sure that I suffer, I only endure distress. But why should I analyse myself? I am analysing the God of *Job*.

I hope the mystery of Effie can be cleared up and when your show's over you can come and see Château Gotham. Ruth will undoubtedly come.

I'm analysing the God of *Job*, as I say. We are back to the Inscrutable. If the answers are valid then it is the questions that are all cock-eyed.

> *Job* 38, 2–3: Who is this that
> darkeneth counsel by words
> without knowledge?
> Gird up now thy loins like
> a man; for I will demand of thee,
> and answer thou me.

It is God who asks the questions in Job's book.

Now I hope you'll tell Ruth she can come here with Clara when the trouble's over, and have her baby. I'm quite willing to take on your old trousers, Edward, and you know I wish you well in your new pair, your new life.

Yours,

Harvey

PART 3

CHAPTER 11

'SO THE LORD blessed the latter end of Job more than his beginning.' It was five days since Stewart Cowper had left for California. He had telephoned once, to say he had difficulty in getting the feature identified which Auntie Pet had seen, but he felt he was on the track of it now. There definitely had been a news item of that nature.

'Ring me as soon as you know,' said Harvey.

Meantime, since he was near the end of his monograph on *Job*, he finished it. The essay had taken him over three years to complete. He was sad to see his duty all ended, his notes in the little room of the cottage now neatly stacked, and his manuscript, all checked and revised, ready to be photocopied and mailed to the typist in London (Stewart Cowper's pretty secretary).

The work was finished and the Lord had blessed the latter end of Job with precisely double the number of sheep, camels, oxen and she-asses that he had started out with. Job now had seven sons and three daughters, as before. The daughters were the most beautiful in the land. They were called Jemima, Kezia and Keren-happuch which means Box of Eye-Paint. Job lived another hundred and forty years. And Harvey wondered again if in real life Job would be satisfied with this plump reward, and doubted it. His tragedy was that of the happy ending.

He took his manuscript to St Dié, had it photocopied and sent one copy off to London to be typed. He was anxious to get back to the château in case Stewart should ring with news. He hadn't told Auntie Pet of Stewart's mission, but somehow she had found out, as was her way, and had mildly lamented that her story should be questioned.

'You're just like the police,' she said. 'They didn't actually say they didn't believe me, but I could see they didn't.'

He got back to the château just in time to hear the telephone. It was from the police at Epinal.

'You have no doubt heard the news, M. Gotham.'

'No. What now?'

'The FLE gang were surrounded and surprised an hour ago in an apartment in Paris. They opened fire on our men. I regret to say your wife has been killed. You will come to Paris to identify the body.'

'I think my wife is in California.'

'We take into account your state of mind, Monsieur, but we should be obliged if –'

Anne-Marie was standing in the doorway with her head buried in her hands.

L'Institut Médico-Légal in Paris. Her head was bound up, turban-wise, so that she looked more than ever like Job's wife. Her mouth was drawn slightly to the side.

'You recognize your wife, Effie Gotham?'

'Yes, but this isn't my wife. Where is she? Bring me my wife's body.'

'M. Gotham, you are overwrought. It displeases us all very much. You must know that this is your wife.'

'Yes, it's my wife, Effie.'

'She opened fire. One of our men was wounded.'

'The boy?'

'Nathan Fox. We have him. He was caught while trying to escape.'

Harvey felt suddenly relieved at the thought that Nathan wasn't in California with Effie.

The telephone rang when, finally, he got back to the château. It was from Stewart. 'I've seen a replay of the feature, Harvey,' he said. 'It looks like Effie but it isn't.'

'I know,' said Harvey.

He said to Auntie Pet, 'Did you really think it was Effie in that mountain commune? How could you have thought so?'

'I did think so,' said Auntie Pet. 'And I still think so. That's the sort of person Effie is.'

Anne-Marie said, 'I'll be saying good-bye, now.'

CHAPTER 12

EDWARD DRIVES ALONG the road between Nancy and St Dié. It is the end of April. All along the way the cherry trees are in flower. He comes to the grass track that he took last year. But this time he passes by the cottage, bleak in its little wilderness, and takes the wider path through a better-tended border of foliage, to the château.

Ruth is there, already showing her pregnancy. Clara staggers around her play-pen. Auntie Pet, wrapped in orange and mauve woollens, sits upright on the edge of the sofa, which forms a background of bright yellow and green English fabrics for her. Harvey is there, too.

'You've cut your hair,' says Harvey.

'I had to,' says Edward, 'for the part.'

It is later, when Clara has gone to bed, that Edward gives Harvey a message he has brought from Ernie Howe.

'He says if you want to adopt Clara, you can. He doesn't want the daughter of a terrorist.'

'How much does he want for the deal?'

'Nothing. That amazed me.'

'It doesn't amaze me. He's a swine. Better he wanted money than for the reason he gives.'

'I quite agree,' says Edward. 'What will you do now that you've finished *Job*?'

'Live another hundred and forty years. I'll have three daughters, Clara, Jemima and Eye-Paint.'

ABOUT THE INTRODUCER

SIR FRANK KERMODE has been Northcliffe Professor of Modern English Literature at University College, London, King Edward VII Professor of English Literature at Cambridge and Charles Eliot Norton Professor of Poetry at Harvard. His many books include *The Sense of an Ending*, *Romantic Image* and a memoir, *Not Entitled*.

CHINUA ACHEBE
Things Fall Apart

AESCHYLUS
The Oresteia

THE ARABIAN NIGHTS
(2 vols, tr. Husain Haddawy)

AUGUSTINE
The Confessions

JANE AUSTEN
Emma
Mansfield Park
Northanger Abbey
Persuasion
Pride and Prejudice
Sanditon and Other Stories
Sense and Sensibility

HONORÉ DE BALZAC
Cousin Bette
Eugénie Grandet
Old Goriot

SIMONE DE BEAUVOIR
The Second Sex

SAMUEL BECKETT
Molloy, Malone Dies,
The Unnamable
(US only)

SAUL BELLOW
The Adventures of Augie March

HECTOR BERLIOZ
The Memoirs of Hector Berlioz

WILLIAM BLAKE
Poems and Prophecies

JORGE LUIS BORGES
Ficciones

JAMES BOSWELL
The Life of Samuel Johnson
The Journal of a Tour to
the Hebrides

CHARLOTTE BRONTË
Jane Eyre
Villette

EMILY BRONTË
Wuthering Heights

MIKHAIL BULGAKOV
The Master and Margarita

SAMUEL BUTLER
The Way of all Flesh

JAMES M. CAIN
The Postman Always Rings Twice
Double Indemnity
Mildred Pierce
Selected Stories
(1 vol. US only)

ITALO CALVINO
If on a winter's night a traveler

ALBERT CAMUS
The Outsider (UK)
The Stranger (US)

WILLA CATHER
Death Comes for the Archbishop
My Ántonia
(US only)

MIGUEL DE CERVANTES
Don Quixote

RAYMOND CHANDLER
The novels (2 vols)
Collected Stories

GEOFFREY CHAUCER
Canterbury Tales

ANTON CHEKHOV
My Life and Other Stories
The Steppe and Other Stories

KATE CHOPIN
The Awakening

CARL VON CLAUSEWITZ
On War

S. T. COLERIDGE
Poems

WILKIE COLLINS
The Moonstone
The Woman in White

IVAN GONCHAROV
Oblomov

GÜNTER GRASS
The Tin Drum

GRAHAM GREENE
Brighton Rock
The Human Factor

DASHIELL HAMMETT
The Maltese Falcon
The Thin Man
Red Harvest
(in 1 vol.)

THOMAS HARDY
Far From the Madding Crowd
Jude the Obscure
The Mayor of Casterbridge
The Return of the Native
Tess of the d'Urbervilles
The Woodlanders

JAROSLAV HAŠEK
The Good Soldier Švejk

NATHANIEL HAWTHORNE
The Scarlet Letter

JOSEPH HELLER
Catch-22

ERNEST HEMINGWAY
A Farewell to Arms
The Collected Stories
(UK only)

GEORGE HERBERT
The Complete English Works

HERODOTUS
The Histories

PATRICIA HIGHSMITH
The Talented Mr. Ripley
Ripley Under Ground
Ripley's Game
(in 1 vol.)

HINDU SCRIPTURES
(tr. R. C. Zaehner)

JAMES HOGG
Confessions of a Justified Sinner

HOMER
The Iliad
The Odyssey

VICTOR HUGO
Les Misérables

HENRY JAMES
The Awkward Age
The Bostonians
The Golden Bowl
The Portrait of a Lady
The Princess Casamassima
The Wings of the Dove
Collected Stories (2 vols)

SAMUEL JOHNSON
A Journey to the Western
Islands of Scotland

JAMES JOYCE
Dubliners
A Portrait of the Artist as
a Young Man
Ulysses

FRANZ KAFKA
Collected Stories
The Castle
The Trial

JOHN KEATS
The Poems

SØREN KIERKEGAARD
Fear and Trembling and
The Book on Adler

RUDYARD KIPLING
Collected Stories
Kim

THE KORAN
(tr. Marmaduke Pickthall)

CHODERLOS DE LACLOS
Les Liaisons dangereuses

GIUSEPPE TOMASI DI
LAMPEDUSA
The Leopard

WILLIAM LANGLAND
Piers Plowman
with (anon.) Sir Gawain and the
Green Knight, Pearl, Sir Orfeo
(UK only)

D. H. LAWRENCE
Collected Stories
The Rainbow
Sons and Lovers
Women in Love

MIKHAIL LERMONTOV
A Hero of Our Time

PRIMO LEVI
If This is a Man and The Truce
(UK only)
The Periodic Table

THE MABINOGION

NICCOLÒ MACHIAVELLI
The Prince

NAGUIB MAHFOUZ
The Cairo Trilogy

THOMAS MANN
Buddenbrooks
Collected Stories (UK only)
Death in Venice and Other Stories
(US only)
Doctor Faustus

KATHERINE MANSFIELD
The Garden Party and Other
Stories

MARCUS AURELIUS
Meditations

GABRIEL GARCÍA MÁRQUEZ
Love in the Time of Cholera
One Hundred Years of Solitude

ANDREW MARVELL
The Complete Poems

CORMAC McCARTHY
The Border Trilogy (US only)

HERMAN MELVILLE
The Complete Shorter Fiction
Moby-Dick

JOHN STUART MILL
On Liberty and Utilitarianism

JOHN MILTON
The Complete English Poems

YUKIO MISHIMA
The Temple of the
Golden Pavilion

MARY WORTLEY MONTAGU
Letters

MICHEL DE MONTAIGNE
The Complete Works

THOMAS MORE
Utopia

TONI MORRISON
Song of Solomon

MURASAKI SHIKIBU
The Tale of Genji

VLADIMIR NABOKOV
Lolita
Pale Fire
Pnin
Speak, Memory

V. S. NAIPAUL
A House for Mr Biswas

THE NEW TESTAMENT
(King James Version)

THE OLD TESTAMENT
(King James Version)

GEORGE ORWELL
Animal Farm
Nineteen Eighty-Four
Essays

THOMAS PAINE
Rights of Man
and Common Sense

BORIS PASTERNAK
Doctor Zhivago

SYLVIA PLATH
The Bell Jar (US only)

PLATO
The Republic
Symposium and Phaedrus

EDGAR ALLAN POE
The Complete Stories

MARCEL PROUST
In Search of Lost Time
(4 vols, UK only)

ALEXANDER PUSHKIN
The Collected Stories

FRANÇOIS RABELAIS
Gargantua and Pantagruel

JOSEPH ROTH
The Radetzky March

VIRGIL
The Aeneid

VOLTAIRE
Candide and Other Stories

EVELYN WAUGH
The Complete Short Stories
Black Mischief, Scoop, The Loved
One, The Ordeal of Gilbert
Pinfold (1 vol.)
Brideshead Revisited
Decline and Fall
A Handful of Dust
The Sword of Honour Trilogy
Waugh Abroad: Collected Travel
Writing

EDITH WHARTON
The Age of Innocence
The Custom of the Country
The House of Mirth
The Reef

OSCAR WILDE
Plays, Prose Writings and Poems

MARY WOLLSTONECRAFT
A Vindication of the Rights of
Woman

VIRGINIA WOOLF
To the Lighthouse
Mrs Dalloway

WILLIAM WORDSWORTH
Selected Poems (UK only)

W. B. YEATS
The Poems (UK only)

ÉMILE ZOLA
Germinal